FRAYED

Donna Roberts

ISBN-10: 150305778X
ISBN-13: 978-1503057784

Edited by: Angela W. Dunn
Cover Art: Steve Cornelius

Acknowledgments

I have been fortunate to live my life wrapped in a cocoon of love, laughter, support and encouragement provided by family and friends. A humble thank you to all those special people in my life who have infused the journey with joy and wonder.

No words can express my gratitude, admiration, respect and love for my mother, Patty Roberts, who has never faltered as my rock. She is a pillar of strength, loyalty and faith on which many have relied. The world has been enriched by her presence, and I have been blessed to call her Mom.

In loving memory of my dad, Bud Roberts, the purest spirit I've ever known. His sensitivity and integrity were admirable traits that ironically burdened his existence. I pray that his life now abounds with the sweetness and gentleness that eluded his time on Earth.

To my sister, Laney Roberts, a singularly imaginative and interesting creature, I must confess that your influence in my life has been crucial in molding me. Your passion for films and books opened doors to new worlds, while your unshackled personality helped me to see the gray in life and occasionally take some steps on the road less traveled.

For my son, Austin Roberts Weeks, who tolerates my grumpiness, you make everything worthwhile. Your dry wit and unflappable demeanor amaze me on a daily basis. Live large and follow your passions. Always know that wherever you are, I am in your corner.

To my zany and talented friend, Chef Antonia Krenza, thank you for adopting me as your big sis and for introducing me to the culture and cuisine of Charleston, South Carolina.

To my brilliant friend, Angela Dunn, thank you for your tireless hours spent editing FRAYED. Your husband was dead on when he dubbed you the Comma Nazi, but your insights and attention to details proved invaluable in completing this work.

To my charming friend, Steve Cornelius, your artistic contribution and patience in creating the cover artwork are deeply appreciated.

To the poised and talented Anne Johnson, sincerest thanks for giving your time and talents to finalize the cover layout.

Prologue

The human race is fascinating, isn't it? A myriad of personalities shaped by genetics, gender, cultures, ethnicity, and economics. With such global diversity, conflict is inevitable and inescapable, despite diligent endeavors to avoid it.

So, life arrives gift-wrapped in conflict – a reality that ultimately allows us to genuinely appreciate our moments in the sun. It's easy to recognize the positive influences of our joyous interactions, but the effects of those experiences marked by conflict can be far more convoluted. The negative experiences can simultaneously rip us to the core and enlighten us with invaluable wisdom. Sometimes, sadly, they can unwittingly mold us into undesirable fragments of ourselves or permanently unravel us.

FRAYED is ripe with subtle and complicated conflicts explored light-heartedly through a group of women who seemingly have little in common other than a desire to play tennis. Like these characters, we all make choices in how we deal with the battles before us. The results make great stories on and off the page.

My wish for you, the reader, is that you enjoy your journey within these pages, but more importantly, your personal journey. I hope that, in some small way, these characters lend camaraderie as you face your own conflicts. Remember that silver linings do exist; there is always something positive to glean from a bad day, even if it's simply a recognition of the next good one.

IS THIS THE BEGINNING...
OR IS THIS THE END?

August 14, 2014

Without warning, a world can be shaken. In the end,
how one processes the tremor is all that matters.

CALLIE

August 14th, 2014 -- 12:15 am. An obnoxiously shrill noise assaulted my ears. I dug deeper beneath my cozy quilt, hiding from the offensive sound. I must be dreaming of the tornado sirens that had erupted intermittently during the afternoon.   The piercing shriek resumed, derailing my blissful descent into slumber.

"Damn it!" I muttered between clenched teeth. Belligerently, I peeled back the covers and peered through the transoms above my bedroom windows. Way too dark to tell if a funnel cloud was headed my way, but I didn't hear any wind howling or the tell-tale sound of a freight train.

When the sound blasted for the third time, I realized that it wasn't the tornado alarm. It was the phone. I picked up my cell and saw that it was 12:15 am. My heart raced. Who could be calling at this hour? Either a drunken misdial or bad news.

"Hello?" I answered tentatively.

"Is this Callie Conrad?" a deep, somber voice inquired.

"Yes," I confirmed meekly.

"I'm sorry to trouble you at this hour, ma'am. This is Officer Bragg of the Homewood Police Department, and we need you to come to UAB Hospital as soon as possible."

I was speechless. No one in my family lived in Birmingham, so I knew this call had to be a mistake. "Why?" I muttered incredulously.

"Do you know a woman by the name of Dallas O'Malley?"

"Yes, sir."

"You're listed as her emergency contact, and I'm sorry to report that there was an incident that has left her in critical condition," the officer explained. In a daze, I promised that I would be there in half an hour.

I frantically threw on a pair of jeans, a bra, a Tennis Rocks T-shirt, and slid into a pair of Volatile sandals. I grabbed my purse and keys and headed for the garage. As I backed onto the street, I wished that I had at least swabbed a toothbrush around my mouth, but more importantly, I wondered why a woman I had met three months ago, a woman with whom I had probably exchanged no more than fifty words, a woman that I felt was a complete enigma, had designated me as her emergency contact.

****

Traveling at 12:30 in the morning spared me the stress of navigating the rush hour traffic that typically paralyzed morning commuters. My mind was free to roam. I remembered the first day I met Dallas O'Malley. It was in late May at a tennis clinic held for the team for which I would serve as captain. I arrived early that beautiful spring morning and stood with our pro, Jake Lenaghan, greeting each woman as she arrived. During the winter months, I asked Jake to select players for a "dream team" that would be poised for state playoffs in September. I instructed him to focus on talent. Who cares about personality, right? I just wanted the best.

As the first clinic revealed, he had clearly delivered. Although not all of us knew each other (our ages and marital statuses varied), most of us knew "of" each other. But no one knew a thing about Dallas O'Malley. To call her intense was an understatement. Nobody on the team possessed the power she did. Whatever the shot, she attacked the ball, and her expression mirrored the physical onslaught -- a diabolical glare -- as if the ball represented something or someone in her life that she passionately despised. I could tell she made most of the ladies feel uncomfortable, which was understandable considering the fact that she didn't speak to anyone or even acknowledge their compliments regarding her skills.

After everyone left, Jake said, "How'd I do? Did I give you what you wanted?"

I smiled at him and thought, *you couldn't imagine what I really want from you*, but I instantly buried that idea. "Definitely, but where the hell did you find Dallas?"

He laughed. "She's intense, isn't she? Actually, she found me. She typically plays out of Pelham Racquet Club, but she came up to me at a local tournament and asked if she could be on this team. I thought it was weird, but she said she had heard how good you and Mary Claire are and wanted to play on your team. I told her I'd watch her match and let her know. Didn't take long to see that she'd be an asset."

"Very odd. Okay, who do I put as her partner? Everybody that got near her looked like a deer in headlights."

Jake grinned. "Ah, there's only one lady who can handle her, and she wasn't here today. Do you know Alex Anderson?"

"I know the name, but we've never met."

8 DONNA ROBERTS

Jake put his arm around my shoulder and pulled me into his chest. "You'll love her. She's funny as hell and nobody, and I mean nobody, gets under her skin. It will be a perfect match."

Awkwardly, I hugged him back, trying to make it a sisterly embrace. "I hope you're right. See you next week."

****

Visions of Jake Lenaghan clouded my head, but the entrance to the UAB parking deck snapped me back to reality. I grabbed a ticket from the automated gate and quickly parked in the barren deck. I hurried to the emergency room desk and asked the on-duty nurse, "Excuse me. I'm here for Dallas O'Malley. A policeman by the name of Bragg called and asked that I come."

As the nurse searched her patient database, a man in police attire approached. "Miss Conrad?" he asked.

I nodded. "Hi, I'm Officer Bragg. I heard you call my name. I thought it would be better to meet you on the main floor. It's so easy to get lost in this place."

I extended my hand, and he took it in a full, confident grip, not one of those wimpy, finger handshakes that I find so insulting. Officer Bragg was clearly not a day over twenty-five but exuded a confidence that demanded respect. He held a small manilla envelope. He looked down at the package and said, "Shall we sit over here and talk? It's quiet at this hour, so we can talk in private." I followed him to the deserted waiting area wondering why we needed privacy.

We sat and stared at each other in awkward silence. Finally, I initiated a dialogue. "Officer Bragg, I have so many questions, but first, how is Dallas? What are her injuries? You said it was critical."

He looked at the envelope again and then back to me. "Ma'am, I don't know how close you two are, but I won't sugarcoat the situation. They took Miss O'Malley to surgery an hour ago, and they told me it would be a miracle if she made it."

I gasped and clutched my chest. "What happened to her?"

"We don't know the full story, but she suffered two gunshot wounds, one to the right shoulder and one to the right hand. We think the shooting occurred in a local residential area, but apparently she fled the scene, and it appears that her shooter chased her down Highway 280 and rammed her vehicle as she cleared the ramp to Hwy 31. The impact made her lose control of her car, and it flipped into oncoming traffic on the other side of the guardrail. An officer was already in pursuit because he had been called to a residence where the chase began. If the accident had not occurred so close to UAB, she never would have made it."

I stared at Officer Bragg, mouth gaping, I'm sure. "Did they catch the one chasing her?"

He shook his head. "No, ma'am. The officer in pursuit was concerned with the injured party; consequently, he had to abandon the chase. He called it in as he stopped to help Miss O'Malley. According to his radio call to dispatch, the fleeing vehicle was a convertible Jag. He didn't get the color or license plate since it was dark, but there can't be too many convertible Jags around town. They'll be able to catch the bastard soon."

All I could say was, "Holy shit!"

****

"Are you okay, ma'am?" Slowly, I looked up at the policeman.

"Sorry. I'm fine. Just shocked. I can't imagine why anyone would shoot Dallas. I met her only a few months ago, and she kept to herself most of the time. She really didn't seem close to anyone."

He extended the packet toward me. "Maybe this will help. We found it in the car with your name and number on it."

I set the package on my lap and looked up at Officer Bragg. "Honestly," I said, "I barely knew her and can't imagine why she named me as her emergency contact."

He stood. "I'll go check on Miss O'Malley while you look through the envelope. I'll be back soon."

"Thanks," I mumbled. I sat there and thought, shit a convertible Jag. Can't be a coincidence. What the hell is going on?

I dumped the contents of the envelope in the chair next to me. There was a letter dated two weeks ago and a small key.

Callie,

If you are reading this letter, then I'm either dead or fleeing for my life. Frankly, I might prefer the former. Maybe not. All I know is that the time has finally come and I feel anxious rather than peaceful, fearful rather than excited, diminished rather than inflated. I've worked toward this moment for so long, patiently planning each step, clawing my way toward this one goal, fighting all the obstacles with a determination that apparently runs genetically deep through my father's family. It kept me going all this time, but now I see that things aren't so black and white.

The enclosed key is to locker no. 44 at The Heights. The contents will explain everything. Tell Mary Claire I'm sorry.

That was it. Nothing made any sense, especially the vague apology to Mary Claire. Despite her distance, Dallas had always seemed cautiously drawn to my doubles partner, Mary Claire Jameson. As I sat waiting for Officer Bragg to return with some news of Dallas's condition, I reflected on our tennis season, hoping that by retracing the moments, I might find some clarity.

THE PLAYERS

MIRROR MIRROR

PRACTICE MATCH - June 1, 2014

A woman is often taunted by the image she sees when standing before a mirror. Rarely does she gaze upon an accurate reflection.

CALLIE

A lime orb floated high above me, momentarily lost in the blinding sun before returning to my now spotty view. As it descended, I drew in a deep breath and muttered, "patience, patience". At precisely the right moment, I struck the sphere with the combined power of every muscle in my body and watched it zoom toward the intended target. The ball slammed into my opponent -- right between her unnaturally perky breasts. I wondered if the pop of a saline sac were imminent.

Although in a doubles match the net person is the intended target, skewering your opponent is not well received, so I apologized profusely for my honestly accidental, yet very gratifying, match winning point. This Maria Sharapova wannabe barely acknowledged my apology as she scurried off the court like a wounded sparrow. She and her equally augmented partner refused to shake hands. Mary Claire, my doubles partner, gave me a subtle look of disapproval and perched on our bench.

I glanced to my left to see how the other courts were performing. It was just a practice match, but I hoped that this USTA tri-level team would have an undefeated season. Our pro had done an excellent job pulling together some fabulous players. Although I had ten on the roster, there were six that I felt would carry the weight. They would pull us into a bid for a state title. Those six "chosen ones" were on the courts now.

Right next to me were my level 3.5 stars, Alex and Dallas. They were deep into their second set and seemed to have a commanding lead (4-2) after an impressive 6-1 first set win. My 3.0 players, Molly Katherine and Katlin, were struggling. They lost the first set 4-6 and were down 1-3 in the second. Their body language bellowed defeat.

I had full confidence that my team would win today with a 2-1 victory; I had zero confidence that this crew would remain solid for the long haul. After five years as partners, Mary Claire was the only one on the team that I truly knew, and there was a part of me that felt I didn't know her at all. Even though all the players except Dallas were from the same club, we were truly a band of strangers. Our team was a meld of diverse personalities and egos that seemed likely to blend into a combustible concoction.

I turned toward our bench and saw that Mary Claire was almost to the locker room. I grabbed my bag and followed.

MARY CLAIRE

I worry so about Callie. She brilliantly projects an image of a successful, career driven, and totally independent woman, but I know that loneliness is consuming her. In the five years we've been tennis partners, I've held her hand through more disastrous relationships than I care to count. She seems to be a magnet for men who will break her heart. Callie always thinks the latest is the greatest -- a massive improvement over the last beau -- but I know the opposite to be true. Each choice seems more desperate -- sacrificing qualities that she wants because she's feeling that her time is running out. She's scared she'll never have a family since she is fast approaching the age of forty. I could tell her that marriage isn't as great as she imagines. She thinks I have the ideal life. I suppose the grass is always greener.

I washed my sweaty hands and began drying them with the exquisitely plush hand towel, a light brown Egyptian cotton with BHCC embroidered in navy script. There must be a stock of at least three hundred in plain sight, so no one reuses a towel. It's extravagant, but then again, the Birmingham Heights Country Club is famous for its excessive attention to the finest amenities. Most people called the club "The Heights". It sounds prestigious, but I think that nickname emerged from the bowels of cynicism toward the privileged rather than the feeling of superiority coveted by many of its members. My husband would consider no other club; he associated with only those things revered by the masses. I preferred a lower profile, but it was not my decision.

I caught sight of a haggard reflection in the unforgiving wall-to-wall mirror above the sinks. The dark circles under my eyes were bleeding through my faded makeup. No concealer could avoid the devastation of 55% humidity and 95 degree heat. My left eye was particularly offensive, so I reached for my makeup kit tucked neatly in my tennis bag.

After correcting my eyes, I gingerly began to pull my shirt away from my left shoulder but quickly released it when I heard Callie calling my name as she opened the door.

"Are you mad at me?" she asked in a toddler voice, through pouty lips.

I laughed. "Not possible, honey. But you will earn quite a reputation for yourself if you aren't careful. And, of course, I will be branded as well -- guilt by association."

Callie rolled her eyes. "You know what Jake says about net play: 'If you hit to them, you'd better hit through them'. Besides, you know half the ladies in the league would love it that I nailed Anna Scully in her boobs. It's her second 'refinement' in three years. Those plastic barbies are on the courts because they look great in the outfits -- certainly not due to their talents. I'm not sure how they made it to a 4.0 ranking. They must have some incriminating photos."

I sighed. "I do agree that their skills are limited, but I'm sure they are nice girls. You have to feel sorry for them. I can't imagine that either of them is over thirty-five, but they have clearly both fattened the pockets of a plastic surgeon. They must have very low self-esteem - really very tragic."

Callie smiled at me. "Mary Claire, you're an angel on Earth. Always the advocate for the potentially down-trodden."

I grabbed my bag, gave Callie a quick hug, and chided as I walked out the door, "And you, my dear girl, always see the worst in humanity. But I'll keep working on you."

"See you later, Mother Teresa," Callie playfully called back to me.

I trilled, "Ha ha ha." I love the way Callie always teases me.

DALLAS

I yanked on the locker room door and a body tumbled into me. It was our team captain, Callie. "Sorry," I muttered.

"It's okay," she responded. "Hey, good job today. I saw some of your points, and you have quite a wicked forehand. Gotta run. See you next week."

"Yeah," I mumbled. As I strolled through the posh locker room, I glanced in the mirror and noticed a stately, older woman staring at me, a condescending expression on her face. I'm sure she thinks I don't belong in such an upscale country club. I answered her with a menacing glare, enjoying the visage of her smug face morph in utter discomfort. She averted her eyes, quickly placed her designer gym bag in her locker, and scurried past me careful not to come too close.

I stood before the mirror and studied myself. I'm no longer pretty, not even cute -- just average looking. I'm not thin, but certainly not fat; however, I am far thicker than I want to be. I have very short brown hair, but not spiked or dyed purple. I'm not freakishly short or tall, but of average height. Just a plain looking thirty-year-old. I should blend easily into the woodwork -- never stand out in the crowd. But wherever I go, I feel eyes on me constantly. It's been like that for a long time now.

I'm so ready to stop looking over my shoulder.

ALEX

As I entered the locker room, Dallas brushed past me looking as if she had the weight of the world on her shoulders.

"Hey," I called as she stormed past. She turned and looked at me vacantly. "Great playing today, Dallas. I think we'll be a kick ass team."

I smiled at her, raised my hand for a high five, but she turned away and mumbled, "Sure. See you," as she headed for the parking lot.

I looked at my upturned right hand, slapped it with my left hand, and said, "Enjoyed playing with you too, Alex. Great down the line shot to take that last game." Wonder what crawled up her ass.

I chuckled to myself and headed into a stall to relieve my aching bladder. I must have downed a gallon of water out there today. As I washed my hands at the sink, I looked in the mirror and sighed with exasperation.

Crap, if I get any fatter, they'll have to roll me onto the court. I stood to the side examining my profile. I longed for my muffin top. Now I look as if I were six months pregnant. I faced the mirror again and began kneading the excess flesh on my face. I could make pigtails with this blubber.

How the hell did this happen? Five years ago I was forty pounds lighter and my husband's friends were making passes behind his back. I'm 51; that's not old. Christie Brinkley is still smokin' hot and she's gotta be 60. Of course, I don't have her money, makeup artists, and plastic surgeons at my disposal, but come on.

"This just sucks," I grumbled.

KATLIN

"What sucks?" I asked as I saw a teammate standing before the mirror. I couldn't remember her name, but I know she played on the court next to me.

The woman turned to me, and grinned. "Aging, little girl. Aging sucks. Enjoy your perfect little body and flawless skin while you can. It sneaks up on you fast!"

I laughed. "I'm Katlin. I played on the 3.0 court next to you. You and your partner won today, didn't you?" She nodded. "We lost. Now that sucks."

"Nice to meet you, Katlin. I'm Alex. And you'll get 'em next time. I gotta run. See you soon."

I waved and watched Alex as she left, wondering how old she was...maybe sixty-five...give or take a couple of years. Really looked solid on the court for her age. I abandoned my reflections and headed for the shower. I had a hot date and had to look my best.

As I let the hot water pour over my body, my mind focused on Sam. We had been out only three times, but I could tell he was smitten. He had already sent me flowers, nothing very original, a dozen red roses, but hey, it's the thought that counts. Sam was older, around the same age as my dad and recently divorced, so really rusty at the dating game. He's so awkward in how he approaches me, like a little boy with his first crush. It's really charming.

I've always liked older men. I grew up at this club and had flirted with the head pro since I was sixteen, but I'd gotten nowhere. Once he found me skinny dipping in the pool after hours. I planned that encounter because I knew he would be there working out. His only reaction was to apologize for catching me unawares and urge me to get dressed and go home because it was not safe to be there alone. I gave up then. He must be gay.

I reached for the soap but found an empty tray. The club provided fancy, scented individual bars rather than liquid soap. No one else in town does that, and I love it. It just adds to the uniqueness of the club. I opened my eyes and looked around the stall. No soap bars hidden anywhere. I was the only one in the showers, so I hopped over to the next stall to grab a bar, but no soap there. None in the remaining three stalls either. "Damn it. Where's all the freakin' soap?" I screamed. The club manager was going to get a piece of my mind.

MOLLY KATHERINE

I heard a shower running when I entered the locker room. I'm not sure how I feel about today's match. We lost, but I know it wasn't my fault. My partner, Katlin, is just not as strong as I am, so it's really her fault. Plus those ladies we played were probably ranked far below their skill level. I know some ladies always want to win, so they keep themselves from moving up in USTA rankings by limiting the number of matches they play. They are cheating the system, and it's simply a travesty.

I dabbed some water on my face and smiled at myself in the mirror. I still looked quite fresh even after two tough sets of tennis in the blazing sun. Good genes, I suppose.

As I exited the locker room, I heard someone curse at the top of her lungs. Something about no soap. How silly is that. It was probably Katlin having a meltdown. She was babbling at the end of the match about how she had to have a shower before her date.

I mean, how rude! Screaming curse words at the city's most prestigious club. But I suppose she feels exempt from any rules. I mean, after all, she's been a member here since birth and is still under daddy's wing. I don't even think she has a job. I just met her last week, but I knew "of her". Everybody's heard of the Hamilton family. She strikes me as a bit of a privileged princess. But I'm not one to judge.

Though I can't escape the feeling that all of us should be judging Dallas. She seems as if she'd relish the idea of using someone's head as a tennis ball. Talk about a woman in need of anger management. I don't really know any of the women on this team well, but I am so thankful she is not my partner. I don't know how anyone can stand playing with her. She always glares at everyone like a demon ready to snatch your soul.

Our captain gave me a thumbs up during our match. We were losing, so I guess she was trying to encourage me. I suppose that was a nice gesture, but I can't really figure her out. I mean, she's so hard to read. I've known her for only two weeks, but I just get the feeling that behind those steel blue eyes, her mind spins nonstop, but she never lets you see what's up. Maybe that's what makes a good leader -- someone unreadable. To me it just comes off as cold, but I'm not one to judge.

THE SEASON

GETTING TO KNOW YOU

MATCH 1 - June 6, 2014

There are those you never really know, those you feel you've always known, and those you wish you had never known.

DALLAS

My alarm sounded for the third time. The final snooze. 7:45 am. I had to get up now to make it to work on time. I had barely slept. I rarely sleep more than a couple of hours at a time, and even then, it's a miserable rest. The voices in my head are too loud and incessant to allow long periods of slumber. Every now and then, I feel the purr of gentle voices -- soft and soothing, but distant -- like a gentle current struggling to pull me out to calmer waters. But most of the time, those kind voices are drowned out by angry ones declaring my guilt with unbridled agony.

I tried desperately to sleep, but my heart kept racing uncontrollably. About the time it would calm down, their faces would parade before me -- their expressions so sad and longing. I felt them all reaching toward me. I tried to catch them, but one by one they all tumbled into an abyss. I failed them and their expressions conveyed the depth of their disappointment. Their screams pierced my soul as they succumbed to darkness.

Long ago when my anxiety levels frequently rendered me barely functional, I researched "dealing with anxiety" on the internet. One article recommended simply finding your "happy place". I envisioned the most peaceful, happiest moment of my life, and I stayed there as long as possible. So, I went to my utopia, running along the sandy white beaches of Santa Rosa Beach, Florida, in front of my grandparents' cottage. I was nine years old, and this was my first summer to visit the grandparents alone. As the oldest of five headstrong kids, it was heaven to be the center of attention for a whole week.

My grandparents watched me from their blanket on the beach. They sat huddled together like love-struck teenagers, occasionally sipping Grandma's rum punch concoction as they watched me run up and down the shoreline flying my prissy, pink, diamond-shaped kite. I loved that kite peppered with dainty tiaras, (probably because of my desire to win a crown and thus upstage my ever so perfect baby sister, Capers). Amazingly, the kite had survived three summers with only a tiny rip caused by a mishap with a crab. The sun was setting, and the rays streamed through the kite making the diamonds in the tiaras sparkle and cast shadows that danced playfully along the sand. I laughed as I dodged the waves crashing around my feet and glanced at my grandparents who stood, raised their glasses to me and bowed. That sent me into a giggling fit.

Grandpa grabbed his Nikon and snapped a photo capturing this slice of heaven. It had always been my favorite childhood photograph. Grandma framed it and placed it in a prominent spot on the mantle. There it stayed for years. It was mine now. I removed it from the drawer of the bedside chest and smiled at the carefree little girl in the picture, longing to be her again.

The clock on my bedside table caught my eye, and my moment of serenity evaporated. The thought of facing a day at work made my stomach turn. I held a temporary job with data entry and mailroom duties at a large insurance company. Even though it was a low stress position, I just couldn't cope with people today.

I practiced my sickly voice and made the call to Nancy Mize, my supervisor, who would be holding vigil over the data entry pool. I heard the tightness in her voice when I told her that I was sick and couldn't make it to work. She curtly wished me a speedy recovery, but I could tell she was angry and probably didn't believe me. I don't blame her. This was the third time in two months that I had done this to her. I'd hate me too. I DO hate me. I hung up the phone and in sheer exhaustion, quickly drifted back into a dreamless (thankfully) sleep.

When I woke up, it was 1:30 pm. Nearly six hours of uninterrupted slumber. That was my lengthiest sleep since moving to Birmingham. I threw back the covers and shuffled to the kitchen. The coffee that had automatically brewed at 7:15 am was far from appealing, so I threw it out and started a fresh pot. While I was waiting, I sat at my laptop and checked my emails. One unopened mail. Big surprise. And it wasn't even personal. It was from Callie Conrad, team captain, regarding the lineup for our first match:

Hello Ladies.

What a great job you all did in our practice match. We took 2 of 3 courts for a solid win. Our first official match is AT home against Riverchase on Friday, June 6th. Match time is 9:30 so be there at 9 for warm up. If you are interested, we could have lunch together after the match. Most of us don't really know each other, so it might be fun to have an opportunity to chat. If you are not in the lineup, feel free to join us. I'll send a text as to time and place once the match is done. It will probably be in the 11:30 to noon time frame. The line up is as follows:

4.0 COURT — CALLIE / MARY CLAIRE
3.5 COURT — DALLAS / ALEX
3.0 COURT — AMY / KELLY

Please confirm that you will be there.

Thanks.
Callie

What would I do without tennis? It's my only outlet; well, I suppose it's a secondary source of focus. I really have only one priority. I'm so much closer now, but more anxious as D-Day draws near.

ALEX

Seated at my desk, I finished reading a string of emails, the last of which gave the details of our first tri-level match. Dallas and I were paired up for the opener. We had rocked in the pre-season practice match. She's intense but wicked good, and I do so love to win.

I heard a car headed up the drive and knew by the sound of the engine that it was Sly. I smiled. Even after twenty-nine years, the thought of that man could make my heart race. Sly barreled through the garage door with a boyish grin on that handsome face. He gave me a bear hug. "What's up, Sly? I know that look. You either closed a big deal, won the lottery, or banged a Victoria's Secret model."

He rubbed against me and gently caressed my arms. "Now what would I want with a Victoria's Secret model when I can have you?"

"A hot body in bed," I responded playfully. "Now, seriously, what's up?"

Sly guided my hand in a southerly direction and nibbled my ear. "You tell me." I blushed.

Now Sly was always an exceptional roll in the hay, but he seriously rocked my world tonight. I propped myself on my arm and stared at his face. He had lots of fine lines, but instead of making him look older, they made him look sexy. Those lines would make a woman look like a bag lady. Funny how gray hair and fine lines are sexy on men, but on women they bring to mind the old saying "rode hard and put away wet".

"Not that I'm complaining, Sly, but you never told me the source of that vigor."

He held my face with both hands and stared into my eyes. "Catching the eye of a beautiful woman." He pecked me on the lips and headed for the bathroom. I admired his muscular body as he entered the shower. I started to join him but then remembered that I resembled the Pillsbury Dough Boy and decided the cover of darkness was the wisest choice. I lay back and smiled as I listened to Sly's off key rendition of *Hot Blooded*, but in the back of my mind I pondered how I would respond to Noah Hargrove's tempting email.

CALLIE

<u>Friday, June 6th, 2014</u>. It was the morning of our first match, and I was behind schedule. 8:15 am. Mary Claire would be here any minute to ride with me (she was never late), and I still had to respond to this work email. My boss, Bob McInish, needed to know when I would have my edits complete on the latest novel assigned for my review. I had been struggling for three weeks on this dismal excuse for writing. Bob thought this girl was a "diamond in the rough", a "burgeoning Bob Dylan of prose". I wanted to tell him that a dung beetle produced better material, but I thought that might be an unwise choice since I had learned that this "diamond in the rough" was Bob's niece. Nepotism at work.

I had thrived as a book editor for Random House for ten years. I love words, and the challenge of restructuring someone else's work to improve a story was always a thrill to me. Bob McInish had been my direct supervisor for the past four years, and I considered his judgment infallible -- until he handed me this manuscript. I couldn't decide if Bob could handle complete candor considering his lack of objectivity. But then again, maybe he was looking for me to get him "off the hook". If his most experienced editor could not salvage the work, then he could shift the blame to me and maybe save face with his family. I opted for an indecisive response:

> *Hey Bob. We need to chat. What times are good for you this week?*
> *Callie*

I heard Mary Claire pull in the driveway. Perfect timing. I closed my laptop, grabbed my gear and headed out the door. We won the match quickly for a 3-0 sweep. By 11:15, I was texting all team members to say that lunch would be at 11:45 at Ashley Mac's. Everyone who played today plus Molly Katherine and Katlin arrived about the same time. I was surprised that Dallas came, but I think Alex convinced her to come and celebrate since they won 6-0/6-0 in a forty-five minute match. Even the grumpiest spirits are a bit festive after such a commanding victory.

Once everyone ordered and settled at an outdoor table, Molly Katherine spoke. "Ladies, I think it is fitting for each of us to take a turn at telling a little about ourselves since we really don't know each other -- except for the fact that we are all outstanding tennis players." She paused, as if waiting for applause, but only awkward silence ensued. "I'll be glad to start us off. I'm Molly Katherine Harriman, and I am a retired second grade school teacher. I have played tennis since I was twelve years old, and without giving away my age, I can tell you I've played for more years than you can count on two hands." She laughed at her joke before continuing in her deep southern drawl. "I have been married to Edward Harriman for a long, long time, and I hail from Brewton, Alabama. Edward and I were childhood sweethearts and have had a wonderful life though we were not blessed with children. Of course, the lack of children was really Edward's fault. He has a low sperm count. We even went to Atlanta for special testing. My reproductive system was deemed a virtual work of art. All deficiency rested with poor Edward."

I looked around the table. Everyone was stone-faced, except Alex, who, as I was learning, never hesitated to speak her mind. "Poor Edward is right! I bet your husband has spent his entire life trying to make up for his 'deficiency'." She made air quotes as she said the word "deficiency" in a condescending tone. I kicked Mary Claire under the table, and she gave me a subtle look of reprimand.

Now everyone at the table looked a bit uncomfortable, fully expecting Molly Katherine to lash out at Alex because of her blatant sarcasm. But Molly Katherine had quite the opposite reaction. "Oh, my dear, Edward did just that. He has devoted his life to making up for not being able to give me children. Every woman wants children. Isn't that why we get married in the first place?"

"Hell, I got married for hot sex," Alex blurted out.

Everyone laughed. But Molly Katherine now seemed offended. "Alex, that is just sinful. The only purpose of sex is for procreation. Anyone who has studied the Bible knows that."

Talk about a conversation stopper. I noticed Dallas bending the tines of her fork as if they were made of paper. Alex's eyes widened abnormally signifying her dismay. Everyone else seemed immobilized, as if just tased, except Katlin who seemed oblivious, head bowed to her iPhone, texting at a feverish pace with a sheepish grin on her face.

Thankfully, our server arrived with our food. As he set a plate in front of Alex, she lightly grasped his arm and said, "Honey, I'm gonna need a big glass of chardonnay just as soon as you can get to it."

As everyone began quietly eating, I felt I had to do something to lighten the mood. "So, Alex, didn't I hear that you have a daughter who is getting married soon?"

Alex smiled as she swallowed a bite of chicken salad. "Yes, my daughter, Avery, is getting married eleven weeks from tomorrow, August 23rd. I can't believe the big day is so close."

"Where are you having the wedding?" Mary Claire asked.

"Avery wanted to have a very intimate wedding, so we're having the ceremony and reception at our house. Hopefully the weather will cooperate because we plan to have everything outside."

"Outside!" Molly Katherine bellowed. "The humidity is horrid that time of year. And the bugs, especially the mosquitos, are out of control. Are you not from these parts? Why, in August, the mosquitos will be gigantic. They'll barely fit in the palm of your hand and suck the life out of you with one bite. What are you thinking, dear?"

As we are fond of saying in the South, you could cut the tension with a knife. Alex took a big gulp from the glass of wine that had just arrived, sat back in her chair in a relaxed posture, and grinned. "I'm thinking, my dear, that it will be a magical evening for my daughter and future son-in-law. I'm thinking, Molly Katherine, that we will take the proper steps to control any bug issue and that the weather will be irrelevant to the people who are there."

"I'm sure it will be lovely, Alex," Mary Claire offered her support.

"Thank you," Alex said without shifting her gaze from Molly Katherine. "You know, Molly Katherine, your name is full of southern charm, but it's quite a mouthful. I think you need a nickname. What about MKat? Ladies, what do you think?"

Everyone, except Katlin, nodded in approval. "Katlin?" Alex implored. Katlin, who had not touched her food, did not respond, apparently hypnotized by her iPhone. "Good Lord, Katlin!" Alex said in a loud voice laced with exasperation. Katlin looked up with an astonished expression. "Have you heard a word we've said? Who's got you so preoccupied on that phone?"

Molly Katherine offered her thoughts. "Really Katlin. You are being quite rude. You've had your head down since we arrived, and you have not participated in the conversation. Did you hear that Alex wants everyone to call me MKat instead of Molly Katherine?"

Her indignation was lost on Katlin. "MKat," Katlin tried it aloud. "I like it. MKat it is." MKat looked disgruntled but didn't get an opportunity to protest.

"I'm intrigued," Alex commented. "What on that phone could possibly be more interesting than us? Or should I say 'who'?"

Katlin blushed. "I'm sorry. I didn't mean to ignore everybody. I've just been texting with this guy I've been seeing for the past few weeks. I think he is different, really special."

"At first they all seem 'special', but in the end they are all the same -- unreliable, selfish SOBs." I felt compelled to impart my wisdom.

"Now Callie," Alex reproached. "Sounds like sour grapes to me. They're not all bad. Sly and I celebrated our twenty-ninth anniversary two months ago, and he's been my best friend and partner in crime the whole time. Sure there have been bumps in the road, but those hiccups just made the ride so much sweeter."

"Well, your husband is the exception to the rule, Alex. I'm happy for you, but life has taught me that celibacy is probably the safest choice."

"Safest choice, yes, but also the most boring," Alex argued.

"Callie's right," Dallas said with conviction. All eyes were on Dallas, stunned that she had spoken. "Men are rarely what they seem."

"Well, you can't convince me that my guy isn't top shelf material," Katlin defended.

"Tell us about him, dear," MKat encouraged. "How did you meet him and what's he like? Does he come from a good family?"

Alex rolled her eyes. "Oh, MKat, you talk as if she needs to check his papers like she's buying a pure bred dog!"

"I like that idea," I said. "Wouldn't it be great if you could shop for men like groceries? Hot but no brain on aisle 1. Smart, excellent earning potential but no personality on aisle 2. Doormats on aisle 3. Total assholes on aisles 4 through 27."

Everybody was laughing, except for Dallas and Mary Claire. Mary Claire smiled weakly; she knew me well enough to know that I was just masking pain and a deeply rooted lack of faith in the opposite sex. Dallas gave me the most penetrating look, like she could see through the humor, straight to my soul where anger and disappointment festered. There was no judgment in her gaze -- just complete solidarity. At that moment, I knew unequivocally that this enigmatic woman had experienced pain that equaled or exceeded my own because she had mistakenly believed in a man.

MKat squelched all levity. "Well, I suppose if there were an aisle for men who cannot bear fruit, I would have been able to steer clear of Edward."

Alex quickly emptied her wine glass and said, "Oh, MKat. I'm quite confident God had a very good reason for you to end up with poor, deficient Edward."

Mary Claire grabbed my knee under the table and squeezed, while we both suppressed our giggles. The true nature of the comment escaped MKat.

Alex signaled for the server to bring her another glass of wine. Then she said, "MKat, I'm curious. Where did you find your tennis skirt? It's a lovely color, but I've never seen one that hits just above the knee."

"Oh, I make my own tennis skirts," MKat confessed with pride. "Skirts keep getting skimpier and skimpier. The lengths are sinfully short, and I refuse to parade around like a common trollop."

Alex chuckled. "Well, you know what they say: 'If you've got it, flaunt it'. I certainly don't have 'it', but as long as everything is covered, I'm comfortable with store bought attire."

"On the contrary," MKat disagreed, "the Lord did not intend for women to expose so much of themselves. It's too tempting to the male population and therefore sinful." Defensively, I pulled my Nike skirt lower on my legs before MKat resumed her soliloquy. "Have you ever noticed that homosexual women tend to cover up their bodies more than normal woman? Their lifestyle is dreadfully sinful, but I have to give their people credit for modest clothing."

Dallas stood abruptly. "I think I'm going to be sick." She threw a bill on the table and said "no change needed". She grabbed her bag and trotted toward the restrooms.

I watched her enter the women's bathroom in the back of the restaurant. Thirty seconds later I saw her sneak out the back exit. I nudged Mary Claire and discreetly nodded to the getaway. Mary Claire looked concerned. I noticed that Dallas had thrown down a $50. Who leaves a $40 tip for a $10 sandwich?

Ever the peacemaker, Mary Claire obviously decided to steer the conversation into a less personal arena. She asked if anyone had ever seen the movie *The Pursuit of Happyness* with Will Smith. She had never seen it, but had rented it the previous night. Everyone shared her evaluations of the story and acting. All seemed moved by this powerful true story of a man who struggled to better his life and his child's life after becoming homeless.

But MKat started rambling unintelligently about how the down trodden were basically responsible for their woes -- that their troubles were a product of their sin. Everyone was squirming in her seat. As if choreographed, wallets were pulled in unison from purses. Three people threw down $20s, thanked me for coordinating a post game lunch, and excused themselves. MKat was waiting for change and Mary Claire, Alex and I had to delay our getaway since we paid with credit cards.

"What happened to Dallas?" MKat asked.

"She texted me and said she had to get home quickly," I lied.

Our server returned with our cards and change. MKat grabbed most of her change. I noticed that she left a generous tip of $1. She stood and said she had to run because Edward was ill. Mary Claire, Alex, and I watched her departure. When she was out of hearing range, Alex declared, "Well, she's fuckin' crazy!"

Mary Claire, who forever takes the high road, couldn't hold back. "She does seem a tad bit opinionated. I do feel sorry for poor Edward."

MARY CLAIRE

<u>Tuesday, June 10th</u>. On Tuesdays, we held our weekly clinic at 10 am. After that bizarre team lunch on Friday, I doubted many players would attend. When I arrived ten minutes early, there was Dallas with a ball hopper practicing her serves. She certainly required no practice. Her speed was phenomenal, and her accuracy was at a professional level. I watched her alternate between hitting the corners of the service boxes and was happy I wasn't on the receiving end.

"Very impressive," I praised as I walked toward her, racquet in hand. She looked up and half grinned -- the first time I had seen her smile since I'd met her. "You think you can teach me how to improve my serve?" I asked.

She gave me a quizzical look. She stared at me -- an awkwardly long pause -- and finally said, "I've watched you serve and don't see a need to adjust. You may not have a ton of speed, but I envy your spin."

Now it was my turn to stare, dumbfounded. Dallas had never uttered more than a few words to anyone, except her partner Alex, and even then exchanges were given grudgingly and void of eye contact. But now she was looking at me with maybe not a friendly gaze, but the hostility that typically surrounded her was absent.

"Well, thank you, dear, for the compliment, but I'd like to have another tool in the shed so to speak. Care to share the secret to your speed?"

Dallas's eyes narrowed to sinister slits. "It's simple really," she began, "just envision the person you hate most in the world and pretend that the ball is his head. Toss it up and slam it with all your strength as you bring your arm across your body." She almost growled as she finished her explanation. "The harder you hit, the greater the pain inflicted."

I noticed that Dallas gripped her racquet until her knuckles turned white. "So hate is your fuel," I surmised aloud.

Dallas looked away, shifting her gaze to my left, but clearly not focusing on anything. "Hate can be a powerful friend."

I was taken aback by this statement and stood there pondering the potential catalyst for such a philosophy, as Dallas continued to stare into the distance.

"What are you ladies chatting about?" The grating voice of Molly Katherine snapped us both out of our pensive states. Dallas simply walked away.

I smiled weakly and responded, "The art of the perfect serve."

"Well, I'm often told mine is simply stellar, so if you want any pointers, I'll be happy to work with you."

I plastered on my best fake smile and said, "That's very kind of you. I see Jake and the others have arrived, so we'd better get started." I hastened to Callie's side seeking a buffer.

CALLIE

Only Mary Claire, Dallas and MKat showed up for clinic. And Mary Claire had on a long-sleeved shirt again. It's 98 degrees. She's been wearing long-sleeved shirts since the start of the season, and I don't see how she doesn't pass out. "Geez, Mary Claire! You might as well have on a parka. Why do you keep covering up so in this heat?"

"I'm taking an antibiotic, and you know they make you more prone to sunburn. I'm just taking precautions." Mary Claire dug into her Cortiglia tennis bag, pulled out a bottle of 50+ Obagi sunscreen and started slathering her face.

I looked at her bare legs. "What about your legs? You're not covering them. Aren't you worried they might sunburn too?"

Mary Claire looked at Jake, who, I did not realize was standing behind me, listening to our conversation. He chimed in. "Conrad, if she covered her legs too she really would pass out. Stop badgering your partner and let's get started." His tone was playful; I noticed that he winked at Mary Claire. She smiled at him as she grabbed her racquet and headed toward me.

Mary Claire had the kindest, most innocent smile. Not the gleeful, carefree innocence of a child, but one that exuded purity; there was no hidden agenda behind her expression. I had often wondered how a woman her age could possess such goodness and purity of spirit. I guess it came from having such an easy life. Being married to one of the most prestigious attorneys in the state allowed her to have anything she wanted. She wore designer clothes down to her underwear, had exquisite jewelry, frequented the finest restaurants, and lived in an exclusive area of Mountain Brook (though, oddly, I had never been to her house). Despite all that, she still seemed down-to-earth, grounded. Seemed like an oxymoron to me.

For the next ninety minutes, Jake drilled us on offensive and defensive net positioning and the art of a successful tiebreaker. Since competitive USTA matches often go to a ten point tiebreak to decide the winner, it was important for all of us to have confidence in our ability to handle what players find to be the most stressful part of the game. I wish attendance had been better today.

As clinic was finishing up, everyone dispersed quickly except Dallas and me. "So, Dallas, how do you like playing with Alex?"

"She's a good partner." She gently bounced a ball on her racquet in perfect rhythm, creating a sound like the distant thud of a drum. "How long has Mary Claire been your partner?" she casually asked.

"Around five years. Don't get any ideas. I'm not letting you steal her," I joked (but I was serious).

Dallas stammered. "Oh, no, that's not why I asked. I mean, I um, I mean I don't really know anyone my age who plays tennis, and I thought maybe she might have children around my age who might want to play singles."

I stood calculating age scenarios in my head and came to the conclusion that Dallas was apparently much younger than I thought. "Sorry, no luck there. Mary Claire doesn't have any children."

"That seems odd. I mean she seems so sweet and maternal. I would think she'd have a house full of kids."

I shrugged. "I asked once, and she said she and her husband decided that they wanted to focus on his career. But after meeting her husband, I'd bet that was far more his decision than hers."

"What do you mean?"

"He came and watched us play together once. He only saw the last half of our second set, but he was very clinical, dissecting what he saw, oblivious to the fact that he might be embarrassing his wife or hurting anyone's feelings. Guess that's what being an attorney for forty years can do to a guy. He didn't win any points with me, but as long as Mary Claire is happy, my opinion doesn't matter."

Abruptly, Dallas put away her ball and racquet. "By the way, why does Mary Claire always wear long sleeves?"

I shook my head. "I asked her that long ago, and she said she was just trying to avoid sunburn. I asked her again before we got started today, and she said she's on antibiotics, and that they make you more prone to sunburn, so she's taking precautions."

Dallas frowned. "That doesn't make any sense. Why are her face and legs so perfectly tanned? And who takes antibiotics for more than ten days? She's been wearing long-sleeved shirts since I joined the team back in April."

"Huh, that's a good point. To be honest, I think she's hiding something, like some skin condition that embarrasses her. She never wore long sleeves until this summer. I've quizzed her about it a few times, but she's always evasive. She's exceedingly private, so I decided to let it go. I don't think she likes to reveal any imperfections -- inside or out."

Dallas shrugged. "I gotta go."

As she departed, I said, "Hey Dallas. I'll play singles with you."

She turned around, looking confused. "Singles?"

"You said you were asking about Mary Claire's children because you were looking for someone to play singles."

"Oh, right. Sure, thanks." She headed off the courts.

"See you at the match Friday."

She simply kept going.

As I packed my bag, Jake approached. "Hey, Conrad. Why the low turnout today?"

"I think most of the girls wanted to avoid MKat if possible."

"Who's MKat?"

I laughed. "Molly Katherine. Alex has dubbed her MKat. She obviously hates it, so I'm sure it will stick. That woman is unique, and that's not a compliment."

Jake chuckled. "She does have a reputation for being annoying, but she delivers, right?"

"So far," I replied. "But she's not half as good as she thinks she is. And what's up with that routine she does before she serves?" I felt compelled to imitate her. I stood sideways assuming the position to serve to the deuce side, then hopped and twisted to face the opponent, pointed my right toe and drug it in a half circle as I pivoted back to the sideways position, jerked the right leg back behind my left and then served. "Did you teach her that move?"

Jake doubled over laughing. "No way. She was doing that when I met her. I told her she was wasting energy with that little jig, but I couldn't get her to stop. You do that quite well, by the way." We both started walking toward the clubhouse. "Hey, want to take in a movie this week?" I stopped in my tracks, and he obviously read my thoughts. "Just as friends," he added. "Totally platonic, I promise." I hesitated. "Oh, come on. It's not like we haven't hung out together before. We always had fun, until you decided to go into hibernation."

I gave him a look. "You know why I stopped hanging out with you."

"That's all in the past," he proclaimed. "I know where your head is and respect your position. I don't agree with it, but I respect it. Come on. I've got lessons late tonight and tomorrow. What about Thursday night? You pick the movie."

As much as I hated to admit it, I really missed spending time with Jake off the court. It was easy to be myself with him. Comfortable. He was a great friend. "Okay. I'll text you the details."

****

As I drove out of the parking lot of The Heights, I felt giddy with anticipation. Not good. I called Mary Claire who picked up immediately. "Hey. It's Callie. What are you doing?"

"I'm driving to Whole Foods. What's going on with you? You sound excited."

"I hate that I'm so transparent," I whined.

Mary Claire laughed. "You are not transparent. I just know you quite well. What's going on?"

"Jake convinced me to go to a movie with him this week, and I feel like a sixteen year old getting ready for the prom. I should cancel."

"No!" Mary Claire reprimanded like a mother scolding her disobedient toddler.

"Mary Claire, I need to keep my distance from him. He's too dangerous for me."

"Dangerous!" Mary Claire laughed. "Honey, you know that you're just looking for excuses. Jake is about as dangerous as a ladybug. You like him, more than a little, and you know the feeling is mutual. You simply lack the courage to explore a relationship with him."

"It's not a lack of courage. History has taught me that relationships end badly for me, and I don't want to jeopardize my friendship with him."

"Look, Callie, you aren't being fair to Jake. I've known him longer than you have, and I can assure you he is a man of good character. Give him a chance. When are you going?"

"Thursday."

"Call me after the movie. Andrew is out of town, so you don't have to worry about waking anyone."

"Okay. Thanks for listening."

****

By Thursday, I had almost cancelled twice, but both times I let Mary Claire talk me out of it. I couldn't focus on work, so I spent the morning cleaning all the windows and plantation shutters in my house.

When I was done, I made myself a salad and tried not to think about Jake. I showered and went online, found a good movie, and texted Jake.

Hey. Meet me at 7:15 at the Summit for "X-Men: Days of Future Past". Starts at 7:40.

I started going through my emails and saw that my boss, Bob McInish, had responded to my earlier mail regarding his niece's work.

12:30 pm
Hi Callie.
"We need to chat" is typically an omen of ill things to follow. I can chat any time today if you like. I am bracing myself.

1:55 pm
Bob,
Interesting that you assume my need to chat correlates with bad tidings :). If you want me to be completely honest with you, I need to know if you would deal with any negative comments better in writing or over the phone. You may not want me to be candid, but you know that is against my nature.

Callie

2:05 pm

Callie,
I know you must feel that I have put you in an awkward position since the author is my niece. To be perfectly frank, I did not want to bring this work in house for fear that it might cause some rifts in the family if the work were not well received. But my wife insisted since Maddie is her brother's only child. I gave it to you because I knew you wouldn't hold back. You are not one to kiss up. Why don't you give me a call after you get this email. Doesn't matter what time it is. I'll be in the office until 8pm but just call my cell regardless of the time. I need resolution to the matter.

Bob

I heard the ping of a text and grabbed my cell. It was Jake:

Got it. See you soon.

It was 2:15 pm. I didn't need to leave the house until 6:45, so I had no excuse not to call Bob. But I could procrastinate. I dried my hair, put on my makeup, and spent twice as long in my closet deciding what to wear. I'm acting like this is a date. It's just two friends going to a movie. Why am I so nervous? I'm an idiot. I wasn't sure if my nerves were due to the call I was about to make or being with Jake. Either way I decided a glass of pinot gris might help.

I downed half a glass and picked up my cell. "Call Bob McInish," I told Siri. I sucked in a deep breath and did not exhale until Bob answered, "Hey Callie. How are you?"

I took a quick sip of liquid fortification. "Hi Bob. I'd be better if you hadn't assigned this one to me."

"I hear you," he said through a laugh. "Just give it to me straight. Don't hold back."

I sighed. "Okay. First I have to ask who encouraged your niece to write. Did she have some crazy English professor who thought it would be the ultimate joke to coax the most untalented student to undertake a novel under the premise that her literary mogul uncle would secure publication?"

"Shit, Callie. No need to sugarcoat it. It totally sucks, huh?"

"Duh-uh. Didn't you pick up on that in the first ten pages? You called her a 'diamond in the rough' and a 'burgeoning Bob Dylan of prose' which led me to believe that you had read some of it and liked it."

Bob cleared his throat. "That was me being optimistic. Actually, I refused to read a word of it. I claimed Switzerland."

"You spineless chickenshit!" I chided.

"Come on. You know that's not fair. I have to spend all my holidays with these people. And I sleep with Maddie's aunt, so cut me some slack, Cruella!"

I couldn't suppress a giggle. "Bob McInish, I don't think I've ever seen you so.....vulnerable. Steel Balls Bob quaking in his tracks. How are you going to buy my silence?"

"By letting you keep your job, missy." His tone was stone cold, but I knew he was just playing.

"There are those balls of steel," I affirmed. "Okay, all kidding aside. Your niece, Miss Madison Hendricks, has absolutely no talent. Not only is the writing some of the worst I've ever seen (spell check and grammar check would have mitigated the offensiveness somewhat), but the story is no good. I've seen great plots that were poorly written and bad plots that were beautifully written, but never a double goose egg."

"That horrendous?"

I drove the nail in the coffin of Madison's ill chosen career. "Even if you paid me an exorbitant fee, I couldn't rewrite the entire book into something remotely interesting."

Bob groaned. "What's the damn thing about anyway?"

"I don't really know," I admitted through a laugh. "It's like a coked out Snow White meets Bilbo Baggins in Disney World but on another planet. It doesn't fit a genre. It's like she tried to create a new one -- sci-fi, romance, porn, mystery all rolled into one."

"Geeeez," Bob moaned. He did not speak, but by the muffled sounds I heard, I knew frustration had driven him to the pack of cigarettes hidden in the back of his left desk drawer. He exhaled slowly and said, "So what do I tell my niece, so that I don't replace the reigning black sheep of my wife's family? And by the way, that poor cousin has held the title for twenty years. Boy, those people can hold a grudge. They just don't seem to be able to let anything go."

I smiled to myself. "Sounds like I might be related. Seriously, you should sit down with Madison, tell her what an amazing accomplishment it is to complete a manuscript. Tell her she should be proud of her efforts, that many start but few finish, and even fewer publish. Tell her that her writing style is not conducive to mass marketing and that you would be doing her a disservice by not being honest and steering her in another direction. I don't think you should tell her you haven't read the book. I would tell her you collaborated with me to get an objective assessment. Then talk to her about what her true interests are and see if you can suggest some different avenues. Bob, you have so many diverse contacts that I'd bet you could get her in the door somewhere doing something that she might really like."

Bob cleared his throat, and I heard the faint sound of an ashtray sliding gently across the desk as he extinguished his cigarette -- a sign that his frustration had faded. "Callie, my dear, you are ever the diplomat. I think that will work. And if I talk to her alone, she'll probably admit that she's really not interested in writing. I think her mother pushed her into it. Maddie is only twenty-three, but her mother thinks she should be sprinting down some lucrative career path."

"Pushy parents are a pain. I feel for her. So when are you going to break the news?"

"This weekend. I won't sit on this one."

"Good luck. Let me know how she takes it."

"I will, Callie. Thanks for plowing through it. I really appreciate your efforts and candor."

"Bye, Bob." I ended the call and saw that it was 6 pm already. I drank a second glass of wine like it was water, brushed my teeth, and headed to meet Jake feeling slightly toasted, but calm.

****

I knew I was in trouble when I saw Jake Lenaghan leaning casually against the wall next to the entrance. I had forgotten how handsome he is. He looks great in tennis wear, but in jeans, Tevas, a red polo, and no hat, Jake jumps to a higher level of hotness. Even his feet were sexy, and I hate feet.

He smiled when he saw me approach. "You look great," he said as he gave me an innocent side hug.

"Thanks. You clean up nicely too, my friend," I responded with an unnatural emphasis on the word 'friend'. Just friends, I had to remind myself constantly.

Jake opened the door for me and held up two tickets. Before I could protest, because, as I kept reminding myself, this is platonic, he said, "You can get the popcorn. That's probably more expensive than the tickets anyway."

I rolled my eyes and said, "Thanks." Once we bought our popcorn and drinks, we got seated and soon lost ourselves in a great movie. As Jake walked me to my car, we shared our thoughts on the merits of the X-Men films. We sat on the hood of my car for half an hour talking about nothing, but it was a great conversation -- relaxed, comfortable, at home.

He looked at his watch. "Wow. Can't believe it's 11:30." He opened my car door. "As always, a pleasure to be with you, Conrad. I have to call it a night. I have clinic at 8 am and don't have a break until 2 pm."

"What's the matter, Mr. Lenaghan? Is it past your bedtime?"

He smiled that sultry smile that made my knees buckle. "Well, I am over forty, you know." I laughed, and he patted my head like I was the family pet. "Drive safely. I had fun, pal."

I drove home, pulled an unopened quart of Ben and Jerry's cookies and cream from the freezer and proceeded to eat in bed while thinking of Jake as anything but a pal. I woke up when I rolled over the soggy ice cream container and spoon. I glanced at my cell lying next to my pillow and saw four texts from Mary Claire. I totally forgot to call her. 4:10 am. I think I'll wait.

DO YOU SEE WHAT I SEE?

MATCH 2 - June 13, 2014

Perception is nine-tenths of reality.

MKAT

I slept fitfully next to Edward. When I was able to drift off for a few minutes, gruesome figures haunted my dreams grabbing at Edward and me until I woke up, my heart racing. This same dream had haunted me more than once over the past few days. Very upsetting.

After those awful dreams, it was hard to return to sleep because of Edward. He has been so sick with the flu that he hasn't had the energy to bathe in five days, and my sponge baths haven't been very effective. Edward was always quick to break out in sweats and pollute the air around him. Very embarrassing for me all these years. I suppose he just wasn't as genetically blessed as I was. Even on the most sweltering southern summer days, when it feels like a sauna outside, I sweat only a little, and it does not affect my natural scent akin to lavender. No cologne or perfume for me, though I am often asked what perfume I am wearing. It's all natural. Exceptional genes, I suppose. Even after all these years with Edward, who has valiantly tried to make amends for his shortcomings, it still deeply saddens me that I was never able to pass those outstanding genes on to offspring.

I looked at Edward lying beside me and frowned. He isn't faring well. He grows paler every day, and he has absolutely no appetite. I got up early and made him his favorite breakfast this morning, eggs benedict, but he didn't touch it. Not a good sign.

I called his boss, Jack Reynolds (a lovely man, I must say), to let him know that Edward would not be able to come to the office. Edward had missed nine days of work, and Jack was concerned and asked to speak to him. "Edward is finally resting, so I hate to disturb him. But you are so dear to be worried about him. I know Edward probably hasn't missed this many days since he joined your office, but at our age, bouncing back from the flu isn't as easy anymore."

"Well, please keep me posted on his condition," Jack conceded. "And if there's something I can do for him, please let me know."

"Thank you, Jack. You are a dear, dear man. Just keeping him in your prayers is all you can do. I will tell Edward that we chatted. You have a wonderful day now."

I hung up the phone and looked at my watch. It was time to leave for the match. I felt guilty about leaving Edward, but he really didn't need anything but rest, and I'd be back in no time. I called out to my ailing husband. "Edward, dear, I'm going now to my tennis match. I hate to leave you, but that Katlin can't win without ME. You just rest and I'll be back soon. I'll make you a nice bowl of chicken soup when I get back. Love you, honey."

MARY CLAIRE

I parked my car in the Wendy's lot fifteen minutes before our agreed upon time to meet so we could carpool to our match. I was the first to arrive which was par for the course. Being punctual was ingrained in my psyche as a child. The polar opposite of his own parents who were carefree and happy, my father was a staunch disciplinarian whose limited capacity for joy evaporated when my mother passed away. He governed unwaveringly by rules that he drilled into my brothers and me. Even though I was the only girl and the baby, there was no "daddy's girl" syndrome to provide an escape clause from his stern demeanor. Any deviations from his rules produced heavy consequences, and being late peeved him more than any other breach of conduct. He believed that even one minute of tardiness was a sign of disrespect.

I decided to close my eyes and relax until the others arrived. Suddenly, Matthew's beautiful face filled my vision. He smiled, and I reached up to touch his cheek. Before my hand made contact, he blew me a kiss. That kiss transported me to the day Matthew, my oldest brother, got held up at basketball practice and arrived home five minutes late for dinner. Matthew was delayed by the coach. They had a state playoff game on Friday. Matthew and Cameron Park were the stars, and the coach wanted to go over some new strategy for the game. Matthew thought that explanation would appeal to my father's rational side. But just the opposite. He said Matthew was being disrespectful to him. Matthew reasoned that wouldn't it be disrespectful to coach to walk out on him? My father chewed him out for insubordination and refused to allow him to play in the state playoffs.

Matthew was such a great kid. With my grandfather's quick wit, he was an excellent student, a great athlete, handsome, and very kind. He was popular, but it didn't go to his head. So many kids looked up to him. Especially me. I adored my big brother. My mother died of cancer when I was six, and he was the most nurturing presence in our house after her passing. When I was upset about something, he would sneak into my room in the middle of the night and hold me while I unloaded whatever was bothering me. He always made me feel better, even when he didn't have the answers.

Despite his great qualities, Matthew never seemed to live up to my father's expectations; consequently, they were often at odds. Ironically, of all the children, Matthew had the most potential. Surely my father recognized this fact. My mother had a way of getting my father to "let it go" when it really didn't matter. Once she died, we had no buffer. He never laid a hand on any of us, but he was quick to anger, uncompromising, and ruled the house like a combat officer. If you bucked, you were sent to the brig.

When my father declared his punishment the day that Matthew was late from basketball practice, I saw a light in my brother's eyes dim. I was too young to understand at that moment, but part of Matthew died. He flatly said, "Yes, Father", ate his dinner in silence, did his kitchen chores and went to bed. Defiance replaced his innocent, eager spirit. On Friday night, Matthew snuck out of the house, played in the playoffs (it was a home game), and snuck back home undetected. But he was the high scoring player with the game winning shot, and his picture headlined the morning paper that proclaimed him a local hero. Saying that my father was livid is an understatement. Matthew had already left for work and when he returned home, he found all of his clothes, trophies, basically all of his belongings packed up and neatly stacked on the front porch. Father told him that if he was too old to follow the rules, he was old enough to live on his own and take care of himself.

That night I crawled into Matthew's bed and cried for hours. Matthew lived with Cameron Park the remaining two months of his senior year and joined the Navy the day after graduation. He wrote me often and sent me little gifts. Fearing that our father would not give me his things, Matthew sent everything to Mrs. Park, and she found a way to get them to me without his detection. I was so proud when I learned that he had become a Navy Seal. We didn't see Matthew again until he was shipped home in a coffin. I was eighteen then. My other brother, Collin, was off at the University of Alabama on a full swim scholarship. I was alone with my increasingly irrational father.

Then my knight arrived and swept me away from the dungeon of my childhood with his charm, generosity and his seemingly endless desire to treat me like a queen. I was smitten in no time and married six months later. Who needs college when you are marrying a handsome attorney ten years older than you? He was someone who could get me away from my father. Andrew Jackson Jameson III was truly a godsend.

I jumped when a noise like a woodpecker at work pulled me out of my reflective state to see Alex rapping on my window.

"Sorry, Mary Claire. I didn't mean to startle you." I unlocked the car, and Alex tossed her bag in the back seat. Then she went around to the passenger side and got in my car.

"You okay?" she asked with concern.

"Yes, yes. I just dozed off for a few minutes." I looked around the parking lot. "No one else here but the two of us?"

"Looks that way. I hope Dallas shows up. I texted her this morning to remind her where we were meeting, but she didn't respond."

"I wouldn't worry about Dallas. She wouldn't miss an opportunity to play."

"What makes you so confident she'll show up? Granted, she's a fabulous player, but none of us really know a thing about her. Being skilled doesn't always mean you're reliable."

"I had lunch with her yesterday, and she talked at length about how important it was for her to play."

"You had a one-on-one lunch with Dallas O'Malley, MY tennis partner?" Alex stared in disbelief. "Did you take her at gunpoint?"

"Actually, she asked me to lunch, Alex." I laughed. "She was a bit awkward socially, but quite pleasant. I got the impression that she hasn't interacted much with anyone in some time."

"Well, do tell. She's quite the mystery, and some ladies are a little scared of her."

"Ironically, I believe Dallas is far more afraid of us than we are of her."

Alex interrupted. "Oh, come on. I love being her partner, but she is one angry woman."

"I agree, but I think her anger stems from fear and suffering. I do know that she has no family. And to be thirty years old and have no one is quite tragic."

"Dallas is only thirty! I thought she was more like forty. She looks so hard to be that young."

"I know. I was shocked as well, but I'm convinced something haunts her. I will admit that I thought her poor social skills simply arose from a more modest upbringing -- a lack of exposure to the social graces. But we ate at The Club, and she was completely familiar with table etiquette. She never hesitated with the utensils; she folded her napkin like a pro. But the entire meal she displayed complete paranoia. She constantly scanned the room, looking over her shoulder like a cat wary of the neighborhood canines."

"Did you ask her why she was doing that?"

"Yes, I asked but she said she thought she saw someone she knew and hadn't seen for some time. She seemed very nervous. I asked if she wanted to go and say hello, but she said it must be her imagination. She said it wasn't who she thought it was."

"How strange. Well, why did she ask you to lunch? What did she want to talk about?"

"I think she's lonely, and maybe she sees something maternal in me. She knows I don't have children and that I am certainly old enough to be her mother. She asked me so many questions about my life."

"Really? What kind of questions?"

"She wanted to know where I was from, had I ever worked, what did my husband do for a living, what was his family like?"

"Wow! That's awfully nosey."

"No, I think she is desperate to connect with someone. She admitted she doesn't have any friends."

"So sad," Alex said. She looked at her phone. "Okay, still no response. I'll text her again."

DALLAS

When I woke up, I was disoriented. How long had I been asleep, I wondered. I turned to my bedside table to look at the clock, but it wasn't there. I looked around the room and realized I was not in my own bedroom. The room was dark, and thick white shades covered the windows; I couldn't tell if it was day or night. The room had no personality -- a sterile environment with stark, white walls and the nauseating smell of a strong cleaning agent.

My head was pounding. Actually, my whole face ached. I needed some Ibuprofen desperately. I brushed my hand over my throbbing forehead and jerked it away when I felt a raised, rough line like a thin rope. I carefully traced the line and estimated that it stretched four inches across my forehead, an inch below my hairline. Stitches. What happened to me? The details were coming together, and I realized that I was in the hospital. Panicked, I shouted out, "Hey!" Immediately the door opened and a young, police officer charged in, looking in all directions before cautiously coming toward me.

"How are you, Miss Sanderson?" he asked in a whisper.

I looked at him as if he had three heads. "Who are YOU? And why am I in a hospital?" I touched my stitches gingerly and demanded, "What happened to me?"

The officer smiled nervously. "Let me find someone who can answer your questions. It might take a half hour or so, though. I'll let the nurse know you're awake."

I drifted back into a restless sleep plagued by images of giant pieces of burning wood falling from the sky. The visions seemed so real that I jerked awake in a cold sweat, breathing heavily as if I had just finished sprinting up several flights of stairs.

A man sat in a chair next to me. His head was bent down studying some papers on his lap. His thinning salt and pepper hair revealed a blossoming bald spot at the crown of his head. Though he was seated, I could tell he was exceptionally tall, maybe over six/four, probably a former high school jock but two to three decades earlier based on his gut. I had no idea who he was. Another stranger. It suddenly dawned on me that everyone around me was a stranger. Where was my family?

I cleared my throat and the man looked up. He smiled, a kind, fatherly smile -- like my dad's. Where was Dad?

"Hello, Miss Sanderson. I'm Detective Hatcher of the Charleston police department."

I grimaced as I tried to sit up higher in the bed. "Detective? Why do I need to see a detective? What happened to me?"

Detective Hatcher furrowed his brow and looked at me with concern. "You don't remember anything?"

I felt my anxiety mount. My questions were only breeding more questions. "Where are my parents?" I demanded.

One of my monitors sounded an alarm. I felt dizzy, and as my head began to spin, a nurse rushed in, and I saw Detective Hatcher hurrying out of the room before it folded into darkness.

I awoke to the chimes of my phone and saw I had a missed call and a text from Alex:

Where are you?

I looked at my watch and realized that I was ten minutes late to meet her at Wendy's so we could ride together to the match in Talladega. Oh shit. I texted her back:

Sorry. Overslept. Will meet you there.

If I left in five minutes I would make it in time, though I wouldn't be able to warm up.

CALLIE

I turned into the Wendy's parking lot and saw that Mary Claire and Alex were already there. Hurriedly, I parked next to Mary Claire and jumped in the backseat of her white Lexus. "Hey ladies," I greeted them. "Sorry I'm late. Where's Dallas?"

"Just got a text from her," Alex answered. "She overslept but will meet us there. She'll arrive right at start time. No warm up for her, but it's not like she needs it."

Mary Claire turned the ignition. "Okay, so we can go now. You said Katlin and Molly Katherine are coming on their own, right?" I nodded.

"Mary Claire, it's MKat not Molly Katherine. Get on board, hon," Alex corrected.

Mary Claire frowned. "Why do you insist on calling her MKat? The woman loathes that nickname."

"That's precisely why I do it," Alex chided. I laughed. Mary Claire endeavored valiantly to appear appalled, but I could tell she was amused. Alex added, "I welcome any chance I get to take that pompous, pious, judgmental hag down a notch!"

"You're a riot, Alex," I said. "Apparently everybody on the team feels that way. I was going to let Kelly and Amy play the 3.0 court today, but Kelly couldn't and Amy said, and I quote, 'no way in hell I'll play with MKat Harriman. She sucks all the fun out of it'."

"Why didn't you just let Amy play with Katlin and sit MKat out?"

Mary Claire and I exchanged a look in the rear view mirror. I thought she could explain the situation more delicately than I could. "Mary Claire, will you please enlighten Alex?"

She sighed. "I don't like to gossip, but frankly I'm shocked that Amy Morard agreed to be on the same team as Katlin Hamilton."

"Do tell," Alex demanded, her curiosity piqued.

Mary Claire began, "Amy is married to Ian Morard, and Ian's second cousin is Brad Morard. Now Brad and his wife, Grace, have been members of Birmingham Heights Country Club since they were married. Their membership was a wedding gift from Brad's parents. In fact, they held their wedding reception at The Heights. Andrew and I attended the wedding -- that was about fifteen years ago. Andrew's law firm represents Morard Industries in all legal matters, so Andrew and Brad Senior have a long business history. All this to say that the Morards are a very social family. And as you know, it's difficult to find a more social family than Katlin's."

I interjected, "To summarize, Katlin's family, the Hamiltons, had been social butterflies with the Morards for at least twenty years."

"That is correct," Mary Claire said, taking command of the story again. "At the time of the wedding, Katlin was ten years old. For years there had been rumors that Katlin, the youngest of the Hamilton offspring, might be the product of a long term affair between Katlin's mom and Brad Morard Senior. Let me reiterate that this was a rumor, not a scandal -- just whisperings without justification. When it reached my ears, I simply ignored it. But a decade later, Katlin, who had blossomed into quite a stunning young girl, captured the attention of thirty-five year old Brad Morard, who was ten years and two kids deep in marriage to Grace, and apparently feeling trapped. Katlin knew Brad was interested, and his wedding band didn't keep her from shameless flirtations which culminated in quite a sordid affair, ninety percent of which took place on the grounds of The Heights."

"No way!" exclaimed Alex.

Mary Claire nodded. "But this affair was not a rumor. There were pictures which were circulated with the caption, 'Hamilton Princess Seduced by Much Older Alleged Half-Brother, Brad Morard'."

Alex whistled and said, "This is straight from *Days of Our Lives*. We moved here five years ago, so I guess all the dust had settled before then."

"Yes, long story short, it was quite a disaster and a miracle that the whole scandal didn't end with three divorces. Katlin's dad, mortified by the possibility that his little princess might not be his biological daughter and by the idea that she might have inadvertently slept with her half brother (the fact that he was married didn't seem to be a problem), demanded a paternity test. Supposedly, tests confirmed that Katlin was indeed a real Hamilton. I don't know how the families came to grips with it all, but eventually it all died down and everyone stayed together."

"Wow," Alex muttered. "Okay, so Amy Morard, who is on our team, is not a blood relative of Brad's. Brad is her husband's second cousin, and all this took place seven years ago. Seems like enough time has passed and that the relative status is distant enough for Amy not to hold a grudge. After all, Brad is just as guilty as Katlin."

"The Morard clan is very tight," I explained. "They stick together like a Mafia family. But I know why Amy joined our team. First of all, she wants to go to state, and Jake drafted her for the team under the premise that he felt that this team had a great shot at going to state. Secondly, she doesn't really get along with Brad's wife, Grace. What better way to needle Grace than to play on a team with her husband's former mistress."

"How do you know that Callie?" Mary Claire asked skeptically.

"I overheard Amy and Kelly talking about it at the beginning of the season. I was in the locker room, but they thought they were alone."

"You know, Katlin is young and very obviously a spoiled brat, but overall she seems like a nice girl," Alex commented. "Maybe this guy she's so crazy about now is the real deal -- someone she can settle down with."

Mary Claire looked doubtful. "I don't know. She said he was about as old as her father and recently divorced. She seems to be repeatedly attracted to older men."

"Oh really," Alex said. "Brad Morard wasn't her only romp down adultery lane?"

"No, her other target was older, but not married." Mary Claire hesitated, as if she were considering not sharing what she knew, but apparently she decided to proceed. "I like Katlin, but I've watched her grow up around The Heights and by the time she was sixteen, she had obviously set her sights on Jake Lenaghan."

My pulse quickened. "Jake had a relationship with Katlin? Gross!" I accused rather than inquired.

"I didn't say that," Mary Claire defended calmly. "Callie, I told you that Jake was a man of tremendous character. He would not go down that road. I simply said it was obvious that she was after him, and her efforts escalated as she grew older."

"How did they escalate?" Alex inquired, clearly soaking in all this juicy gossip.

"Obviously while she was involved with Brad Morard, she abandoned her pursuit of Jake. After that scandal faded away, and she had graduated from college, she resumed her efforts."

"Mary Claire, how do you know all this?" I asked.

"I have considered Jake not only a wonderful tennis pro but a valued friend for at least ten years. He came to me and asked my advice when things got out of hand."

"What do you mean by 'out of hand'?" I was incensed. I don't know why, but I just couldn't keep my indignation out of my tone.

I saw Mary Claire glance back at me. She looked amused. "Jake told me that Katlin had repeatedly invited him to meet her out at local bars and had even asked him to be her 'companion' over the weekend play at the US Open -- all expenses paid."

"And he passed on the US Open?" Alex asked incredulously.

"Absolutely," Mary Claire answered. "There was never any question in his mind. I'm telling you both that Jake is a man of quality. He told me he was not going to take advantage of a young girl. But, he was concerned that although he had declined all of her advances, she wasn't going away. The advances were just becoming more elaborate. He wasn't sure what he should do. Her daddy paid the bills, so she scheduled private lessons with him almost daily, and she wore the most provocative apparel. I told him he was handling it appropriately and that, unless Katlin was completely unbalanced, she would eventually take a hint. But when he caught her skinny dipping in the pool, he was so upset."

"Oh, good Lord. A man can resist only so long. Did he cave?" Alex was salivating over this story.

Mary Claire laughed. "No, he didn't cave. He told me about it the next day. He said he apologized for catching her because he knew she did not intend for that to happen. He turned his back and told her she should get dressed and go home because it was not safe for her to be alone at night in a pool. Apparently that rejection was enough to squelch her quest. She hasn't bothered him since, except I have heard her suggest that Jake might be gay."

I declared emphatically, "That's a joke."

"And how would you know, missy?" asked Alex in a sassy tone. "Katlin is a hot little thing. Most men would sample the goods after repeated offers."

"Yes, tell us how you would know, Callie," Mary Claire seconded.

I blushed. Hopefully, they didn't notice since I was in the backseat. "I mean, we're good friends and spend time together. There is nothing about his behavior that would make me think he's gay. Trust me, he is 100% heterosexual."

"Oh, so you are an authority on Jake's sexuality?" Alex probed.

"By the way, Callie," Mary Claire interjected, "I texted you several times last night. Were you too busy verifying Jake's sexuality to answer my texts?"

"You had a date with Jake last night?" Alex asked excitedly.

At this point, we were exiting I-20, and in less than two minutes we would be at the Talladega YMCA. "Alex, I just said we were friends and that we hang out together. We went to a movie last night. I'm sorry, Mary Claire. I meant to call you when I got home, but I fell asleep before I did."

"Oh, honey," interjected Alex. "That man is a prize. You oughta go for that."

I cleared my throat as we turned into the parking lot. "We're here now. Let's go."

After a quick trip to the bathroom, we reached the courts and began our warm up. Mary Claire and I hit some balls to Katlin and Alex. I hit as hard as I could to Katlin. She couldn't handle my pace. I just kept pounding her with no mercy. When we warmed up volleys, I aimed at her body most of the time.

"OMG, Callie, are you trying to kill me?" Katlin whined.

Immediately, I realized I was punishing her for coveting Jake. And I had no right. She was a beautiful, young, single female who went after a handsome, single man, although way too old for her, but I had no right to be annoyed. So why was I thoroughly unglued?

"Sorry, Katlin. Just taking out frustrations on the ball. Nothing personal. I see MKat heading this way. Have a great match." With that said, I headed to the bathroom, splashed water on my face, and tried to shake off my unsettling feelings. I hated the fact that anything to do with Jake Lenaghan affected me so deeply. Like I said, he was dangerous for me.

KATLIN

I watched Callie walk away as MKat approached. I guess I had a weird expression on my face because MKat said, "What's wrong, dear?"

"Oh, nothing." I had no desire to discuss anything with MKat. "How's your husband? Is he feeling any better?"

"Well, thank you for asking, dear, but I don't think he's much better. I really felt guilty leaving him. His coloring is bad, and he's so listless. I hated to leave him, but I knew that the team needed me to pull off the win, so here I am."

I wanted to punch the old bag, but just then I heard the ping of a text. It was my boyfriend, Sam. Perfect timing. He wanted to wish me a happy day. What a sweet man. I smiled and immediately felt calm. I had never felt so positively about any relationship in the past. Sam is good medicine for me. He keeps me even-tempered and truly happy. Peaceful. Those are feelings that I'd never experienced until I met him.

It was 9:25 am. We had five minutes left to warm up. We hit a few groundstrokes, served on each side four times, and went to meet our opponents who were waiting on the side of the court. Constance was a very tall, large woman, who greeted us with firm handshakes and a friendly smile. Her petite, much younger partner, Andi, looked disgusted when Constance smiled. And then I saw why. Constance had a big hole where her two front, top teeth should be. I guess we all looked a little shocked, because suddenly her hand flew up to cover her mouth. "Oh, ladies, do forgive me. My partial plate cracked last night, so my teeth are missing this morning. I keep forgetting."

"My dear, how is that possible to forget? I would think it would be quite drafty in there." MKat just had to comment. "Well, you are quite a trooper to come out and play. I would have been inclined to forfeit a court before I would have embarrassed myself in public." Andi, standing slightly behind her partner, nodded in agreement.

"MKat!" I exclaimed. I knew my voice had hit that whiny pitch that always came out when I was really angry. "You are so rude." I turned to Constance, who looked as if she had just been slapped in the face. "Constance, just ignore MKat. She didn't mean to be so insulting. Her husband is very ill, and she hasn't been herself lately."

MKat poked me on the shoulder. "Excuse me, but I don't need a spoiled, little debutant speaking for me, Miss Katlin Hamilton."

Before I could react, our petite opponent, Andi, spoke up. "Katlin Hamilton. You're the rich bitch that almost destroyed my cousin's marriage. You remember Grace Morard, don't you?"

I stood like a statue unable to speak or move. Constance glared at her partner and lashed out. "Andi, that was uncalled for and completely out of place. You should apologize right now." Her speech was a little slurred due to the missing teeth.

"Don't tell me what to do, Constance. You're not my mother, thank God. How embarrassing that would be!"

By this time the other two courts had stopped playing and everybody was staring. They probably overheard most of the conversation since our voices were so loud. Callie, who was two courts away, started walking in our direction. I could tell she was ticked. But as she reached the court between us where Alex and Dallas were playing, Alex stopped Callie and said, "I got this, captain."

Alex walked over with a big smile on her face. "Ladies. Now I have heard your conversation, well everybody on my court has. How could they not? It appears there's a lot of PMS going on over here," her tone was casual and friendly, and she circled her hands as she spoke as if drawing us all into a ring of guilt. "This is no place for a cat fight. Y'all just need to put on your big girl panties, forget every silly word just said, and play your match. Y'all aren't here to make friends or enemies. Just keep your opinions to yourself and play. Got it?" Everybody nodded. "Good," she stated as she turned back to her court, "because I don't want to have to come back over here and put anybody in time out!"

No words were spoken from that point, except the mandatory scores and line calls. Every time MKat and Constance were up at the net, Constance would look at MKat and smile. From the baseline, I couldn't resist giving Constance a thumbs up. That smile unraveled MKat, and she played worse than I'd ever seen her play.

It was an ugly match, but somehow we pulled out the win, 2-6, 7-5, and a 10-8 tiebreak. Our team ended up winning the match 3-0, but it was really a close match, except, of course, Dallas and Alex who won in two sets, 6-4, 6-3. They always win. Dallas is a tennis machine. I stuck around to watch Mary Claire and Callie finish their match. They lost the first set 6-7, won the second 7-6 and won the tiebreak 21-19. It was a marathon.

I congratulated Callie and apologized for the altercation on our court. She told me she knew that I wasn't the instigator. I just smiled and said, "To be honest, if there is any way I can avoid playing with MKat, I'd appreciate it. She was so condescending to that sweet lady. Callie, MKat is a good player, but she's not half as good as she thinks she is. And her personality is hard to take."

"I know," Callie agreed. "I'll see what I can do. But next week I have no choice but to play y'all together. The other 3.0s aren't available."

"Okay," I conceded. "But even if I have to sit out, if you could give me a few breaks from her, I'd appreciate it."

"I promise I'll make that happen," Callie said. "And thanks for putting up with her."

I was glad that Callie didn't seem annoyed with me like she did during warm up. That was bizarre. But I was even happier that she said she would try to keep me away from MKat.

ALEX

After the match, Mary Claire, Callie and I ran through the Chick-fil-a drive-through on our way out of town. We had originally planned to stop somewhere and enjoy a leisurely lunch, but it was late, and we all needed to get back home and tend to our personal business. Starving, we ate in silence, but once I collected all the empty wrappers, I couldn't help myself. From the back, I leaned forward and wedged myself between the front seats. "So, Callie. Let's talk about Jake."

Callie sighed, then grinned. "Okay, I'll tell you something about Jake. I'm going to find a way to make him pay for drafting MKat for this team."

"That was some crazy business on her court today," I responded, fully aware that Callie was trying to divert my attention. "The funny thing is that Katlin seemed like the most mature one on the court."

"Yes, she even apologized for the scene which is more than MKat did. But she asked if she could avoid playing with MKat. Nobody wants to play with her. We have six matches left. Not sure what to do about that."

"Play Amy and Kelly next week," Mary Claire suggested.

Callie shook her head. "Amy and Kelly aren't around next week. I told Katlin she'd have to play with MKat again, but I would give her a break as soon as possible."

Mary Claire added, "Katlin is so in love that she's in a perpetually forgiving mood. She'll be fine with whatever you do."

"She is smitten," I interjected. "So cute how she blushes when you mention 'the boyfriend'. And speaking of boyfriends, Callie, when is your next date with Jake?"

"Geez, Alex! You're relentless! Like I said earlier, we are great friends, nothing more."

Her tone told me to shut up. Mama didn't raise no fool, so I changed the subject. "So what's the deal with MKat's husband? Since we had our preseason match, MKat has said he was sick. And that was two weeks ago. Seems like if he's that sick, he might need to be in a hospital."

"Surely Molly Katherine wouldn't drive all the way to Talladega and play tennis if he were deathly ill," Mary Claire commented.

Callie agreed. "Yeah. She's a wicked piece of work, but she's an old school southern woman."

"What exactly does that mean?" I asked.

"That she'll be there 'til his dying breath," Callie explained.

All I could say was, "Poor Edward."

IF LOOKS COULD KILL

MATCH 3 - June 20, 2014

Karma's a bitch.

CALLIE

On Tuesday, June 17th, after the match in Talladega where MKat and Katlin almost erupted in a catfight with their opponents, we had clinic with Jake at 10am. As I speculated, Katlin and MKat did not attend. In fact, no one came except Alex, Mary Claire, and me. Dallas's absence surprised me, but it's not like she needed to practice. She continued to be a dominant force on the team.

"Hello, ladies. How are things going?" Jake asked as we started warming up at the net. "Did you have a good match last week?"

"Well, I've got no complaints," offered Alex. "Dallas may be an odd bird, but damn, can that girl play some tennis. So thanks, Jake, for putting me with the 'terminator'."

"I knew you could handle her, Alex." Jake turned to Mary Claire who once again wore a long-sleeved shirt -- and it was 98 degrees with 67% humidity. "Mary Claire, you've got to be burning up. Aren't you done with that round of antibiotics? Can't you go back to short sleeves?"

Mary Claire looked away and coughed. "Had to start another round of meds. Unfortunately, I suffered another flare-up the other day."

Jake missed the net shot I returned to him and pushed the ball cart to the back with unnecessary vigor. "Everybody move to the baseline," he ordered, his voice clearly irritated. He kept his back to us, bouncing a ball for an unusually long time.

Alex looked at me and whispered, "What's up with your boyfriend?"

"I don't know, and he's not my boyfriend," I whispered emphatically.

Alex gave me an exaggerated wink. Jake turned toward us with a smile on his face and seemed to be himself again. We continued with some drills, good point play, and overhead work.

When clinic was over, I lingered by repacking my tennis bag (which I had cleaned out last night). "Hey you," Jake called from the net. "Let me buy you lunch."

I suspended my ever so important repacking process. "That sounds like a date," I responded with an accusatory tone.

"Well, we wouldn't want that now would we? Come on, Conrad. I'm free for two hours. I could use some pleasant conversation with a friend. Your choice."

"Okay. Taziki's?" Jake nodded. "I'll just meet you there."

"See you in a minute," he agreed.

We went through the line and ordered our food -- a roasted pork loin sandwich for Jake and a Greek salad with chicken for me. We set our number on an outside table nestled under an awning, so the temperature was almost pleasant.

"So what was that all about?" I asked after we sat.

"What was what all about?" Jake responded.

"After Mary Claire said she was taking more antibiotics, you acted uptight for a few minutes."

Jake popped his knuckles, looked away, and remained silent for a long time. "Something's up with her," he finally said as he turned back to make eye contact. "You need to make her confide in you. She's so damn stoic, you'll have to push her."

"She's very private, Jake. I don't want to pry."

"Sometimes prying is justified."

He was so serious. "Okay. I'll try to get her to open up." Just then our food arrived.

Jake seemed to refocus his attention on his sandwich. "How did your match go Friday? It was in Talladega, right?"

I nodded as I chewed a bite of salad. "We won 3 and 0, but it was a battle on every court except for Alex and Dallas. Dallas is unreal. She could play 4.5 easily. I still can't believe she found you and sought out this team."

"Why is that so strange? You and Mary Claire have been partners for what, five years, and players know who you are and respect you. I'm not surprised that someone wants to play on your team. What's odd is how little anyone knows about her."

"What do you mean?"

"After I agreed to put her on this team, I started asking around about her. She's been playing out of Pelham Racquet Club, so I made some inquiries there. Everybody knows that she's an awesome player, but no one seems to know anything about her. According to my contacts, Dallas channels a boatload of energy into her game, but off the court she's a zombie. She really doesn't speak to anyone or divulge any personal information. The pro there described her as 'intensely passionate on the court and completely lifeless off the court'."

I nodded. "That's a perfect description."

"Except she does seem to harbor some fascination with Mary Claire," Jake added. "She's asked me about Mary Claire's personal life, which I found rather strange."

"Really? She's quizzed me about Mary Claire, too."

"Strange. Maybe you should ask Mary Claire about that when you approach her about her long-sleeved shirts."

We ate in silence for a few minutes. I couldn't resist poking at Jake. "I did learn something interesting during my drive to Talladega."

"What's that?" Jake inquired nonchalantly.

"I heard that Katlin Hamilton chased you for years like a dog in heat."

Jake choked a little as he swallowed a sip of water. "Oh God, yes. It started when she was sixteen and really didn't stop until a few years ago. And thank God she finally stopped."

"Is it really true that she asked you to go as her guest to the US Open?"

"Yes."

"I have to ask. Why did you turn her down? That had to be tempting."

"Definitely tempting. Especially since she had phenomenal seats and passes to several parties that tennis icons would attend. But if I accepted, I knew I would just be using her. I have never had any interest in Katlin. She's a beautiful girl, but to me she's just a kid, who, quite frankly, seems a little vacuous. She reminds me of someone I dated in college, and I have no desire to go down that road again."

"Well, apparently she's gotten over you and seems quite smitten with some older guy she's been dating."

"Good for her," Jake declared. "I hope she is blissfully happy with her new target."

"So, tell me again why you picked Molly Katherine Harriman for this team. You know she's playing with your jilted Katlin."

Jake laughed. "That's a match destined for trouble. The puritanical and the promiscuous."

"Yes, they just about ignited on the court on Friday." I relayed the details of the altercation with their opponents.

"Wow. Sounds like Katlin handled herself with a little maturity. Maybe she's grown up a bit."

"Sounds like you might be interested in a matured Katlin."

Jake snickered. "No way. I'm only interested in women who demand platonic interaction. Gotta love a challenge."

With that comment, he rose and discarded the crumbs of his lunch. I stared at my empty plate wondering, yet again, why I was adamantly opposed to getting romantically involved with this guy. As I stood to leave, I saw Alex sitting with some man in the back corner of the restaurant. She gave me a thumbs-up and winked.

ALEX

"Morning, Mom." Ah, the sweet sound of my daughter's voice. Truly music to my ears. Avery was home for a weekend of wedding planning. I couldn't believe my baby girl was getting married. But she was marrying a fabulous young man. The only negative comment I could honestly make about this union was that Avery and her children would be branded with a heinous last name.

Avery walked into the kitchen. "Well, if it isn't the future Mrs. TIT-man," I teased as I wrapped my arms around her. Avery rolled her eyes and clasped my face tightly between her palms. "Oh, Mother, there is no exaggerated pronunciation of the first syllable."

I smiled. "Well, I guess it could be worse, like Mrs. Asswipe."

Avery gave that one a fake laugh and asked, "Where's Izzy?"

"You mean Easy?" I responded.

"Huh?" Avery's nose crinkled -- a reflex so adorable as a child and equally endearing as an adult.

Izzy was a Boykin Spaniel that Avery's last boyfriend (aka, Lord Voldemort) had given her three Christmases ago. Avery left her with us after they broke up six months later, claiming Izzy was a painful reminder of the man who broke her heart. No big surprise to me. I knew his parents, the Prince and Princess of Darkness. "Your dog, my dear, has been whoring it up. She must really put out. I've seen more than one canine sneaking into the yard. Figures Mr. Gabriel Holloway the Fourth would give you a dog as sleazy as he is."

Avery smirked and grabbed an apple from the fruit bowl on the counter. "Oh, Mom. That's all part of the past. You know Gabe ended up marrying Emma three months after I caught them in bed." She tossed the apple gingerly from hand to hand. "I hear they are miserable. Dreadful, isn't it?" she feigned concern and bit a chunk from the apple.

In Scarlet O'Hara fashion, I cooed, "Breaks my heart, darlin'."

"Well, finding my boyfriend in the sack with my roommate did help me choose more wisely next time around. Travis Titman runs circles around Gabe Holloway on every level. And when it comes to sex, Gabe is just in the kiddie leagues."

"TMI ! TMI !" I shouted. "There are just some things a mother doesn't want to know. Even one as cool as me."

Avery laughed. "Okay, but seriously, where do you think Izzy is? I've checked all her favorite spots in the house and can't find her. She must have stayed outside last night. Does she have a favorite outdoor hideout?"

Just then Izzy poked her head through the doggy door of the back deck door. She saw Avery and yelped with glee. She bolted through the hole and went straight to Avery who scooped her up and received a shower of slobbering kisses. "Izzy baby. You feel so heavy. Look at your fat belly. Mom, what are you feeding her?"

I walked over to Avery and patted Izzy's chocolate head. "Yeah, I noticed that she's gained weight lately. Happens to the best of us," I said as I patted my belly. "Your dad's probably sneaking her too many treats. She has him wrapped. I just put her on a Purina food for overweight dogs. I'm sure she'll lose it."

"I hope so. It's so bad for her joints to be overweight. And she's still young."

"I know, sweetie. Please feel free to take her back at any time. Obviously, it's no longer painful for you to love on Lord Voldemort's final offering."

Avery grinned. "I know, Mom. Thanks for keeping her for so long. I promise that once Travis and I get settled, we will take her back."

"No hurry. I'm attached now."

"So, what's on tap for today?" Avery asked as she snuggled with an elated Izzy.

"I play tennis on Fridays, and today we have a match at Mountain Brook Club. If you want to come watch, we can go grab a bite to eat at Olexa's after the match, and then we can head over to the caterers at four to finalize the menu. Gabby said she had a few more dishes she wanted you to sample."

"Sounds good. I haven't seen you play in years. Have you improved at all?"

"Smarty pants," I teased as I punched her arm.

"I'm just kidding, Mom. I'm sure you're probably ready to turn pro by now."

"Damn straight, little girl. We'll need to leave in about half an hour."

Avery headed toward the staircase. "I'll just run upstairs and change."

"Don't forget to 'slather up' with sunscreen," I yelled as she disappeared from view.

"Mother, I am twenty-seven. Don't need my mommy to remind me that my skin goes up in flames without sunscreen."

"Sorry, IVORY. Hard to turn off the mommy switch." Sly nicknamed her Ivory because of her lily white, untannable skin. At least she won't have skin like a Shar Pei when she's forty.

I changed into my favorite tennis skirt. It felt snug. Thank goodness the material stretches. I thought about the beautiful dress I bought to wear to Avery's wedding. I found it in Atlanta three months ago. Three months ago my tennis clothes didn't feel tight. Would it still fit?

My cell phone rang and thankfully disrupted my disturbing train of thought. I dug it out of my purse but didn't recognize the number. "Hello?"

"Is this Alex?" the caller asked.

"Yes."

"Hey, Alex. This is Molly Katherine Harriman."

"Hi MKat," I responded. I snarled at the phone just as Avery walked into my bedroom. She gave me a look, and I just waved her away.

"Alex, I hate to bother you, dear, but I need a ride to the match today. My car won't start, and my husband is still under the weather. You are the closest teammate to me, so it just makes sense that you be the one to pick me up."

"Okay. Give me your address and I'll be there shortly, but you'll have to find someone else to take you home. My daughter is with me, and we have some places to go directly after the match."

"Thank you, dear. I'm sure no one would mind taking me home."

"Yeah, right. They'll all be fighting for the chance," I muttered as I hung up.

"What was that all about?" Avery asked.

I grabbed my bag and motioned for her to follow. "We have to pick up one of my teammates," I groaned as I tossed my purse into my tennis bag.

"I take it you don't care for this person."

I found my keys on the kitchen table, and we headed toward the garage. "Well, you remember your Grandpa's #1 rule?"

Avery did her best impersonation of my dad. While speaking in a deep, gruff voice, she pumped her fists for emphasis. "If you don't have anything nice to say about someone, don't say anything at all."

I chuckled because she always nailed it. "Let's just say Mrs. Harriman renders me mute."

MKAT

I saw Alex's loud, crimson Audi SUV turn into the driveway, so I hurried from my perch on the front porch, tennis bag in hand.

I got into the backseat and placed my bag to my right. I was quite surprised that her daughter did not give me, the elder adult and the guest in the car, the front seat, but I was gracious and kept silent on the subject of bad manners. You know what they say, like mother like daughter.

"Thank you for picking me up, Alex. I hope it wasn't too much trouble."

"Only ten miles out of the way, MKat. This is my daughter, Avery. Avery, meet Molly Katherine Harriman."

Alex's daughter turned toward me. "Nice to meet you, Mrs. Harriman."

"Likewise, dear."

"By the way, MKat, what made you think that I was the closest person to come pick you up?"

I pulled my pink address book out of my pocketbook. "When Callie gave us the team roster, I looked everybody up and recorded their telephone numbers and addresses in my little book." I held it up so Alex could see it in the rearview mirror. "Then I drove to each house just to see how close I was to everyone and based on the calculations I recorded, you were the closest."

Alex and her daughter were silent. It's not like Alex to be quiet. She is an overly chatty, rather crass woman, so the silence felt awkward. I decided I needed to stimulate a conversation. "Avery, have you met your mother's doubles partner on this team?"

Avery turned to me. "No, ma'am. I look forward to meeting her today."

"Well, maybe she'll be cordial to you. I think she is downright sinister."

Alex found her voice. "MKat, Dallas is not sinister. She is very reserved. Yes, she's hard to get to know, but she is an outstanding player. I'm lucky to have her as a partner."

I saw Alex and her daughter smile at each other. They must be close. "Avery, can you believe your mother has butchered my lovely southern name and dubbed me MKat? MKat. Sounds like a nasty medical procedure. And now all the ladies on the team call me MKat. Shame on your mother."

"Mrs. Harriman, you should be flattered that my mom gave you a nickname. A nickname is a genuine sign of affection, a term of endearment."

I saw Alex wink at Avery. What a sweet relationship they seem to share. If Edward had been able to give me children, I'm sure I would have had a girl, and we would have been two peas in a pod. But, I was barren because of my unfortunate union with Edward.

ALEX

After I introduced Avery to the girls, she found a shady spot on the clubhouse porch with a good view of all the courts. Avery never had an interest in playing tennis but liked to watch the major tournaments with me and observe on occasion. Today, we clearly entertained her.

Dallas was quieter than usual, if that's even possible. She was silent to the point of rudeness, ignoring direct questions from our opponents. I made light of her mood by saying she was so focused when she played that she barely spoke to me. Dallas was by far the most intense personality I'd dealt with as a partner, but nothing ever affected her game. In fact, it seemed that the darker her mood, the more dangerous an opponent she was. I'd never had a partner who took so many risks -- long shot poaches, low percentage shots -- yet her unforced error rate was in the single digits every match. She played with the confidence of one protected by the tennis gods, but I knew she was mortal and had an Achilles heel. Everybody does. I just hadn't discovered hers yet.

We were leading in the first set 4-0, and Dallas returned a serve. Her shot was beautifully placed as it hit the outside doubles line and ricocheted off the tape. If we were pros, it would be one of those shots the tennis commentators would dub "the shot of the day"-- hard, low, fast, unreturnable. Our opponent called it out. I said with disbelief, "Excuse me." The ball was clearly in because no ball, even one with wicked spin, takes a bounce like that unless it hits the tape on a soft court.

"That ball was out," our opponent repeated emphatically.

Dallas looked like a bull ready to charge. She started moving forward with a demonic look on her face. Holy shit, I knew I had to diffuse the situation and fast. I blocked her and put my hand on her shoulder. "Dallas," I said calmly, "that ball was clearly in, but let me handle this okay. Even if we give them the point, we are way ahead, and we will win. I promise. What goes around comes around. Just watch."

While I was talking to her, she was giving our opponents (who had approached the net) a death stare. Finally she refocused her gaze on me and said in a low, guttural voice, "Fine."

Dallas returned to the baseline, and I approached the net. Now, playing as many years as I have, I know there is such a thing as karma. Our opponent, Mimi, had called the ball out, so I calmly turned to Cara, her partner, and said, "Do you really support your partner's call? That ball was clearly in."

Cara looked scared and turned toward Mimi, who gave her a look that would deflate the strongest of souls. Meekly she responded, "I really didn't see the ball. I just didn't have a good angle."

Mimi gave me an "eat shit" grin and I calmly replied, "Okay, ladies. It's your call and Mimi, if you can live with that blatant lie, the point's all yours." I turned and walked back to the baseline and whispered to Dallas, "Just watch now. That Mimi will screw up every ball that comes her way in the next five minutes, so hit everything at her. Notice I said 'at' not 'to'." Dallas gave me a subtle, but clearly evil, grin.

It was my service game, and I served out wide to Cara. My serve is by no means strong, but I think my chat had rattled her, and she hit a weak, high floater that Dallas attacked at the net. It landed at Mimi's feet and died. She had no chance to return it. We bombarded Mimi with every return, and she blundered all. In four minutes the set was over -- a 6-0 victory for us. Silence ruled the break between sets. No friendly banter about children and personal lives erupted as is typical at these club matches. The tension was as suffocating as the humidity, but it worked to our advantage. The second set was over in twenty minutes. I played well, but Dallas was freakin' unbelievable. I swear I think she hit one ball out and that was it for unforced errors. We walked away from the match with a 6-0/6-0 win. Needless to say, our opponents' handshakes lacked sincerity.

Dallas and I walked up to the porch where Avery watched, and she greeted us with enthusiastic applause. She hugged me and said, "Mom, you have improved, but I think the best improvement is your partner. Wow, Dallas, you make my mom look good."

Dallas awkwardly acknowledged the compliment with a nod. She looked at the other courts in play. At the moment, it appeared that our team would win 3-0. Dallas picked up her bag. "Looks like this match is in the bag. I need to head out."

"Looks can be deceiving, partner," I said playfully. "A match can turn quickly. Don't you want to stay and watch? You are welcome to join Avery and me for lunch afterwards."

"Thanks, but I have a ton of stuff to do." She hoisted her bag on her shoulder and started to walk away. "Thanks for keeping me from strangling that bitch today, Alex. Nothing I hate more than liars and cheaters."

Avery called after her, "Nice to meet you, Dallas." Dallas did not respond.

Avery stared after her, dumbfounded. "Wow, she's a rude one, isn't she?"

"I don't think she's intentionally rude, sweetie. Mary Claire is the only one of us who has spent any time with her away from the courts, and she thinks Dallas has suffered some serious tragedy that has damaged her social skills."

"What happened to her?" Avery asked.

"I don't know any details, but I do know that she has no family. My gut tells me that whatever happened was dark and has taken hold of her in a dangerous way."

"That sounds a little melodramatic, Mom, even for you."

I ignored that little dig. "Oh, come on now. You know my gut is as good as LeRoy Jethro Gibbs. But, for once, I do hope I'm wrong and reading too much into her style on the court. You saw her in action. She's like that in clinic, too -- like an animal addicted to the hunt -- especially the kill. Her court personality is just a bit unsettling to most of the ladies. I'd like to help Dallas, and you know I don't mind being nosey, but for some reason, I don't think I can pry her open. Apparently Mary Claire is the only one on the team who may have any influence. Dallas seems very interested in her. She even asked her to lunch recently. I love Mary Claire, but she's about the least interesting of the whole group. She's calm, cool, unflappable. I've never seen her get rattled. She always seems completely in control, but I've never heard her really voice an opinion with passion. She's just the perfectly lovely, gentile wife -- the devoted spouse of a successful attorney. She reminds me of a Stepford Wife -- always impeccable, always does and says the right things."

"Well, well, aren't you Miss Critical?"

"Not criticisms, just observations. And the only reason I mentioned those things is because it seems odd to me that Dallas reaches out to someone much older who, personality wise, doesn't seem to have her own identity. I would think Dallas would gravitate to someone closer to her own age, like Katlin."

I saw that comment register with Avery as her eyes widened. "Dallas and Katlin are the same age? I thought Dallas was your age."

"I thought so, too," I replied, nodding, "but no, she's thirty, just a couple of years older than you. So, if you're trying to improve yourself socially, wouldn't you want to hang out with someone around your own age who clearly has lots of connections in town?"

"If Dallas doesn't have any family, maybe Mary Claire just reminds her of her own mother. And maybe the fact that she is on edge and Mary Claire is so calm attracts her. If she wants to curb her anger, Mary Claire might be a good teacher."

"Maybe," I pondered, "but I think there's more to it." I turned my attention to the match being played by MKat and Katlin. "Now, you talk about interesting." I pointed to MKat. "That woman is certifiable. She wins most of her matches, but I swear I think it's because she irritates the shit out of her opponents. And did you notice her serve? Her rituals are about as ridiculous as Nadal's."

Avery laughed. "That car ride over here was enough to send me over the edge. I don't know how her partner tolerates her."

I chuckled. "Her partner, Miss Katlin, is oblivious. Katlin is so in love, nothing affects her, which is probably a blessing in disguise. Talk about living on cloud nine. But it's sweet how smitten she is. Hope he's a good guy."

"Yeah, she told me she had a serious boyfriend when I met her before the match. You know she was only a year behind me in school. We actually have a mutual friend. You remember Chloe Kennedy? They were neighbors before Chloe's family moved to our area of Atlanta. Katlin seems nice. We talked about getting together with Chloe."

"Small world, isn't it?" I mused. "Geez, would you look at MKat bossing Katlin around like a servant. Katlin's boyfriend must be giving her some good lovin' because that abuse just seems to fall on deaf ears."

"Mom!" Avery responded with an indignation rolled in amusement.

I just ignored her. "Come on, precious. Your fat mama is hungry. Let's head to Olexa's."

DALLAS

When I got home from the match, I went directly to the shower. I don't know how long I stayed there torturing myself with images of Parker Fielding. I could have sworn I saw him last week when I was at lunch with Mary Claire. Surely it was just my imagination.

Even after everything, I could see his face so clearly. He was stunningly handsome, with unbelievably intense blue eyes. I remembered every detail of our first encounter. He stood with his back to the bar when I walked into FIG to meet my sister and her fiancé for dinner. It was as if he were waiting for me, for when I walked in, he turned and our eyes locked. He stared at me with a disarming grin. He was definitely older than me, but not too old for me. He was staggeringly sexy.

A moth to a flame, I was literally drawn in, unable to avoid the pull of his charismatic force. He extended his hand, and I grasped it. "Hi. I'm Parker Fielding."

Our hands remained in a handshake that morphed into a tender grasp. "Hello," I managed to speak. "I'm Providence Sanderson."

"Providence? That's an unusual name. What's the story there?"

I rolled my eyes. "A family tradition. My parents loved to travel. Before they had kids, they traveled extensively. When they started the family, they named all of the kids after their favorite places."

"How big is your family?"

"Five kids," I said as I held up my hand.

"Do tell their names, please. I'm intrigued. Let me guess, there is girl named Sydney and a boy named Denver."

I shook my head. "You're partially right. One of my siblings does have Sydney as a middle name."

"Okay, tell me everybody's name. This is fascinating."

"Well, I think you should buy me a drink before I spill the family secrets."

"Ah, where are my manners. What's your pleasure?"

"Cosmopolitan, please."

"Does your choice of libation reflect your nature?"

"Some might consider me a bit cosmopolitan."

Parker handed me my drink. "You have your poison now. Spill it."

"Okay, I'll go in birth order: Providence Sanibel; Rio Nepal; London Roma, Jackson Sydney and..." I felt a tap on my shoulder. "And last, but definitely not least, my baby sister, Capers Curacao Sanderson." I hugged her close to my side. "And this is her fiancé, Derek Woodley. He has been embraced by the family despite his drab name."

"Who's your friend, Prov?" Derek whispered in my ear as we hugged.

"I'm Parker Fielding." Parker shook hands with both Capers and Derek. "I've been enchanted by your lovely sister. But don't let me keep you from your dinner. I just stopped in for a drink. I'm here on a business trip and head back home to Philly tomorrow."

"You're from Philly? Me too. Capers and Derek live here in Charleston. I'm just here for a quick visit. I head home tomorrow, too."

"By chance are you on the 4:50 pm flight?"

"No way!"

"I guess it's divine providence."

"Clever."

He kissed my hand. "Until tomorrow."

Even now I could feel that kiss singe my hand. I scrubbed the spot that his lips had tainted until the water turned icy cold and forced me out of the shower. Did I really see Parker last week? Maybe I should call Detective Hatcher. Surely he would know.

IN THE NAME OF LOVE

NO MATCHES - June 27 and July 4, 2014

Love is patient. Love is kind. Love is blind. Love is a
four-letter word.

CALLIE

June 27th. On the Saturday following our Mountain Brook match, Jake and I met at 10 am at Pepper Place to peruse the Farmers Market. During the summer months, local growers set up stands each Saturday to sell their fresh produce: corn, yams, potatoes, tomatoes, eggplant, cucumbers, zucchini, onions, beans, multiple varieties of squash and peppers. I love to support local growers.

A date at the Farmers Market -- that's a first. But, it wasn't a date, I had to remind myself. We were just friends doing a little outdoor grocery shopping together. We hadn't seen each other since our lunch on Tuesday, but we had texted and chatted on the phone daily since then. Jake asked what I was doing over the weekend. When he said he'd never been to a Farmers Market, naturally I told him he was welcome to join me.

I texted Jake when I found a parking place, and he met me at my car. "How is it that you've never been to a Farmers Market?" I asked as we walked toward a bin of tomatoes.

He shrugged. "Guess I never saw a need. Grocery stores always have what I need, and I eat out a lot."

"Yes, but when you buy in the grocery store, you really don't know how long ago it was pulled off the farm and put on a truck. If you buy locally, you know it's fresher."

"I'm not much of a vegetable guy, so I'm probably not missing out."

"So what do you eat? Potato chips and dip?"

"Only for breakfast."

I laughed. "Seriously, what do you eat?"

"Really? You want to dissect my diet?"

I smiled. "Indulge me."

"You're a pain," Jake pronounced as he lightly punched my arm. "Okay. With my schedule, I usually leave work after seven, so about three times a week I swing by Five Guys and grab a burger and fries." I grimaced. He ignored me. "Every now and then, I'll stop at Bob Baumhower's and have some wings. If I go straight home, I might make a cheese omelet. And, if I'm feeling really creative, I'll chop up an onion and throw it in the omelet."

"What about breakfast and lunch?"

"Breakfast is usually coffee, a banana, and a bagel or breakfast bar. And lunch is typically a PB&J sandwich and a bag of chips."

"So you really never cook, I mean, besides the omelet?"

"Not true," Jake protested. "I'm a master at the grill, and I'll grill some steaks and potatoes or corn on the weekends if I'm not working."

"So steak, potatoes, and corn make you a grill master? Pretty shallow title, my friend."

"Hey, I can grill ribs, lamb, tenderloins, roast, steaks, fish. You name it; I can grill it."

I rolled my eyes. "Okay, okay. Do you ever eat anything green?"

"Green?"

"Maybe a salad."

Jake cocked his head as he pondered. "Mmmm, maybe a salad every now and then when I'm eating out -- but not often."

"What about a salad at home. Don't you ever make one to go with your grilled meal?"

Jake waved the idea away. "All that stuff goes bad too fast. You know what it's like when you live alone."

"That's a really nasty diet, my friend."

Jake stopped and displayed his body with a sweep of his hand. "Look at me, Conrad. I'm the picture of health."

"Maybe on the outside, but your insides can't be healthy on that diet. I don't want to be involved with someone who's a walking heart attack."

"Involved? Why, Miss Conrad, are you saying you're involved with me?"

"I meant attached, you know, how good friends care about each other." I was totally flustered and fidgeted, twisting my hair into tight ringlets. "I just meant I want you to be healthy, so I can keep hanging out with you and abusing you."

"Of course, of course." Jake walked up to a bin of white produce. He picked up one item and studied it. 'What the hell is this?" he asked as he shoved it two inches from my face.

"This, my friend, is a scalloped squash. They are delicious."

"You mean you can actually eat this crazy looking thing?" He placed the squash back in the bin.

"All it takes is a little know-how."

"Aren't you the cocky cook." I gave him a nasty look. Jake picked up an eggplant and tossed it back and forth in his hands. "Are you up for a challenge, Conrad?"

"What kind of challenge?"

"A cook off. You come over to my house tonight and bring with you any meat or seafood of your choice, and I'll grill it. Don't tell me ahead of time. I'll be prepared for anything, except I must veto ribs since they take too long -- unless you want to eat at 2 am."

"I'll pass. So, what am I cooking?"

"You leave now, and I'll pick out a few things from these bins. When you come over, you can work your magic to make these 'healthy' things taste good."

"Why don't you come to my house, Jake? The tools of the trade vary with the vegetable and you might not have what I need."

"Do you have a grill?" Jake asked. I shook my head. "Then you have to come to me. Just pack up what you think you might need, because I can't pack up my grill. And there's a grocery store ten minutes from my house."

"A convenience store or a full grocery store?"

"A real store -- a Publix."

I deliberated internally, but only briefly. "Okay, text me your address. What time?"

"Five o'clock."

"A little early, don't you think?"

"You'll probably need plenty of time to make this crap taste good."

"Don't underestimate me, Lenaghan."

"Move along, Conrad," Jake demanded as he gently pushed me away from the produce. "I have work to do."

I laughed and obeyed. "See you later."

****

Promptly at five, I rang the bell at Jake's house. He opened the door, and I could tell he was fresh out of the shower; shampoo and soap aromas drifted in my direction. With towel dried wet hair, Jake stood before me in charcoal gray cargo shorts and a royal blue polo. Damn, he looked and smelled delectable. He welcomed me with a hug. "Come on in. Aren't you prompt."

"Tardiness is my pet peeve. Actually one of many, but you probably know that."

"Yes, I've picked up on a few over the years. I'm confident it's a long list."

I shrugged. "You know me, always thorough." I walked into the house and was impressed by the decor. Definitely masculine, but very tasteful. "So, where is the bag of veggies that I must transform into edible bliss?"

"Edible bliss? Sounds like an aphrodisiac. You planning on dropping your platonic rule tonight, Conrad?"

I felt flushed and could tell Jake noticed. I needed a quick recovery. I sauntered up to Jake and caressed his arms. "I don't know? Would it be worth it?"

"Absolutely," he responded, holding my gaze until I felt completely unglued. He grabbed my hand and led me to the kitchen. "Close your eyes, please." I obeyed. "Okay, palms up. Take this, but don't open your eyes." He put something small in my hands. "So tell me what it is, without looking."

"Oh, so we're playing a game?"

"Don't we always, Callie?"

I knew that comment was a dig because Jake calls me Callie only when he is serious. I decided to play dumb and keep the mood light. "I'll win, of course," I declared confidently.

"Of course. Have you ever NOT gotten your way?"

I gave Jake the finger and started gently exploring the object in my hand, careful not to bruise it. "It's slightly fuzzy and textured, small, soft, tubular." Grinning, I announced, "It's okra, and I hope you bought more than one."

I started to open my eyes but Jake yelled. "Hey! No cheating. We're not done yet. Yes, it's okra, and I bought one for you, too. Okay, here's the next item."

The object was heavy, thick, smooth, long and circular. One end was bigger than the other. "Butternut squash."

"Impressive." Jake placed a third object in my hand.

"How many things did you buy?"

"Just four. Hush up and guess."

He placed a small, smooth, round object in my hand. Small leaves grew from the top. "I'm disappointed, Jake. This one is too easy -- a tomato."

"Ah, but what kind of tomato? This one is special."

I felt along the top of the item and discovered that it had ridges. "Heirloom tomato! Oh, I'm so excited; I haven't had one in a few years."

"Glad I excite you, Conrad."

"Shut up, Lenaghan. What's the last item? I'm batting a thousand. Hope you have a true challenge left."

"Smart-ass. Here's the last one." It was light, smooth, circular, spongy, and one end was slightly bigger than the other. "It's an eggplant," I declared as I opened my eyes. "So, of the four items, you bought three phallic symbols for dinner."

Jake laughed. "You're a pervert. Now where is my bag of goods?"

"In my car in a box with all my magic tools. Be back in a minute."

"Relax," Jake said as he threw something at me. It turned out to be an apron. "I'll get it. I think you have work to do."

"Car's locked," I called out as he left the kitchen. "My keys are by my bag on the sofa."

A few minutes later, Jake returned to the kitchen and set the box on the table. "So what's my challenge?"

"Surf and turf," I answered as I handed him a grocery bag.

Jake emptied the contents of the sack. "Filet and grouper."

"Not very original, I know. I didn't challenge you so well. I, on the other hand, have my work cut out for me."

"I'll be your sous chef and bartender. We're in no hurry. What do I do first?"

I surveyed the contents of my box. "First, I think you'll have to make a trip to the store."

"No problem. What do you need?"

"A carton of vegetable stock."

What's that?"

"You'll find it in the soup section."

"Okay. What else?" he asked as he started a written list.

"Do you have any Jack Daniels?"

"Yes, ma'am."

"Great. Okay. I need some arugula salad, some balsamic vinaigrette -- that would be salad dressing. Also some Italian bread crumbs." He looked lost. "Jake, I think I'd better go."

Now, he looked relieved. "I think you might be right. What can I do for you while you're gone?"

I handed him a peeler that I had brought from home. Start peeling the skin from the butternut squash. Take your time. When you get to the orange part, you know you've peeled enough."

He saluted me. "Anything else?"

"Yes, have a drink waiting for me when I get back."

Thirty minutes later I returned, and Jake met me at the door with a generous pour of red wine.

"Perfect." I took the glass from his hand and set it by the cutting board where a freshly defrocked butternut squash sat.

"How'd I do?" he asked as he saw me studying the squash. "Good. You probably went a little deeper than necessary but a good job." I took a sip of wine, pulled my chef's knife from the box, and began cutting the squash into cubes. Jake walked over, put the apron over my head and tied it loosely around my waist. I felt my heartbeat escalate during the process.

"You're pretty good with a knife," Jake observed. "So what do you want me to do now?"

"As my sous chef, you must do all the nasty little tasks that I despise." I had reached the base of the squash where all the seeds and gooey matter resided. I handed it to him. "Here you go. Get a spoon and dig out the seeds and yucky stuff."

"It's like a pumpkin," Jake commented as he worked. "Orange and full of sticky, slimy, seedy goo."

I laughed. "I know. Not a fun job. So, here's some trivia. What is a pumpkin? A vegetable or a fruit?"

"Hmm. Never thought about it. But probably a fruit since most people would say a vegetable."

"Very astute of you, Lenaghan. Do you know why it's a fruit?"

"The seeds?" Jake answered with a question. He handed the deseeded squash back to me.

"Thank you. And yes, it's the seeds. So, technically squash is a fruit, but I doubt that fact can ever be embraced by the general public."

"You're a nerd, Conrad," Jake proclaimed playfully as he popped me with a dishtowel. I ignored him. "So what are you making?" he asked as he watched me dice an onion. He saw that my wine glass was low and replenished it.

"Thank you. I'm making butternut squash soup."

"No offense, but sounds disgusting."

"Oh, really?" I said defensively.

"Just being honest, but I'll try it. I'm open-minded."

"I promise you'll be pleasantly surprised. It's time for you to get back to work. Get a pan. It needs to be wide and at least two inches deep."

I heated the pan, added butter, and the diced onions. I sautéed the mixture, stirring frequently and adding some bottled water to prevent burning.

"I never knew you were a cuisine expert."

"You give me too much credit, but I did want to be a chef."

"Really?"

"Yep. When I was growing up, I was always experimenting in the kitchen. By the time I was fourteen, I was probably cooking about seventy-five percent of all the family meals. I thought my mom was so great for giving me free reign in the kitchen, but in retrospect, she probably surrendered the kitchen because she hated to cook."

"Smart woman. So, why didn't you become a chef?"

"Because I knew that path would make it hard to have a family. But here I am, almost forty and still single, so it appears it would have been fine to be a chef. Ironic, isn't it?"

"Callie, you're thirty-seven years old. Not exactly over the hill. You shouldn't give up on the white picket fence just yet. Better to wait for the right person than be with the wrong one. Trust me, that's worse."

"Sounds like you're speaking from experience," I commented as I added the cubed squash and some vegetable stock to the sautéed onions.

"Indeed. I dated this girl in college, Camilla Sutherland. She was from South Africa and had a full scholarship on the women's tennis team. Camilla played brilliantly. She was aggressive as hell, and, at 5' 10", she dominated the net."

"You played on scholarship as well, right? At the University of Georgia?" Jake nodded.

"So, we were both freshman, and I fell hard and fast. Camilla was stunning and with that accent, she was intoxicating. When she entered a room, every male stared, even the gay ones. She would smile sweetly and be so charming with every guy that approached. There were many who tried to gain her affection. I was apparently invisible because none of the guys acknowledged my presence. But she always stayed with me. Her devotion fed my ego, sucked me in deeper. I was the guy with the most sought after girl on campus. Not really sure why she picked me, but how could I want anything else. I was living the dream.

In retrospect, I was her obedient little puppy. Nothing she requested seemed unreasonable."

"It's hard to imagine you as some girl's 'boy toy'," I commented as I began slicing the heirloom tomatoes.

"Well, I was young, stupid and vain. Totally focused on the wrong things. We both were at the top of our game. Our statistics were great. We walked around campus like royalty. I was so full of myself that I wonder how I ever got my head through a door."

I placed a bed of arugula on a plate, then layered mozzarella rounds on the arugula, and topped them with the tomato slices. As I turned to stir the squash mixture, I asked, "So what finally deflated your ego?"

"Two years into the relationship, my sister sat me down and started asking questions. Jackie was older and wiser and had been around Camilla several times. She asked who Camilla's female friends were -- who she hung out with besides me. I couldn't think of anyone. She asked if I had ever noticed that Camilla's teammates didn't seem to include her in off court activities. They didn't talk to her much. I just chalked that up to jealousy. Camilla was the top player and drop dead gorgeous, so, of course, her teammates were jealous. Jackie shook her head and warned me. 'I'm telling you, Jake, a woman who has no girlfriends is a bad egg. It means she doesn't play well with others -- doesn't want to get along'. I told Jackie she was being too hard on her. I reminded her that Mom and Dad loved her. Jackie said, 'That's because Camilla works a room like a presidential candidate at a fund raiser. Jake, she may truly care about you, but I can assure you that her needs will always outweigh yours. You need to get out before you're in too deep'. Of course, I totally forgot that Jackie had always been a fantastic judge of character. I decided she was jealous of Camilla, and at Christmas of our senior year, I proposed. My family was thrilled, everyone, that is, except Jackie. She was cordial but cool, clearly unhappy about my engagement."

By now, I had finished preparing my tomato salad with a few capers added and a drizzling of balsamic vinaigrette. Jake paused his story while he set the table, put a rub on the steaks and grouper, and opened another bottle of wine. Where did the first bottle go?

We sat down. "Just a little tomato appetizer. Okay, now continue your story. I'm mesmerized."

"This looks great." Jake took a bite. "It's fabulous."

"Glad you like it. Please go on. You just got engaged."

"Right. So Camilla wanted a big wedding, but her parents didn't have the ability to finance it. They couldn't even come to the wedding, which we all thought was rather strange. But even stranger was the fact that Camilla didn't seem upset about it. So my parents, because they just adored her, paid for the wedding. My mother indulged Camilla's relentless requests for every minute detail. Camilla was an infection that paralyzed your ability to think clearly, though her female peers seemed immune to her disease. But when Camilla asked Jackie to be her maid of honor, I felt a momentary fracture in my image of this goddess."

"This is starting to sound like a soap opera. Did you tell Camilla that Jackie thought she was a conniving bitch?"

"Of course not, and Jackie never said that, but I suppose that was the gist of her message. I had told Camilla that Jackie had concerns about our relationship."

"So how did Camilla react to that?"

"Well," Jake began as he refilled our wine glasses, "she smiled, and gently stroked my face, and said 'darling, you know I love your sister, but I think she's jealous. She's much older and doesn't even have a boyfriend. And her baby brother is blissfully happy. I understand, and I promise I won't hold it against her'."

"What a bitch." Jake looked surprised. I couldn't help myself. Wine made me far more likely to speak my mind. "And you believed that BS?"

"Sadly, yes. I decided that she asked Jackie as a kind gesture, an opportunity to bond with her future sister-in-law. And that's what I told Jackie when she informed me there was no way in hell she was going to be a hypocrite and be maid of honor. Eventually, I convinced Jackie that she would be doing it for me, not Camilla."

"Your sister obviously loves her baby brother."

"Yes, she does, and she was a trooper throughout the rest of the process. She even tried to throw Camilla a bachelorette party, but she couldn't find anyone willing to come."

"Did Camilla know?"

"No, Jackie tried to make it a surprise. When she couldn't find anyone, she decided to have a surprise spa day with Camilla and Mom. Mom was thrilled to be included as one of the girls, and Camilla was in her element since a spa is all about pampering the customer."

"Jake, why did Camilla want a fancy wedding if no friends or family would be there to share her big day?"

"Because for her, it wasn't about who was there or not there, it was about being the center of attention for a crowd of onlookers admiring her dress and beauty."

"You seem quite clear in your perception of her now."

"The fog has cleared over the years, and hindsight is 20/20. So, the wedding went perfectly, except Jackie's expression was as solemn as one attending a funeral. Funny thing is, she got really drunk and ended up passing out in the men's bathroom. She misread the restroom signs and went in the wrong one. Anyway, one of my groomsmen, Reed Sawyer, found her. He took care of Jackie and made sure that my parents and I didn't know she was over the edge. Reed Sawyer is now not only one of my best friends, but also my brother-in-law. Now those two have something special. I can always see that union as the silver lining in my Camilla disaster.

"I digress. After a honeymoon in St. John's, we settled in a little apartment in a suburb of Raleigh, North Carolina. I worked as a high school history teacher and coached the boys' tennis team. Camilla was miserable in no time. Nothing satisfied her. She didn't want to work, and I was fine with that but couldn't understand how she was going to avoid boredom. The apartment was too small, the neighborhood too average. My job was lowly. She wanted me to be head pro of a ritzy country club. The concept of 'paying your dues' was lost on her. She couldn't be bothered to clean or cook. Such chores were beneath her. She wanted a maid or else I had to do everything. I soon realized that our bond had been tennis, and while that's a great activity to have in common, it's not enough to build a marriage. Camilla was no longer the center of attention, and married life was mundane. She thought we should be going to country club parties and being high profile socialites. I told her that wasn't the real world. She told me that was the only world she wanted.

"Needless to say, things went from bad to worse. On our first anniversary, I came home to find that she had packed her bags and left. She did leave a note saying how she had wasted years of her life on me. That I was not the man that she thought I was, and that I could not provide her the lifestyle that she deserved. She said, and I quote, 'I was born to live like a queen'. Of course, I was devastated. As time passed, some things came to light that deepened the wound but also fortified me with anger. A few weeks after she left, the credit card bill arrived. She had been abusing it from day one -- buying expensive clothes and makeup. We fought about this, and I told her to get a job, but it was, of course, my fault. But this last bill had a substantial charge from an abortion clinic. I remembered that a few weeks before, she spent an entire weekend in bed with a stomach virus. I waited on her like a dog and even took Monday off because she was still sick. When I saw that credit card charge, I knew that I nursed back to health the woman that murdered my child."

"Oh, Jake. How horrible."

"I finally tracked her down and confronted her. She said that motherhood had never entered her plan and that she was not about to ruin her body by being pregnant. I told her she had no right to have an abortion without discussing it with me first. She screamed at me that it was her body, and she would do whatever she wanted and that it was my fault that I did not take proper precautions."

He smiled weakly. "It was a long time ago. I often think about my child that never had a chance, and it makes me sad, but no child deserved that woman as a mother."

I poured the rest of the wine into his glass, kissed the top of his head, and moved to the stove. "I don't know how we got off on that subject, but we need to lighten things up. I need my sous chef back in the kitchen."

"Sorry." Jake picked up the plates on the table and brought them to the kitchen. "Didn't mean to go to the dark side on you. How can I help?"

I ignored his apology and set him to work. "If you could please wash the okra and peel the eggplant, I'll finish up the soup. Where's your bottle of Jack?"

Jake entered a closet, obviously a pantry, and returned with a bottle of Jack Daniels. It was a big bottle, and I didn't need much. I opened the cabinets until I found what I wanted. I grabbed two shot glasses and loaded them with the whiskey. Jake had his back to me. "Hey you," I called. He turned around, and I handed him a shot glass.

"What's this for?"

"I think you need it." I raised my glass and toasted, "Here's to silver linings."

Jake smiled. "To silver linings."

We both tossed back our glasses. "Shit!" I cried out in agony. "I think my esophagus disintegrated."

Jake laughed. "Give it a sec. It'll pass."

I pressed three cloves of garlic into the squash mixture and added a little bottled water. Then I pulled out the immersion stick that I brought from home. Jake saw it and grinned. "And you accused me of bringing phallic symbols to the table."

I smiled. "Intimidated are you?"

"Not in the least," Jake replied with a straight face.

"Gotta respect a confident man," I answered with a giggle.

"Seriously, what are you doing with that?"

"It's an immersion stick. Watch." I submerged the device in the squash mixture and worked it around the pan blending the soft squash into pulp. I stopped to add more vegetable broth and a little water.

"So, it's a blender on a stick," Jake surmised. "Clever device."

"Yep. A lot easier than pulling out a heavy blender. And much easier to clean." When the mixture was to the thickness I wanted, I added a little Jack Daniels. I tasted it, and added a little more. I tasted it again. "Perfection," I declared. "Two soup bowls, please."

I filled two small bowls and set them on the table. I grabbed a small tub of goat cheese that I had picked up during my earlier trip to the store. We sat, and I noticed that a new bottle of wine had miraculously appeared on the table.

Jake savored a spoonful of soup. He looked at me with a surprised expression. "I thought I would hate this, but it's great. I always hated squash, so I knew this would stink, but I was wrong."

"Glad you like it. I should have let you taste it before I added the whiskey. I don't add much, but it makes all the difference. You have to be careful though. Add a little, taste. Repeat as necessary. If you add too much, it ruins the soup. All you taste is Jack." I opened the tub of crumbled goat cheese. "I almost forgot. Try a little of this on top."

Jake sprinkled a little in a small section and tasted. "It's good, but I think I like it better without it."

"I like it, but I agree that it's not a necessity." As we finished our soup, I looked at my watch. "Oh my gosh, it's 8:30. We'll both pass out before we get to the main course. Go work your grill magic. I've got the eggplant and okra under control."

For me the only way to eat okra is fried, and it's my favorite way to eat eggplant as well. So I followed my grandma's recipe for breading and frying, except that I used olive oil instead of Crisco. I grew up eating the okra pods chopped into several slices, but I kept them whole to create okra fries. I opted for fry style for the eggplant as well. My brother always wanted them thinly sliced so that all you really tasted was the fried batter, but then you missed out on the flavor of the vegetable.

Our timing was perfect. Just as I was turning off the stove, Jake arrived with his smoked filet and grouper. "You up for eating on the screened porch? With the fan on, it's really nice."

"Sounds great." We set up on the porch. Jake's surf and turf were both exquisite. "I don't know if it's the rub you used or all the wine I've consumed, but this is the best grouper and the best filet I've ever had. Excellent job."

"The secret weapon is a great grill, and a lot of patience."

"Patience?"

"If you slow cook, you have to make sure the fire isn't too hot. It takes a lot longer than direct heat, but the results are spectacular. Seems that the best things in life come your way when you're patient."

"Like a win on the tennis court?"

"Among other things."

I felt exposed by his penetrating stare. Time to change the subject. "I love your house, by the way. And the neighborhood is charming. How is it that I've never been here? We used to spend a lot of time together, but I've never darkened your door."

Jake sat back in his chair and dropped his fork. "Seriously? I must have invited you here twenty times, but you always had an excuse."

"An excuse? For what?"

"To keep the ball in your court. To keep control. If you dictated the environment, you controlled the outcome."

"Oh, come on Jake. I'm not that bad."

"I didn't say you were. That's just your way. Callie Conrad's method of self-preservation. You try to keep the upper hand so things go according to your plan. I figured that out when you stopped returning my calls two years ago."

Jake refilled our glasses. Was that the end of bottle number three? I definitely felt light-headed but retained enough cognitive ability to be offended. I savored my final bite of grouper and leaned forward on the table, arms folded. "You know why I stopped returning your calls, Jake."

He leaned forward, mirroring my posture. Less than a quarter of an inch separated our folded arms. The proximity threatened an eruption of goose bumps. If that happened, I knew that the hairs on my arms would tickle him. "Yes, but no sense rehashing all that. Did you ever talk to Mary Claire about her long sleeved shirts?"

"I haven't been able to have any time with her. I asked her to lunch for Thursday or Friday, but she left for the beach Wednesday afternoon. She needed to supervise some work being done on their beach house."

"Really? Where's their place? She's never mentioned that they owned one."

"It was news to me, too," I confessed. "I think she said it was at Alys Beach. Apparently her husband bought it for rental property. I don't think he has any intention of using it for pleasure."

"Figures," Jake mumbled.

"What do you mean?"

"Nothing. He just strikes me as way too uptight to ever relax and lounge at the beach."

"I met him a couple of years ago, and he did seem rather stuffy. Probably sleeps in a tie." Jake laughed. I started clearing the table. "I'll help you clean up before I head out. I've made quite a mess in there."

"Oh, no you don't. You've worked a lot harder than I have. I'll take care of the kitchen later. For now, come relax." He led me to the hammock on the porch. Only it wasn't a hammock after all -- more like a suspended twin bed.

"Cozy," I said as I settled into the swinging bed. The temperature had dropped into the low seventies and the humidity was low. Jake covered me with a light blanket. "Thank you." I snuggled under the blanket, relaxed and comfortable.

I heard dishes clanking and water running. I felt a little guilty that Jake was cleaning up, but not enough to leave my cocoon.

Just before I drifted off, Jake returned. "Scoot over, Conrad. You're hogging the space."

I complied in silence, eyes closed. Once Jake settled, I spoke. "You know, I'm not sure sharing this legless bed qualifies as platonic behavior."

"Oh, please. You never crawled into a hammock with a buddy on a sunny afternoon and planned your future?"

My eyes remained closed. "Can't say I have, but I'm too content in this spot to move." We lounged in silence, bodies innocently touching. I absorbed his warmth, soaked in the essence of Jake. Heaven. I wanted to slip my hand into his, but that would be dangerous; lines might be crossed.

Suddenly, I propped myself on my elbow and looked at Jake. His eyes were closed, but I could tell he was still awake.

"Jake, what happened to Camilla? I mean after she left, where did she end up?"

Jake didn't move; his eyes remained closed. "That's a bit of a mystery. About a year after the divorce, her mom called. She had no idea that we had split up. I suppose that's no surprise, because this was the first time I had ever talked to her, and Camilla never mentioned talking to her parents. Anyway, her mom called to inform Camilla that her dad had suffered a massive heart attack. He would have triple bypass surgery the next day. She thought Camilla might want to talk to him before the surgery. She asked why the marriage had been so short, and I explained, truthfully, but left out the part about the secret abortion."

"How did she react?"

Jake moved his arms to cradle his head while he stared at the ceiling. "How did she react? Her tone was sad, defeated. And then she apologized."

"For what?"

"That's what I asked. She said that she should have told me about Camilla's background before I married her. She asked me how Camilla explained their absence from the wedding. When I told her that Camilla said they couldn't afford to come, she laughed. She said 'You and your family must have thought us dreadful people. While it is true that our finances were tight, we would have found a way to travel to the US to see our only child get married. But Camilla called and said you had eloped. We told her that we still wanted to come for a visit to meet our son-in-law, but she said it wasn't a good time right then. We haven't heard from her since that conversation'.

"She couldn't hide the pain in her voice when I explained that we had an elaborate wedding which my parents funded. She offered to repay them, which was kind, but I politely refused. Her mother explained that she thought our marriage was a sign that Camilla had found a good man and put aside her devious ways. She told me that Camilla learned the value of a good lie at an early age. When she was six, she hated the lunch that her mother packed, so she threw away the contents of the lunch box before she entered school. Her mother witnessed the disposal from the car. When her class went to lunch, her classmates asked her why her lunch box was empty. She was mad at her mother, so she said that her mom must have forgotten. Everybody felt so sorry for her that they shared things from their lunch boxes and were extra attentive to her the rest of the day. She continued to tell more lies that made her the center of attention, mostly the type of lies that gave the appearance of a neglected home life.

"Of course, Camilla's parents were oblivious until they were summoned to a meeting with school officials investigating her neglect. Eventually the school staff and parents were able to see how Camilla manipulated her environment, but Camilla never stopped the process. She just shifted the targets of her lies when she was close to being caught. She would say anything to make herself the center of attention. Camilla's mom said that she was a chronic liar before she hit middle school. Her mom said she truly believed that her daughter had become incapable of distinguishing fact from fiction. They tried to get her professional help, but all the experts said Camilla was completely aware of what she was doing and only she could make the choice to stop. Unless she physically hurt herself or someone else, there was nothing they could do. By the time she was in high school, everybody had clued into her game, so they all ignored her. With nothing else to do, she poured her energy into tennis and flourished. By the time she was a senior and an outcast, she was desperate to go to college in the States so she could escape her web of lies and start a new life in the US."

"Good gosh, Jake. Camilla may have been worse than all my mistakes combined."

"Crazy, huh? I felt so sorry for her mother. She said if only she had warned me about her ways before the wedding, maybe it would have spared me and my family some grief. I told her it wouldn't have mattered because I was completely under her spell. I would have found some excuse for her. I told her I had no idea where Camilla was, but I gave her the last cell phone number I had. I'll never forget the last thing she said to me before she hung up, 'Once Camilla is done with you, she discards you like a used paper towel -- totally disposable and insignificant'."

"So you haven't heard from Camilla or her family since then? How long has it been?"

"That was in 1998. I actually called Mrs. Sutherland a couple of weeks later to see how her husband was, and if I'm honest with myself, I wanted to know about Camilla. Not because I missed her. I wanted to know what she had found that was so much better than me."

"I know exactly how you felt." I had been rejected more than once and fully understood the desire to know what trumped you as a partner. Being left behind, even if the guy is doing you a favor and you're too stupid to see it (as Mary Claire repeatedly said), is deflating. "So what did Camilla's mom say?"

Jake rolled over and faced me. "We had a brief but sad chat. The cell number I gave her was no longer in service, and she had no luck trying to track her down. Since Camilla had no friends in South Africa or the US, Mrs. Sutherland didn't know who to call. But Mr. Sutherland had developed post surgical complications and passed away a week after the surgery. Her poor mother was completely alone in the world."

"How awful."

"I called the divorce attorney to see if he had any contact information, but he didn't."

"So, Camilla just disappeared?"

"Oh, I'm sure she found her queen's life," Jake answered with a laugh, "but I haven't a clue where she is or what poor fool she is torturing. My mom swears that a few years ago she saw Camilla on TV on the arm of some older actor during the red carpet ceremony of the Oscars."

"No way."

Jake rolled onto his back and closed his eyes. "It wouldn't surprise me if it were true. That woman excelled at getting what she wanted."

"Jake? How do I not know this story or any facet of it?"

Jake turned his head and stared at me with such seriousness. "Because I've never shared it with anyone outside of my family."

"Why? Are you embarrassed about being divorced?"

"No, but the part of my life involving Camilla is not relevant to my job, so I don't see the point in disclosing my personal life. All that was behind me years before I started working at The Heights."

"Then why did you share it with me?"

"Because, Callie, I know you have trust issues. And I wanted you to see that just like you, I have been completely deceived by someone I loved. But I also learned from the experience and am willing to take a chance on someone else." Jake stood and helped me off the hammock bed. "I also know that we're good together, but you won't let your guard down so we can see just how good it could be."

He took my hand and led me into the house, down a hallway and into a bedroom. He turned on a light in a bathroom and then grabbed a t-shirt from a closet. He guided me in silence to the bed. Jake pulled back the covers but just stood staring at me. I couldn't look away. I knew he wanted to kiss me, and I ached for him to do so. I wanted to see just how good it could be with Jake. I just needed to take the proverbial leap of faith. Jake gently took my face in both hands and leaned in for a kiss. When his lips were an inch from mine, he hesitated and moved to the left planting a gentle peck on my cheek. "It's 2 am, and we've had way too much to drink for you to be driving home. You can stay here and sleep in as long as you want." He handed me the t-shirt. "Here. You'll be more comfortable in this."

Jake headed for the door. I wanted to call out to him, ask him to stay and hold me all night, but I couldn't find the courage. He turned back as he started to close the door and gave me his casual yet disarming grin. "Let me know if you need anything. Sleep well, Conrad."

I stood in my tracks, immobile and mute. Finally, I took off my clothes, put on Jake's t-shirt, and crawled into bed. Within a couple of minutes, I drifted easily to sleep, feeling as if I were blanketed by the warmth of Jake Lenaghan.

MKAT

"Edward, dear, I'm back." I put my grocery bag on the kitchen counter and returned to the living room where Edward lounged in his recliner in front of the TV. Golf network was on. "I'm so glad we moved you to the living room. You look much more comfortable, and the sunlight is helping improve your color."

I sat across from him and pulled his paycheck from my billfold. "I stopped by your office and picked up your check. Honestly, Edward, that human resources manager, Brenda Horton, is simply a shrew. I can tell by her accent that she's a Yankee, but that's no excuse for rudeness. Do you know that before she gave me the check, she practically accused us both of stealing from the bank! She gave me a cold stare the whole time she was talking to me. I don't even think she blinked. Not even once. She said, 'Mrs. Harriman, your husband has exhausted his six-week sick leave bank and is now tapping into his accumulated vacation reserve. After this check, he has only five weeks remaining in his vacation account. Please let Mr. Harriman know that once his vacation account is gone, there will be no more paychecks issued, and quite frankly, since no one has heard from him, I certainly cannot guarantee that his position will be available. There is work to be done, and we have already burdened other employees with covering his desk for eight weeks now. Please tell him to check in as soon as possible.'"

I stood and tucked in the blanket that was loose around Edward's feet. I smiled and patted his shoulder. "The nerve of that woman. Well, let me just tell you that I set snippy Miss Horton straight. I snatched that check out of her hand and let her have it. 'Listen here, lady,' I started in, 'You act like we are some charity case trying to rob this bank. My husband has been a devoted and respected manager here for several years. He has been very ill, and as his caregiver, I have put his health first and let him rest, undisturbed. I check in regularly with Mr. Jack Reynolds. You are familiar with him, aren't you -- Jack Reynolds, the man in charge of this bank? Jack is fully aware of Edward's condition, and I trust that Jack, not you, will handle any issues regarding my husband's future with this bank. In fact, I think I'll go visit Jack now and let him know exactly how his human resources manager treats valued employees and their wives.' I marched right out of that office before she could say a word, slammed her door and went straight upstairs. Jack was out of the office, but I will call him later and give him a piece of my mind. The very idea of that woman suggesting any wrongdoing on our part purely makes my blood boil!"

Edward looked so exhausted. I felt guilty for unloading my woes. "I'm sorry, dear. I shouldn't have burdened you with my mistreatment. You just rest now and I'll work on dinner."

The things I go through to look after Edward. When my time comes, why Jesus himself will meet me at the Pearly Gates.

DALLAS

<u>Monday, June 23rd.</u> As I lay in bed, I saw the clock roll over to 3:30 am. I had been staring at the clock, the walls, the ceiling or the TV for three hours. Frustrated, I got up and started a pot of coffee. While I waited for it to brew, I contemplated, for the hundredth time, calling Detective Hatcher. I picked up my cell and found him in my contact list: D. Hatcher. D for detective. Suddenly it struck me that I had no idea what his first name was -- as if his identity stretched no further than his role as a Charleston PD detective. How odd that I didn't know anything personal about the only link to my past.

After I poured my cup of coffee, I went to my bedroom closet and stood on the step stool. From the top shelf, I retrieved the small fire safe hidden beneath a pile of blankets. With the key that I kept taped to the bottom, I opened the safe and removed the small packet of photos. I flipped through these precious keepsakes, filled with emotion from memories rekindled. I came to the picture of Parker and me, faces smashed together laughing at something that now escapes me. It had been my favorite snapshot of us, and I had kept it on the mantle in my apartment. My brother, Rio, took it with his cell camera and gave me a copy a few days later. I turned over the photo and read Rio's note: *What a handsome couple. You both look immeasurably happy and totally in love. I think he's "the one", sis. Be happy. Love, Rio.*

Rio was right. We really did look like the happy couple. Enviable. But personalities often have multiple layers, and apparently I had not peeled back Parker's outer layer of infectious charisma. My encounters with Detective Hatcher revealed the deeper, darker layers -- Parker's true nature. In my mind, I replayed my second meeting with Detective Hatcher.

"So, the first time you met Parker Fielding was in the restaurant in Charleston?" asked Detective Hatcher. The tall, kindly man was seated in the chair next to my hospital bed as I awoke on day five of my hospital confinement. This was the first day I engaged in a formal interview with him. His line of questioning baffled me, but quite frankly, I was easily confused these days. My waking moments during the past five days had been brief and far from lucid. All I knew was that I was in an accident, but I was still unclear as to the details.

I nodded in confirmation, and he continued. "How did your relationship progress from there? Are you okay to continue? Is this too much for you?"

I looked at him, resigned. "I don't understand why you need to know about my fiancé. Why hasn't he come to see me?"

"Look Miss Sanderson, I'm not going to insult you by saying something stupid like 'I understand'. I've been a homicide detective for over twenty years, and this is the most tragic case I've ever worked, but I would think that you'd want justice."

"Justice? Homicide? Did someone try to kill me? I thought I was in an accident. Did someone try to kill Parker? Is he dead? Is that why he hasn't visited?" I frantically asked this string of questions. "Who would want to kill Parker?"

He attempted to console me. "We don't think Parker Fielding was the target."

"Then I was the target? Why would anybody want to kill me?"

Detective Hatcher uncrossed his legs, shifted his weight and re-crossed his legs in the opposite direction. "We think you were one of many targets, but we don't know why at this point."

My frustration grew, and my tone conveyed every ounce. "Why am I being isolated? I feel like a prisoner. I've been here five days with a guard at my door, and no one has allowed my family to come visit."

"Miss Sanderson, may I call you Providence?" I nodded. "I need you to take me back to the morning of July 4th, the day you were brought to the hospital. How did you start your day? What did you have for breakfast?"

"We didn't eat breakfast. On the Fourth of July, we load the boat by 7 am and sail over to Capers Island for a breakfast packed the night before. We've been doing that since I was a little girl. Everybody has to make something. If you are four or older, you pitch in. Mom packs bloody marys and mimosas, and we explore the shores of Capers Island after we eat."

"Sounds like a great tradition," he commented with a sad smile.

"It is. The whole family is together, and it's a great time."

"Did Parker go with you?"

"No. He received a call late the night before and had to go deal with an emergency back home."

"What kind of emergency?"

"A good friend of his had been seriously injured in a car accident, and Parker was listed as his emergency contact. Parker felt like he needed to go back to Philly immediately."

"So what time did he leave?"

"Around 11:30," I answered slowly. "Wait. He did leave, so that means he's alive and well. When can I see him?" I was excited to remember that Parker wasn't involved. I was happy to know that I was alone, and no one else got hurt.

"We do think he's alive."

"What do you mean 'you think he's alive'?"

"It's complicated. First, please go on with your story. Tell me about your trip to Capers Island. Were you able to leave right on time?"

"No."

"What caused the delay?"

I hesitated as I tried to recall the details. "I know we all loaded up and Skylar, Rio's four-year-old daughter, was bouncing around because she couldn't wait for everyone to try her special cinnamon rolls."

"So did you cast off?"

"No, I told Dad to wait a sec, and I hopped out to get my beach bag that I left in a lounge chair on the dock."

"What happened next?"

"I remember grabbing the bag and then feeling the sensation of flying backwards," I answered slowly and paused to collect my thoughts. In my mind, everything was fuzzy. Then I relived a horrific sight, landed with a thud on my back and saw a burning chunk of wood hurtling toward me. I screamed -- a blood curdling wail born of intense pain, not fear. Detective Hatcher looked terrified. I was still screaming when two nurses held me down and inserted a sedative into my IV.

ALEX

<u>Friday, June 27th</u>. No match today. I missed playing, but plenty of things needed my attention before tonight, and I had been running errands all day. Avery and Travis were coming in town for a wedding shower hosted by some of their married friends. The party was on Saturday evening, so Sly and I were taking them to dinner tonight.

When I walked in the house, I called out, "Izzy, baby. Mama's home." No pitter-patter of canine paws. "Izzy?" Usually she greeted me in the kitchen within seconds of opening the door. "Izzy?" I called out again. Maybe she was out back playing. I walked on the deck but didn't see her. I called out a few times but nothing. I decided she must be curled up napping in her favorite spot -- the back corner of Avery's closet which is piled high with college t-shirts that she just can't bring herself to discard. I decided to check my email before searching further for Izzy.

In my inbox, there was a big red flag by another email from Noah Hargrove. I had never responded to his first email. The latest mail simply said, *"Why are you ignoring me :("* Typical Noah.

I really wasn't ignoring him. I just didn't know how to respond. His offer tempted me, but I had avoided discussing it with Sly. He seemed so preoccupied lately that I never found a good time to discuss it with him. Plus, I knew that Noah was not one of his favorite people. Sly has never said that, but I can tell. And the feeling seemed mutual. Noah was always polite to Sly, but their interaction felt forced. There was no warmth between those two though neither spoke ill of the other. Maybe tonight at dinner with Avery and Travis would be a good time to bring it up. They could serve as buffers and offer feedback.

Noah and I went way back -- almost to the womb. Noah was my first cousin. My mother, Bridget, had a twin sister, Brenda, and the Baker twins gave birth to their first and only children on the same day -- April 15, 1963. Around our hometown of Hartford, Alabama, Noah and I were known as the Tax Twins. Of course, we weren't twins, but everybody said we might as well be. We were inseparable. No sibling could have been any closer. Hell, we even got in trouble at the same time. Our moms sent us both to what we called Baker Boot Camp the summer before our senior year. Baker Boot Camp was at MawMaw and PawPaw Baker's house on Compass Lake. Talk about a backwoods swamp.   Snakes and gators were our closet friends. Memories of that summer still made me shudder, but Baker Boot Camp did little to curb our rebellious natures. I smiled remembering all the shit Noah and I did that summer. It's a wonder we escaped with our sanity and limbs intact.

I looked at the email and hit reply.

Hello, my other half...notice I did not say "better half". Much to your dismay, Sly still holds that title. You know Avery's wedding is 8 weeks from this Saturday, so your skinny ass better be here several days before. And you can stay at the house as long as you don't bring your "bimbo of the month". :) :)

As for your question, I'm pondering, thus the delay in answering your email. I'm intrigued but still mulling it over. It might be the perfect adventure to lull me out of the depression that will certainly engulf me once Avery is married and off to start her life with Travis in Italy. (Poor things, such a dismal spot to start a marriage..haha).

Anyway, precious, I'll write you back next week and let you know where I stand. I do admit, I think it would be exciting and so much fun to get to spend more time with you again. We were "something" at 17...imagine what kind of trouble we could cause at 51!

Love you and can't wait to see you soon.
XXXXXXOOOOOOO

I hit the send button and went to the fridge to get a Coke. I thought I heard a faint whimper and remembered Izzy. I headed upstairs. "Izzy?" I cooed as I entered Avery's room. I pulled back the partially open closet door and about peed in my pants.

"What have you done, girl?" There she lay on her side with seven of the strangest looking pups snuggled against her belly. "Izzy!" I cried as I bent down. "You didn't get fat after all. You little tramp. As MawMaw Baker used to say, 'if you play, you gonna pay'."

I patted her head, and she licked my hand. "May I?" I asked as I gently picked up a pup. He was so warm and cuddly, but as I gazed upon his tiny face I muttered, "Lawdy, who's your daddy? That's a face only a mother could love." Izzy barked as if I had offended her. I laughed and went to get a box big enough to serve as a kennel and plenty of newspaper to provide lining for multiple potty adventures.

After I got Izzy and her babies settled, I showered, put on my robe, dried my hair and put on my makeup. Now for the hard part -- finding clothes that fit. I decided if I wore jeans and a long, dressy, and most importantly, loose fitting, top, I might not look so fat. I had only one pair of jeans with possibility.

As I stood before the full length mirror in my bedroom in my bra and undies, I wanted to hurl. My belly looked like a wave pool, and my thighs were tattooed with cellulite and varicose veins that reminded me of country roads peppered with potholes. "How the hell did this happen," I whispered aloud.

I grunted and started to pull on my jeans. I was thrilled that they made it past my hips with only minor yanking, wiggling and groaning. But I lost the wind in my sails when I tried to zip them. "Holy shit, I'm a cow." I sucked in as much as possible and managed to zip them all the way. It was painful. I couldn't imagine sitting down for dinner. Surely the waistband would sever my torso in half. A boa constrictor wrapped around my waist would be more comfortable.

I needed to stretch this instrument of torture. I sucked in again and buttoned the waist. I squatted up and down three times and felt the waist suddenly loosen as the button broke free and rocketed straight into the mirror where it imbedded itself like a dagger in the center. Dismayed, I watched cracks radiate in every direction. "Mother fucker!" I screamed at the top of my lungs.

"Mom! Mom!" Avery was in the house obviously taking the stairs at a sprint. I quickly put on my top just as Avery burst into the room. "Are you okay?" she exclaimed.

"Yes, honey. I'm fine. Just having trouble in the wardrobe department."

Avery spotted the cracked mirror. "What happened here?" she asked as her eyes fixated on the imbedded button.

"Don't ask," I answered emphatically and exited the room.

At the foot of the stairs stood Travis Titman, Avery's future husband. Those dark eyes looked full of concern for his future mother-in-law. Gosh, I loved that sweet boy. "Did my foul mouth scare you, honey?" I said as I embraced him. "I was having a serious wardrobe malfunction and lost my temper. All is well," I said as I patted his cheeks. "Go ahead and take your bags upstairs. You know you are technically in the guest room, but I'm no dumb-ass."

"Mother!" Avery reprimanded.

"Hey, you may not want to sneak your betrothed into your room anyway. You're already sharing it. It may be too crowded."

"What?" Avery asked, crinkling her nose.

I laughed. "Just go on upstairs and see for yourself."

Avery and Travis bolted up the stairs and within thirty seconds, I heard them both ooing and ahing over the puppies. "We leave for dinner in an hour," I called up. "Be ready. We're meeting your dad at Hot 'n Hot, and you know how grumpy he gets if we're late."

****

At 6:30 pm on the dot, Avery, Travis and I entered the Hot 'n Hot Fish Club. Sly sat at the bar slinging back a Newcastle. Avery wrapped her arms around her dad. His face lit up like a Christmas tree. Avery was such a daddy's girl. That always made me smile. Sly stood, shook Travis's hand affectionately, and gave me a peck on the cheek.

The hostess seated us, and Sly ordered a bottle of cabernet for the table. We were all salivating over the menu when suddenly Avery said, "Mom. Who do you think the dad is?"

"Excuse me," Sly interjected.

Avery looked at me with wide eyes. "Dad doesn't know?"

"Baby, I barely knew an hour before you got home."

"Knew what, ladies?" Sly demanded.

"Izzy had babies today," I said in a matter-of-fact tone.

"Babies?" Sly blurted out.

"Yes, honey. There are seven pups in Avery's closet."

"No way!"

"I know. Here we are only eight weeks away from getting rid of Avery, and now we have seven new babies in the house."

"Hurtful!" Avery exclaimed. I winked at her.

"Those puppies are really strange looking." Travis joined the conversation. "Honestly, they're so unattractive it might be hard to give them away."

"How did this happen?" Sly seemed perplexed. "The yard is fenced, and she doesn't dig out."

"No, but the fence is only four feet high and that's not much for a big dog to jump over."

"Well, there is a leash law. It shouldn't be too difficult to figure out who the scoundrel is."

"I don't know who the father is, babe, but based on his offspring, there's no denying the fact that he's not a looker. There's no accounting for taste. I married you, didn't I?"

Travis and Avery failed to suppress their giggles. Unflappable, Sly spouted back, "I'll have you know, missy, that I've still got it. On more than one occasion, I've caught the eye of some young thing about Avery's age."

"Gross, Dad. That makes my skin crawl. When have you been out trolling for girls young enough to be your daughter?"

"Come on, Avery. Don't give your old man grief. Every now and then I have to entertain clients, generally all men, and I just notice at bars that, on occasion, some younger women are drawn to me."

"You take your clients bar hopping, Sly, while you leave me at home alone?" I was totally kidding but had to mess with him.

"No, honey," Sly defended. "You know I take clients to excellent restaurants, like this, and they all have nice bars."

Travis spoke up. "How did the conversation go from solving the mystery of Izzy's mate to this?"

Avery put her arm around Travis. "That's the Anderson way, honey. Conversations always bounce around like crazy. And it's worse when the extended family is together. Wait 'til you meet Uncle Noah."

Perfect lead in for me. "Speaking of Noah," I began, "we've exchanged a couple of emails this week."

Avery looked alarmed. "He isn't bailing on the wedding, is he?"

"No, sweetie. He'll be here in full party mode."

"So, what crazy adventure is Noah up to these days?" Sly couldn't keep the sarcasm out of his voice.

"Actually, he wants me to work with him again." Avery looked excited, while Sly looked alarmed. "He's doing a National Geographic article covering a remote area of Arizona. He wants me as his photographer. He would write the article, and I would edit."

"That's awesome, Mom. It'll be like old times. When do you get started?"

"Well, I haven't agreed, but if I did, I would leave three days after the wedding."

"Dad, isn't that fabulous?"

Sly didn't seem to share Avery's enthusiasm. "How long would you be gone?"

"Just four days. I'm thinking it might help ease the post wedding blues."

"I think it's a great idea, Mom."

"What about dear old dad?" Sly whined. "What about my post wedding blues?"

Avery squeezed Sly's arm. "Oh, you'll be fine. A day on the golf course, and you'll be good as new. Get on board, Dad. This would be really good for Mom."

"Well, it's just one project. Go for it. Have a blast," Sly conceded. "It's not like you're going back to work full time."

I didn't bother to share the rest of the email. Noah wanted me to work with him on several more projects, and I really liked the idea.

Sly switched topics. "So, what's left on the wedding to-do list?"

"Nothing really. I think we've got it all under control. Except I'm still on the fence about having someone sing during the service."

"Really?" Sly asked. "You know I'd be happy to sing at your wedding."

Avery and I both broke into hysterics. "You, Dad? Sing? Like, in front of people -- who are alive?"

"Is he that bad?" Travis asked.

Avery and I lost it again. "Travis, honey," I began, "Sly gets an A for enthusiasm and an F for talent."

"That's harsh, honey. You're just jealous because your pipes aren't as pure as mine."

"Yeah, right. I'm jealous of your croaking."

"Thanks for the offer, Dad, but I think I'll stick with instrumentalists."

By the time we left Hot 'n Hot and got home, it was 10:30 pm. Sly and I said goodnight and retired to our room. About twenty minutes later, there was a light tap on the door. "Hey. Are you awake?" whispered Travis.

I opened the door. "Yes. We were both reading. What do you need, sweetie?"

"Thought you guys might want to see this," he said as he motioned for us to follow. "But we have to be very quiet."

He led us to Avery's room. There on the bed, Avery lay on her side curled up in the shape of a C with Izzy and her babies cuddled inside the curve. All were sound asleep.

"Priceless," I whispered and asked Sly to get my camera. Travis leaned against the doorframe smiling as he gazed upon his future wife, eyes filled with wonder and joy. I knew my daughter would have a husband who cherished her.

CALLIE

<u>Tuesday, July 1st.</u> I was the first to arrive at clinic. Jake was collecting balls from his previous lesson when I walked up. "Hey," I called out from the opposite side of the court. "Want some help?"

When he looked up and smiled, the butterflies took flight. Did he smile like that at everyone or just me? "Get a grip, Callie," I reprimanded myself in a whisper.

"Morning, Conrad. It would be great if you could start on that side. I'm almost done over here."

I grabbed a hopper and started picking up balls behind the baseline. Jake was by my side with his hopper within a couple of minutes. "I had a great time with you Saturday."

"Me, too," I said through an unsolicited smile.

"What are you two doing all huddled up in the corner?" We both turned to see Alex standing at the edge of the court, a mischievous expression on her face. "Looks like y'all are up to something highly inappropriate."

I felt like I did when my dad caught me stealing a beer from the fridge when I was sixteen. My face flushed instantly. Jake laughed. "Inappropriate? I'm not that lucky, Alex. I don't think Miss Conrad does inappropriate."

"What's that supposed to mean?" I asked, in an offended tone. "I think you just called me a prude."

Alex jumped in before Jake had a chance to defend himself. "Don't get all bent out of shape, Callie. Even if he did just call you a prude, he clearly meant it as a compliment. But Jake, don't forget that it's the prudish girls who are typically the wildest ride behind closed doors."

"Alex!" I growled.

Jake grinned sheepishly and mumbled something inaudible. "Come on you two. Let's warm up at the net until the others arrive." I gave Alex a nasty look, and she stuck out her tongue. "How many matches have you had so far?"

"Three," I answered.

Jake nodded. "Alex, what do you think of Dallas as a partner?"

"Oh, honey, you done good. Dallas could take on Serena and not be rattled. She's definitely a keeper."

While Alex and I volleyed Jake's feeds, MKat arrived. "Come join me over here, Molly Katherine," Jake instructed.

Alex and I both acknowledged her presence, but neither of us was overly friendly. I decided to take the high road. "MKat, how's your husband doing?"

"Thanks for asking, dear. He seems a bit better over these past few days. It was such a lovely weekend, so he sat out on the deck in the morning, you know before the heat kicked in, and he seemed to revive a bit. He's got a little color back in his cheeks."

"That's good."

"Yes, and just in the knick of time. That hateful human resources manager at the bank implied that if Edward did not return to work very soon, he wouldn't have a job."

"What!" Alex was appalled. "MKat, I doubt they can do that."

"I certainly hope not. That would be simply tragic. We would be in quite a pickle if Edward lost his job."

I chimed in. "If you have any trouble, we can have Mary Claire get her husband involved. From what I hear, Andrew Jameson is damn near invincible in the courtroom."

"By the way, where is Mary Claire?" Jake asked. "She's never late."

"She's not coming today, " I responded. "She said she had a bad flare-up of her arthritis last night and that she was still not feeling 'up to speed', as she put it."

Jake looked concerned.

"She's okay, Jake. You know this is nothing new. As long as I've known her, she's had joint issues, though they seem more frequent over the past few months. I guess that's just due to age."

"Guess so," he muttered. At that point we were joined by Amy Morard and her partner, Kelly Lancaster. "You think this is it for today?" Jake looked at me.

"Probably. Dallas had to work, and Katlin is out of town."

He sent us to the baseline and explained a poaching drill. It was a great clinic today, but Jake seemed quieter than usual, distracted. I lingered after everyone dispersed because I wanted to find out what was bothering him. I saw him on his cell in the back corner of the court. He seemed very serious. I felt like my presence was an intrusion, so I left.

I went to the locker room and found Alex and Amy deep in conversation. The minute I walked in, Alex grabbed my arm and pulled me close. "Amy, let's ask Callie what she thinks?"

"Ask me what?"

Alex giggled and said, "Amy thinks Jake is, and I quote, 'smokin' hot'."

"I was under the impression that you were married, Amy." There was no denying my judgmental tone.

Amy waved her arms as if warding off evil spirits. "I am! I am! I'm not after Jake, but I do think he's hot. I have this friend that I was thinking of setting up with Jake. Her name is Olivia Dunn, and she is stunning. Thirty-five, naturally glamorous, and very smart. She has a great job as an estate planning attorney with some big firm in Atlanta. Anyway, she's coming to visit this weekend, and I thought my husband and I could double date with them. That way neither of them feels any pressure if there's no chemistry. But I really think they would hit it off. I think I'll go back out there now and ask Jake."

"I wouldn't do that," I hurriedly interjected.

"Why not?" Amy asked.

"Yes, why not, Callie?" Alex asked not so innocently. "Sounds like a fabulous idea," she oozed with enthusiasm. She winked at me. I wanted to slap the bitch.

"He was starting a private lesson when I left the court. Besides, I'm pretty sure he's seeing someone," I foolishly commented.

"Who?" Amy said.

"Yes, do tell. Who is the lucky lady?" Alex encouraged.

I started washing my hands. "I don't know who. Jake and I are friends, and he mentioned that he'd been chatting regularly with someone."

"Chatting? Oh, that's nothing serious. It won't hurt to ask. The worst he can do is say no. I just hope he's available Saturday night, because Olivia is here only that evening. I'll leave a message for him to call me. I don't want to interrupt his lesson. Bye ladies."

"Bye now," Alex chirped. Alex inspected the showers and stalls to make sure we were alone. Then she crossed her arms and glared at me. "Well now, missy. Why the long face? Seems you weren't totally honest with us the other day in the car. So you and Jake ARE more than friends."

"I can't believe I just did that." I slapped my forehead with the palm of my hand. "I'm so selfish."

"I disagree, hon. You were simply protecting your territory."

"No. I'm just an ass. I've always had feelings for Jake, but I'm not about to screw up a wonderful friendship by getting romantically involved with him. It will only end badly. They always do."

"Maybe this could be different, Callie. Maybe all the bad breakups just make you recognize a good thing. Make you appreciate what you've found. You should go for it."

"No," I shook my head. "It's too late to be more than friends. I set the rules of engagement, and he understands that platonic is the only relationship we can have. There have been a few moments that I've felt weak and know I would have caved. He had to see it, but he didn't seize the opportunity. Trust me when I say he has fully embraced my rules, and I have only myself to blame."

Alex put her arm around me and squeezed. "Callie, honey, rules were made to broken." With that she patted my cheek and departed.

DALLAS

I stood in the break room at work, staring at the cubicle to the left of the doorway where I had delivered mail to a claims adjustor, Darren Thomas. His wife had made a surprise visit with their six-week-old baby boy. Darren beamed as his peers popped in to greet his son. They were such a cute couple -- both in love with, and at the same time intimidated by, their first baby. That's the future I thought I would have with Parker Fielding.

I looked at my watch. 11 am on July 1st -- as if I didn't know the date. Only sixty-eight hours until the second anniversary of the day that changed my life forever. I noticed a vase of flowers that sat askew on a break room table. Clearly it was from someone's garden, but it was quite charming in its simplicity -- a small, clear vase filled with a dozen yellow daisies. I wondered who left them behind. Was there an unpleasant story connected to those flowers? I remembered the first and only time someone gave me daisies. The memory of that day made me shaky, so I sat at the table with the flowers and tortured myself by reliving it.

When I awoke in my hospital bed on July 10, 2012, I remembered it all. My new reality. The pain was indescribable, unbearable. If they would just let Parker see me, it would help. Why were they keeping my fiancé away? I ignored all pleasantries attempted by the doctors and hospital staff. I refused to listen to the soothing words of the hospital psychologist. My physical wounds healed slowly, but the mental ones festered. In time, they would become a cancer that ravaged my soul.

On that day, Detective Hatcher walked into my hospital room with a vase of black-eyed susans. "May I?" he asked as he started to place them on the window-sill adjacent to my bed. I nodded. "I thought you could use some color in this room," he commented as he glanced around. "It's rather drab."

"Thank you," I responded without sincerity.

"The nurses tell me that your memory has stayed with you." Again, I nodded. "I don't know how to convey how sorry I am." His tone oozed genuine compassion, and his eyes welled with tears. As much as I wanted to keep him at bay, I could not shut out his kindness, and the tears spilled quietly but freely down my cheeks.

"I know this is hard, but do you think you are up for answering a few questions?"

"Yes, but I need to understand why you are not letting anyone visit me. I have a fiancé and friends who certainly know what's happened, but I've not been allowed any visitors. I'm being guarded as if I'm royalty or a prisoner. Why the isolation? I'm not contagious."

Detective Hatcher pulled a chair next to my bed. "I know your situation is frustrating, but I think that once you answer my questions, we will be able to address yours. I beg your patience, please."

"Fine," I said, exasperated.

Detective Hatcher pulled a document from a file folder in his briefcase and handed it to me. "Do you recognize this man?" he asked, almost in a whisper. It was a headshot of a man wearing an elated expression. His fist was raised in the air as if celebrating a huge victory.

"Yes. This is my fiancé, Parker Fielding. Is he here? How did you get that picture? Where was it taken?"

Detective Hatcher looked as if the wind had been knocked out of him. "This image was taken about five seconds after flying debris knocked you out on the dock."

That's not possible, I thought, my mind swimming. "There must be some mistake. Parker wasn't in town. I told you he left around 11:30 the night before the accident."

"Providence, this will be difficult to hear, but we actually have a video of the chain of events. Noah Hargrove is a freelance writer/photographer who was working on an article about Fourth of July family traditions in the Carolinas. He had heard about the Sanderson family ritual and wanted to capture the tradition without your knowledge -- to preserve authenticity. He had planned to interview you after you dined at Capers Island and ask permission to include your story in his article. He rented a simple fishing skiff and anchored fifty yards off your family's property about thirty minutes before you were scheduled to leave. When he started filming, he scanned the property as he said 'to capture the solitude of the moment just before the pot was stirred'. He was surprised to see movement in a patch of woods to the right of your property. Mr. Hargrove saw this young man move to the shoreline with a net, and he thought the guy was crabbing.

"Mr. Hargrove captured your world in solitude and the joy of your little niece racing toward the boat screaming that she was the first one on board. He was not aware of Parker Fielding's movements because he was focused on your family. He turned over the video to the police, and our experts were able to enhance it to see everything that Fielding did."

I turned to Detective Hatcher, a figure distorted by my pooling tears. "Are you trying to tell me that my fiancé murdered my family?"

"All circumstantial evidence points in that direction. We have to assume he intended for you to die as well. In the video, you were the last one to board the boat, and within three seconds, we can see him depress what we assume to be a trigger switch. Mr. Hargrove immediately called 911 and came to shore to see if there were any survivors. He had enough wits about him to slow the bleeding of your wounds until the paramedics arrived. You would have died if he hadn't been there."

"I wish I had." I stared at the ceiling, and tears rolled down my face. "I guess I should thank him for being a good samaritan, but my heart isn't in it."

"He thinks you're dead anyway. Everybody does."

"What?"

"We decided that it would be best for the world to believe that the entire family had died, because we didn't want Fielding to come after you. To him, you're a loose end. He triggered the bomb after you got in the boat, but it exploded after you had hopped out to retrieve the beach bag you forgot. That's the only thing that saved you."

My entire family was dead, my friends thought I was dead, and the man that I was planning to marry in six months was behind it all. I let Parker Fielding into my world. It was my fault that my family was dead, yet I was still alive. In less than thirty seconds, the essence of my being, everyone that I cherished, every dream that I treasured was obliterated. I felt an unbearable weight, as if a steady stream of cement was being poured over me. I didn't fight it. I welcomed the suffocation. I turned my back to Detective Hatcher and whispered, "Please leave."

"Okay," he answered somberly. "But I have to ask you one more thing before I go. We found remnants of professional grade explosives at the site. We were hoping for at least a partial print but no luck. If we can get a print or DNA of Parker Fielding, we are hoping it may lead us to him, and we can find a way to prove that he was responsible. Do you have anything that would have his DNA on it?"

"He spent two days at the beach house. His prints are probably all over the place."

"That makes perfect sense, but our efforts came up empty. We think he wiped down the place before he left your house the night of July 3rd, or maybe he snuck back in the house after the explosion and cleaned up. Or possibly he had something covering his fingertips that prevented him from leaving prints behind. We thought maybe you would have something personal that we could use."

I was such a sentimental fool. I kept the very first thing he ever gave me -- a silly Delta Airlines cocktail napkin that he had pressed to his lips. I kept it in my apartment tucked in the pages of my favorite book -- a signed copy of *The Help*.

He thanked me and promised to return when he had more information. I didn't respond. I heard him whispering with the nurse at the door. All I heard were two words, "suicide watch". I cranked up the morphine drip as high as possible and prayed that I would never wake up again.

****

"Dallas! Dallas!" A shrill voice called my name. It was my supervisor, Nancy Mize, standing beside me. I suppose I had a blank look on my face. "What are you doing in here, Dallas?"

I rose quickly and apologized. "Sorry, I came in here to rest a minute and got sidetracked by these flowers. Someone left them behind." I pointed to the table.

She was livid. The veins in her neck stood at full attention. "I don't care about the flowers, Dallas. Let the cleaning service take care of that and get back to work. I don't know what's wrong with you, but you are skating on thin ice. We will discuss your performance issues later. Now go!"

I hurried out of the room wishing I had called in sick today.

MARY CLAIRE

July 5th, Saturday. I sat at a corner table next to the window overlooking The Heights' golf course watching a family of geese waddle toward the lake just to the left of the eighteenth hole. Such an orderly procession, feathered soldiers dutifully marching behind their commander. The last one had a bit of attitude, occasionally wandering laterally until reprimands were shrieked to force him back in line. I wondered if he would be abandoned if he continued his rebellious ways. Apparently he longed to stand apart, but could he stand alone?

"Hey. You look deep in thought," Callie said as she sat opposite me.

"Only if you consider watching geese an exercise in depth," I replied. "I'm glad we have a match next week. It feels like an eternity since I've played, and I miss seeing you and the rest of the ladies."

"I know. But it wouldn't be so bad if you'd been coming to clinic. We really missed you. Are you feeling better?"

"Much better, thank you," I replied as I refolded the napkin on my lap several times until the ends perfectly aligned. "I plan to be there on Tuesday. I'll certainly need to practice before our match on Friday. I don't want to embarrass you."

"Not possible. Even on your off days you're an asset. It's your calm spirit that's the key. If we could bottle and sell your patience, we'd be disgustingly wealthy. We could buy a private island and escape our troubles whenever we wanted."

"An escape." I pondered the word as I watched the rebel goose swim away from the flock. "I like the sound of that," I muttered more to myself than to Callie.

"Excuse me, ladies," interrupted the server. "Are you ready to order?"

I focused my attention on the table again. "I'm ready. Do you need a little more time, Callie?"

"No. I know what I want."

I ordered the grilled halibut lunch special, and Callie ordered grilled fish tacos. When the waiter departed, I turned to Callie. "So, how did you spend your Fourth of July?"

"Mostly working. But I did meet a friend in Homewood last night to watch the fireworks."

Callie picked up a piece of bread and spent far too much time spreading butter on it. She was hiding something, so I smiled and asked, "Did Jake enjoy the fireworks?"

Callie glared at me, butter knife and bread frozen in her hands. "Why do you assume I was with Jake?" She returned to lavishly painting her bread.

"Because he is your only friend that makes you blush." Callie abandoned her food art and touched her flushed cheeks. "Very funny, Mary Claire. You know, Jake is worried about you."

"Don't try to change the subject, Callie. You need to update me on your relationship with Jake. We haven't talked in two weeks."

"I'm serious, Mary Claire. He's worried about you, and quite frankly, so am I."

I refolded my napkin as I responded. "I'm perfectly fine, Callie. Why are you worried about me?"

"Wearing long sleeves while playing tennis in this heat? It's a wonder you haven't had a heat stroke. And you rarely miss any clinics, but you've missed several. What are you hiding? You say you've been on antibiotics. What's wrong?"

As I listened to her voice, her anguish was unmistakable. "Callie, you know that I'm a very private person. But if you are worried that I have some terminal illness, let me put your mind at ease. I'm perfectly healthy. Since I graduated from high school, I've been living with certain impediments that flare up on occasion. When that happens, I have to take the proper precautions, like the long-sleeved shirts. We all have our crosses to bear, and we find ways to carry them. But I don't have any life-threatening conditions and plan to be your doubles partner as long as you'll have me."

"I wouldn't want another partner. But you know you can talk to me, right? I respect your privacy. I mean you can trust that if you need to confide in me, what you tell me will go no further. Everybody needs a sounding board every now and then. I'm here for you any time."

I patted Callie's hand. "I know that. You are a dear friend, and I appreciate your concern. But now I want to hear more about you and Jake." Our food arrived as I spoke.

Callie took a bite of her slaw before answering. "There's nothing to tell, really. We've been spending a lot of time together and texting and talking daily. It's very comfortable to be with him. Not comfortable as in boring, but comfortable like a favorite pair of shoes. The more you wear them, the better the fit. They mold to you, and soon all other shoes pale in comparison. There are no other shoes in the closet that you want to wear. We laugh a lot. Which is good for me."

As she spoke, Callie's eyes lit up. Clearly she was falling for Jake. Actually she fell for him long ago but pushed him away. Maybe now she was ready to admit it. Of course, I knew Jake was in love with Callie, but he had been waiting a long time for her to come around. I wasn't sure how much longer his patience would last. We ate in silence for a few minutes before I shared my thoughts. "Callie, it is blatantly obvious that you and Jake have an amazing connection. Two years ago, when you two were unofficially dating, you pushed him away. No disrespect intended, but your reasons defied logic, so please tell me you are not going to shut him out again."

Callie shook her head. "I have no intention of doing that. He's really the best male friend I've ever had. He really gets me, and I understand him as well. I just wish he were less attractive, so I wouldn't be constantly aching for him on a physical level. It would be far better if the attraction were solely cerebral."

"My dear, sweet, misguided friend," I began as l laid down my fork. "Don't you see that you have just described the most ideal relationship? A man to whom you are intensely attracted, and at the same time, a man that you consider to be a best friend. And I know Jake feels the same about you. What is holding you back?"

"Jake told you how he feels about me?"

"He doesn't have to, Callie. It's obvious. So, I ask again, what's holding you back?"

"Mary Claire," Callie began, arms folded in a defensive posture, "you've witnessed the ugly ends to relationships I've had over the past five years. The process has left me numb. Jake's friendship is so important to me. If that relationship crosses the line and things don't work out, then I've lost a friend, and I couldn't bear that loss."

"Callie, you can't be so naive as to believe that two people who are intensely attracted to each other can successfully repress those desires one hundred percent of the time."

"So far we have. And trust me, there have been some moments where crossing the line would have been easy. I have to admit that I've wanted him to cross it, but he respects my philosophy and retreats when things get a little...heated."

"Jake's a good man, but he's no saint. If you keep expecting him to act like a monk, he will eventually resent you, and your friendship will be permanently damaged."

"He exhibits more willpower than I do. Maybe he isn't as attracted to me as you think."

"You're dead wrong." She's so stubborn. "You cannot deny your feelings for him, so why not take that leap of faith?"

"Because I've taken that jump more than once, and I'm tired of being crushed when I hit the canyon floor."

"This time is different. You're right; I've witnessed your many disappointments, but I can tell you that none of your former boyfriends elicited the responses that Jake does. Even when the relationships were in their infancies, when things tend to be so blissful, you never spoke of them with the admiration and respect that you do when you talk about Jake. You blush at the mention of his name. Not so with the others. You never described any of them as your friend. I think those in the past looked good on paper but turned out not to be right for you in reality. Those were the ones you should have pushed off the cliff rather than leaping first."

Callie fidgeted. "You might be right. You've certainly had a long, happy marriage, so maybe you recognize the ingredients that blend into a successful relationship."

"You give me too much credit," I snickered. "But I know unequivocally that I am right about you and Jake. Promise you'll think about exploring your feelings. I think you'll regret it for the rest of your life if you don't."

"Okay," Callie promised. "Not to change the subject, but have you heard from Dallas lately?"

"We were supposed to meet for lunch a couple of times, but she cancelled at the last minute in both instances."

"If it were anyone other than Dallas, I'd think that was odd. I don't mean to be nosey, but what do y'all talk about? I know you've had lunch a few times, and I can't imagine what you have in common."

"Not much really. I think she's lonely and needs someone to talk to. I think since I'm old enough to be her mother, I'm a safe harbor for her."

"She picked a good harbor. I know you've been my safety net on many dark occasions."

"I don't know that I'm helping her. To be such a bull on the court, she's as timid as a mouse off the court. She truly seems troubled. I don't mean like mentally disturbed, but emotionally burdened."

"You're probably helping more than you think."

"I hope so."

Callie rose. "I need to visit the ladies room. Be right back." The bill arrived, and I charged it to our account. Callie would fuss, but she'd get over it. I looked in the direction of the pond, searching for the rebel goose. A young man stood leaning against an ancient oak near the edge of the pond.

"What are you looking at?" Callie asked as she followed my gaze while taking her seat at our table.

"Do you see that man against the tree?" She nodded. "Do you know who he is?"

"No, I don't recognize him."

"He looks so familiar, but I can't put a name to the face."

"Where's the bill, Mary Claire?" Callie asked in an agitated tone.

I raised my index finger to my mouth and whispered, "Shhh. Just say thank you."

Callie rolled her eyes. "You are maddening. Thank you, though. Next time is on me. I have to go now, but this was fun. We need to do this more often. So, I'll see you Tuesday for sure?"

"Absolutely." I turned back to see if one more look at the young man would jog my memory, but he was gone.

FRACTURES

Match 4 - July 11, 2014

If a crack in the soul remains unchecked, fissures spread allowing discontent, doubt and destruction to seep to the surface.

ALEX

<u>Tuesday, July 8th</u>. I arrived at the club for clinic and saw Mary Claire already headed to our court. I grabbed my bag and jogged toward her. "Hello, stranger," I called out as I caught up with her and wrapped my arm around her shoulders. "So good to see you, Mary Claire." I squeezed her toward me, but she grimaced and pulled away. "Oh no, did I hurt you? I was so excited to see you; I just hugged you too tight."

Mary Claire breathed deeply and waved off my concern. "No, honey, I'm fine. I just have a tender place on my arm, and you accidentally anchored on that spot. It's fine."

"I'm so sorry." I carefully removed her tennis bag from her shoulder. "The least I can do is carry your bag for you."

"That's not necessary. You know what it's like when you hit a bruise the wrong way. It hurts for only a second."

She reached for the bag, but I stepped out of her grasp. "I don't care. It will make me feel better. Come on." We walked in silence for a few steps. "Do you know if Dallas is coming today?" I asked. "Not that she needs the practice, but I was hoping we could work on some strategy. I'm ready to add something new to the mix."

"Yes, she'll be here. We're going to have lunch after clinic. I spoke with her over the weekend, and she said that she had a very difficult week and was looking forward to taking out her frustrations on a tennis ball."

"Katy bar the door! Hope everybody's wearing big girl panties today."

Mary Claire snickered. We were the first to arrive. Jake seemed very happy to see Mary Claire. He hugged her gingerly, as if he knew to avoid her bruise. "So happy you're back. We've missed you."

"I'm glad to be here. I've missed everyone. It's been far too long since we played a match. I'm afraid I'll be a bit rusty today."

"I'll go easy on you," Jake responded with a wink. "Let's do some easy volleys while we wait for the others."

"Did you ladies have a nice Fourth of July?" Jake asked.

"Sly and I spent the long weekend working in the yard. The wedding is less than two months away and since everything is going to be outside, we've been 'kickin' it up a notch' -- adding more bedding plants and stone pathways. The yard looked nice before, but it's amazing how much more inviting it looks now."

"What looks inviting?" Amy Morard asked as she joined them on the court. Callie was two steps behind her. Jake motioned for them to join him on his side so that they could volley with Mary Claire and me.

"We were just talking about how Sly and I had worked in the yard over the holiday weekend sprucing it up for my daughter's wedding." I stopped and looked around before continuing. "Y'all put it on your calendar, August 23rd, because all of you are invited. It will be tons of fun -- open bar, great food, live band. Jake, I expect to see you at my house as well. Invitations will go out very soon."

"Well, Jake, if you need a date to Avery's wedding," Amy interjected, "I'm POSITIVE that my friend, Olivia Dunn, will be more than happy to go with you. She was quite impressed with you at dinner Saturday night. I knew the two of you would hit it off."

Just as Amy finished speaking, I hit a solid volley to Callie. She didn't even move her racquet. Her eyes were still locked on Amy when the ball hit her square in the stomach. "Damn, Callie. Are you okay?" I called as I hurried to her side. Mary Claire was just behind me, and Jake was already there looking painfully concerned. I'm not sure if he was more concerned about an injury or Amy's comments.

"You okay?" Jake asked. She didn't respond. Jake turned to the others. "Everybody take a two minute water break and head to the baseline."

Dallas arrived as the others were getting water. "Dallas," I called as I saw her, "will you please bring some water for Callie?"

Callie waved her arms in protest. "I'm fine. Knocked the breath out of me. Need a minute." Jake tried to guide her to the bench, but Callie jerked her arm away. "I'm not an invalid, Jake." If looks could kill, Jake Lenaghan would have instantly vaporized. He turned around, and I swear the man was grinning from ear to ear. At first, I thought he was being a dick, and then I realized why he was smiling. Ah, what a twisted little game he was playing.

"Who is Olivia Dunn?" I heard Mary Claire ask Jake under her breath.

"Tell you later," he whispered in return. He raised his voice and said, "Everybody to the baseline, one line on the deuce side. This is a backhand drill. I'll feed you three balls. First ball is coming as a deep backhand. Return it deep crosscourt. Second ball is a backhand approach shot. Take it down the line. Third ball is a backhand volley.

You should already be in position from the approach shot. Take the volley crosscourt aiming at my feet, but try to get behind me. Callie, feed in when you're ready."

Callie joined us in less than five minutes and completed the entire clinic in silence. And she didn't miss anything. She and Dallas were like twins -- silent but deadly. As she was packing up to leave, Amy asked her who we played in Friday's match. She looked blank as she answered. "I don't remember. It's a home match. I'll send out a line up later tonight." Then she turned and high tailed it to her car at quite a clip. I saw Jake discreetly watching her as he picked up balls with his hopper, the whole time looking like the cat who swallowed the canary. I couldn't decide if I should give him the finger or applaud.

MARY CLAIRE

As everyone departed, I told Dallas that I needed a moment to chat with Jake, so I'd meet her in the clubhouse dining room in about ten minutes.

I sat on the bench and summoned Jake, who was picking up the last of the balls. "Jake?" He turned and I patted the spot next to me.

He jogged over and took the appointed seat. "So, how are you, really?" he implored.

"No sir, we are not speaking of my unyielding woes today. You're dating someone named Olivia Dunn? What's this all about? I thought you and Callie had reconnected. What's going on?"

Jake clutched his chest. "Mary Claire, of all people to jump to conclusions, you are typically the last. How disappointing." His tone was quite playful.

"Stop toying with me, young man. Explain yourself."

He laughed. "Okay. The weekend before the Fourth, Callie and I grilled out at my house, and we had a great time. Very relaxing, very comfortable. Great conversation, lots of wine. When we're together, everything feels right. I know that we're good for each other, and she knows it too, but she just won't admit it. That evening, there was a point that I started to kiss her, and I don't mean to sound cocky, but there is no doubt in my mind that she wanted me to. But right before I did, I remembered how she shut down two years ago when I went beyond the friendship zone. When we started hanging out again a few weeks ago, she made it very clear that our relationship had to remain platonic. So, I can't be the one to cross the line that she so adamantly drew."

"I understand, but who is Olivia?"

"I'm getting there. Like I said, Callie has to break the barriers, not me. Anyway, last week after clinic, Amy left me a message to call her. She said that she had this gorgeous, smart friend coming to visit over the weekend and would I be interested in going to dinner with her and Ian and this friend, Olivia, like a casual double date -- no pressure. When I started to decline, she volunteered that Callie told her it wasn't a good idea because I was interested in someone right now. Callie told Amy that we are good friends, and I had mentioned that I had been chatting with someone regularly."

"Oh my goodness," I interjected.

"Oh my indeed," Jake responded. "So I decided to accept the offer thinking that if it got back to Callie, maybe it would help her cross that stupid, self-imposed line."

"The revelation clearly unglued Callie, but Jake, you have to remember that her thought processes are absurdly complicated. I hope this little tactic doesn't backfire."

"Me, too. She was mad as hell at me," Jake declared through a grin. "I hate to admit that I enjoyed watching her squirm."

"I know you're not going to wait on her forever. Honestly, what did you think of this Olivia woman?"

"Amy didn't oversell her. Olivia is drop dead gorgeous, bright, quite charming. She's a catch by any standard except for one thing."

"What's that?" I asked.

"She's not Callie Conrad."

I smiled. "Callie is one of a kind. I'm sure she'll stew over this a few days and then hash it out with me. If she's misinterpreted anything, I'll steer her in the right direction. Or at least, I'll make an attempt."

"Thank you," Jake said and kissed my forehead. "Here's my next lesson now. You take care of yourself, and call me if you need me."

I blew him a kiss and headed toward the clubhouse to meet Dallas.

****

I spotted Dallas seated at the same table Callie and I had occupied a few days before. I followed her gaze as I took my chair. The same geese that I had watched that day now mesmerized Dallas. I spotted the rebel goose and pointed to it. "That one, second from the left, is my favorite."

"Really?" Dallas responded with surprise. "Mine, too."

"And why is he your favorite?" I asked.

Dallas continued to study the rebel goose, who was exploring the reeds along the shoreline while his siblings swam as a synchronized team behind their mother. "He's a misfit. He doesn't belong. I can relate." She gave me an awkward smile. "Why do you like him?"

"Hmm," I pondered her response. "What an interesting perception you have. Mine is totally different. I see him as a rebel -- a nonconformist who wants to break the mold and seek his own path. I envy that quality," I commented longingly. "So, we both are drawn to his solitude, but we each interpret his singularity as it relates to us personally. Fascinating how the mind works, isn't it?"

Dallas stared at me for a moment before speaking. "Mary Claire, I know you don't work, but what is your degree?"

I sipped my water before responding. "Regrettably, I don't possess a degree."

"Ah, so you left college early to get married," Dallas surmised. "What were you studying? What university did you attend?"

I folded the napkin in my lap taking great care to make sure that the edges aligned perfectly. I kept my eyes focused on my task as I spoke. "I didn't attend college, Dallas. I met my husband shortly after I graduated from high school, and we were married six months later."

"I'm shocked," Dallas replied. "Your demeanor, your vocabulary, everything about you, suggests a well educated woman. Quite frankly, I expected you to tell me you attended an ivy league school and that's where you met your husband."

"Well, I'll take that as a compliment," I chuckled.

"What's so funny?" Dallas inquired.

"Oh, I was just thinking that Andrew would give me an 'I told you so' look if he heard what you just said."

Dallas crinkled her brow. "I don't understand."

"It's a long story," I answered, thinking it best to keep my personal history to myself.

"I really want to hear it. Let's order, and you can tell me."

The server arrived shortly, and we placed our orders. I requested a glass of chardonnay, totally out of character for me in the middle of the day, but Dallas had unwittingly struck a nerve.

After the server departed, I turned my attention to Dallas. "So you really want to understand why I seem well educated without the degree?" She nodded. "It's really a boring story, but okay. College was always my plan. In fact, I had a swim scholarship to Auburn University and aspired to become a veterinarian. Auburn has a fabulous veterinary school. But that's a long road, and I knew my father couldn't afford it. I would have to earn substantial scholarship money to be able to go to veterinary school. Leaving for college had the added perk of getting me away from my increasingly tyrannical father. Being the only one left at home had been very stressful under his tireless scrutiny. Anyway, as soon as I graduated from high school, I started my summer job as a lifeguard at The Heights."

"You were a lifeguard here?" Dallas interrupted.

I smiled. "Seems like a lifetime ago, but yes, I was. It was my third summer in that position, so I knew all of the regulars. That summer, Andrew Jameson was a new face in the crowd, and my, what a handsome face it was. The first time I saw him, he was here with a woman. She was striking, but they didn't seem smitten with each other. After that day, he came every Sunday but always alone. He started talking to me during my breaks. I suppose I was naive, but he was charming and obviously very successful. In assessing Andrew Jameson as a suitor, I had no basis for comparison, since I had never had a boyfriend. In retrospect, he was quite boastful; he bragged about the fact that at the age of twenty-nine, he was the youngest attorney to ever make full partner in his firm and that membership at The Heights was a perk of being partner. He often dropped names of prominent clients and regaled me with stories of his courtroom victories and his 98% win rate. He loved to talk about all the nice things he owned -- his car, his house, his clothes. He seemed so certain of what he wanted for his future and the type of woman he wanted by his side. His self-confidence impressed me, probably because I had very little of my own. I liked the fact that he was ten years older than me -- more mature and settled. He showered me with flowers and expensive gifts, and took me to the finest restaurants. Shockingly, he won favor with my father. Andrew treated me like a queen, and my utter lack of experience with men ironically appealed to him. When it came to physical contact, he was a perfect gentleman. I didn't offer him anything more than a good night kiss on our dates, but it seemed very important to him to preserve my innocence. He admitted that he had experienced some seedy relationships with loose women and no longer desired 'unsavory dalliances' but craved a 'lasting, meaningful relationship'."

While I paused to take a few bites of my meal, Dallas reflected with a hint of sarcasm. "Sounds like a fairy tale. Was there anything about him that you didn't find utterly perfect?"

"Indeed, I felt like Cinderella. But there was one facet of his persona that troubled me. Andrew was very intense; rarely did he smile, much less laugh. He was so serious all the time. That fact troubled me a bit, because it reminded me of my father, but then I found a photograph of him and realized that there was another, lighter component of his personality, and that eventually, I would experience that side of him."

"What was so special about this photograph?" Dallas inquired.

"I found it underneath his car seat and knew he had intended to throw it away. But it struck me so deeply that I kept it. Anyway, I was already ridiculously infatuated with him, and I masked his seriousness as mysterious and alluring. By the time summer was over, I was completely in love. The week before I was to leave for Auburn, he took me to dinner. It was no ordinary dinner. He had hired a harpist to play for us while we dined in a restaurant that Andrew had rented for the night. He told me that he couldn't bear the thought of my leaving for Auburn. He said that he knew college life would poison me, and we would lose each other forever. He slipped this ruby and diamond ring on my finger," I held up the exquisite jewel for her to see, "and begged me to marry him before Christmas."

"You gave up a swim scholarship, your entire college career, to get married at the ripe old age of eighteen?" Dallas was appalled.

"You have to weigh all the parameters, Dallas. Here I was a very insecure, naive, inexperienced eighteen-year-old being wooed by an older, handsome, successful man who promised to give me the best of everything. I was an eighteen-year-old with an overbearing father who told me that I would be a fool to pass up the chance to marry Andrew Jameson. I suppose, using his skills as a litigator, Andrew persuaded me that he could educate me with far greater efficiency than a university. He also promised to take care of my father's financial needs as he aged. He promised to provide the best medical care and in-home care if he ever fell ill or debilitated."

"But what about your dream of being a veterinarian? How could you give that up?"

"Oh, I'm not sure I was really that serious about it. Working with animals seemed like a peaceful occupation free of the demands of people. I'm fifty-five years old, and I've never owned a pet. I seriously doubt I would have pursued a veterinary career. Now back to your original question about my education. Andrew and I married in December of that year, and within two days of returning from our honeymoon, he had scheduled my itinerary for the next twelve months. He developed a curriculum to provide the most well-rounded education he deemed necessary. He detailed the books to read -- the classics, historical novels about different regions of the world. He enrolled me in cooking classes at the Culinard, refinement classes with a personal coach, and gardening classes at the Botanical Gardens. His selections centered upon an education that would refine my skills as a homemaker and facilitate my ability to converse on a variety of topics at those dreadful firm functions. While he built his career, I followed his plan to morph into his image of the perfect wife. Basically he molded me, meticulously chipping away at my undefined core until he had sculpted me into his perfect statue -- one that he could proudly parade before his partners and clients."

"Wow," Dallas muttered under her breath. We sat in silence, both looking at the geese.

"I'm not complaining. I have been given much, but I have experienced little."

"That sounds like a regret to me."

"Possibly. But enough about me. You told me you had a very difficult week. Are you better now? Can I help?"

"Actually, you have helped. For some reason, you sharing your story helped me a little. At least it got my mind off things."

"Did you do anything fun to celebrate the 4th?"

Dallas's demeanor darkened, and I felt her anguish erupt. "The Fourth of July used to be my favorite holiday. Now I hate it."

"I'm sorry. I didn't mean to upset you."

"You didn't know. How could you know that it was the second anniversary of the worst day of my life? But I don't want to talk about that. Do you mind if we chat about you some more?"

"Well, I'm quite dull, but certainly."

"What do you think about marriage, Mary Claire?"

The question puzzled me. "What do you mean?"

"I mean, do you like being married? Is he the man you thought he was?"

"Why do you ask?" I replied with a question, eager to avoid a direct answer.

"Oh, I suppose because I was engaged once."

"What happened? Did you call it off?"

"Me? No, no. I was madly in love. No, he turned out to be a far different person than I thought he was. He was quite an actor."

"I'm sorry, Dallas. That must have been a painful experience for you. Did things end on somewhat amicable terms?"

Dallas laughed, a disturbed cackle that drew a few curious looks. "Amicable? Not at all."

"I'm sorry. It sounds as if the wounds are fresh. How long has it been?"

"A little over two years, but you still haven't answered my question."

I sipped my wine. "My memory is going, Dallas. What was the question?"

"You've been married a long time, forty years, right? Is your husband the man you thought he was, or did he fool you?"

I began folding and refolding my napkin, unable to succeed in producing satisfactory folds. "When you are young and in love, you tend to be a bit blind to the faults of those who hold your affections. I think it's normal for our faults to emerge after being married for a while -- when the newness fades and the mundane nature of everyday life settles in. Marriage is difficult and requires a great deal of work to make it successful."

"Do you think all faults are forgivable?"

"What do you mean?"

"Do you believe that if you discover severe character flaws in your spouse -- deceptions -- that you just work through them? Or do you leave?"

"I suppose it depends on the situation. Inevitably, one person tends to compromise more than the other."

"Yes, but one can compromise so much that eventually there is nothing left, and you don't even know who you are anymore."

I looked off into the distance, fighting back the tears pooling in my eyes.

"Are you okay?" Dallas recognized my anguish, but I couldn't respond. "Mary Claire, are you okay?"

I took a moment to compose myself and patted her arm. "Sorry, Dallas, sometimes I feel as if you know far more about me than you should. You are too young to lose faith in love. It sounds as if your guy treated you poorly, but sometimes the bad ones get their due. Then again, some get away with treating women poorly longer than others. But don't give up. Your ex is probably miserable. Do you know where he is now?"

"No, but I can assure you that if he ever darkens my door again, I will kill him."

The tone of her voice was defiant and finite, so I chose to ignore the comment.

As I pulled my wallet from my purse, something fell out. I looked down and saw that it was the picture of Andrew that I loved. Dallas was already bending to retrieve it. As she righted herself, I noticed that the hand gripping the photo was trembling.

"Is this the picture you were talking about earlier? The one that you said made you realize that your husband had a lighter side?"

"Yes. It's weird. I know it's him, but it's almost as if he is a different person. He looks so happy and carefree. His eyes appear less intense and kinder. I think there's a pivotal story here, but one that I'll never know. See how the picture is cut? You can tell he had his arm around someone who has been cut out. My theory is that the person removed from the picture was a woman. Someone he fell in love with in law school. Someone as bright and ambitious as he was. She broke his heart, and the pain left him colder, more removed than the carefree, kind man in the picture. I wish I had known this Andrew. The one with the gentle kindness in his eyes. Sometimes, when I feel that he is being harsh, I'll take out this picture and remember that somewhere deep inside, there is a different side of him that may come out one day. But after so many years of marriage, I've never seen a glimpse of the man in the photograph."

"And you never will," Dallas declared emphatically as she returned the picture to me.

"Excuse me," I responded, taken aback by her statement.

Dallas fidgeted. "I'm sorry, Mary Claire. That was a rude comment. I think after forty years of marriage, if you've never seen that side of him, then I doubt you ever will. But I was out of line to say that, and I apologize."

"It's alright, dear. I suppose you're right."

Dallas looked at her watch and stood. "I didn't realize it was so late. I have to go now. Thanks for lunch."

She scurried away before I could utter a word.

DALLAS

I left Mary Claire so abruptly at lunch that I felt guilty, but that picture completely unglued me. She doesn't know. She's not complicit. Mary Claire is a victim, too. But I can't allow this twist to complicate the plan.

Again, I thought about calling Detective Hatcher. Maybe he had useful information about Parker. But making contact might jeopardize everything. Eventually Parker would pay. I would see to that.

Just the thought of Parker Fielding deepened the blackness in my soul. He had played me so easily. I mean what were the chances that we would meet on a Saturday night in Charleston and be on the same flight to Philadelphia the next day? We had talked nonstop from the moment we met at the gate until we landed. He had doted on me, not in a suffocating way, just completely charming. We seemed to share the same interests in music, movies, books, and politics.

When I look back now, I see that it was too good to be true -- that I had been completely gullible. My parents were clearly soul mates, but they didn't agree on everything. "A little controversy keeps the spark alive," my dad used to say. I suppose Parker studied my habits and interests since I was his target. Isn't that what accomplished con artists do -- research their marks? I thought he was totally sincere, but his interest in my family should have been a red flag. What guy wants to know details about a girl's family right away? I thought his interest stemmed from the absence of family in his own life. He said he was originally from Minneapolis and that he was the only child of older parents who were killed in a car accident when he was in college.

After that flight, we were together constantly. The relationship quickly became romantic. I remembered that first kiss -- more passionate than any I had ever experienced. I thought that passion sprang from our deep connection. I craved more, and his touch was tender, yet seductive. I remembered how exhilarating it felt to give myself to him completely and how that surrender pleased him so deeply.

As I relived those images of intimacy, I barely made it to the toilet before I threw up. I brushed my teeth rigorously. My hands were shaking as I cleaned my face with a cool cloth. I needed a diversion. I sat at my computer to play a game of Solitaire, when a message popped up. It was from Callie giving the lineup for Friday. Friday could not arrive soon enough.

ALEX

<u>Friday, July 11th</u>. I was driving to The Heights for our match against Vestavia Country Club, when my cell phone rang. I smiled as I recognized the ring tone, *Sweet Child of Mine*.

"Good morning, baby girl."

"Hey, Mom," Avery greeted.

"Do you realize your big day is six weeks from tomorrow?"

"No, I'd forgotten all about it," Avery teased.

"Haha."

"Actually, that's why I was calling. Invitations go out next week, right?"

"Right. Did we forget someone?"

"No, I just wondered if you're inviting your tennis buddies."

"Several, yes. Is that a problem?"

"No, but you aren't inviting that crazy lady, are you?"

"MKat? Heavens no."

"What about Katlin?"

"Well no, she wasn't on my radar."

"If it's not any trouble, can we add her plus a guest? We've been chatting up a storm since we met at your match and realized we had mutual friends. I really like her. And she has this serious, older boyfriend that she'd like to bring. Is that okay?"

"Sure. Consider it done."

"Thanks, Mom. What are you up to this morning?"

"Just pulling into the club for a match."

"Okay. I won't keep you. But how are Izzy and the pups doing?"

"Izzy's a good little mom, and those pups are getting uglier by the minute."

"Mom!"

"Oh stop. You know I love 'em to death. They'll be old enough to leave Izzy in a few weeks, so if you know anyone who wants a dog that looks like he's been dipped in ugly, just let me know."

"You're awful."

"I know. Your dad wants to give one to some little girl in his office, but other than that, no takers."

"I'll ask around. Good luck with your match."

"I don't need luck, missy. I have Dallas."

"Bye, crazy Mom. Love you."

"Love you too, baby girl."

****

Callie parked beside me as I pulled my tennis bag from the trunk. "Morning, Callie."

"Hey." Callie grabbed her bag from the backseat, and we started walking toward the courts. "Are you ready for this one? This is a big match."

"Can't wait to play, but what's so special about this match?"

"We're 3 and 0, as you know. Vestavia is 4 and 0 and the only other team in our bracket that is undefeated."

"I didn't realize that."

"Maybe I shouldn't have mentioned it. Didn't mean to unleash a cloud of pressure."

"You didn't. Stuff like that doesn't get in my head. But, I'm surprised you didn't put your A-team in the lineup for the 3.0 court. As much as I hate to give MKat a compliment, I think she and Katlin are a stronger team than Amy and Kelly."

"They are stronger, but I promised Katlin I would give her a break from MKat. And I have to play MKat and Katlin next week because Amy is not available. The pressure is on you and Dallas and Mary Claire and me to get the win. Just between you and me, I don't think Amy and Kelly can beat the team they're playing. I checked their history on the website, and they've played together for a few years and have wiped out their opponents this season."

"I'll give it 110%, captain."

"I know you and Dallas will be fine. I'm worried about my court. Mary Claire has played only once since our match three weeks ago, and I feel a little rattled thinking about what's at stake."

"I understand, but you know you can't produce when you're tight."

"I know. I've just got to focus on the game and not the score."

We joined Dallas and Mary Claire who were already warming up from the baseline. About five minutes later, Jake walked over to wish us luck. "Stay aggressive ladies and watch the middle. I'll be able to watch the first hour, so I'll be taking mental notes for our next clinic."

As he turned away, I warned him. "Stay hidden, Jake. You might be distracting if we see you lurking around in our peripheral vision."

"You'll never know I'm there."

As Jake headed back toward the clubhouse, I saw Amy and Kelly stop to chat with him, but they weren't alone. An immaculately dressed, very attractive blonde flashed a radiant smile at Jake and greeted him confidently with a peck on the lips. I turned to Callie, but thankfully she missed the entire exchange.

Amy and Kelly joined the warm-up. "Sorry we're late," Amy apologized. "My good friend, Olivia, showed up at my door unannounced this morning. She has a business meeting here this afternoon, so she decided to surprise me so we could hang out before her meeting. I fussed and said she should have called first because I had this match. But she loved the idea of coming here and watching us play. Personally, I think she came in town early hoping to maneuver some time with Jake. I haven't seen Olivia this excited about a guy since college, but who can blame her. Jake's a catch. Can't believe no one has snatched him up by now."

Callie walked up and ordered, "Go to your courts. It's time to play." Her tone was all business, but I knew she was all bent out of shape by the surprise visitor.

Dallas and I took the court and stayed the course. My partner was true to form, and at the risk of sounding a bit cocky, I was superhuman. Best match ever. And our opponents were strong, but Dallas and I moved like a perfectly oiled machine. We anticipated each other's moves flawlessly, and in thirty minutes we had sealed the first set 6-2. Between sets, our opponents took a bathroom break, so Dallas and I were able to watch the other courts. Amy and Kelly were getting drilled. They kept coming up to the net, but their opponents consistently unleashed perfect lobs. Talk about gluttons for punishment. They needed to regroup and try a new strategy. Then we turned our attention to Mary Claire and Callie. I was playing in the zone, but Callie was playing in another dimension. Her shots were spectacular -- deep, well placed and largely impossible to return with any authority. She was oblivious to not only her opponents, but also her partner.

Dallas commented. "Look at those ladies. They look scared. Callie is playing out of her head. I've never seen her attack the ball so aggressively."

I laughed. "It's like looking in the mirror, isn't it, Dallas?" I patted her knee. "Come on, partner. Here they come back from the bathroom. Let's put this one to bed."

We had to work a bit harder to take the second set, but we managed to close out at 6-4.   By the time we were done, Amy and Kelly were down 1-5 in the second set and looked like decimated rag dolls.

Dallas and I joined Jake who was tucked away out of sight but with a good view of Callie and Mary Claire. "Good playing, ladies," he whispered.

"Thanks," I said. "Looks like this match is all up to Mary Claire and Callie. Are they still in the first set?"

"No, they won the first set 7-5. This is the first game of the second set. Callie is playing like her life is on the line. Wonder what lit a fire under her butt?"

"Oh, now come on, Jake. I think you know EXACTLY what ignited that fire."

Jake shot me a puzzled look. We both turned as we heard movement behind us. Amy, Kelly and Olivia were headed our way.

"Look. Here comes the walking match stick now."

Jake studied me, confused. I watched his expression mellow as the meaning of my words took hold.

"Well, that was embarrassing," Amy declared softly. "Sorry we couldn't deliver."

"Don't feel bad," Jake consoled. "Those women you played knew how to take control. They were clearly very experienced. Just look at them as inspiration."

I looked at my watch. "Jake, you said you could watch for only an hour. We've been out here ninety minutes."

"My 10:30 cancelled. Glad I get to watch this battle play out." Both opponents had come up to the net, and Mary Claire hit a low, flat ball directly between the two to tie the set at one game each.

"Yes," Jake whispered enthusiastically with a fist pump.

"Fabulous shot," Amy complimented.

We watched, mesmerized by the impressive level of tennis displayed by all players. Soon it was a 4 all match.

"Why is that woman playing tennis in a long-sleeved shirt?" Olivia asked.

"More importantly, why does she keep stretching and rubbing her left arm?" Dallas spoke for the first time since we began watching. "And she looks really pale? Do you think she needs to take a break for medical reasons. She could be overheating or worse."

Jake reassured. "She's okay. She's had issues with that arm for a long time. But I think it's bothering her today because this is a tough match. I think she's tired, too. She doesn't need to go three sets. Callie needs to make sure they get these next two games."

I watched Callie take the balls from her opponents and then hand one to Mary Claire. It looked to me as if Callie were seeing her partner for the first time today. I think it registered with her that Mary Claire was fading. Callie put her arm around Mary Claire and turned her back on her opponents, talking to her as they leisurely walked to the baseline. The conversation lasted less than thirty seconds, but it seemed to have brightened Mary Claire, for she was smiling and looked more invigorated as she took her place at the net. Callie, who hadn't missed a first serve since we'd been watching, had trained her opponents to stand at or behind the baseline. When she took her first serve, she hit a weak short serve that died before the receiving party could get to it. 15-0. By mixing up her serve, Callie threw the opponents completely off guard and forced them to either hit out or hit weak, floating returns that Mary Claire was able to easily poach and put away at the net. Now they were up 5-4.

Vestavia served to stay in the match. The pressure must have gotten to the server because she missed most of her first serves and gave weak, lob-like second serves which were easy to manipulate into drop shots. Two drop shot returns on the first two serves, and our girls were up 30-0. Anticipating a short return on the third serve, the net person stood close to the T because she knew that she would have to pick up the short shot; her partner couldn't make it up to the net fast enough. When Mary Claire returned the next serve, she took it down the unguarded alley. 40 - 0. Next, Callie returned serve. Their opponents both charged the net as they saw Callie position her racquet for yet another drop shot. Suddenly, Callie repositioned and lobbed high over their heads deep into the back right corner of the doubles alley. Game, set, match.

They shook hands, and the Vestavia team quickly left. We rushed to their court. "Brilliant match ladies," I applauded. Mary Claire looked happy but weak. "Come sit down, Mary Claire," I said as I guided her to a bench. "I think you've overheated a little."

Jake jogged over with a cup in his hand. "Here, drink this. It's my special brew." He handed the cup to Mary Claire who silently obeyed.

"What did you give her?" Callie demanded snippily.

"It doesn't matter," Mary Claire protested. "I'm sure it will help." She turned to Jake and handed him the empty cup. "Thanks, Jake."

"Did we win the match?" Callie asked.

"We lost our court," Amy began, "but Dallas and Alex rocked, so we won 2-1."

"Awesome. We are now the only undefeated team in our division."

"Jake?" Olivia interrupted. "I have to leave now. Could you walk me to my car?"

Jake looked torn, but Mary Claire reassured him. "I'm fine, Jake. You don't need to babysit me. I promise."

He studied her expression, gauging her sincerity. "Okay, but I'll be right back." Olivia said it was a pleasure meeting everyone and watching our exciting match. Jake turned and started walking with Olivia toward the parking lot.

"Oh my, Olivia is on the prowl," Amy volunteered. "I always admired her determination and self-confidence in college, and it hasn't faded. If she locks on something she wants, she goes for it. And she has definitely locked on Jake. I bet she manages to get him to take her out tonight."

Callie stood abruptly and strolled away. "Where are you going?" I asked.

Callie turned around but kept walking backwards as she spoke. "I'm going to get Mary Claire something to eat. Be back in a minute."

Dallas wet a tennis towel from her bag, rolled it up, and placed it across Mary Claire's forehead. "This will help cool you down."

"Thank you, Dallas. No need to fuss. I'm fine."

"You sure?"

"Absolutely. It's just really hot and that match was tough. After I rest a bit, I'll be fine." Mary Claire looked at her watch. "Dallas, you need to be headed for work soon, don't you? I don't want you to be late. Run on. I'll call you later."

Dallas departed without goodbyes to anyone else, and Amy and Kelly left thirty seconds later. I sat on the bench next to Mary Claire. "You played quite well today."

"Thank you, Alex, but all credit goes to Callie."

"Don't sell yourself short, now, but I agree that Callie played out of her mind. You think she was jealous about that Olivia showing up?"

"There's no doubt in my mind."

"That's some serious competition for Callie, don't you think?"

Mary Claire smiled. "Only if Callie fails to see Jake's true motives."

"You mean trying to make Callie jealous?"

"You caught that, I see," Mary Claire observed. "Jake's playing with fire."

Callie approached with a large bottle of water and a plate filled with grapes, crackers, various cheeses and some pastrami. "Thank you, Callie," Mary Claire said as she took the plate.

Jake returned and sat on the other side of Mary Claire. "Are you sure you're okay?"

"Would you all stop doting on me like I'm a hundred years old. I just got too hot. I'm perfectly fine now."

"Good," Jake declared as he gently patted her knee. "Let me just say that you two played with complete abandon today. Total rock stars. By the way, when y'all were tied 4 all in that second set, what did Callie say to you?"

Mary Claire grinned. "She said, 'we're taking them down in 8 points, so follow my lead and stay ready', and oh my, did she make good on that promise."

"Way to go, Conrad. I liked seeing you take those big risks today."

"I'm not the only one taking big risks today, Lenaghan."

I saw Jake glance at Mary Claire who mouthed the words, "I told you so." He shrugged and grinned.

CALLIE

I left Mary Claire, Jake and Alex sitting on the bench and made it to my car two seconds before my considerable efforts to repress a good cry crumbled. I let the floodgates open as the weight of my stupidity bared down upon me. Why didn't I tell Jake how I felt about him when I had the chance? Now this Olivia Dunn is in the picture, and I don't stand a chance. Though I was around her only a few minutes today, it was clear that she was bright, poised, gorgeous, and confident. Apparently, she was a woman skilled in successfully pursuing her desires, and obviously she desired Jake. The tears spilled forth, and I buried my face in my tennis towel.

MARY CLAIRE

I sat on the bench finally feeling like I might have recovered enough to leave the court and drive home. Alex had departed five minutes earlier, but Jake still sat next to me keeping vigil. Dear, kind, thoughtful Jake.

"Feeling better?" he asked.

"Yes, I'm okay. Please stop treating me like a fragile old lady. I'm only fifty-five."

"You are fragile, and it has nothing to do with your age. Has something else happened? We all noticed how much you were rubbing your left arm -- how uncomfortable you seemed. Is there something I should know?"

"No. Nothing new. I don't remember having a match this taxing in years. It took its toll physically, and, of course, the heat made it much worse."

"And that long-sleeved shirt didn't help," he commented icily.

"Jake, you know why I'm wearing this. It can't be avoided."

"Sure it can. You just don't want to do what's necessary to avoid it."

I took Jake's hand and squeezed. "Let's not speak of this anymore. It only upsets me and angers you. Tell me about your surprise visitor today. She's quite impressive."

"Yes, that certainly caught me off guard," Jake responded as he clasped his hands together in a prayer like position.

"Did you enjoy visiting with her today?"

"Actually, no. On one hand, I'm flattered by the gesture, but on the other, I'm put off by the intrusion. It was distracting."

"You certainly weren't the only person distracted by her presence. Callie clearly felt threatened."

"Really?" Jake said. "Not sure I agree. I've never seen Callie so focused. Her game was damn near flawless today."

"That's why I know unequivocally that Olivia's presence unnerved her to the core."

"I don't understand."

"Jake," I began, "Callie is a survivor. When something rattles her emotionally, she redirects all of her energy to the task at hand. That's how she blocks out what's bothering her and protects herself. Not that it's a healthy approach to self-preservation, but I can't criticize. I'm certainly no expert on the proper ways of protecting one's self."

"Isn't that the truth," Jake commented sarcastically.

"So, do you plan to see Olivia tonight?" I asked, ignoring his reprimand. "Amy seemed quite confident that she would convince you to spend time with her this evening."

"I don't know. I told her I'd text or call later today. I do enjoy her company, but she seems very interested, and I don't want to mislead her. Don't get me wrong. My ego is loving the attention, but I feel a bit deceitful because the only reason I agreed to meet her was to hopefully push Callie into admitting her feelings for me. I may have succeeded in only pushing her further away."

"Hmm, I'm not so sure about that." I looked at my watch. "It's five 'til twelve. Don't you have a lesson at noon."

"Yes," Jake replied as he stood. "Let me walk you to your car first."

"Jake, that's not necessary."

"It's necessary to me." He grabbed my bag. "Come on, my fragile friend," he teased as he offered his arm.

"So gallant."

Jake smiled, and we walked in silence to my car. I had forgotten that I parked next to Callie and was surprised to see her still there. As we came closer, I saw Callie behind the wheel with her face buried in a towel. Jake saw her too and was alarmed. He quickened his pace, but I stopped him.

"Jake, I've got this. You go now."

"Do you think she's sick?" he asked, alarmed.

"Heartsick, yes, but she doesn't need to see you now. She would be mortified if you saw her in this state. I'll take care of her."

The concern in his eyes, the pain in his expression, touched me. "If I ever had a son, I would have wanted him to be just like you. Now go. I'll call you later."

Reluctantly, he turned and walked away.

CALLIE

A tap at my passenger window startled me. I lowered the towel just below my eyes and saw Mary Claire motioning for me to unlock the door. Thank God no one else found me blubbering like a fool. I dropped the towel, unlocked the door and she sat in the passenger seat.

"I'm fine," I declared as she settled. "I'm an idiot, and I'm venting. Don't worry about me. How are you? Do you want me to drive you home?"

"Callie, honey, I'm in a far better state to drive than you are." She smiled and said, "The ball is in your court, dear."

I shook my head. "No, I think I already tanked it in the net. I screwed up. I didn't tell Jake how I felt when I had the chance, and now he's moved on."

"You're wrong, Callie. The ball is still in play, but it's all up to you now."

"Did you see that woman, Mary Claire? She's perfect for him, and she has the guts to go after him. More than I can say for myself."

"You're right. By all appearances, that woman is perfect for Jake, but as unlikely as you may think it is, you, Callie Conrad, are the woman he wants. But Jake will not break your silly platonic rule. You have to do it. He needs that from you. You want him to do it for you, so you don't feel as if you're going out on a limb. He already tried that two years ago, and you cut him off. The only way that he will have confidence in your feelings for him is if you shatter the barriers. He has emphatically expressed that fact to me."

"Really?"

"Really. But this is your last chance. Jake didn't say that to me, but I'm telling you that you've made him wait long enough for you to grow confident in your feelings. If you don't take that leap of faith now, you don't deserve him, and I would encourage him to pursue Olivia or anybody else that he finds appealing."

"Mary Claire!" I was shocked and hurt by her comments. "I thought you were on my side."

"I am," she soothed. "But he's given far more to you than you have to him. It's time for you to give back. Make a decision. Actually, your decision was made long ago, but you're too afraid to take a chance. I'm telling you this for your own good. The man is in love with you, and I know you're in love with him. Tell him how you feel NOW. Take a chance before it's too late. Jake is probably the finest man I've ever known. Maybe I feel so strongly for him because he reminds me so much of my late brother, Matthew -- a confident but kind and tender-hearted soul. Callie, you are family to me, and I want only the best for you. Please don't be stupid. You'll regret it for the rest of your life."

"Okay," I replied weakly.

"Okay," Mary Claire reiterated in a finite tone. "I have to go now. You call me if you need me."

"Thanks." I waved goodbye as she shut the car door.

I sat in my car another ten minutes just staring out the window. Mary Claire was right, and I didn't intend to go down without a fight.

DON'T GO STICKIN' YOUR NOSE IN OTHER PEOPLE'S BUSINESS

Match 5 -- July 18, 2014

Curiosity, like most things, is best in moderation.

KATLIN

I was disappointed, but not surprised, when Callie partnered me with MKat for the Tuscaloosa match on July 18th. I hadn't played in almost a month, so I wanted to play, and MKat was the only player at my level willing to be my partner. I wasn't exactly on friendly terms with Amy Morard, and Kelly was Amy's sidekick, so she wouldn't be thrilled about having me as a partner either. I suppose MKat and I formed the misfit partnership; no one wanted to play with either of us.

I resigned myself to the reality of the situation and decided I could tolerate MKat as a partner for the rest of the season. But two days before the match, she called and insisted that I ride with her. No way I could stand being cooped up with that old bat for an hour. I tried every excuse except the truth to avoid it, but she wouldn't stop badgering me. She said that she had some very important things to discuss with me.

I finally caved, but I don't think even nosey, judgmental MKat could ruin my day. Sam texted me late last night and said he was bringing me a very special present tonight. I wonder if it could be a ring? That's crazy. I've been dating him for six weeks -- way too soon to get engaged. But I think he's the one. He's twenty-three years older than me, only seven years younger than my dad, but I don't care. I'm crazy about him.

I met MKat at the parking lot in front of Edgar's Bakery on Highway 119. She wanted to drive, so I transferred my gear to her car and got in the passenger seat. "How's your husband doing?" I asked.

"Thank you for asking, dear. He is much better. I think he'll be able to return to work next week. This illness has been quite an ordeal. I wouldn't have agreed to travel to Tuscaloosa if he weren't so much better. He insisted, and from what I can gather, we are very much needed today."

"What do you mean?"

"I looked up the match results from last week, and Amy and Kelly were simply blown off the court. Have they even won a match this season? We are obviously a much better team."

"Maybe," I muttered and fell into silence. I studied the landscape and dreamed about the big surprise Sam promised to bring me this evening.

"Katlin. Katlin. KATLIN." MKat was looking at me with those bulbous, accusing eyes. "Dear, where did you go just now?"

Confused, I asked, "What?"

"I've been talking to you for five minutes, and it is clear that you haven't heard a word I've uttered."

"Sorry, MKat. I was just thinking about my boyfriend."

MKat perked up. "Oh, is that the same young man you were so busy texting during that luncheon after the first match? You know you missed the 'episode'." She exaggerated the word with a tone of condemnation.

"Episode? What are you talking about?"

She reprimanded, "See, if you weren't so busy being rude with your phone, dear, you would be enlightened."

I tried to indulge her. "Oh, come on. You're my tennis partner. What did I miss?"

"Well," she began, "I was commenting on the style of dress that the female homosexuals follow, and Dallas abruptly tossed down a fifty dollar bill and said she had to go to the bathroom."

"Why is that an episode? Maybe she just had an upset stomach."

"Because, Katlin, she never went to the bathroom. I saw her slip out the back exit, and she never returned."

I was clueless. "I still don't get why you call that an episode. What's the big deal?"

MKat rolled her eyes and looked at me with pity. "Dear, sweet, naive Katlin. It was the point of exit that is the issue. I was commenting on homosexuality when she suddenly departed. I referred to homosexuals as sinful."

"So?" I replied with impatience.

"Katlin, child, how can you be so oblivious? Dallas is a LEEEESS-bian and was angered by my biblically factual commentary against her kind."

Okay, this conversation stunned me, and quite frankly it was laughable. Was this the important thing MKat had to discuss with me? "I'm sorry, but why do you think she's gay just because she left the table during your discussion? Don't you think you're a bit hasty in your judgment?"

She sighed dramatically, exhausted by my ignorance. "Dear, you must have lived a sheltered life. I know who your parents are and that you were born with a silver spoon in your mouth. But I must say that I admire your parents' protectiveness because you seem completely unaware of the signs."

"The signs?" I questioned, feeling as if MKat needed a long stay in a padded cell.

"Honey," she patiently began my education, "haven't you noticed Dallas's hairstyle?" She paused for the light bulb to illuminate my feeble brain. After a few seconds, she could see that darkness still lingered. "You know, she's got that really short cut. It's almost manly."

I stared at her blankly. "You said 'signs'...plural. What else is a sign?"

We were at a red light now, so she turned to me and continued. "Haven't you noticed how she is built? She's not fat but thick like a man. She keeps her nails super short and when she plays tennis," she gasped, "she attacks the ball. She moves as if she were a soldier in battle attacking the enemy. That is not the behavior of a woman."

"MKat, you've got to be kidding me!" That really wasn't the extent of what I wanted to say, but I controlled myself. How could so much ignorance be rolled up in one petty person? "She's just an aggressive player. Short hair, short nails and a powerful tennis game do not mean she is gay. She's just a tom-boy. And who cares anyway?" My indignant tone obviously escaped her notice.

"But Katlin, haven't you seen how she stares at Mary Claire? She's always watching her. Like some obsession."

Maybe I was wrong. Maybe MKat really could ruin my day despite the thought of Sam's surprise. "Look, I'll admit that she is intense, removed, maybe even unfriendly, but that's all. Like I said, even if she is gay, who cares?"

MKat's expression clearly showed that she was appalled by my indifference to Dallas's sexual orientation. I could tell she was about to explore the subject further, but something diverted her attention.

"There they are." She pointed to the side of the road. "Do you see those strange boxes over there?"

I glanced to the left and saw a stack of what appeared to be natural colored plastic boxes sitting on two concrete blocks. It looked like a cheap chest of drawers, and there was a brick sitting on top. "What is that?" I asked, staring at the bizarre roadside scene as we passed.

"I don't know, but it is an abomination!" she answered indignantly. "That tacky roadside rubble has been there for years. Such an eyesore. But I've made up my mind that I'm going to find out what it is."

"How are you going to do that? Go ring the doorbell of the house and demand to know?"

"Oh, I don't think it belongs to that house. I think it belongs to the city because it appears to be on an easement."

I didn't know what an easement was, but I didn't care. "So why don't you just call whatever government agency handles the roads in this area and ask?"

"Oh, I'm sure they'd just feed me some government propaganda. I'll get to the truth on my own. You just wait and see."

The interstate was still miles away, and I was already feeling like jumping out of a moving car. "So, what important things did you need to discuss with me?"

She giggled. "Well, Katlin, I suppose I'm guilty of a little white lie. I just wanted to have company."

"You lied to me!" I wanted to strangle her.

"Oh, please don't be mad, dear. I'm just a bit lonely. You know Edward has been sick for so long that I haven't had anybody to talk to lately. I'm sorry. I thought we could have fun getting to know each other better."

She seemed pitiful now, so I tried hard to find my happy place. Sam's face popped into my head, and I instantly calmed.

"It's okay, but in the future I'd much prefer that you be honest with me."

"I am sorry, Katlin. Thank you for forgiving me. Now tell me about your boyfriend. Is it serious?"

"I think so," I answered through a smile. "We haven't dated that long, but I'm twenty-seven, and I've had a few boyfriends. Sam is different. This relationship feels right."

"I'm happy for you, dear. But I wouldn't be a good friend if I didn't broach a rather delicate subject regarding your gentleman friend."

"What's that?" I asked, morbidly curious.

"How do you know he really loves you, dear?"

"What?"

"Don't be naive now. You are from a very wealthy, prominent family. How do you know that he's not after your money?"

"Geez, you really know how to hit below the belt. I have to admit, though, that with past boyfriends, I felt it was my name, not me, that attracted them. So, when I met Sam, I didn't give him my real name. I told him my name was Kate Carter from Little Rock, Arkansas, and that I moved to Birmingham two years ago."

MKat gave me an admiring glance. "Good for you, dear. It would be simply tragic if he were only after your family money and position. As Kate Carter, you will know if he really loves the person you are."

"True. But if things progress like I think they will, I'll be introducing him to my family. I hope he doesn't feel too deceived when I tell him the truth."

"Certainly not, Katlin. By the time you reveal your true identity, you will know that he really loves you, so he should understand your deception and realize that the Hamilton connection is an added bonus to having you."

****

By the time we arrived in Tuscaloosa, I knew far more about MKat than I wanted to know in ten lifetimes. I found the idea of hitchhiking back to Birmingham tremendously appealing.

Callie, Mary Claire, Dallas and Alex were already there warming up. I joined Alex on the court and she asked, "Did you actually drive over with MKat?" I nodded, but gave her a look that spoke volumes.

"Oh, Katlin, you've moved to the top of the line toward sainthood. That must have been like spending an hour in hell."

"You have no idea," I confirmed. "And you should have heard her talk about Dallas."

"What did she say about Dallas?"

"Trust me. You don't want to know. The woman's a total fruitcake. I'm telling you, she's not wired right."

"You can ride back with me, if you'd like. I had planned to carpool with Callie and Mary Claire, but I was running late this morning and told them to go on without me. Funny thing is, I arrived five minutes before they did. I guess Avery's right. I do drive like a bat out of hell."

I laughed. "Thanks for the offer, but I don't want to hurt her feelings and switch cars. She seems a bit desperate to have some company. I'll survive."

"That's a mature attitude. And a kind gesture as well."

"By the way, I'm really looking forward to coming to Avery's wedding. And, thanks for letting me bring a guest. You'll like Sam."

"I'm looking forward to meeting him. Avery says y'all are pretty serious."

"I think so. I hope so. I'm crazy about him."

"I'm happy for you, Katlin. When you find the right one, you know in your gut." I looked at my watch. "It's 9:25. I'd better take a few serves now and head to the potty before the match starts."

"Have a good match, Alex."

"You, too."

It was an uneventful day on the courts. We all sailed through our matches in two sets to win 3-0. There was no drama, no controversy. We got the job done and headed home.

On the way back, I closed my eyes and pretended to sleep, but that tactic silenced MKat for only fifteen minutes. She proceeded to dissect our match, point by point. Finally I snapped. "MKat, what does it matter? We won, and we won big."

"I find it helpful to review my matches in detail. It reduces the chance of repeating the same mistakes."

"I can't believe you can even remember such detail." I looked at my watch. We'd been traveling for forty minutes. I saw the exit for Highway 119 and knew that I would be back in my own, perfectly silent car in fifteen minutes. I breathed a premature sigh of relief.

MKat seemed very focused on the road during our drive down Highway 119, almost as if she were searching for something. Ahead, I saw the roadside plastic chest that MKat found so offensive. As we approached, she slowed and turned on her hazard lights.

"What are you doing?" I asked as she parked the car on the side of the road a few yards from the odd chest of drawers.

"I told you I'm going to find out what this tacky thing is. It has littered this road far too long. It's an embarrassment. A blight on the community. Might as well be a refrigerator in a front yard."

I had a bad feeling. "I really don't think this is a good idea. This is private property and that could be something dangerous. You never know."

As MKat turned off the car, she reassured me. "Dear, I told you this is on an easement which really makes it public property, and they are not stupid enough to put something dangerous right in the public's line of view. Think of how easy it would be for a car to swerve off the road and hit it. They just wouldn't be that careless. They don't want to be sued."

I wondered who "they" were and why she had so much faith in their good judgment. "I'll be right back." MKat patted my knee and smiled. "Unless you care to be a little adventurous with me?"

I shook my head decisively. "No, thanks. I think this is a really bad idea."

"Oh, don't be silly. I'll be back in a flash."

I watched as MKat marched forward with determination, her ridiculously long tennis skirt swooshing from side to side. When she reached the chest of drawers, I could tell she was studying the exterior.

I got out of the car and stood by the door. "Change your mind?" I teased.

MKat turned around and reported, "It's odd. There are lots of tiny holes on the sides."

Before I could respond, she raised her hand and yanked open a drawer. Her body blocked the chest, but a blood-curdling scream filled the air.

ALEX

I left Tuscaloosa just ahead of MKat and Katlin, but I stopped briefly to get gas. Katlin impressed me more and more as I got to know her. I don't think I could have convinced myself to make this trip with MKat. That would be a fate worse than death.

After I gassed up the car and got back on the road, I went through my wedding to-do list in my mind. The wedding was five weeks from tomorrow. I put the invitations in the mail today on my way out of town. What else did I have to do this weekend? Well, Alex, it might be wise for you to see if you can fit your fat ass in that dress, I thought. I knew it wasn't going to fit. I had paid a fortune for the dress, but it was beautiful. I didn't want to buy a new one. I loved the one I bought. I was in a pickle, and I hadn't a clue as to how to get myself out of this mess.

As I traveled down Hwy 119, I saw MKat pulled over on the side of the road and thought she must have car trouble. I stopped behind her car to see if she needed help. As I opened my door, I heard a piercing scream. I couldn't tell if it came from MKat, who was several yards away, or from Katlin, who was running toward MKat. Then I realized they were both screaming.

I started to run towards them but stopped, frozen in my tracks when I saw MKat flailing. It was all so surreal, like watching a B horror film. When she turned toward me, I saw a four foot tail swinging from her nose. She was pulling frantically at the tail and gyrating like a bad dancer. In the process of all her spasms, she tipped over what looked like a cheap chest of drawers. When the contents spewed forth, Katlin, who was about ten feet from MKat, simply collapsed in a lifeless puddle.

The scene was mesmerizing...like the rags in the Publix checkout lane. When I unload my grocery cart, they just captivate me. I want to look away, but I just keep reading all the headlines about Will and Kate, Brad and Angelina, Kim and Khloe, Selena and Justin. It sucks me in.

As I gazed at the ground, I realized why Katlin had melted like a pat of butter in a frying pan. The ground was moving like that dreaded floor in the Indiana Jones movie. Oh shit, there were snakes everywhere.

Now, I have to admit that I have a respectful, but passionate hatred of snakes born from a brief stint of teenage stupidity that I have shared with few in my life, mainly because I am embarrassed by my lack of sound judgment. Chills ran down my spine as I momentarily revisited that period, but at least I knew how to handle this crisis. Daddy always said something good eventually comes out of every bad experience. I'll be damned, over thirty years have passed since I dove head first into the pool of stupidity, and now the good was about to unfold. Daddy was far wiser than I gave him credit.

First, I knew Katlin was okay, because even if the snakes crawled all over her, as long as she didn't move, they wouldn't strike. I didn't think they would move to her area; most were headed away from the chaos toward the woods, but MKat was in deep shit. I silently prayed that the snake clamped to her nose was not a copperhead or a rattlesnake. Quickly, I grabbed the scissors that I stored in my glove compartment. I ran to MKat, making sure there were no reptiles slithering in the vicinity.

I screamed at MKat, "STOP MOVING." I must have succeeded in only scaring her further, because she became more frantic, pulling and screaming at the same time. I'm surprised she hadn't suffered a heart attack from the stress. Too bad she hadn't passed out.

Since yelling didn't work, I tried to calm her with a slow soothing voice (which was difficult to do over her eardrum splitting wails). "MKat. It's Alex." I cooed as if hushing a fussy baby. "Honey, if you will just be still, I can help you, but you must be calm. I know how to remove the snake, okay. I promise I know what I'm doing." Her eyes were stretched so wide I thought they might pop out of their sockets. She turned those bulbous orbs in my direction, and recognition seemed to spread gradually, like a sunrise. She stopped moving and closed her eyes, tears sliding down her reddened cheeks.

"That's good. Just be perfectly still and keep your eyes closed. Now don't look. You'll be much better off not watching." Her mouth quivered. I reached up and firmly grasped the snake just behind the mouth and squeezed to loosen his hold. Damn thing had its fangs in so deep. I squeezed harder, took my scissors and inserted them under a fang. Once I was able to pry out one fang, the other came out easily. "Okay, you can open your eyes now."

MKat gingerly rubbed her nose which was already severely swollen. She looked at me helplessly and whispered, "Am I going to die?"

"No, ma'am. You were lucky. It's a non-venomous snake. I don't know what kind it is, but you can tell by the eyes. See?" I extended the snake toward her. She yelped and jumped back. "Oh, sorry. I was trying to show you its eyes. The pupils are round, like ours, so that means non-venomous. But you still need to get to the hospital because the punctures can cause infection."

"I thought you said it wasn't poisonous," she cried out in horror.

"It's not poisonous or venomous, but it's a bite, a wound, and untreated wounds get infected, especially those from wildlife." I inspected the ground around our feet. No reptiles. Good. The snake still struggled in my hand. I laid it on the ground and secured one end by stepping on it. "MKat, hand me that brick." Once I held the brick in my free hand, I quickly removed the hand holding the head and replaced it with the brick. I couldn't believe I still had the skill. Then I took a large stone and smashed it against the snake's head. It continued to wriggle for at least a minute before dying.

I know not five minutes had passed since I parked my car, but there was already a crowd of onlookers. Apparently someone had called the police and an ambulance. I heard Katlin groan and went to help her up.

Shit, I'm going to be in the news for another damn snake incident, I stressed internally. I hope no connection is made. Infamous yet again!

I motioned for the EMTs. They came over and gasped when they saw MKat's nose. Not very professional of them, but I have to admit it was a frightful sight. A clown's nose would be considered petite in comparison.

"Guys, do you have a plastic bag or extra pillowcase?" One EMT returned to the ambulance and quickly produced a plastic bag. "This is Mrs. Harriman. That snake over there tried to make a meal of her nose." I picked up the carcass and walked toward the EMTs. They backed up, eyes wide. "Oh, man up boys. It's dead, but you may need it at the hospital. Open the bag, and I'll put the snake in." Reluctantly the younger EMT held the bag, then quickly tied it shut. "You don't have to worry about an escape, sweetie." I asked which hospital they were headed to so we could follow.

As MKat climbed in the ambulance, she started ranting about a lawsuit. I didn't get so much as a "thank you" from the old bag. How the hell did this fiasco happen anyway?

Katlin stood immobile, feet anchored to the ground. I walked over and took her arm. "Come on, sweetie. Let's get your things from

MKat's car. You need to get checked out too. I think you're in shock."

I put Katlin in my car and buckled her up. Then I moved all her things from MKat's car to mine and did the same with MKat's purse and tennis gear. The keys were still in the ignition, so I grabbed those and locked the car.

After using half a container of Wet Wipes to sterilize my hands, I began driving to St. Vincent's Hospital. I was really worried about Katlin, because I couldn't get her to talk. She was catatonic. I was concerned that she might have sustained a head injury when she fell. Or maybe she was bitten, and I didn't know it. I kept talking in a calm, steady voice until she finally snapped out of her trance.

"MKat," she muttered feebly, "is she dead?"

"No, we're not that lucky. She's alive and kicking even with a nose the size of a grapefruit. She was already screaming lawsuit before the ambulance doors closed. Apparently the experience did not humble her one ounce. What about you, Katlin? Did you hit your head? Do you have any knots, cuts, or bruises? Check your whole body." I refrained from using the words punctures or bites for fear she would freak.

She didn't find anything of concern and seemed more coherent. I handed her a bottle of water from my tennis bag. "Here. Drink this."

"Thanks."

"Do you remember what happened?" Slowly, Katlin described the chain of events to the point where she passed out. Then I revealed the events that occurred after she fainted.

"Alex, how do you know how to handle snakes?"

"From another lifetime, Katlin. Another lifetime."

After I got Katlin settled in the emergency waiting room, I checked on MKat. She was resting comfortably in an examining area. "Hey, MKat," I greeted. "Have you seen the doctor yet?" She shook her head. "I'm sure they'll be with you soon. I have all your things in my car. I grabbed your keys and locked your car before we left the scene. Here's your purse. You probably need your insurance card. I put your car keys in the inside pocket."

She took the purse and said, "Yes, they did ask for my insurance card."

I'll stick around until you and Katlin are released, and then I'll take both of you home."

"That's not necessary, but thanks. I've already called someone to pick me up."

"You sure? I don't mind."

"No, my friend will be here shortly."

"Okay. Do you want me to bring your tennis bag in here or just keep it with me, and you can get it later?"

"I don't think I'll need it any time soon. You can leave it at the clubhouse the next time you're there."

"Okay. You get some rest now." I left her room. Still not a word of thanks. Unbelievable.

I returned to the waiting room, but Katlin had been moved to an examining area. I found her and told her I would wait for her and take her home when she was done.

"No need," she said. "My parents are on the way."

"I'll wait with you until they arrive."

"Thanks, Alex. I'd really appreciate that."

Thirty minutes later the Hamiltons arrived. They were both quite kind and thanked me for helping their daughter. Very gracious and down to earth. Not what I expected from multimillionaires.

I finally arrived home around 4 pm. I knew Sly was working late tonight. Izzy and the babies were ready to go out and play for a bit. When I got them settled, I emailed Noah.

> *You'll never believe the day I had. Headed to the shower to sterilize myself and then drink a bottle of wine while soaking in a bubble bath. Might not bother with a glass. xxoo*

I relaxed in the tub feeling fortunate that no local news crews had hounded us for a story. I didn't want to explain myself on camera. And if an eager beaver reporter did a little research, woe is me. Little did I know that a bystander filmed the whole incident.

LET'S GET IT STARTED

Match 6 -- July 25, 2014

In the words of Will.i.am., I gotta feeling, that tonight's gonna be a good good night....or not.

ALEX

<u>Tuesday, July 22nd</u>. As I put my tennis gear into the car, *Sweet Child of Mine* started playing on my cell.

"Hi, baby girl."

"Mom, what happened to you last week?" Avery asked in a frantic voice.

"What?"

"I swear I saw you on an episode of Equals Three."

"What the hell is Equals Three?"

"Never mind. You're too old to know about that."

"Well, you know what you can kiss, little girl."

"Oh, don't get your panties in a wad, Mom. I saw a video on YouTube with you wrestling a snake from that crazy lady's nose. If it wasn't you, you have an identical twin."

"I don't know what you're talking about," I lied.

"Do you want me to send you the link so you can see for yourself? I sent it to Uncle Noah an hour ago, and his only response was 'holy hell'."

Why didn't Noah keep his big mouth shut? Now I'm busted. Better review the evidence for damage control. "Yes, ma'am, please send the link. I'm heading to my computer right now. Hang on a minute."

The moment I opened my email, I saw a red flag in the inbox next to the name Noah Hargrove. All it said was:

Call me, you snake charming southern hick.

Nice. As I closed his email, Avery's arrived. I opened the link. To my horror, there was a thumbnail of MKat's face with a snake dangling between bulging eyes. The title below was "SNAKE BITES WOMANS FACE".

"Did you get my link yet?" Avery broke the silence.

"Yes, I'm watching it now," I replied reluctantly. "Is this true? Over two million views since Friday afternoon. Is that really possible?"

"That's why they call it 'going viral', Mom."

"Ugh. I was hoping this little drama would escape any media. I'd appreciate if you wouldn't mention this to anyone, and that includes Travis and your dad."

"Why? You've got nothing to be embarrassed about.   You're not the one with a snake dangling from your nose. You're the hero of the video. How did you know what to do anyway? You look like a pro removing that snake."

"I don't know.   I suppose I've seen so many episodes of Wild Kingdom and the Crocodile Hunter that I did what I'd seen on TV.   I hate snakes, and if you keep making me talk about this, I'll have nightmares."

Avery didn't buy it. "Tell you what. If you promise to explain what happened AND how you knew what to do, I'll keep it between us, and the two million other viewers."

"It's a deal, but I can't explain right now. I'm on my way to clinic. I'll call you later."

"Okay, but who was the woman lying on the ground?"

"That would be your friend, Katlin. She passed out the moment all the snakes fell to the ground."

"What! Please tell me now what happened. I'm dying to know."

"You'll have to wait. I'm running late for clinic. Call you tonight when I have more time. Love you."

I knew Avery would call Katlin the moment I hung up.

KATLIN

As I headed to The Heights for our Tuesday clinic, I felt the stress leave my body. I'd been cooped up in my parents' house since Friday. When they picked me up at the hospital after the reptile incident, they insisted that I come home with them. Although I wanted to go to my own house, see Sam and find out what his surprise was, I was actually relieved that my parents took control. This bizarre episode with my insane partner rattled me, so I liked the idea of having some TLC. After three days though, I felt like a caged rabbit.

As I drove to the club, my cell rang. It was Avery Anderson. Her mom must have told her about the incident. "Hello?" I answered.

"Hi, Katlin. It's Avery. Are you okay?"

"I'm okay. I guess your mom told you what happened?"

"Actually, no. She doesn't want to talk about it at all. The only reason I know about it is from YouTube."

"YouTube?"

"Yep. Somebody filmed it, and it's gone viral. Over two million hits."

"No way! I must look like a total wimp passed out during the whole thing."

"No. I'll send you the link. No one can recognize you. The only reason I know it was you is because I asked Mom."

"Good. I've always been terrified of snakes, and when they all fell on the ground, I fainted."

"I understand," Avery consoled. "So what happened?"

I told Avery the whole story as I drove to the club and finished just as I parked.

"Wow," Avery commented.

"I know. Crazy, right? Never in a million years. But how did your mom know what to do?"

"Not a clue, but when I find out, I'll let you know. Hey, I'd better get back to work now. Talk to you soon."

CALLIE

Walking briskly to the court, I rehearsed for the thousandth time what I would say to Jake. I knew I could have his undivided attention, because I had booked a private lesson with him right after clinic. The thought of baring my soul made me nauseous.

My nerves were quickly distracted soon after I arrived. Turnout was strong: Mary Claire, Dallas, Alex, Katlin, Kelly, Amy and me. "This is great. If MKat comes, we'll have a full house."

"I doubt MKat will make it," Katlin volunteered. "In fact, you should probably go ahead and count her out of this week's lineup."

"Why?"

Katlin took out her phone. "Everybody grab your phone and look for my text. I'm sending you a link to a YouTube video."

"Katlin, you've been talking to my daughter this morning, haven't you?" Alex sounded perturbed. "I don't think it's necessary to share that video."

"Oh, come on, Alex. This is some serious entertainment. Besides, you're the hero of the story." Katlin finished texting and continued. "Before you open the link, let me give you the back story." Once Katlin explained why the snakes were freed in the first place, she told everyone to open the link.

Jake didn't have his phone out, so I motioned for him to come over and watch on mine. What followed on camera was simultaneously horrifying and comical. If I didn't know it was a real, I would have pegged it for a crazy SNL skit.

"How is Molly Katherine doing?" Mary Claire asked with concern.

Neither Alex nor Katlin answered.

"Katlin, she's your partner," Mary Claire began, "you haven't checked on her condition? I realize that Molly Katherine is completely responsible for her own misfortune, but regardless, it was a traumatic event for her. Her husband has been very ill for weeks and is probably in no shape to take care of her."

Katlin looked like a scolded child.

"Well, I feel like a heartless bitch, and I'm the one who removed the snake from her nose," Alex commented.

I wanted to diffuse the situation. "Look, MKat's a pain, but Mary Claire is right. She's been through a lot, and we need to show a little compassion. Amy and Kelly, you'll be playing in the match this week. I'll check on her today and send an email with an update on her condition. Let's get this clinic going now."

After clinic, I sat on a bench and tried to call MKat, but voicemail picked up. I didn't think she texted, so I sent her an email basically saying that the team missed her at clinic and was sorry to hear about her unfortunate accident. We all hoped that she was feeling better. I asked her to let me know how she was doing, and if there was anything we could do for her.

As I finished my email, Jake sat next to me and my nerves surged to high alert. "Trying to reach Molly Katherine?" he asked.

"Yes, but no luck. I sent her an email." I tucked my phone in the outer pocket of my tennis bag. "Can you believe that actually happened? I feel sorry for her, but what possessed her to do something so ridiculously stupid?"

Jake shrugged. "Had to hurt like hell. I overheard Alex telling Mary Claire that Molly Katherine was threatening to sue. I don't think she deserves it, but she'd probably win a sizable settlement."

"Maybe Mary Claire's husband will take the case."

"Not a chance," Jake smirked. "This is small potatoes. Andrew Jameson only deals in highbrow litigation. He defends big corporate clients."

I studied Jake's expression. He seemed tense. "You don't sound like a fan, Jake."

"I think he's an ass, and Mary Claire deserves far better."

"I have the feeling that you know much more about my partner than I do."

"Possibly," Jake responded. "I've known her a lot longer than you have. And she was different when I first met her."

"How so?"

"Ten years ago, she was a bit more carefree, more open. Now she's closed off, uptight. She keeps everything in."

I knocked my shoulder into his. "You're quite observant, Mr. Lenaghan."

"A regular Dr. Phil." Jake stood. "Now, let's get this lesson started. I must say I'm honored that you booked a private session. Can't remember the last time you did that. I haven't heard much from you lately."

The nausea returned. "I had an ulterior motive for this lesson." He looked intrigued. "Please sit down for a minute before we start." I grabbed my tennis towel and twisted it back and forth.

"Okay. What's up?"

My heart raced. I felt short of breath. The color in my cheeks erupted. I felt like a teenager.

"You okay, Conrad? You look a little flushed."

I touched my burning cheeks, buried my head between my knees and let out a frustrated scream into the towel. "Jake, you drive me crazy."

"What did I do?" Jake asked innocently.

I glared at him. "You're enjoying my anguish, aren't you?"

"No, not at all. I'm in the dark here. No clue what's going on in that twisted mind of yours."

"Sure," I replied sarcastically. I paused, collecting my thoughts. "Look, this is hard for me, so please be patient as I try to express myself coherently."

"Okay. Take your time."

Jake continued to sit on the bench, but I stood and paced as I began. "Jake, I know that I emphatically declared that our relationship had to remain platonic, and you've done a fabulous job respecting that rule. But when I'm with you, I want more. I've always been reluctant to cross lines because your friendship is so important to me. But I'm tired of trying to repress my feelings. I guess what I'm really trying to say is that when we're spending time together, if there is a moment when you want to explore a different level, you don't have to hold back. I'm officially removing the wall." Jake was listening attentively, but I couldn't read his face. At that moment, I thought I might have made a colossal mistake. I felt compelled to back peddle. "No pressure. You might not feel the same way anymore. If so, it's okay."

Jake's expression was serious, but still unreadable. "Callie, sit down, please." I did as he asked, thinking that in about thirty seconds I would wish that I had never opened my mouth. "Thank you for telling me this. Obviously it was hard for you to let your guard down, but I sincerely appreciate it. If you are truly confident in what you said, then maybe you will agree to do something I've wanted to do for a long time."

"What's that?"

"Would you do me the honor of going on a real date with me? I come to your house and pick you up, we go out and have a nice time. I bring you home and if we are both interested in a goodnight kiss, then we go for it."

"Sounds wonderful. I accept your offer."

"Great. Does Saturday, 7 pm, work for you?"

"Yes."

"Fabulous. I'll let you know details later in the week. Now, do you really want to have a private lesson or was it just an excuse to chat with me?"

"A little of both. I do want to work on my kick serve and on disguising my drop shot."

Jake grabbed my hand and pulled me off the bench. "Let's get started."

DALLAS

Friday, July 25th. It was 4 am and no surprise that I couldn't sleep. I would leave for our match in a little over four hours, but I could think of ways to occupy my mind until then. It was almost time to trigger the end of my journey, and selecting the proper catalyst required preparation.

I went to my closet and removed the fire safe from the top shelf. Odd how the only possessions that matter to me can all be stored in such a small space. I dumped the contents on my bed and sat in front of the pile. I started going through each document and photo, determining which items would be most effective in achieving my desired result. Ultimately, I opted for the "less is more" approach. On a piece of printer paper, I wrote "YOU DID THIS" with a red sharpie and attached it by gem clip to the chosen document.

After I sealed it in an envelope, I began carefully replacing the contents of my safe. I replaced the identity documents without a glance: birth certificates, social security cards, passports. I gave the snapshot of Parker and me a cursory glance before quickly tucking it away. I felt hatred rise in me like an erupting volcano incinerating every form of life in its path. It had happened so many times over the past two years; there was nothing left to kill. Now, I felt as if I were nothing more than a vessel of hatred sustained by only a desire to avenge my family.

From my nightstand, I retrieved the picture of me running on the beach with my prissy tiara kite. It was time to put it in the fire safe since I would be leaving soon. I felt a surge of emotion as I looked at the image (maybe there was a morsel of life left in me after all). It was still in the original frame in which it sat for years on the mantle in my grandparents' beach house. I studied the expression on my nine-year-old face -- sheer innocence, unbridled joy. Who could imagine that this carefree, dainty child would grow into a self-loathing, angry, masculine-looking woman. If you posted photos of me then and now, the most appropriate caption would be "derailed by life".

Next I came to a picture of Raven with the beautiful chestnut foal named Olive. This was the only photo I had taken in two years -- the only moment I had believed worth capturing since my family had been murdered.

Olive was born a few months after Detective Hatcher had relocated me. I remembered the day my new life began. After weeks in the hospital, Detective Hatcher, now my only friend on the planet, escorted me back into the world. Once in his car, we didn't head north toward Philly. When it was obvious that his route would not lead home, I asked, "Are you kidnapping me?"

He smiled. "No, I'm keeping you safe." I looked at him, confused. He squirmed. "Providence, you know you have to start over. We've had very little progress on this case, and although everyone thinks you're dead, we need to keep it that way. You have to leave behind your identity. If you use your real name, there's always a slight chance that it will resurface around the wrong people. I don't want to take that risk. I've gotten all new records for you -- passport, driver's license, social security card, the works. Grab that file in the backseat. You'll need to memorize it. It's your new history. You are an only child born and raised on Sanibel Island."

"My family vacationed there for years. It was like a second home to us," I explained, an ache of longing in my voice.

Hatcher smiled. "I know. That's why I picked it as your hometown. In case anyone asks questions, it will be easier for you to answer since you're already familiar with the island."

"How did you know my family vacationed there?"

"It's my job to know everything about you."

"That's creepy. So what's my name now?" I asked blandly.

"Dallas O'Malley."

"O'Malley, huh? Do I have Irish parents back in Sanibel, or did I sprout from an alien pod?" There was no hiding the malice in my voice.

"Parents are Ryan and Eva O'Malley, who are real people by the way. Eva is my first cousin."

"The Witness Protection Program lets you use your own family for cover?"

"You're not in the Witness Protection Program. I'm doing this off book."

"What?"

"You don't qualify for the program. It exists to protect witnesses who have testified or will testify in high profile cases awaiting trail. And only for cases where the witness is at great risk of being eliminated by associates of the accused in order to sabotage the case. Typically you're talking about organized crime, drug syndicates."

"Are you telling me that in a case where a lunatic murders an entire family, ten adults and two children, with the push of a button, they don't offer protection for the only witness, the only survivor of the attack?" My voice steadily rose as I spoke.

"Typically no, because Fielding is a one man show; he's not part of some network of criminals endangering the general public."

"So, you're telling me that my family doesn't matter. The Sanderson family isn't worth the effort." I fought back my tears as I stated this harsh reality. Anger boiled within me -- the only emotion I felt these days.

"Providence, that's far from the truth. No one thinks that. But the Witness Protection Program is a government program that costs a ton of money to operate. Without parameters, it couldn't function. The government exists to protect the general public; they can't create programs that drill down to the individual. I realize that philosophy can leave out deserving people, but a program that offers some protection is better than no program at all."

"Wow, you should run for office. Red, white and blue ooze from your mouth."

Detective Hatcher ignored my sarcasm and continued. "The problem is that Fielding is missing, and in my opinion, until he's behind bars, you need to stay under the radar. Providence, I want you to be able to reclaim your life, but I don't think it's worth the risk until we know more about Fielding's location and his motive. He wouldn't have done this if there wasn't something that he expected to get out of it."

"Maybe the sick bastard just enjoys killing. Maybe that's what he got out of it."

Hatcher shook his head. "No, the whole thing was meticulously planned. He spent months orchestrating this tragedy. There is no doubt in my mind that he targeted your family. He had a reason. If we can determine that reason, we can make some progress."

I stared out the window watching the cars whiz by, all holding people oblivious to my plight. My existence was no more important to the world than that of a pitiful, old homeless woman roaming the streets of downtown Philly. I couldn't imagine why Detective Hatcher was sticking his neck out for me.

"Won't you get in trouble for doing this?"

"Why would I get in trouble? I'm not doing anything illegal, and nothing has been done on your behalf in the name of the Charleston

PD. I've done everything on my own time. I've taken a vacation day here and there, like today and tomorrow, to get things set up. I simply performed tasks on your behalf as a private citizen -- a friend taking care of another friend who is in desperate need."

"Why are you sticking your neck out for me, Hatcher?"

"Because you deserve a fresh start. I had great respect for your parents."

"You knew my parents? Why haven't you mentioned that before?"

"I knew of them; I didn't know them personally. My investigation required me to dig into your parents' backgrounds, and my contacts at the Philly PD praised them both as exceptional people. They both contributed their time and talents to the community. Your dad, as you probably know, was very supportive of the Philly PD. He defended several officers who were wrongfully accused of misconduct, and he never charged a fee. Your dad was smart. If he interviewed an accused officer, and his gut told him the officer was guilty, he walked away. Even if the officer's family offered to pay full fees, he declined. Your dad was all about doing the right thing. And your mom was equally kind and fair. She was the best advocate of children's rights Philly has ever seen. She revamped the DHR system so kids didn't get caught up in legal loopholes that left them unprotected. They were champions of Philadelphia."

My tears flowed unchecked, not the gut wrenching sobs of one who has just learned of a tragedy, but the controlled tears of one who recognizes the depth of her loss. My tears were as much for me as they were for my family, for I realized that with each tear shed, I lost another fragment of myself.

"Providence?" Detective Hatcher gently called.

"Yes," I replied weakly without looking at him.

"After explaining all this to you, I realize that I've handled this all wrong. Here I am, a private citizen that you barely know, driving you away from Philadelphia without your consent. Technically, I have kidnapped you, and you could probably press charges. Ironic, huh?" I didn't answer, so he continued. "You do have a choice. You are free to resume your life as Providence Sanderson in Philadelphia. I can guarantee you that the woman who came back to life, the sole survivor of the Sanderson family extermination, will be big news. It will be national news because the original story made national headlines. And even though the crime occurred in South Carolina, your parents were prominent, beloved citizens of Philadelphia. What I'm trying to say is, you have two options. I can turn this car around and take you back to your parents' house or your apartment. But you have to know that the media will hound you and make it very easy for Parker Fielding to know that you're alive. I guarantee you he will follow this investigation religiously until he's confident that it's turned into a cold case. Or you can disappear for a while as Dallas O'Malley and give us an opportunity to bring Fielding to justice without endangering you. The choice should have always been yours, and I apologize for making it for you. I was wrong to do that."

I felt numb. Is numb a feeling? Doesn't numb mean you feel nothing? Maybe it's a diminished state of emotion, one notch above no emotion. Whatever it's called, that's where I was -- just shy of feeling nothing. I turned to Detective Hatcher and calmly asked, "If I disappear, what will happen to my parents' assets?"

"That's a good question, and I've been in contact with your parents' attorney, Olivia Dunn. Do you know her?"

"I know the name. I've never met her. Didn't she work for my dad for several years, but then moved to Atlanta to head up an estate planning group in a large law firm? I seem to recall that she was from Atlanta and wanted to be closer to her family."

"That's right. Your parents were her first clients when she moved to Atlanta. Anyway, I've talked to her, and she knows that you're alive, and is, of course, sworn to secrecy. I've explained the complexities of this situation, and she thinks she can find a legal way to redirect your parents' assets to you as Dallas O'Malley. But it will take several months to make it happen."

"Tell her not to sell the house. Just have someone take care of it until I can return."

"So you don't want me to take you home."

"No. I think disappearing sounds easier, and safer for now. I don't have the energy to deal with media and all my friends feeling sorry for me. I don't want to deal with anything or anybody."

"I understand. Thanks for not getting mad at me."

"It's okay. Your heart was in the right place. Thanks for caring."

"I promise we'll get the SOB, and I'll personally escort you home once that happens."

I turned and stared out the window, feeling not one ounce of enthusiasm for starting my life as Dallas O'Malley.

****

I must have fallen asleep, for when I looked out the window again, my view had drastically changed. The grass was lush, and simple wooden fences stretched without end into the horizon.

"Where are we?"

"Lexington, Kentucky. Bluegrass country."

"Why here?"

"I did a little digging and found out that you worked summers during college as a trainer at a large horse ranch in Sacramento."

"Like you said," I snickered, "you know everything about me."

"Thought it might help you to be around animals that you love. Some friends of mine, Trevor and Katie Roberts, own a small ranch. They breed, board and train. They need someone to live on property and train. They like to travel and want someone responsible to look after things when they're gone."

"I really don't want to live with strangers. That would be too awkward."

"You'll have your own place. They have a great little cabin on property." I must have given him a doubtful glance because he elaborated. "I promise it's not a bunkhouse with a wooden cot, pee pot and two-burner stove. It's updated, quaint. You'll be pleasantly surprised."

"Do your friends know anything about me? I mean, do they know that I'm basically hiding out on their property?"

"No. They don't know any details, just that you are Dallas O'Malley, the daughter of my cousin from Sanibel Island. I told them that you needed to get away for a while because you are quite sad due to the death of your fiancé. I explained that he was killed when he fell underneath a combine tractor and was painfully mulched."

I laughed hysterically.

"You like that, huh? I thought it was a nice touch."

I had difficulty regaining composure. "If they ask me about it, I might start laughing again."

"Oh, don't worry about that. I told them that under no circumstances should they mention the tragic mulching of your fiancé."

I lost composure again, and Detective Hatcher laughed as well. That would be my last genuine laugh for a very long time.

Within an hour, we pulled into the ranch. It was beautiful, very inviting. At least a dozen horses frolicked through the lush pastures. It was dusk, so I knew that soon they would all return to the barn. It was peaceful here. Possibly a good place to try to heal.

It was 8 pm when we arrived, so Detective Hatcher called ahead and told his friends that I was exhausted and not up for visitors. He would get me settled in the cabin and then join them at the house. He would spend the night with them and head home in the morning very early. It was a long drive back to Charleston.

Detective Hatcher had not exaggerated. The cabin was charming -- very open with a half bath, kitchen, and living area downstairs and a loft bedroom and full bath upstairs. The entire cabin was floored with wide, pine planks. The living room was warm and inviting with its cozy sofa and chairs upholstered in a soft taupe fabric. Bursts of color were provided by a mix of pillows, a throw rug, and blankets. The room centered around a massive stone fireplace.

A bar separated the living room from the kitchen. The kitchen had stainless appliances and granite countertops. The refrigerator was fully stocked, and the cabinets and drawers had every imaginable utensil, china and kitchen appliance. On the bar was a bottle of merlot next to a plate of assorted cheeses and crackers. There was a note:

Welcome, Dallas. Trevor and I look forward to meeting you tomorrow. Rest well and sleep in. We'll come by at noon and show you around. So happy you are here.

Detective Hatcher joined me at the bar as I read the note. "I'm overwhelmed by their kindness. This place is amazing."

"I knew you'd like it. And you'll love Katie and Trevor. They won't intrude, either. They'll invite you to do things with them, but they won't pressure you, and they won't be offended if you decline any social offer. You're in good hands. Why don't you go wash up while I bring in your luggage."

"I have luggage?"

"I snuck into your apartment during the dead of night and picked up a few things."

"You went to Philly just to get my clothes? How did you get in?"

"I was going to Philly anyway to research this case further -- so two birds, one stone. I'm skilled at picking locks. Huh, so much for my above-board conduct. I've admitted to kidnapping and unlawful entry today."

"I won't tell," I promised quietly.

I closed the door to the bathroom. It was equally charming and updated. It was fully stocked with a hair dryer, comb, brush, Lancome makeup, sunscreen, Aveda shampoo and conditioner, bath salts, plush towels, a thick bathrobe, an assortment of ponytail holders and barrettes. A five-star hotel couldn't have provided better service. I washed my face and returned to the living room where Detective Hatcher patiently waited.

"Okay. Provi..I mean Dallas. Gotta get used to that. We both do. I put all your things upstairs. I'll take off in the morning, so I won't see you, but I'll be back at some point." He reached in his pocket and handed me an iPhone. "I picked this up for you."

"Who am I going to call?" I asked as I took it. "I'm dead, remember?"

"You call me whenever you need to talk. And I'll be checking in on you frequently. I've already entered my number under contacts as well as Katie and Trevor's house number and their individual cells. You get some rest now."

"Detective, thank you for all you've done. I know you've gone above and beyond the call of duty and I am grateful, even though I probably don't seem like it."

"I know you are." He hugged me awkwardly and departed.

I walked upstairs for the first time. It was beautiful. A king-sized pine sleigh bed was the focal point. It had a white quilt and white European shams, with a sky blue afghan neatly folded across the foot of the bed. Floral accent pillows were propped against the shams. Built-in bookshelves flanked a large window directly opposite the bed. A plush leather chair and ottoman were nestled between the bookcases. The cabin was a tasteful combination of Pottery Barn and Pier I Imports. I couldn't have done better myself.

On the ottoman sat a large, gift-wrapped box with a packet on top. I emptied the packet on the chair. There was a card and a thick, smaller envelope labeled: *A loan until you get on your feet. Hatcher.* I counted the contents -- 100 $50 bills. Detective Hatcher left me $5,000 of his own money.

I could not fathom the extent of his kindness and that of my new employers. They went to excessive lengths to make me feel safe and welcome. And I'm a perfect stranger to all of them. I needed to soak in the unsolicited goodness bestowed upon me. I needed to remember that there was still good in the world.

I opened the card: *I have gathered important documents and some more personal items that I thought might be precious to you. Keep them safe. Take care of yourself. Hatcher*. There was a key in the card. The gift was heavy. I opened the present and found a small fire safe. I inserted the key and examined the contents.

****

Now, in my apartment in Birmingham, I was reviewing the identical contents. With the exception of the picture of Raven and Olive, there had been no change in the items protected by the safe since I had received it two years ago.

I picked up my cell, a replacement for the one Detective Hatcher had given me long ago, and saw that it was 8 am. Time to start preparing for today's match. I returned the fire safe to its hiding place and headed to the kitchen to make a pot of coffee.

MARY CLAIRE

I arrived at the club at 8:50 am ready to warm up for the match. Unfortunately, but not surprisingly, none of my teammates had arrived. I decided to warm up my serve. Within five minutes, Callie joined me on the court.

"Good morning, partner," I greeted.

"Morning, Mary Claire. You ready for the match?"

"I'd better be after that email you sent out Monday."

"What do you mean?" Callie asked as we began some warm-up volleys. "Are you referring to the line-up email or the one I sent just to you, Alex and Dallas?"

"The latter, of course. You really put the pressure on us today."

"Honestly, Mary Claire, that was not my intention. Greystone YMCA is a tough team, and our 3.0 court is not that strong since we can't use Katlin and MKat. I wanted the four of us to understand what's at stake. We're undefeated and so close to a state bid."

"I know, sweetie. We'll all give it our best. By the way, what did MKat have to say? Did you ever speak with her?"

"She called me," Callie replied, "and I thought she'd never stop talking."

"Has she recovered from her reptile encounter?" I asked.

"Oh, she seems quite recovered. She said she felt fine to play but too embarrassed to be seen since her nose is still swollen. She's taking some antibiotics to knock out any infection from the bite. Most of the conversation centered around her plans to sue the people who owned the snakes. She's hired a lawyer, and despite the fact that she was way out of line to go snooping around those boxes, he thinks she has a strong case."

"Interesting, though it hardly seems right," I commented. By now Alex, Dallas, Amy and Kelly were on the court next to us.

We hit groundstrokes and serves for another ten minutes before I announced, "Okay, Callie. I'm sufficiently warmed up. I'm going to the restroom."

"Take your time."

As I made my way down the path, I noticed a man sitting against a pine tree between the 4.0 and 3.5 courts. He seemed so familiar, and then I realized that it was the same young man I had seen reclining against the giant oak by the pond while I had lunch with Callie a few weeks ago.

"What are you looking at, Mary Claire?" Jake was standing beside me.

"Hey, Jake," I greeted him with a smile. "Do you know that man sitting against the tree?" I pointed discreetly. "Does he work here?"

Jake followed my direction, but he shook his head. "No, I don't know him. He could work here, I suppose, but I've never seen him before. Why?"

"This is the second time I've seen him here at the club. I don't know him, but there is something about his demeanor that makes him seem as if I should know him. He seems oddly familiar to me."

"Sorry I can't help. Good luck with your match today. I'll check in later to see how it's going."

I returned from the bathroom to find my team huddled together exchanging good wishes for their matches. "Ladies," Callie called out, "time to get started."

****

Callie and I found our stride early. We quickly determined that our opponents were phenomenally strong baseline players who relied solely on their impressive groundstrokes to win points. Rather odd at the 4.0 level. After the first game, we decided to charge the net from the first point. They were totally intimidated, and we used our finesse shots to end points quickly.

Within twenty minutes we were up 4-1. During the changeover, I noticed that the man still sat perched against the tree watching our match. I turned to watch Dallas and Alex play a few points and was shocked to see that they were down 2-4. They've never played a set where they didn't lead.

"What's up with them?" I asked Callie.

Callie glanced at their scoreboard and shook her head. "I don't know, but I hope they can pull it together. Look at the 3.0 court. Amy and Kelly are down 1-5. Maybe Alex is having an off day. I know she has so much on her mind with the wedding only a few weeks away."

We returned to our match and continued our aggressive strategy. Our opponents adjusted and started lobbing over us, so I started staying back to pick up the lobs since I'm a stronger lobber than Callie. My lobs were much deeper and better placed than those of our

opponents. Consequently, their return lobs were weaker and shorter --
easy overheads for Callie, who at 5' 9", could easily pluck them from
the air and convert them to winners.

We won the set 6-2. During the break, our opponents went to the
restroom, so Callie and I watched Alex and Dallas. Alex was calm and
playing well. All the unforced errors were coming from Dallas. I
noticed that she kept glancing toward the unidentified man against the
tree. But the man wasn't watching her, his attention was focused on
me and Callie. Suddenly, I felt very uneasy. Why was some young guy
who nobody knew lounging there? If he worked here, it seemed odd
that he had such a long break. Something felt off.

"Callie, does Jake have a lesson right now?"

She turned toward his teaching court and saw that it was empty.
"Doesn't look like it. Why?"

"Call him and see if he can get rid of that guy sitting up there. I
think he's the reason Dallas is playing so poorly. She keeps glancing
that way. I don't know why he's such a distraction, but it's strange that
he's camped out there."

Callie texted Jake, and within five minutes, I saw Jake headed
toward the stranger. By this time, Dallas and Alex had lost their first
set 4-6. I watched Jake as he chatted with the stranger for a few
minutes. The man rose and started walking with Jake toward the
clubhouse. They seemed engaged in a friendly exchange. Dallas's
attention did not leave them until they were totally out of sight. His
departure seemed to relax her a good bit.

We returned to our court for a lively second set. Our opponents
had adjusted to our game plan and gave us some serious competition.
But we pulled out the second set 7-5 and sat on the bench to watch the
remaining matches. On the 3.0 court, Amy and Kelly apparently dug in
because it appeared that they were about to win their second set 7-6.
Dallas and Alex were tied up at 2 all in their second, but Dallas seemed
to be gaining her composure.

"Things look a little brighter. Chances are one of these two courts
will pull us to a win."

"I hope so," Callie commented. "It would be a shame to lose when
we are so close to the finish line. Only two more matches."

"I agree, but it's only tennis. There are more important successes in
life to seek. Speaking of more important things, did you confess to
Jake that you actually have feelings for him?" Callie's grin and rising

color in her cheeks told me all I needed to know. I was elated without knowing any details.

"Yes, I told him after clinic on Tuesday. I was so nervous. Thought I might throw up a few times," she shared through a laugh.

"So, what's the next step?" I inquired. "That is, if you don't mind my asking."

"Don't be silly. Of course, I don't mind. Actually, we have a real date tomorrow night."

"Like he comes and picks you up at your house? He drives? He decides what you're doing?" She nodded. "Wow. That is a real date."

"I know," Callie squirmed beside me. "I'm very excited."

"I can tell," I said through a giggle. "Do you know what you're doing? What are you wearing?"

"Well," Callie began as she tried to answer and watch the matches simultaneously, " I don't know what we're doing, but Jake said that dinner was part of the plan and to dress up, like for a cocktail party." Her eyes were riveted on the 3.0 court. "Damn, Kelly and Amy just lost the third set tiebreaker. It's all up to Dallas and Alex."

"No need to worry. It appears that Dallas has fully recovered. Her last few shots have been clear winners."

"I hope so."

"So, what are you wearing?"

"I think I've settled on a fitted, straight silk skirt and some sexy heels. And the top is sleeveless, black silk with some subtle black beading on the front. The back is completely open. It's a bit daring for me. I'd describe it as tastefully risque."

"Sounds lovely."

Callie whispered, "I can't wear a bra with it. Does that make me a little slutty?"

"Scandalous. Simply scandalous," I teased. We both giggled in hushed tones.

"What's scandalous, ladies?" Jake had snuck up behind us while we were giggling like teenagers.

We both jumped. "Jake! Shame on you for sneaking up on us."

"Sorry, ladies." We slid apart so he could sit between us. "So, what's the scandal?"

"Girl talk, Jake." I shut him down and winked at Callie. "Thanks for chasing off that man. What's his story?"

"No problem. He was actually a nice guy. He was quite polished and engaging. I told him sometimes even an audience of one can make you ladies nervous and that this was a big match. He was very apologetic. I don't know why he made Dallas nervous, because he was watching your match not hers."

"I noticed that, too, but why was he here in the first place?" I inquired.

"He said he was new in town, and was thinking of taking up tennis. He's checking out various clubs and thought he'd watch for a while before taking a tour of the place."

"Why was he interested in our match?" Callie asked.

"I asked that question as well, and he pointed to Mary Claire and said that she looked a lot like his mother who had passed away many years ago."

"That's a bit morbid, don't you think?" I asked.

Jake shrugged. "It did strike me as a bit odd, but he seemed harmless."

"Yes!" Callie grunted with a fist pump. "Alex and Dallas are up 6-3 in the third set tiebreak."

"Tiebreak?" Jake asked incredulously. "You mean those two lost a set? Has that ever happened?"

"First time all season," Callie confirmed. "That guy unnerved Dallas for some reason. Glad you got rid of him."

They won their tiebreak 10-7, but before we could congratulate them, Dallas had literally run out to the parking lot.

"Alex, what was wrong with Dallas today?" I asked with concern.

"I don't know, Mary Claire. Something was under her skin. Her anxiety level was so high she could barely breathe. I thought she might hyperventilate. Seriously. But once Jake ran off that man, she composed herself, but not quite to the level she typically plays."

"Why did she run out of here so fast?" Callie asked.

"She said she had to get home and take care of something."

"I'll check on her," I volunteered.

"Good job, ladies," Jake praised. "Glad you got the win. See you Tuesday at clinic, I hope."

As he walked away, I saw Jake graze Callie's hand with his fingers and whisper something in her ear. She grinned like a little girl.

DALLAS

I peeled out of The Heights parking lot. Four blocks later, I was still shaking. That man lingering around the club today derailed my game. After moving to Birmingham, my paranoia had steadily escalated since I anticipated that at some point Parker Fielding would surface. I knew he was smart enough to put the pieces together, and I wanted him to do so; but at the same time, I was constantly looking over my shoulder worried that he would blindside me. If Detective Hatcher were right, I was a loose end, and Parker would track me down to tidy up his crime.

The man I saw today stood quite a distance from me, but he seemed so familiar. He was much thinner than Parker with longer and darker hair, but something about his demeanor reminded me of him. Plus, I think he was the same man I saw the first time I had lunch with Mary Claire several weeks ago. If it were Parker, he could have eliminated me by now. Maybe my paranoia had graduated to mental instability.

My cell rang, and I almost wrecked. I picked it up and saw that it was Mary Claire. "I'm okay, Mary Claire," I answered.

"I don't think so, Dallas. Why did you run off like that after the match? That man is obviously someone you know if he upset you so much, because I know having someone watch you play tennis doesn't bother you. You tune everybody out, but not this guy. Who is he?"

I didn't know how to answer. I couldn't very well tell her I was worried that my fiancé, the man who murdered my family, had resurfaced to eliminate the one family member still living. "I don't know him. This is the second time I've seen him, and he gives me the creeps because he reminds me of someone from my past."

"Does he remind you of your fiancé?" Mary Claire speculated. "Based on your comments, you obviously didn't have a favorable parting."

Her deductive reasoning impressed me. "No," I lied. "He wouldn't darken my door. No, he reminds me of this guy my sister dated several years ago. He hit on me, and the whole episode caused a lot of problems between my sister and me for a long time. Seeing him, or his look-alike, brought back a lot of bad memories."

The line was silent. "Mary Claire?"

"I'm here," she answered, "but I doubt you're being honest with me." Silence prevailed. "Anyway, I agree that it's creepy for some total stranger to hang out watching a ladies' match for so long. But you can rest easy that whoever he is, he didn't know you. Every time I looked up he was watching my match. And Jake said the same thing; he was watching our match, not yours."

Suddenly, a new idea clouded my paranoid mind. What if it were Parker and he was not there for me but for Mary Claire? After all, he most likely still thought I was dead. Maybe Mary Claire was his target, not me. Just as he had done when I was his patsy, maybe he was studying Mary Claire -- determining her habits and patterns. Maybe he was here to finish what he started since he got it wrong the first time. Detective Hatcher was right; Parker's ego was too big to admit defeat. And with his background, he was mission-oriented and would not stop until his mission succeeded.

"Hello? Hello? Dallas, are you there?"

"Sorry. I lost you for a moment there. I'll be okay. I guess I overreacted a bit, but I still think it's creepy."

"Me, too."

"Thanks for checking on me, Mary Claire. I'll see you at clinic Tuesday."

"Okay. You have a good weekend."

As I hung up the phone, I decided that I could delay no longer. I had planned to set things in motion after the last match in two weeks, but the possibility that I might not be paranoid changed everything.

CALLIE

<u>Saturday, July 26th, 6:45 pm.</u> I stood before the full-length mirror assessing the merits of my exhaustive afternoon preparing for my date with Jake. Manicure, pedicure, facial, shower, shave, lotion, hair, makeup, jewelry, skirt, blouse, heels. I hadn't put this much effort into prom night. As I looked at my reflection, I had to say, "Not bad, Conrad. Not bad at all."

For the next fifteen minutes, I sat as still as a cat poised to pounce a mouse, adrenaline surging in anticipation. When the doorbell rang at 7 pm, I jumped up, almost breaking an ankle as my left heel slid sideways on the hardwood floor. "Shit," I growled through a grimace.

Once I worked my ankle around a few times to confirm that it was okay, I hurried to the door. When I saw what was on the other side, all I could do was stare. Jake wore a charcoal gray suit, pale pink oxford, and a striking paisley tie with subtle flecks of pink. I swear he could be a model. Why in the world was this man interested in me?

"Wow," he greeted me. "You look stunning."

"Thank you." I openly surveyed his physique and commented, "but you look a lot better than I do. Wow, yourself."

"Oh please," he responded waving off my compliment. "You ready?"

"Yes, let me grab my purse." As I turned toward the living room, Jake groaned. "What's wrong?" I asked with concern.

"Nothing. I didn't realize the view of you from the back could be as captivating as from the front. That top is..."

"Sleazy?" I finished his sentence apprehensively.

"I was going to say sexy."

I now felt a little uncomfortable with my wardrobe choice. "If you think it's too much, or maybe not enough, I can change. It won't take but a sec."

"I think it's just right," Jake reassured with that grin that brings me to my proverbial knees.

He walked over to the sofa, retrieved my purse, handed it to me, and lightly kissed my cheek. I felt goose bumps race down my arms. How can a kiss on the cheek be that seductive? Maybe it's the lingering factor, maybe it's just Jake, but I felt like putty.

He took my hand. "Let's go."

I smiled and followed. At that moment, I would have followed him anywhere.

****

We arrived at Chez Fonfon a little early, so the hostess seated us at the bar until our table was ready. "What can I get you, Ms. Conrad?" Jake asked.

I pondered momentarily and grinned. "Surprise me."

Jake looked stunned. "You're letting me decide for you? Callie Conrad is relinquishing control? Are you ill?" he asked as he placed his hand over my forehead.

"Ha ha," I replied. "You planned the evening. I'm in the dark. Might as well enjoy a little more mystery."

"Fair enough."

When the bartender came our way, Jake ordered. "One Highlands martini and one Havana Sidecar, please."

"That was decisive. You've had those drinks before?"

"Never, but I thought they sounded interesting."

The drinks arrived momentarily, and Jake handed me the martini. He raised his glass and toasted, "Here's to a new direction."

"Cheers," I said as we clinked our glasses. I tasted my drink. "This is delicious. Want to try it?"

"Let's swap," he suggested. We exchanged glasses, and I took a sip of his Havana sidecar. I puckered my lips. "Ugh. Not for me. How do you drink this?"

"It may be an acquired taste," he said through a laugh. "It'll take the edge off."

"Are you implying that you are on edge tonight, Jake?" I asked as we returned each other's cocktails.

"I'll have to admit I was a little nervous."

"Really? Why? It's not like we don't know each other."

"True, but this is our first official date. We've had lots of interaction as friends, but tonight is the first time you've sanctioned a date."

I laughed. "I have to admit that as much as we've hung out over the years, I couldn't believe how nervous I was about tonight. Funny how labeling an event alters your perception."

Jake nodded. "Insightful comment. And dead on. I think that's why I chose a more formal setting for our first official date --

something new for us -- something to change the perception from 'just friends' to 'more than friends'."

"I like the way you think, Jake." At that moment, the hostess came to seat us.

As we perused our menus, Jake casually inquired, "See anything you like?"

"Definitely," I responded lustily as I closed the menu and stared at him. "Most definitely."

Jake looked over the top of his menu and caught me leering. He grinned bashfully and cleared his throat. "How about the menu? Do you see anything on the menu that interests you?"

I actually rattled him. That was a first. "You know what," I replied, "you did quite well with my drink order, so I'll let you do the honors."

"Who are you?" Jake teased.

"Just giving you a different perspective. Contrary to popular opinion, I don't always have to be in control."

"This is definitely a side of you I've never seen."

"Nice to know I can surprise you."

"I never doubted that for a minute."

Jake ordered an appetizer -- duck rillettes with celery root and arugula. "So how's your team holding up under the pressure of an undefeated season? You're 6 and 0 now, right?"

"Right. I thought yesterday would be our downfall. Alex and Dallas form the one partnership that I don't ever worry about. I don't think they'll always win, I know they will. I've never seen a better partnership. That pairing, if you recall, was your idea, so thanks for that."

"My pleasure."

"Yesterday was bizarre, though. That's the first time they've ever lost a set. Dallas was like a different player until you ran off that guy. I don't know why he unnerved her so much. People watch her play all the time, and it's never seemed to bother her."

"But he wasn't watching Dallas and Alex, he was watching you and Mary Claire, and really, he was focused on Mary Claire which struck me as odd. Even though he was a nice guy and gave me a reasonable explanation as to why he was there, the whole thing rubbed me the wrong way. So I decided to follow up with management to see how his tour went. They told me they didn't do any tours yesterday. I looked in the guest book, and he didn't sign it."

"Now he seems more like a stalker. What did you say his name was?"

"It was Cavanaugh. James Cavanaugh."

"I wonder if he could somehow be associated with her husband's practice. I think I'll tell Mary Claire to ask her husband if he knows that name. I'm sure he's made more than a few enemies during his legal career."

"I'm quite sure you're right about that," Jake stated sardonically as he shifted in his chair. "How's Molly Katherine doing? Do you expect her back next week?"

"She said she would be at clinic on Tuesday and fine to play next week. Never thought I'd say it, but I'll be so glad to have MKat and Katlin back on the court. By the way, have you ever met MKat's husband?"

"Edward Harriman? Yes, I've met him a few times over the years. Why?"

"Just wondering what he was like."

"He's nice, very quiet. A small man, rather short and thin. Molly Katherine appears to wear the pants in that marriage. He seems very subservient to her."

"That doesn't surprise me. She constantly bosses Katlin around the court. The next time I ask you to assemble a team, ignore me if I say I don't care about personalities. Big mistake on my part. We'll be lucky to make it through the last two matches without some catastrophic event."

Just before our meals arrived, I pulled out my cell. "I'd better text Mary Claire now before I forget to tell her to ask her husband about that man at the club. What was his name again? James ...?"

"James Cavanaugh," Jake reminded me.

"James Cavanaugh. Got it."

****

For dinner, Jake selected veal shank with mushrooms, tarragon and white wine, trout amandine with brown butter and brabant potatoes, and kale slaw. After a few bites, I said, "This is delicious. You make good choices, Jake."

"I like to think so," he said, through a grin. "I'm glad you like it." He took a sip of his wine and said, "Here's a loaded question for you. Where do you see yourself in ten years?"

"That is loaded. Am I being interviewed?"

"I know it sounds contrived, but's it's a good way for us to get to know each other on a deeper level. This may be a first date, but we've been friends for several years, and we know each other well. However, I really don't know what your long term plans are. You've never really shared your dreams, not that I'm surprised since sharing doesn't come easily to you."

I started to protest, but Jake interrupted. "It's an observation, not a criticism. I like that about you. Your demeanor intrigues me. Most personalities have levels. Every now and then, I'll meet someone who truly is one-dimensional, but the majority of people have multiple levels."

"I agree with that assessment."

"But you, Miss Conrad, have more levels than you even know exist."

"Oh really," I commented in a sassy tone. I leaned forwarded and dared, "and do you think you possess the ability to unlock those hidden levels?"

"I think I'd have a hell of a good time trying," he answered through a laugh.

"It works both ways, Lenaghan. You start dissecting my brain, and I'll do the same to you."

"No, I'm far less complicated than you. A simple man with simple needs."

"You, simple? Far from it. But I'll answer your question. Where do I see myself in ten years? I hope to be exactly where I thought I would have been by now -- married to a spectacular man, with a couple of kids. We would be a close knit family that takes fun trips, but a family that can also enjoy and cherish small moments together on a daily basis."

"And how do you define a spectacular man?"

I started to say that I was looking at one but refrained. "To me, spectacular is smart, kind, generous, appreciative, attentive, compassionate, balanced, fun, spontaneous, and really hot." I laughed.

"What do you mean by balanced?"

"I mean he has his priorities in line. He's not consumed by his work. He doesn't miss a ton of family events because of work or an excessive number of nights out with the boys."

"You know, Callie, some men would say you'd have to be a lesbian to get what you want."

I chuckled. "Or marry a gay guy, right? Heard that one before. Do you believe my expectations are too lofty?"

"Not at all," Jake replied. "I think you should always set your sights high but realize that nobody's going to meet those expectations 100% of the time. That would be unrealistic. I think, or maybe I should say I hope, that you're able to know instinctively where you're comfortable comprising."

"What about you, Jake? Where do you see yourself in ten years?"

"I hate to sound like an echo, but basically the same place you want to be, sans the spectacular man. I'll opt for a really hot, spectacular woman."

"Really hot is already part of the definition of spectacular, remember?"

"Yes, but I'd prefer a double dose of hotness."

"You shallow man," I teased.

"I'm a guy. Shallow goes with the gender," he conceded. "But I do have a couple of deviations to the dream. Maybe not deviations, just enhancements."

"Do tell," I encouraged as I sipped my wine.

"Might add to the kid count, if I'm not too old. And I'd definitely add a couple of dogs to the mix -- labs, goldens, or huskies. But the biggest item would be my work. I love being head pro at The Heights, but I can't see it as the end of the line. I'd really like to run a tennis academy. Maybe team up with a retired pro to start a school that helps kids who can't afford the well-established places. Find a way to subsidize the fees of some underprivileged kids as well as give scholarships. I'm starting to itch for something a little more rewarding. Don't misunderstand me. It's rewarding to see players at the club improve after working with them, but working with kids would have a deeper impact."

"I understand. So have you explored any opportunities?"

"I've been putting feelers out over the past year. It's a slow process, but I'm patient."

"You know, you could spearhead a local tournament to raise scholarship money. That would help some kids now and raise awareness of your interests."

"Not a bad idea. But ultimately, I'll probably have to relocate. What about you? If you become a mom, will you want to stop working?"

"No, I can't imagine not working. The great thing about being an editor is that, if you're really good, you can go part-time with lots of flexibility and work from basically any location. Of course, I have no concept of how difficult it is to manage work and parenting, but the thought of not making my own money feels unsettling. I don't like the idea of feeling dependent."

"Now that doesn't surprise me," Jake teased. "But a spectacular guy would not see you as dependent. He would be in awe of the woman tirelessly raising his children. Watching my sister, Jackie, go through the parenting process elevated her to sainthood in my eyes. But I understand your concerns. Jackie went back to work part-time when her youngest started school. She said she really missed the intellectual stimulation of other adults. She said going back to work was more about preservation of sanity than money."

"I know having a family changes everything. I think that's why I'd like to have a couple of selfish years in the beginning of a marriage. I'd like to take the time to travel and really soak up each other before the kids come. At my age, though, that might not be an option."

"You've got more time than you think," he reassured. "What's your biggest fear about starting a family?"

I sat thinking for a long time before responding. "I hate to appear vacant, but I don't know."

Jake shook his head. "I don't buy that."

"Honestly, nothing specific comes to mind. In general, the whole idea of such monumental change is daunting, but I can't drill down to any particular fear."

"Oh, there's something specific; you're just not tapping into your dark side," he argued playfully.

"It's probably in one of those hidden levels that you claim exists in my muddled mind."

"I didn't call your mind muddled, Conrad, just complicated," Jake clarified.

"Okay, since I'm giving you lots of control tonight, hazard a guess. What do you think I'm afraid of in regards to having a family?"

Jake placed his cutlery in the four o'clock position -- tines up, knife blade inward -- lifted his wine glass and sat back comfortably in his chair. "I think risk is your biggest fear."

"Risk?" I repeated. "How so?"

"When you're single, basically working for yourself, and living alone, there aren't many outside factors to upset your world. Granted, it's impossible to isolate yourself to the point that you have total control, but when you have a family, there are so many things that can go wrong. And so many ways your surroundings can snatch away what little control you do have."

"That's a frightening thought."

"Ah, but remember, the greater the risk, the greater the reward."

"So risk doesn't bother you, Jake?" I probed.

"Honestly, no. It's part of life. Living without risk makes you boring. Without risk, there are few highs and lows; you spend most of your time on a flatline. And that's existing, not living."

I pondered the merits of his supposition. "So what about you? You asked the question which tells me that you must have a specific fear about starting a family."

"You're right. I do. My fear is complacency. I see so many people rest on the flatline once they have a family. It's less trouble that way. Things become mundane, and spouses take each other for granted. They opt for the ordinary."

"I never knew you were such a philosopher."

"A regular Aristotle," he teased. Jake looked at his watch and saw that it was 10:30 pm. We were the only people remaining in the dining room, and he had settled the bill long ago. "We'd better clear out."

"You in the mood for dessert?" I asked as we headed for the car.

"Absolutely," he replied as he opened the passenger door for me.

After he got in the car, I said, "There's a great yogurt place not far from my house. They're open late on weekends."

"Okay," he said as he pulled away from the curb. "Tell me where it is."

At Yogurt Mountain, I had a small cup of cheesecake yogurt, while Jake had a cone of red velvet cake. He carefully licked the cone so that no drips would be wasted. Lord, that man made eating ice cream sexy. I never thought I'd be jealous of an ice cream cone.

We got back to my house around 11:15, and I invited him in for a drink.

"Feel free to put on some music and get comfortable."

Jake tossed his coat on the back of a barstool. "Where's the music?" he asked as I got the ingredients together for a cocktail.

"Here," I said as I handed him my phone. "Find something you like in my playlist. There's a docking station by the sofa."

As I brought two martini glasses into the living room, *Take the World* blared through the speakers. Jake quickly turned down the volume.

"Sorry. That was a little loud."

"Good choice. Can't beat Johnnyswim," I commented as I handed him a drink.

"Thanks," he replied. "This looks refreshing. What is it?"

"An Absolut Berri Acai cosmo."

"Very nice," he complimented after he took a sip. "I want to see some pictures of you as a teenager. Do you have any high school yearbooks here?"

"That sounds embarrassing, but yes, I know I have my senior yearbook in that bookcase." Jake rose. "It's on the third shelf."

Jake came back to the sofa and sat next to me. He quickly found the senior section. "Here you are. Calista Amarah Conrad. Unusual names. What's the origin?"

"Greek," I replied. "My parents met in a Greek mythology class at the University of Alabama, so they thought it would be charming to use Greek names for their first born."

"Ah, look," Jake instructed as he pointed to my senior portrait. "You were captain of the tennis team and yearbook editor. How fitting. And look at your picture. The only thing that's really changed is your hairstyle. You're well-preserved, Conrad."

I punched him in the bicep. He started reading the yearbook signings, so I snatched it from him. "Enough of this." I returned the book to the shelf.

As I turned back, Jake was beside me. He circled his arm around my waist and drew me into him. With his free hand, he held the back of my head and slowly moved his lips toward mine. At first he kissed me softly, slowly, and I felt myself melt into him. He focused his attention on my top lip, then the bottom one, cradling each lip between his own. He broke away for a few seconds, studied my face, changed direction, and made contact again. He started softly, but as he opened his mouth, the urgency grew. He pulled me tighter against him as the kiss intensified. It was amazing. I never knew a kiss could be this erotic.

When he broke away, I expressed myself quite eloquently in a breathy whisper. "Wow. Did you see those fireworks?"

Jake grinned, started to kiss me again, but stopped and stepped away.

"What's wrong?"

"Are you sure about this?"

"What do you mean?"

"Callie, the last time I kissed you, you ignored me for months. I never understood why, unless it was a really bad kiss, but my ego says that wasn't the case. I don't want to go there again."

"I don't want to go there either. Jake, the first and only other time you kissed me, I was terrified of screwing up our friendship. I suppose I felt like I couldn't have both friendship and romance with you. At that moment, I chose friendship. I needed it more. But now I see things more clearly. I think that was the problem with my past relationships. I never considered anyone I dated to be a friend. I see now that romance and friendship aren't mutually exclusive, and that they actually enhance each other. I promise I won't ignore your texts tomorrow. I would love for you to kiss me again, if you so desire."

"I so desire," Jake replied confidently as he pulled me into him. The second kiss was equally incredible, but this time I sensed his passion mount to a boiling point. It was as if the depth of his emotions flowed from his lips to mine, and we both felt an insatiable thirst. The longer we kissed, the more I craved his touch.

After several minutes spent lost in each other, Jake said, "I'd better go now."

"Why?" I asked incredulously.

"Because, Callie, I'm only human. One more kiss like that, and I might get out of line. Tonight has been amazing. Truly the start of the kind of relationship that I've wanted with you for a long time. I don't want to screw it up by letting my desires take control. I respect you and don't want to do anything to make you think differently."

"You know," I said as I squeezed him in a hug, "this honorable behavior of yours is really hot."

Jake laughed and put on his coat. He took my hand as he walked toward the door. I leaned against the doorframe, battling a plethora of emotions. Jake braced one hand on the frame above my head, leaned down and lightly kissed my cheek. "I had so much fun with you tonight."

"Me, too, Jake. Thank you for a fabulous evening."

"My pleasure. You busy tomorrow night? We could hang out at my place, grill out. I'd do all the work, maybe watch some Tennis Channel. Totally low key. Doesn't matter to me. I think I'd have fun with you watching paint dry."

"You're nuts," I responded. "Yes, I'd love that. But I'll pass on watching the paint dry."

Jake gave me that signature, sexy grin and kissed my hand. "I'll call you tomorrow afternoon.'"

He let go of my hand and walked through the door. He was almost to his car now, and I ached for him to turn around.

"Jake. Wait." I hoped my voice didn't sound as unraveled as I felt. He turned and looked at me. "Don't go."

"What?"

"I want you to stay."

Jake returned to the door, his expression torn. "Callie, you know we've had a lot to drink. If things escalate, I'd feel like I'd be taking advantage of you."

"Jake, I appreciate your chivalry, seriously, but I'm not drunk. The alcohol came over the course of several hours and with plenty of food. I'm fully in control of my faculties at the moment."

Gently, Jake cradled my face in both hands and looked longingly into my eyes. "Honestly, I don't think I can behave if I stay here much longer."

I placed my hand gingerly at the back of his neck. As I began slowly working my fingers through his hair, I whispered, "Who says I want you to behave?" I leaned into his body, curled my head under his chin, and lightly kissed the back of his jawline. He exhaled a sigh of pleasure.

"I don't want to fight it anymore, Jake. You told me several weeks ago that you felt like I knew we'd be good together but just wouldn't admit it. You were right. I've repressed my feelings for you for years, always struggling to keep us in the friendship zone. I was stupid. I know we're great for each other. And I know that I want you. Whether it's tonight or not is irrelevant. I'm just not ready for you to leave now. So stay. Please."

Without a word, Jake closed the door behind him and followed me into the living room. I removed his jacket and placed it neatly on the back of a chair. Jake sat on the sofa and pulled me down onto his lap. I cradled my head against his chest, and he began tenderly caressing my arm. We sat that way in silence for a long time. In his arms, I felt peaceful, safe, and loved. For me, it was a perfect existence.

"Callie, are you sure your wall is completely down? You worked for years to establish that damn line of demarcation. Are there any rock fragments lingering to slice me open when I least expect it?"

I sat up, turned to face him so I could look him directly in the eyes. I wanted him to be completely confident in my response. "Jake, not even a pebble of that wall remains."

I held his face and in slow motion kissed each eye, the tip of his nose, each cheek and then rested my lips against his. He reacted without hesitation. He pressed harder against my lips, commanding them to part. Our tongues intertwined, circling each other in an erotic dance that compelled my back to arch in anticipation. He embraced me with a confidence and appreciation that I had not felt in other relationships. His kisses exuded intense passion and desire, but it was clear that his motivation was to please me as much as himself.

We broke apart, each breathing heavily, taking a moment to savor our primal urges. I untucked his shirt, put my right hand underneath, and tentatively moved from his belt line up to his pecs. I flattened my hand against his chest so I could feel his warm skin as I moved my hand from his pecs to his waistline. Jake closed his eyes as I worked my way down. I took my time, diverting from the path, exploring the smooth skin over rippling muscles. My breathing had steadied, but my pulse quickened.

When I reached his waistline, I put my other hand inside his shirt and moved both hands slowly up his back. I closed my eyes soaking in the warmth of his skin. It was soothing, like the comfort of warming my hands at the perfect distance from a roaring fire. I was so lost in the warmth of that blaze that I gasped when I felt a hand slowly meander from my neck to my waist in the open back of my blouse.

I opened my eyes to find Jake watching my reaction. I smiled.

"I've wanted to do this since the moment I saw the back of your shirt," he admitted sheepishly.

"Maybe that's why I wore it," I suggested as I moved my hands down his back, pressing hard against his skin, pulling myself closer to him until there was no space between our bodies. He kissed me again, fiercely, while he buried his hands in my hair.

Time slipped away. We stayed intertwined, locked in an intense embrace. Our hands roamed, but only teased, pushing arousal to the edge, and retreating before that pivotal point. It was like having a door slammed in your face the moment you start to cross the threshold. It was a sensual dance of maddening intimacy.

I wasn't inexperienced, but I had never experienced anything like this. His kisses flowed like waves, swelling with a fierce passion that pushed me to the edge, and ebbing to a softer, slower pace just before

I reached the point of no return. I couldn't imagine our interaction being more fulfilling, erotic or sensual, and I still had on all of my clothes.

"Damn, Jake," I whispered, "if it gets any better than this it might kill me."

He laughed and buried his head in my chest. "This is amazing, isn't it? I can assure you I've never felt this kind of intensity with anyone."

I stood and playfully picked him up by his tie. I led him to my bedroom where I loosened the windsor knot and removed the tie. I placed it over my head and tightened it around my neck. "What do you think?"

Jake shook his head. "No fair. I'm losing clothes and you're adding them."

I removed my heels. "Better?"

He shook his head.

"Trust me," I offered, "there's not much left on my body."

"Let's find out," Jake teased as he quickly scooped me up and placed me on the bed. I settled into the pillows while Jake removed his shoes. He lay down beside me and propped himself on his elbow so he could face me. I rolled over on my side to face him.

"What's on your mind?"

"Shallow thoughts, I must admit," he answered.

"How shallow?"

"You really want to know?"

I nodded.

"This top, shirt, whatever you call it, is so sexy," he observed as he lightly rubbed my back.

"Glad you approve."

"But I'm wondering how I can take it off without being ridiculously inept. I've been studying this thing, and there's nothing to untie and no sign of buttons."

"It's a chastity belt for the upper body. It's magic," I surmised through a sultry grin.

"Oh, come on. Help me out here."

I shook my head. "Sorry. You're a smart guy. Figure it out."

"Cruel, Conrad. Very cruel." He pulled me into him and began kissing me in that rhythmic method of ever changing intensity. He rolled on his back and lifted me on top of him. I bent my left leg so that my knee grazed his crotch and rested there. He moaned, and his kisses became greedier.

I lost myself in Jake. I couldn't get close enough, and I sensed he felt the same way. I had never felt this way. I wanted to meld not only physically, but also mentally and emotionally. It was as if the only way to get close enough was to totally immerse myself in him. This feeling was simultaneously intoxicating and suffocating. In one way, it was great to feel lost, carefree, uninhibited, completely at the mercy of Jake. But in another way, the vulnerability, exposure, the loss of self was scary as hell. The degree of closeness I craved required a temporary loss of identity. We had to simply become extensions of one another.

"Jake, I'm fairly confident that you just unlocked one of those hidden levels."

He nibbled my neck and played with my hair. "Maybe I cracked the door a little."

I sighed in blissful agony. "I think you're about to kick it wide open."

"I'll try," he promised as he discovered the tiny clasp that held my blouse together at the waist. He deftly unhooked the clasp and carefully slipped his hand underneath my blouse. He grazed my skin ever so slightly as his hand traveled toward my chest. My heart raced with nervous anticipation. Suddenly, a phone rang. I knew by the ring tone it was not mine.

"Just ignore it," Jake said. "I'm sure it's a wrong number."

I sat up, straddling him, and started unbuttoning his shirt. Jake sat up and let me take off the button down as well as the shirt underneath. If I were standing, I would have fainted. I knew the man had great legs, but I never knew he had such a chiseled upper body. I pushed him down lightly so I could explore this magnificent wonderland. I ran my tongue up the center of his chest while sliding my hand down his right side stopping at his hip bone. He brought his hand back under my shirt to conduct his own exploration, but once again the phone rang as he approached my chest.

"Maybe you should get that. It's late and it might be an emergency."

"I'm sure it's a misdial," he said as he rolled me onto my back. He began kissing me, tongue probing with unparalleled sensuality, arousal mounting. My heart was racing as he wedged his right leg between mine, and bent my left leg. He was still mesmerizing me with his lips as he caressed my calf. Then he started at my ankle and slowly traveled up the back of my leg stopping only when he reached my waist.

Between his kisses and his touch, I could not suppress a moan of longing and desire.

"Oh, my," he exhaled deeply and buried his head in my neck. "You've been commando all night!"

I gave him a sultry grin. There was no denying the determination and desire in his expression. He lifted me to my knees. Jake pressed into me, allowing no space between us, making it impossible to hide his growing pleasure. He never broke eye contact as he unzipped my skirt. But before he could remove it, four texts pinged on his phone. He stopped and picked up his cell from the nightstand. His face darkened as he read them.

"Son of a bitch," he shouted angrily. "Damn it." He jumped up and frantically redressed. "Callie, I have to go," he said as he put on his shoes. "You were right. Those calls weren't misdials. It's an emergency."

"What kind of emergency?" I asked as I began zipping up my skirt and refastening my blouse. "Can I help? I'll go with you."

"No, you can't come with me," Jake answered with a heavy dose of frustration. "I need to hurry. I'll call you tomorrow. I'm sorry." Without giving me a chance to reply, Jake ran out the door. As I stared at him from the open doorway, I could hear him mutter, "Damn son of a bitch. That fucking asshole."

As I watched Jake drive off without a backward glance, I felt as if someone had shoved a dagger in my gut.

OLYMPUS IS FALLING

Match 7 -- August 1, 2014

All dynasties eventually fall into decay.

MARY CLAIRE

While in the process of creating a masterpiece of a meal, I heard the familiar ping of a text message. It was almost 8 pm, so I thought it must be Andrew letting me know when he'd be home. I wiped my hands on a dish towel and picked up the phone. The text was from Callie. How odd that she would text me tonight. I knew her first real date with Jake began at seven, so I feared something must be wrong. Her text was strange:

Ask your husband if he ever had a disgruntled client/affiliation named James Cavanaugh. Details later.

Though the message was peculiar, I knew Callie would not ask unless it was important. Fearing I would forget, I wrote the question on a post-it note and left it on the counter. My thoughts returned to Callie. I hoped that the evening turned out well for them. My long desired image of Jake and Callie as a couple filled my heart with pure happiness.

After today's match, I decided to prepare my husband's favorite dinner, beef wellington. Andrew had been trying a case in Nashville all week, and I was confident that a special, home-cooked meal would be well received. I knew his plane arrived around 8:00 pm, so I timed everything to be ready by 8:45 pm. But at 8:10 pm, he called to say that he changed his flight so he could entertain some potential clients in Nashville. It would be well after midnight when he arrived home.

Without eating, I stored the food in plastic containers and cleaned up the kitchen. This was a familiar disappointment -- the last minute, work-related event that left me alone, too late to make other plans. I understood, though. Andrew worked very hard, and I could not begrudge him, as he frequently reminded me. After all these years, though, being stood up had grown tiresome. If we had a dog or cat, I would have some company, but Andrew would not allow pets. He considered them an unnecessary burden and expense. Over the years, I tried to soften him by surprising him with cuddly bundles of canine and feline joy, but his consistently vehement opposition taught me that this subject was unequivocally non-negotiable.

As I surveyed the kitchen to make sure nothing was out of order, my eyes rested upon today's mail. Amongst the pile of documents from the mailbox, there was a large envelope that apparently circumvented the postal service. It had no return address and no postage; it was simply addressed to ANDREW JAMESON. My curiosity soared, but I knew better than to snoop into my husband's business. I left it with his other mail, as I did without fail each day, on the left side of the place setting where he would typically eat each meal. I stuck the post-it note about James Cavanaugh on top of the stack.

Once positive all was in order, I retired to my room with a good book, but quickly fell asleep. I'm not exactly sure what occurred to abruptly pull me from my deep slumber, but my husband stood over me grasping a manilla envelope in his clenched fist. He was livid.

"Where did you get this?" he shouted as he shook the envelope in my face.

"It was in the mailbox, Andrew," I explained meekly. I was not fully awake, but I had seen that look more times than I cared to remember and knew that it was imperative to assuage his rising anger. "Honey, what is it? Why are you so upset?"

He growled -- the enraged cry of a wild animal unwittingly trapped. Fear engulfed me like a thick, morning fog.

DALLAS

An unsettling fog crept into my soul as I initiated my plan. I felt a surge of evil pleasure thundering through my body. Was I ironically morphing into a mirror image of the maleficent being I obsessively sought to destroy? Ethan warned me not to let my demons consume me. At the moment, I felt far past consumption.

I was scheduled to work but couldn't focus, so I called in sick. Nancy Mize, my supervisor, calmly explained that I should not bother coming in ever again. I was fired. Not a big surprise. The surprise was that she hadn't fired me earlier. I was an unreliable employee, but I didn't care. My job was not my life; my mission was my passion.

Could that really have been Parker Fielding I saw yesterday during my match? Granted, the man had been at a distance from me and clearly had no idea who I was. Did I look that different than I did two years ago? I suppose I did. But I was drawn to this stranger even if I couldn't confirm his identity. If it were Parker, I would think that he would be drawn to me as well. Clearly, if he had ever had genuine feelings for me, he would have felt some inexplicable connection when he saw me, despite the drastic change in my physical appearance. Even knowing his true connection to my family and me, he felt absolutely nothing for any of us.

Maybe it wasn't him after all. Maybe it was just a random stranger with a freak resemblance to Parker. This guy was much thinner than Parker. Parker was not heavy, but he worked out religiously and was thick with muscles. And this guy had dark hair that was shoulder length and wavy. Parker had blonde hair that he kept meticulously cut short. But he moved like Parker.

If there were ever a time I should call Detective Hatcher, this was it. Yet, I hesitated. I wanted to be able to have my say without his interference. I deserved my own brand of justice. It was the only thing that kept me going. I wondered if Detective Hatcher had ever considered not sharing Parker's true identity. If he hadn't, I might have been able to heal somewhat in my new life as Dallas O'Malley at the ranch in Kentucky. I liked the simplicity of that life and the relationships that were developing there, but my anger simmered quietly. I don't think he knew that. Of course he didn't, neither did I. Hatcher's revelation was the catalyst that ignited my rage.

As I lay in my bed, newly unemployed with nothing to do but reflect, I revisited my life in Kentucky. After Detective Hatcher relocated me to the Roberts Ranch, I genuinely endeavored to embrace all the changes. My first night at the cabin, I lay in my cozy bed repeating my new name. "Dallas O'Malley. Hi, I'm Dallas O'Malley. I'm Dallas O'Malley from Sanibel Island." I suppose Hatcher picked O'Malley because of my Irish appearance -- light blue eyes (like my dad's), fair skin (a mystery), and long, thick strawberry blonde hair (like my mom's). I suppose he chose Dallas since all the Sanderson kids were named after cities. Nice of him to honor that family tradition.

The day after Detective Hatcher dropped me at the ranch, Trevor and Katie Roberts, the owners, took me on a tour, introduced me to the horses, and explained how the ranch operated. They were both wonderful, clearly in love with their life and each other. They described my responsibilities but did not burden me with them all at once. They added a couple of new things each week, until two months later, I had mastered all the tasks on their initial list.

The job was therapeutic, and I quickly settled into a routine. But I remained introverted. Katie and Trevor invited me to dinner at their house several times a week, but most of the time I declined. Though they never made me feel bad about my refusals, Katie insisted on bringing me a plate of food so I wouldn't have to cook. Detective Hatcher called once a week to check on me, and I told him that things were fine. I always asked about the case, and he always answered with evasive responses like "making baby steps" or "got some strong leads we're running down". The idea of Parker Fielding being free, living his life as he pleased, ate at my soul.

Nights proved to be the most difficult part of my day. Memories of my family collided in my head. Rather than provide comfort, they harassed me, chastising me for surviving the blast -- like angry clouds converging and melding together into one wicked storm. I slept fitfully, plagued by nightmares of the explosion and always ending with the vision of Parker Fielding thrusting his arm in the air as a sign of victory when he wiped out my family.

Would I ever know why he had targeted us? I needed to understand, even though it wouldn't alter reality. Hatcher kept me updated on the search for Parker, but I always felt that he was holding something back. Shortly after they did the DNA testing on the napkin, they determined that Parker Fielding was an alias. He was really James Cavanaugh, a former Navy Seal, who, according to Hatcher's research, was exceptional on all levels -- intelligence, cunning, and physical strength. His skills were unparalleled in missions, but after two years he was dishonorably discharged for his chronic insubordination. According to his military records, Cavanaugh simply "does not comprehend the concept of teamwork. Self preservation was his top priority and that mentality endangered his fellow Seals".

Parker's background explained how he had pulled off the explosion and eluded the authorities for so long, but they had no idea why he targeted my family. At least that's what Hatcher kept telling me. Something in his voice told me there was more to the story, but he denied it when I asked.

In early October, Trevor and Katie announced their complete confidence in my ability to handle things on my own. They wanted to take a long weekend in Atlanta to celebrate their anniversary. The only pending issue was that one of their mares, Cocoa, was pregnant with her first foal. Her due date was November 1st, but their veterinarian, Ethan Moore, would be available if Cocoa went into labor early.

They departed on a Friday morning in mid-October but not before giving me all relevant contact information, Dr. Moore's cell number, and a promise to check in daily. Friday went smoothly, and I assured Trevor that all was well on Saturday morning when he touched base. By early evening, however, I found Cocoa in her stall, and I didn't like the way she acted. Not that I had any experience with the birth of horses, but my gut told me that all was not well.

I called Dr. Moore and he arrived an hour later. I had met him a couple of times when he was at the ranch for routine check ups of Cocoa and the other horses. He seemed nice but shy. I stood quietly as he examined Cocoa. "Is she okay?" I asked after several silent moments.

"Oh, she's fine," he answered as he stroked her head. "She's definitely in labor though. Have you ever seen a foaling?" I shook my head. "Don't worry," he reassured. "I'm here for the duration. She should have a normal delivery. We just have to let nature take its course and monitor her."

My expression, obviously dumbfounded, inspired Dr. Moore to say, "Don't worry, Dallas. I've got this covered. There's nothing you need to do."

"Actually, I'd like to stay with Cocoa, unless you prefer to be alone." God knows I certainly understood choosing solitude over the company of strangers.

"No, you're welcome to stay. I didn't want you to feel obligated. I'm going to grab some more gear from my truck and call home. This may take a while."

When Dr. Moore returned, I was still riveted to the same spot. "You okay?" he inquired as he walked past me. I followed him like an eager puppy and watched as he set up two portable chairs as if preparing for a tailgate party before a college football game.

We sat in awkward silence until I felt compelled to be social. "So, Dr. Moore," I began.

"Please, call me Ethan," he interrupted.

"Okay, Ethan. How long have you been the vet for the ranch?"

"Oh, probably close to eight years now. I've been their primary vet since my father retired."

"So, you've known Katie and Trevor for a long time."

Ethan chuckled. "Katie was my babysitter when I was in elementary school, so you could say that."

"Really? They don't seem that much older than you."

"They're not. When I was nine, Katie was eighteen, and I told all my buddies she was my girlfriend, not my sitter."

"Bet they didn't buy that," I commented through a smile. "Do you think I should call them and tell them Cocoa's in labor? You know, Cocoa is Katie's favorite."

"I know, but there's no reason to call. They'll be home tomorrow and even if you called now, they wouldn't make it home in time for the delivery. No reason to worry them."

I nodded. We continued our silent vigil.

"Katie tells me you're from Sanibel Island," Ethan commented awkwardly. "That must have been difficult for you to grow up in that climate."

"What do you mean?" I inquired, perplexed.

"That's some intense year-round sun, and you're very fair skinned."

"Ah, yes," I responded. "Sunscreen was my best friend."

"So, what brought you here?" Ethan asked casually. "Kentucky is certainly a change of pace."

"Oh. Well, I umm," I mumbled as I squirmed in my seat.

Sensing my discomfort, Ethan said, "You don't have to answer. I didn't mean to pry."

"No, it's a valid question," I assured him. "It's just a complicated story, and I can't share it right now."

"I understand. I was just making conversation. I suppose we all have stories that we can't bring ourselves to share for one reason or another. I certainly do."

The comment piqued my interest, but I couldn't ask for details since I wasn't willing to reciprocate. Ethan was easy to talk to, and I sensed no judgment in his demeanor. I felt comfortable giving him a little information, even if rather ambiguous. "Ethan, I can assure you that you aren't sitting next to a fugitive, but there is no question that I am hiding here."

"Okay," he commented easily. "I can appreciate that."

"The problem is," I found myself admitting freely, "that you can't escape your own demons."

Ethan gave me the kindest smile. "I know all about demons that haunt you 24-7. Eventually, you have to find a way to cage them so they don't cage you anymore."

"Can you tell me how to do that?" I pleaded.

"I wish I could," he commiserated, "but every personality is unique as are the demons that haunt it; so, there's no magic formula to rope them in. I can, however, tell you that if you don't find a way to squash them, they will eat you alive in an excruciatingly slow repast."

I don't know if his words chilled me to the bone or the unseasonably cool night air hit me, but I suddenly shivered and rubbed my arms.

"Here. This should help." Ethan dug into his box of gear and retrieved a fleece blanket. He stood and spread it over me so that only my head was exposed.

"Thank you. You're prepared for anything, huh?"

"No way to prepare for everything. Just when you think you've got it all under control, life will kick you square in the ass." His response was laced with sarcasm.

I stared at him, unsure of a response.

"Oh, God, I'm sorry," he apologized as my expression registered with him. "Just one of my demons rearing its ugly head." Ethan rose to check on Cocoa. I decided not to follow. I thought he needed a few moments of solitude to wrestle his demon into submission.

"How is she?" I asked when he returned.

"She's good. I think two to three hours and she'll be a mom."

We sat in a compatible silence for a while. My stomach growled, and I realized that I hadn't eaten since breakfast. "Hey, are you hungry? It's no trouble to bring some snacks out here."

"That would be great. You need some help?"

"No, I'm fine. How do you like your coffee?"

"Black, please."

"Be back shortly."

I returned fifteen minutes later with a pot of coffee, some turkey wraps with lettuce, tomatoes, and Swiss cheese on the side, as well as a plate of decadent brownies that Katie gave me before they left town.

"Thank you. This looks great. I didn't realize how hungry I am. But I need to wash up first."

"Sure. Go to my place. The bathroom's downstairs. You can't miss it."

"Thanks."

Within an hour after we ate, Cocoa's delivery escalated. Ethan described the foaling process as it occurred, but those details escaped my mind almost instantaneously. The emergence of this gangly foal, however, etched itself permanently in my memory. I must admit that I'd like to edit that memory and discard the afterbirth portion, but no luck there.

Ethan declared that the foal was a healthy filly and that both mother and daughter were doing great. It was 1 am, and he started packing up his gear.

"What are you doing? You're not leaving, are you?" I asked frantically.

"There's nothing more to do here, Dallas. Cocoa knows how to take care of her baby."

I wasn't convinced. "But don't we need to help her?"

"No, she's got it all under control. It's not like we need to heat some bottles for her. Cocoa will provide all the nutrition and warmth she needs. You should get some sleep now. I'll come back first thing tomorrow morning and check on them."

"Okay," I agreed hesitantly. "Thanks for everything. I'll see you in the morning."

"When do you expect Katie and Trevor back?"

"They said they'd call when they hit the road tomorrow, but probably late afternoon."

Ethan grinned. "They'll be thrilled." He headed toward his truck. "Good night and thanks for dinner."

I waved and watched as he drove away. I turned back toward mother and child. There was no way I was leaving them unprotected. Ethan reclaimed his portable chair and blanket before he left, so I half-carried and half-drug a rocker from the porch of my cabin and parked it in front of Cocoa's stall. I jogged back to the cabin, put on a sweatshirt, grabbed a bottle of water, a notepad, pen and two fleece throws from the sofa. Within three minutes I was back in the barn, wrapped in blankets, staring at Cocoa and her baby.

Ethan was right; they didn't need me. I busied myself by making a list of potential names for the filly. Flax, Fennel, Vidalia, Cherry, Olive, Saffron, Pepper, Basil. All were crazy names my baby sister, Capers, had suggested as potential names for her firstborn. She always said she got a raw deal on the name. Like all of my siblings, Capers was named for a place that my parents loved, in her case Capers Island, South Carolina, but she claimed that her name was always associated with the spices rather than the island. "But capers aren't spices, silly," I had reminded her. "They come from the bud of a flower."

I stirred slightly at the sound of a car door slamming, but quickly drifted back into a restless sleep.

"Dallas? Hey, Dallas?" Someone whispered softly while gently shaking my shoulder.

I looked up and saw Ethan Moore. "Hi, doc. Back already?"

"Did you stay out here all night?"

"Guilty. I couldn't leave them, but of course you were right. They didn't need me." I looked around, disoriented. "What time is it?"

"Nine," Ethan answered. "Why don't you go rest in a prone position? I'm sure you'd be more comfortable in your bed."

"I have to feed the horses first."

"I'll take care of it. I know the routine around here. Get some sleep. I'll wake you up before I leave."

I rose unsteadily. "You sure?" I asked as I began to drag the rocker behind me.

"I'm sure," Ethan responded. He removed my hand from the rocker. "I'll take that back to the porch. Go now," he commanded.

****

I awoke to the enchanting melody of innocence -- a child's unrestrained laughter. I always loved it when my niece, Skylar, laughed as my siblings scooped her up and tickled her into hysterics. Her dad, my brother Rio, would warn "you know, Skylar has been known to give pee pee showers to tickle monsters" at which point a wriggling Skylar would be promptly deposited into Rio's arms.

I smiled at the memory as I got out of bed and walked to the window to discover the source. Ethan Moore was chasing a little girl around the trees. Several small children came to the ranch to ride, but I had never seen this girl. I hurriedly dressed and went outside.

Ethan picked up the giggling child when he saw me. "We didn't wake you, did we?" he asked as he placed the girl on his shoulders.

"No, it was time for me to get up. Who's your friend?" I inquired pointing to the girl who had buried her head in Ethan's hair.

"This little parasite," he teased as he extracted her clinging frame from his body, "is Raven, my daughter."

I felt inexplicably deflated by the realization that Ethan was married. No mention of a wife and child occurred during the vigil of Cocoa. "Nice to meet you, Raven," I said.

She looked at me with big, dark eyes and studied me. She squirmed out of her father's arms and ran to the barn.

"Raven, come back and say hello," Ethan called after her. "You're being very rude."

"It's okay," I assured him. "I used to be shy around strangers, too."

Ethan shook his head. "It's deeper than just being a stranger," he explained in a worried tone. He gazed in his daughter's direction, lost in thought. Then he recovered and turned back to me. "She wanted to see a one-day-old horse, so my parents dropped her off about an hour ago."

"And how is the newborn?" I asked.

"She's great, but I think she needs a name." He pulled a folded paper from his pocket. I recognized my handwriting and knew Ethan had found my list of names that my sister and I had giggled over only a few months before. "At first I thought this was your grocery list. Then I decided it must be a list of possible, interesting names for Cocoa's filly."

"And you would be right," I confirmed as I took the paper he offered.

"So, why do you want to name her from a list of condiments?"

I thought of Capers and smiled sadly. "It's a long story."

Ethan obviously detected the sadness in my tone. "Something tells me it's a story connected to those demons."

"Something like that," I muttered as I headed to the barn.

Ethan stepped in front of me. "Can you wait just a sec, please?" he asked as he extracted his phone. "Let me check on something."

He returned quickly, smiling as he looked down at his phone. "This is why I wanted you to wait," he explained as he handed me his phone. It was an overcast day, so I had no problem seeing the image on the screen. Raven stood face to face with the filly, rubbing her head. They were the same height, and it was a precious photo.

"Raven's been trying to make friends with 'the baby', as she calls her, since she arrived. I thought she might have succeeded since she's been quiet for more than two seconds."

"Priceless moment. Glad you were able to capture it," I commented as I returned his cell. He gazed at the image lovingly before pocketing his phone. "Do you think Katie and Trevor would let Raven and me name her?"

"Good chance they would. Raven has T and K, as she calls them, wrapped around her little finger. I don't think there's much of anything they would deny her."

Once in the barn, Raven turned and gave her dad a huge grin, but when she saw me, she stiffened. I never had a problem with kids in the past. Experts say kids are far more perceptive than adults realize. Maybe Raven sensed my broken spirit.

I must have worn a wounded expression, because Ethan whispered in my ear, "Don't take it personally. It's not you. Raven isn't very trusting of women at the moment. I'm hoping it will pass soon."

"It's okay." I approached her slowly and asked, "Raven, would you like to name the horse?"

She inched away from me, backing up into her dad's legs. He bent down and wrapped his arms around her. "It's okay, Raven. Miss Dallas is a nice lady. You want to help her name the baby?" he gently asked. She nodded.

I stayed where I was and said, "Good. I have a list of ideas for names. How about I read them to you, and you tell me which one you like?" Hesitantly, she nodded.

"Okay, how about Flax?"

Raven made a face and shook her head. Then she shrank deeper into her dad's embrace. He stroked her dark curls.

"Fennel?" I continued. Same response. "What about Pepper?"

"I don't like pepper, " she whispered to Ethan. "It makes me sneeze."

"Let's definitely mark that one off the list," I said cheerfully. "Do you like the name Saffron?"

"Yuck!" Raven said with vigor. "That's a silly name." She loosened her grip on Ethan.

"Well, let's strike the silly name from the list. What about Olive?"

Raven lit up. "I love olives. That's her name. Olive." Raven squirmed out of her dad's arms, ran to the filly and proclaimed, "I named you Olive, and we'll be best friends."

"Olive's a lucky girl," I observed. "She's been in the world less than 24 hours and already has a best friend."

"I'll never leave you, Olive. I promise," Raven vowed as she hugged her new best friend. As I glanced at Ethan watching his daughter, I caught the shimmer of a tear sliding down the side of his face.

****

By the time Katie and Trevor returned from their trip, Ethan and Raven were gone. Hopping out of the car before Trevor had even turned off the engine, Katie couldn't contain her excitement. Trevor joined us in the barn a few minutes later and shared his wife's enthusiasm.

"She's beautiful," he commented as he examined the newborn. Then he turned to Cocoa and rubbed her head. "You did good, girl."

"I hope you don't mind, but today Raven and I picked out a name for her. Raven picked Olive." Trevor and Katie stared at each other, mouths ajar. "Oh, I'm sorry. I didn't mean to overstep my boundaries. Of course, you name her whatever you like. I'm sure Raven will understand."

Trevor eased my concern. "Olive is a great name. Katie and I are shocked that you met Raven. And she actually spoke to you?"

"I wouldn't say we had a conversation. She seemed afraid of me. But once I started talking about potential names, she responded. She directed her responses to her dad, but she seemed to loosen up."

Katie hugged Trevor. "Well, I'll be. Miracles do happen. That settles it. This Saturday night, we're having a party. Trevor, you tell Ethan that his whole crew better be here at 7 pm ready for some fun. And you, Miss O'Malley," Katie pointed at me accusingly, "will not be allowed to say 'no'."

"Okay," I responded meekly.

"Come on, bossy," Trevor teased as he put his arm around his wife. "Let's get unpacked. Dallas, thanks for taking care of everything while we were gone. We really appreciate it."

"Oh, yes, thank you," Katie seconded as she gave me a brisk hug. "Trevor and I had so much fun and that's because we could relax knowing you were in charge."

"You're welcome."

As they headed out of the barn, I heard Katie whispering excitedly, "Can you believe it, Trevor?" He grinned and pecked her happily on the lips.

****

When Saturday evening arrived and I started dressing for dinner, my anxiety mounted. The idea of spending the evening being social did not appeal to me. I knew that I would excuse myself as soon as I could do so without appearing rude. But I was curious to meet Ethan's wife.

I walked up to the house and rang the bell. Katie opened the door and exclaimed, "Come in! You look lovely. What an adorable dress. Looks fabulous on your tiny frame."

"Hello, Dallas," Trevor greeted as Katie led me to the living room. "Don't you clean up well."

"Thanks," I responded feeling painfully self-conscious.

"Trevor, honey, please get Dallas a drink. I've got to finish up a few things in the kitchen."

"Do you need some help, Katie?" I asked.

"No. I'm fine, thanks. Just visit with Trevor."

I heard a car drive up. "Looks like the rest of our guests have arrived," Trevor called to Katie.

He went to answer the door, and I stood waiting to greet Ethan and his family. A short, portly man sauntered into the room. "Well, hello, little lady." His voice filled the room as he waddled toward me, arms extended. I thought he would crush me, his embrace was so tight. "You must be Miss Dallas. We've heard such good things about you. You can call me Big E."

"Good Lord, Pop, you're going to break her," Ethan reprimanded jokingly as he entered the room. His father chuckled and released me. "Hi, Dallas," Ethan greeted softly. A petite, raven-haired woman entered the room. There was no doubt that Ethan was her offspring. "Mom, come meet Dallas."

The polar opposite of her husband, the dainty Mrs. Moore was the personification of demure. She extended her hand and softly said, "Hello, dear. Lovely to finally meet you."

"Nice to meet you, too, Mrs. Moore."

"Please call me Caroline."

Trevor arrived carrying Raven. "Hi, Raven," I greeted.

She waved to me and gave me a shy smile. Trevor put Raven in his leather recliner and went to get everyone drinks. We exchanged pleasantries for a while, but I never saw Ethan's wife. I assumed she had joined Katie in the kitchen. When Katie seated everyone for dinner, however, there was no addition to the party. I started to ask, but something held me back. I found it odd that no one offered an explanation for her absence.

Spending the evening with strangers proved more enjoyable than anticipated. Big E and Caroline were warm and engaging. Katie had prepared a feast akin to a Christmas celebration. Raven sat between Katie and Trevor, who discreetly entertained her during the meal. But, after an hour, she could no longer control her fidgeting.

"Miss Dallas? Will you take me to see Olive?" Raven asked suddenly.

Everyone looked as if they had seen a ghost. Confused, I responded hesitantly. "Sure, if it's okay with your dad." I turned to Ethan for reassurance. "Ethan?"

Ethan turned to me. "Sure. If you don't mind."

"Not at all," I answered as I rose.

Raven ran to my side, grabbed my hand, and started pulling me toward the door.

As we left the room, I glanced back and saw that all sat staring at us, mouths ajar. Bizarre.

When we entered the barn, Olive trotted toward us and stuck her head over the railing. Raven immediately buried her head in Olive's face. "Miss Dallas, can we let her out?"

"Hm. I don't know. Cocoa may not like it. Mommas don't like to be away from their babies."

"Some mommies do." Raven's tone was flat, and her eyes were vacant. Suddenly the absence of her mom tonight made sense. Raven's sadness was palpable.

Thinking the filly might help, I opened the gate, and Olive pranced her way out of her stall. Cocoa seemed undisturbed. "Cocoa seems okay with it. But just for a few minutes."

Raven and Olive frolicked in the wide hallway of the barn playing a game of chase. When they grew tired of running, Raven wrapped her arms around Olive and stroked her long back.

"Miss Dallas, K says you can teach people to ride. Will you teach me?"

I walked over and rubbed Olive's nose. "I would love to Raven, but Olive's not old enough."

"I know. I mean when she's older."

"If I'm still here, it would be my pleasure to teach you."

Raven looked at me with pleading eyes. "What do you mean? Are you leaving?" Her tone was frantic.

What demons tortured this poor child? I felt compelled to be delicate. "Well, you see, Raven, I'm supposed to be here for only a short time. I'm from a city that's a long way from here, and I miss my friends and family."

"Then why did you leave them?" she asked with an accusatory tone.

"I didn't want to, Raven. I had no choice. You remind me of my niece, Skylar. She's a little bit younger than you, and she loves horses. I wish you could meet her. I have a feeling you two would have been great friends."

Raven must have sensed my sadness. "Maybe she'll come visit you here. That will cheer you up, won't it?"

I smiled and took her hand. "Sky won't be able to come visit, but I wish she could. It would make me so happy." I struggled unsuccessfully to fight back tears. I hoped that Raven didn't notice. "Okay, let's get Olive back to bed." Olive followed Raven into the stall, and Cocoa nuzzled her.

"I guess we'd better get you back inside, too."

Raven took my hand, but stopped and reached up for me to carry her. I picked her up and she studied my face. She wiped away my tears and said, "Don't be sad, Miss Dallas. I bet you get to see your family soon."

Sobs came uncontrollably. I looked up to see Ethan and Trevor coming into the barn. I turned around quickly and let Raven down gently. "You go to Daddy now, okay?"

She squeezed my hand and scurried off. I heard whispers but could not make out the words. Then I heard Trevor request, "Come on, my little wild thing. Let's go swing on the front porch."

I kept my back turned until they departed. When I heard voices fade away, I dropped to my knees and let go of my emotions. I jumped when someone put an arm around my shoulder. "What's wrong, Dallas?" It was Ethan, his face burdened with concern. "What happened?"

I shook my head. "I want to go home," I cried like a four-year-old.

Ethan lifted me up by supporting my waist. "I'll walk you home."

With the exception of my sobs, we walked in silence. When we reached the cabin, I said, "I'm so embarrassed. I apologize for my breakdown."

"Did Raven say something to upset you?"

"No, Ethan. She's a little angel. She reminds me of someone I miss, and our conversation triggered some memories. I just lost it."

"Does it have anything to do with why you're hiding here?"

"Yes," I admitted through quivering lips.

Ethan opened the cabin door and led me inside. "Do you want to talk about it?" he asked gently. I shook my head. "What can I do to help?" he persisted.

I didn't want to talk, but I felt scared and lonely. I didn't want to be alone. "Could you stay with me for a little while? You don't have to do anything."

"Of course, I can." He led me to the sofa, and I sat. "I'll be right back." Ethan went to the bathroom and returned with a wet wash-cloth. He sat beside me and gently wiped my face with the warm cloth.

"I'm so tired." My tears returned, but thankfully without the wretched sobs.

Ethan spread a blanket over me, sat beside me and put his arm around me. He pulled me into his chest and stroked my hair. "Keep fighting your demons, Dallas. Some days are better than others. Eventually, you'll have more good days than bad. I promise."

****

I suppose Ethan stayed until I fell asleep, because I was stretched out on the sofa, a pillow under my head and a blanket over my body, when I woke up. There was a note on the floor beside me:

Hope today's a demon-free day. Ethan.

I was so embarrassed. Breaking down like that in front of a total stranger. I went to the bathroom and saw my mascara streaked face.

Lovely. Another source of embarrassment. Nothing to be done about it now. It was time to face another day.

I threw on jeans and a t-shirt, pulled my hair back, grabbed a jacket and headed to the barn to start my daily routine. I smiled as I remembered the kind note that Ethan left me. A demon-free day. I liked the idea, but at this point it seemed like a fantasy.

I entered the barn and found Katie already hard at work doing my job. "Dallas!" Katie seemed surprised to see me. "I wasn't expecting you to be out of bed yet. Ethan said you were under the weather and that's why you didn't come back to the house with him last night. He told us we should let you sleep in because he thought you might not be up to doing much work today. He said he thought you had a really nasty stomach bug."

I stood staring at Katie, touched that Ethan had spared me the humiliation of everyone knowing that I had emotionally derailed. "You look pale. Why don't you take the day off and rest?"

"I'm really fine, Katie. I promise. Thanks for getting started, but I need to work. It keeps my mind off things."

Katie looked skeptical. "I'm not convinced you're 100%, so I'll make you a deal. We'll handle all the chores together. That way I can keep an eye on you. I insist."

I shrugged, knowing it was useless to fight her. Actually, I was glad to have the distraction. Having company would probably keep me from getting lost in my own twisted head. "It's not necessary, but I know better than to argue with you." Katie grinned. "Thanks again for having me to dinner. It was fun. The Moores are all so nice."

"Yes, they are lovely, aren't they? Trevor and I truly think of them as family. We're blessed to have them in our lives."

"Katie, I don't want to pry, but why does everyone seem so shocked that Raven talks to me?"

She had been filling the feeding troughs but paused to answer. "Raven has been extremely withdrawn, particularly from females, for a couple of years now. Her grandmother and I are really the only women that she trusts." Katie spoke slowly, carefully choosing her words. I suppose my expression made her realize that her explanation was like throwing a match in an open gas can. "Raven endured some tragedy. She was five -- old enough to remember the pain but too young to understand the circumstances. The experience will never leave her. We just pray that the scars won't run too deep."

I was curious enough to be more direct. "Do her issues have anything to do with the fact that her mom didn't come to dinner last night?"

Katie seemed torn as she hesitantly answered, "Yes, but I can't elaborate. It's Ethan's story to share, and although he seems good now, he doesn't talk about it. So don't ask. I think he's found a way to accept the past and not dwell on it, but I know he worries about Raven."

"I definitely won't bring it up."

We finished the work in the barn in silence. As we were leaving she said, "He likes you."

"Who?"

"Ethan, who else?"

"He's a kind, thoughtful man. I think he likes everyone."

Katie laughed. "Well, you're right, but I mean, he likes you like he's interested in you. I can tell. I know the look."

"So I hear," I teased.

"What do you mean?" Katie asked innocently.

I smiled. "I heard about his crush on you when you were his sitter."

"So true. What prompted him to share that story?"

"We had lots of time to kill while we waited for Olive to arrive."

"Ah. So you know I've watched him grow up. He's like a little brother to me. I know all his looks and moods, and I'm telling you, Dallas, he likes you."

"I'm a bit of a train wreck, Katie. He deserves better than me."

Katie stopped and grabbed my hand. "Dallas, you know Hatch explained to Trevor and me why you came here. I never pressed you to talk about it, but I think you know that my door is always open if you ever need an ear. Ethan has been through some equally bad things. It's not as fresh for him as it is for you, but it scarred him, and he's vulnerable. I think he sees that same vulnerability in you. You might be able to help each other work through your issues if you both open up. If nothing more, you two could be great friends."

"Did you tell Ethan why I'm here?"

She shook her head. "Absolutely not. He knows as much about your story as you do about his. It's your story to share when and if you decide to share. Same with him." She hugged me. "Enough of the heavy stuff. I'm headed back to the house. You go rest until your training session with the Brody twins. If you're not up for it, you call me, and I'll handle that lesson. I know those boys are a handful!"

"Thanks. I'll be okay."

Back at the cabin, I made myself a ham and Swiss wrap, while I pondered my conversation with Katie. Assuming she was right, I felt a little giddy, almost excited, about the prospect of Ethan having an interest in me. Yet, it was a terrifying thought for more than one reason. First, I had already proven that my ability to assess character was severely deficient. Ethan was gentle, thoughtful and very aware of the needs of those around him. But maybe, deep down, he was really a horrible person. I fell hard for Parker Fielding, couldn't wait to marry him, but turned out our whole relationship was based on his elaborate plan to murder my entire family. Then there's the issue of me living a lie. No small thing to live under a false identity with the looming possibility that a crazy man might show up to erase my existence. Granted the chances are slim since he thinks I'm dead, but anyone close to me would be in danger as well. Finally, the whole idea of trusting anyone I really don't know just wasn't worth the risk. I could be nice to Ethan, but I had to keep my distance.

I kept thinking about him and felt that it would be rude not to thank him for taking care of me during my meltdown last night. I had stored his number in my cell during the weekend that Trevor and Katie were out of town. I started to call, but decided a text was more appropriate.

After sending a brief but heartfelt text, I cleaned up the kitchen. Ethan's note was still on the counter. I smiled as I read it again:

Hope you have a demon-free day. Ethan.

I put it under a refrigerator magnet and read it every day when I made my morning coffee. It never failed to ignite a spark of hope. That is, until the next time I saw Detective Hatcher.

****

November through February were dismal months. It was cold, so the number of riding lessons dwindled, and the ranch was fairly quiet. I had far too much unstructured time to torment myself with detailed images of Parker Fielding's life. I wondered where he was and if he had even a spark of remorse. I envisioned him sipping margaritas on the beaches of Bermuda, frolicking in the waves with his personal harem. I anguished over the injustice of the situation and bemoaned the fact that I had been left behind to live alone in fear and misery. I pickled my mind in anger, negativity and self-pity.

Dealing with the first Thanksgiving and Christmas without my family was excruciating and intensified my mental decline. I knew Katie would insist that I spend the holidays with them, so I lied and said I was going to Florida to spend both holidays with my parents on Sanibel Island. Over Thanksgiving, I took a cab to a Marriott in downtown Lexington and spent four days holed up in a hotel room renting movies, dining exclusively from the mini bar, and crying myself to sleep every night. Over Christmas, I repeated this routine but did so on Sanibel Island at a resort that my family frequented when I was a child. I did venture outside to torture myself by revisiting all the spots that my family loved when we vacationed here. I found a full bottle of Percocet that a prior guest had inadvertently left behind a telephone book in the nightstand. The only thing that kept me from washing down those pills was the nagging feeling that Hatcher really did have more information to share regarding his search for Parker Fielding.

During this dreary period, I saw very little of the Moore family. Big E suffered a mild heart attack, and about the time he was cleared for normal activity, Caroline came down with pneumonia and spent three weeks in the hospital. But in March, the depression lifted. Ethan and Raven become regular visitors to the ranch. Every Thursday afternoon at four, they arrived for Raven to have a riding lesson on Cocoa. I worked with her for two hours, and typically they would stay and eat with Trevor and Katie. At first, I declined their invitations to join them, but then I gave in, and it became a Thursday ritual.

I found myself looking forward to Thursdays. Raven's personality grew exponentially after a few riding lessons. She learned to trust both Cocoa and me. Once she reached that point, she relaxed and quickly became quite an accomplished young rider.

After the first Thursday dinner I attended, I said my goodbyes, but Trevor suggested that Ethan walk me back to the cabin. Raven grabbed my hand and offered to help her dad escort me home, but Katie insisted that Raven stay behind to help with a secret project. The same scenario occurred after the second dinner, and a pattern emerged. I often wondered if it was Katie or Trevor that instigated this chivalrous routine.

As part of the Thursday ritual, the walk back to my cabin ended with us sitting in the rockers on the porch for an hour or more. Sometimes we shared snippets of our day, or discussed our favorite movies and books, or shared college war stories. We often talked about Raven and how much she had blossomed over the past few months. Sometimes, we simply sat in compatible silence with our eyes closed, soaking in the sounds of our surroundings, each lost in our own thoughts. To a passerby, we probably looked like an old married couple enjoying our nightly routine before bedtime. But neither of us ever broached topics of family, future or the nature of our demons. Boundaries had been set instinctually.

Two months passed quickly, and summer rolled in with the subtlety of a freight train. My first taste of a southern summer was as paralyzing as my first bite of a habanero pepper. With sweat perpetually rolling down my neck, I felt as if I were being baked in a soggy tortilla. I complained about how miserably sticky it was. They all laughed and said it was a mild May -- that I needed to brace myself for August.

One Thursday in late May, Katie came to watch Raven's lesson. She stood with Ethan admiring how well this seven-year-old could handle Cocoa. Soon they were engaged in heated conversation, though I could tell it was friendly banter.

Katie was smiling as she pointed a finger in Ethan's face and declared, "No is not an option, Ethan" to which he replied, "You sound exactly like you did when you were my sitter". "Somebody needs to push you in the right direction," Katie pressed. "You old hag," he said affectionately. "Now that's just mean, Dr. Moore," Katie remarked as she blew him a kiss and walked away.

"Are K and Daddy fighting?" Raven asked worriedly.

"No, I think they're teasing each other. A little like brothers and sisters pick at each other."

"I don't know what that's like, but most of my friends say they don't like their baby brothers and sisters," Raven reflected.

I laughed. "That's typical. But at some point, brothers and sisters usually become good friends."

"Do you have brothers and sisters, Miss Dallas?"

My throat tightened, but I refused to fall apart. "Yes, I do."

"Can I meet them when they come to visit you?"

"Unfortunately, it's not possible for them to come for a visit." My eyes filled with tears. Sadness sat on my heart like a forty-pound weight.

Witnessing the change in my mood, Raven asked, "Why are you crying, Miss Dallas?"

I rubbed my eyes and replied, "Some dirt blew in my eyes. It's gone now." I helped Raven off Cocoa. "Let's get Cocoa to bed and get washed up. I bet you're hungry, and you know K will have something delicious ready for us to eat."

"Correction. K will have something delicious for Raven to eat, but Dallas has been uninvited to dinner," announced Katie who was standing with her hands on her hips by the edge of the barn. Ethan stood beside her rolling his eyes.

I was speechless. "Don't feel bad, Dallas," Ethan commiserated, "I've been kicked to the curb as well."

"Dallas, you haven't left this ranch since you've been here. And I can't remember the last time Ethan took a night out. You two are going to The Bluegrass Barn, and Trevor and I are making homemade pizza with Raven."

"Yay!" exclaimed Raven who ran and jumped into Katie's arms.

Panic descended as the idea of going out in public sunk in. I scrambled for an excuse. "Look at me. I'm sweaty and dirty. I can't go out like this. I'd embarrass Ethan in front of his friends."

I couldn't tell if Ethan's expression conveyed relief or sadness. "Unless there's been a significant upgrade at The Bluegrass Barn, you look better than 95% of the patrons as you are right now, but it's okay if you don't want to go. Katie thinks we're both introverts who need to be forced into a public outing." Ethan gave Katie a look that said "look what you've done -- embarrassed us both".

I could feel a little tension building between them and didn't want to be the cause. "You know what," I spoke cheerily, "if you can get a cold beer at this Bluegrass Barn, then I'm in. Let me go wash my face and change into something clean. I'll only be a few minutes."

"You sure?" Ethan asked warily.

"Absolutely. I'll meet you at your truck in ten minutes."

I washed my face and changed into some lightweight khaki shorts and a simple shirt with spaghetti straps. I was so tired of being hot; I thought the fresh, lightweight clothes might alleviate the discomfort.

The Bluegrass Barn was only ten minutes from the ranch. On the drive over, Ethan described it as a "classic dive". We pulled into a parking lot, well more like a dirt field, packed with pickup trucks. I don't think I saw a single sedan -- just a sea of Ford and Chevy trucks. The restaurant itself was no more than a massive shack that appeared one click away from being labeled a condemned building. But once we stepped inside, I felt the appeal. Television screens were mounted around the massive bar. There was a large open area with pool tables and ping pong tables. Country music filled the air. Everything was basic, but inviting.

We found a bistro table in a corner of the dining room and ordered a pitcher of Corona. In silence, we surveyed our surroundings, avoiding eye contact -- like teenagers on a blind date destined to be miserably awkward. Once the pitcher arrived, Ethan filled two chilled mugs and raised his glass. "Here's to us, Katie's social misfits." I laughed and we clinked mugs. We both drank until we were out of breath, and the mugs were two-thirds drained. As we set our glasses down in unison, we made eye contact and laughed. "Impressive," Ethan lauded as he pointed to my mug. "Did you win a lot of chugging contests in college?"

"No," I said and belched. "Oh my, excuse me. I'm so embarrassed." Thankfully the music was loud enough that no one else heard my blunder.

Ethan hid his face in his paper napkin and howled. "That was awesome. Bet you won belching contests, too."

"Hush! I was nervous and drank it too fast. I'm mortified."

"Don't worry about it. I like being out with a real woman. So you were nervous too, huh?"

"Yes. I don't know why. What were you nervous about?"

"Didn't you hear? I'm a social introvert. Makes me nervous to be in public with a pretty girl."

I blushed, and Ethan smiled. "The ranch is my sanctuary," I explained. "Everything feels safe there. I haven't ventured out even to the grocery store since I've been there. I've made lists and paid one of the ranch hands to do my shopping for me."

"Haven't you been here for about a year?"

"Ten months, actually," I corrected.

"And you haven't left the ranch, not even once?" I shook my head. "Okay, you're officially worse than me." I gave him a knowing smile. "But why? Aren't you going stir-crazy?"

"I'm hiding, remember?" I reminded him.

"Fair enough," he replied. "So, seriously, how goes your battle?"

Ethan waited patiently while I caressed my beer mug. I looked up and saw such concern in his dark eyes. There was no hidden agenda, or at least I didn't think so. I thought about Parker, how much I loved his piercing blue eyes. I thought they were so intoxicating and sexy. Now I realized they were void of emotion; they conveyed no warmth like Ethan's. I smiled. "My demons," I began, "are still there, but they're mostly nocturnal. I don't sleep well. I have a lot of nightmares."

He looked at me, as if he wasn't sure whether or not to delve deeper. "I don't want to pry, but you know you can tell me anything, confidentially. I just want you to know that I'm here for you if you need to talk. Even if I can't help, sometimes it's good just to talk."

"Thank you, Ethan. I truly believe that you, Katie and Trevor are all willing to help me in any way. And I appreciate that. It's comforting to know that the people around me genuinely care."

"Okay. Just making sure you knew. So where are you really from? And don't say Sanibel Island, because there is no way you grew up in Florida."

"Why do you say that?" I demanded.

"First of all, you have a completely neutral accent. Not a trace of any southern origins."

"Oh, please. Haven't you ever heard south Florida called the New York of the South? Half of New York migrates to southern Florida when they're over sixty-five. And don't forget about the snowbirds. There are no accents native to southern Florida. Seventy percent of the population is migratory."

Ethan took a swig of beer and said, "Okay. Maybe I'll have to concede that point, but you seem completely unaccustomed to the temperatures here. Kentucky is far less hot and humid than Florida. You act is if you've never experienced this type of weather."

I rolled my eyes, even though I knew Ethan was dead on. Then something occurred to me. "Well, I suppose I can understand why you would think that; however, you have to remember that Sanibel Island is very small. It's not like Hilton Head where it never feels like an island. The breezes hit you at any location, and I grew up on the beach. We had constant breezes which masked all that humidity."

He shrugged, defeated. "You have an answer for everything, don't you? I call bullshit on the whole thing, but I'll let it go. You're a bit of a mystery girl."

By now our meat lover's pizza had arrived, and we dove in. I was thinking about my secrets and decided that Ethan had plenty of his own. "What about your demons, Ethan?"

Ethan stopped chewing and looked up. "Mine? For the most part, they're caged. I've had a couple of years to get control, but I'm always vigilant. They've left their mark, trust me. I used to be a far more carefree guy."

I looked doubtful. "Really?"

"Yes, ma'am. I was once the life of the party, but I've become very boring in recent years."

I took a chance. "Do your demons have anything to do with Raven's mother?"

Ethan dropped his pizza and folded his hands together. I noticed his knuckles turned white. Very calmly, he stated, "I don't want to talk about that."

Ethan drained his beer, and I could tell he was trying to decompress. I took a healthy swig from my mug, and he refilled both glasses. I wasn't offended by his response, but I felt as if I needed to offer some concession. Ethan had been a good friend to me, lending unconditional support. I grabbed my beer and took another substantial drought to fortify myself. The cool liquid soothed my throat and strengthened my resolve. "I'll make a deal with you. We both have secrets that neither of us is comfortable discussing. But I do trust you, Ethan, and am willing to open up a little if you will, too."

"I'm listening," he answered as he grabbed another slice of pizza. "What do you have in mind?"

"I'll tell you a little something about myself that I haven't shared with anyone since I moved here, and you do the same. The magnitude of the secret is totally up to you. But you can't ask questions once the secret is revealed. Not now anyway. AND you cannot, under any circumstances, share the secret with anyone else. Maybe, if we're both comfortable with this process, we can share a little more when we have our porch time."

Ethan smiled. "I like our porch time."

"Me, too," I admitted. "It's been good for my soul."

Ethan looked touched. "I do believe that's the nicest compliment I've ever received." He grabbed my hand, squeezed and let go. Then he rubbed his hands together. "I'm in on this secret swapping gig. Ladies first."

"So chivalrous," I chided. "Just remember one thing as I reveal information since we have the 'no questions' rule. I am hiding, but I am not a fugitive."

"I remember."

"Okay, you were right. I'm not a southern girl. I grew up in the northeastern part of the country and am completely out of my element in this horrid humidity. I can't breathe."

"I knew it."

"Your turn, doc."

Ethan looked as if he were deciding which secret to share. "I used to sleep in your bed."

"Excuse me," I exclaimed.

"I mean, I used to live in your cabin. I moved out about a year before you moved in."

"Really? Why?"

Ethan shook his head. "No questions, remember? That was your rule."

We ordered a second pitcher of beer and finished our pizza. The rest of the evening we talked lovingly about the people we had in common. Then Ethan challenged me to a game of ping pong. He was excellent, though I held my own. I saw a bit of the fun Ethan, the one he claimed the demons had driven away.

"So how did you get so good at ping pong, doc?" I asked after he beat me 21-18.

"I really haven't played much ping pong, honestly. I used to play a lot of tennis. Maybe that's where the skills emerged."

"You play tennis?" I exclaimed. "I used to play a lot. I played on our high school team, and then I used to play a round robin with..." I stopped short as I remembered how much fun I used to have every Fourth of July in our late afternoon Sanderson family round robin. My mood plummeted.

"Secrets?" Ethan asked softly.

Lips quivering, I nodded and buried my face in my hands. I felt arms gently encircle me.

"It's okay," Ethan cooed as he rocked me back and forth.

After a few minutes, I regained my composure. "Sorry about that," I apologized as I left his warm embrace.

"My shoulder's yours any time you need it," he reassured. "You ready to head home? I'm sure Raven has exhausted Katie and Trevor by now."

I laughed. "Might be the other way around. Katie is a live wire. I've never seen her give even the slightest appearance of fatigue."

"It's rare to see Katie Roberts less than giddy." Ethan looked reflective after he made that comment.

"But you have seen her that way, haven't you?" I asked.

Ethan steered me to the truck as he answered. "On a few occasions, yes. Even Katie can't always keep everything in a cookies and ice cream mode, though she certainly tries." He smiled affectionately. "And you can't fault her for that. She wants everyone to be happy. She's such a sweetheart."

After I strapped myself into the truck, I inquired, "How did Katie and Trevor meet?"

"You don't know that story?" he asked incredulously.

"Sorry, no," I answered as if I had failed some test. "Should I?"

"I figured Katie told you by now. She's such a motor mouth, and she loves to tell that story. Even Trevor likes to spin that tale."

I shook my head. "I'm completely in the dark."

"It's a good one. Katie, or Miss Priss, as I used to call her, was a senior at UT and was the rush chairman for her sorority, Chi O. They had a swap with the KA house, and she was responsible for working with the fraternity rush chairman to pair up freshman pledges in the two houses. As is often the case at college frat parties, things got a little out of hand, and the Long Island teas were way too plentiful. Katie got a call at 3am from a frantic freshman whose swap date had taken her back to his place but passed out ten minutes after they arrived. She couldn't wake him or his roommate. She was stranded, worried about her reputation, and had no idea where she was. It was a massive apartment complex, and there was no identifying sign in sight.

"Now Katie told all her pledges that if they were ever in trouble, they should call her, day or night. When this pledge called Katie, she was hysterical. Katie told her to remain calm, stay inside and she would be rescued within the hour. Katie was pissed. Some dumb-ass boy had not treated her pledge with respect, not to mention the fact that she had a huge biology exam at 8am.

"So Katie marched herself over to the KA house and beat on the door. After five minutes of constant pounding, and as I hear it, yelling some unladylike phrases, a guy opens the door, grumpy and half asleep. Wearing only his Mickey Mouse boxers, this guy says, 'Are you trying to wake up the whole city of Knoxville? What the fuck do you want?' That was the first time Trevor and Katie laid eyes on each other, and if you hear Trevor's version, he swears that he had no idea a girl was at the door. He thought it was a drunk pledge who needed his ass kicked, or he never would have spoken that way. Katie, being the kick-ass bitch that she still is, said, 'I am the fucking rush chairman for Chi Omega, and one of your dumb-ass pledges has kidnapped one of my pledges. She's stranded at an unknown apartment complex with a drunken, passed out KA pledge, and if somebody doesn't help me find her, I'm going to bring the KA house to its knees'.

"Of course, she was screaming by now and making quite a scene. Other members of the fraternity had emerged and groggily witnessed her tirade. But Trevor was a man of composure. 'Okay, ma'am. Now I can see you're upset, but I promise we'll have this situation under control in no time. Who is the KA dumb-ass that has kidnapped your Chi Omega angel?' Katie took a deep breath and replied, 'Grant Patterson'. Trevor said, 'Grant Patterson! Oh hell, he can't drink two sips without losing his mind. I know where he lives. His roommate is a bigger pansy than Grant. Give me two secs to put on some clothes, and we'll go get her'.

"Katie, who was quite bossy even then, responded, 'I am perfectly capable of extricating my own pledge, thank you. Just give me the address, and I'll be on my way'. Trevor sized her up and argued, 'Ma'am, I am the president of this presently suspect group of men, and I will not allow a lady to go unescorted on a rescue mission at 3:30 in the morning. It's my dumb-ass pledge that didn't take proper care of your impressionable young freshman, so I must make sure that the matter is properly handled'. Katie hopped in the car of Kappa Alpha president Trevor Roberts on a mission to rescue her virginal pledge from the dumb-ass KA. Katie was smitten with this chivalrous KA gentleman, and the rest is history."

Ethan finished his story as we pulled in front of my cabin. "I love it," I commented. "A true story of a southern gentleman saving a damsel in distress."

Ethan walked me to my door. "I'm glad Katie forced us out tonight. It was a fun evening."

"It was fun. Thanks for treating."

"My pleasure. Playing ping pong made me remember how much fun I used to have playing tennis. I'd like to resurrect my game. It's been a while, but I'm sure it will come back quickly. Are you interested in joining me?"

I hesitated. "I don't know. Besides, I don't have a racquet."

"I can cover you there.   Think about it," Ethan encouraged. "Better get Raven now."

"Goodnight, Ethan. Thanks again." I don't know if it was the beer or the company, but I slept through the night. No demons.

****

A couple of weeks later, on a Sunday afternoon, Ethan convinced me to play tennis with him at a public park. I didn't have proper attire, and Ethan had to loan me a racquet, but the court was in worse shape than me. Despite the sagging net and cracks that meandered around the court like varicose veins, it was good enough to hit some balls. We lacked consistency, but it was obvious we both had skills.

It felt good to hit something and proved to be an excellent outlet for my frustration over the lack of progress in the search for Parker Fielding. Detective Hatcher still called faithfully every couple of weeks, but I got the feeling his vague comments about the case were just false hopes for my benefit. Deep down, I knew the case was dying as were the chances of Parker being brought to justice. I also knew that I couldn't live with that.

If not for Ethan's steady kindness, I would have drowned in a pool of bitter frustration. After a few weeks of playing tennis for fun, he convinced me to sign up as his partner to play in a mixed doubles USTA league. I ordered tennis apparel, shoes, a bag and a racquet online. Our first match was a blast. Initially I was nervous, but once I settled in, I played fairly well and thrived on the competition. Ethan always seemed relaxed on the court, but surprisingly, he was just as competitive as I was. After a 7-5, 6-2 victory, we celebrated with a beer on the porch.

Ethan raised his bottle and said, "Here's to you, partner. Way to play today."

"Thanks. You played quite well yourself."

"What's Raven up to today?"

"Big E took her to the movies. She'll come back with a stomach ache because he'll buy her anything she wants."

"Ah. The joy of being a grandparent. Spoil them rotten then give them back to the parents."

"I suppose, but it makes it tough since we're all under the same roof."

"I didn't realize your parents lived with you."

"Actually, we live with them." Ethan seemed embarrassed. He rose from his rocker, leaned against a post and faced me. "We haven't shared any secrets since our Bluegrass Barn outing." He looked off into the distance. I could tell he was gathering strength. "I had a wife. Her departure was unexpected and devastating to both Raven and me. My parents helped us pick up the pieces."

Ethan looked down at his feet, shuffling them uncomfortably. I couldn't tell from his comments if she died or left him, but the rules prohibited me from asking. I wanted to offer comfort, but I knew there was nothing I could do other than say something that would show him that I was intimately familiar with loss. "I had a fiancé before I came here. Katie and Trevor think he was tragically killed in a mulching accident." Ethan looked up, stunned. "That's not true, but I wish it were."

We stared at each other, neither of us knowing what to say. Finally, I said, "Too bad we didn't have this conversation before we played tennis. I really feel like hitting something right now."

Suddenly Ethan started laughing, a deep uncontrollable laugh, void of humor, born of irony. "How about another beer?" I asked. "I think we could both use one."

****

The weeks passed, and despite my frustration with the stagnant status of my case, I looked forward to each Thursday and Sunday -- my set times spent with Ethan and Raven. I wasn't sure if my growing feelings for Ethan went beyond friendship. Considering how Parker had completely fooled me, I didn't trust my judgment. All I knew was that I enjoyed his friendship and welcomed his calming influence. My demons were always with me, and my anger constantly stewed, but on days spent with him, I had a reprieve from their destructive powers. Somehow he inspired hope. He and his adorable daughter kept me from being completely consumed.

But the approach of July 4th heightened my anxiety. I gave Detective Hatcher a severe lecture reminding him that the first anniversary of my family's annihilation was approaching, and he had failed miserably to find Parker Fielding. Later, I felt horrible because I knew he had gone above and beyond the call of duty to protect me. I was confident that he was doing everything in his power to apprehend Parker, but Parker's freedom crippled me. I couldn't move forward.

Katie and Trevor planned their fifth annual Fourth of July party. Not only Ethan and his family, but also other ranchers in the area were invited. Ethan said it was a celebration that started around four and ended around midnight. Beer, BBQ, kid friendly games and fireworks fueled the event. Katie was pushing hard for me to attend despite my perpetual objections. "But even Hatch might come, Dallas," she pleaded.

I was stunned. Detective Hatcher had not mentioned any plans for a visit. Of course, I barely allowed him to speak during our last call. "Oh dear," Katie said with alarm. "He hasn't mentioned it to you? Maybe he wanted to surprise you, and now I've ruined it."

"It's okay, Katie. He probably won't come anyway. We had a bit of a disagreement the last time we chatted. I was probably unfairly hard on him."

She waved away my concern. "I'm sure he's forgotten all about it. Everything you throw at Hatch just rolls away like water off a duck's back. He'll be here. He hasn't missed a year yet. Besides, I get the impression he wants to check on you."

The last Sunday before the Fourth, the whole clan came to watch us play our mixed doubles match. Big E and Caroline brought Raven, Katie and Trevor to serve as our personal cheering squad. We both focused on showing off a bit for our supporters, so we played out of our minds and rolled over our opponents 6-1, 6-0.

"You two are an impressive duo," Trevor congratulated. "Dallas, I don't see how it's humanly possible for someone as tiny as you to produce that kind of power. You hit as hard as the men."

"It's a great way to release frustration," I responded.

"Well goodness, honey," Big E chimed in, "you must be all clogged up with frustration."

Everybody laughed, and I gave Big E a hug.

The Fourth of July arrived despite my resistance. I rose early, fed the horses, and snuck back to my cabin all before the sun came up. I hadn't slept the night before, so it was easy to get things done early. Once home, I took a steaming hot shower and couldn't avoid reliving the details of the last Fourth of July. I awoke to the sounds of laughter -- a house full of people eagerly awaiting a boat ride to Capers Island. At this moment, one year ago, I had exactly thirty-eight minutes left with my entire family. Why did I survive? I shouldn't be here.

I pulled an old t-shirt over my head, crawled back in bed and cried until I was numb. Eventually I dozed. I awoke to a pounding on my door. I glanced at the clock. 4 pm. Probably Katie here to drag me to her party. I decided to ignore her, but Raven's high-pitched plea compelled me to open the door.

I must have looked frightful based on Raven's reaction when I opened the door. "Miss Dallas, what's wrong? You look terrible."

"Hi, sweetie. I must look a little scary. I'm a bit under the weather, so I don't think I'll make it to the party."

"K sent me and Daddy to come get you, and she said 'don't take no for an answer'. But I can tell you don't feel good. Sorry you're sick. I'll tell K you need to rest and get well."

"Thanks, Raven. You have fun okay." I could see that Ethan had stayed in the truck. I waved to him as Raven ran back to the passenger side.

Halfway up the stairs, I stopped and pivoted as I heard heavy footsteps on the porch. I opened the door as Ethan lowered his fist to knock.

He looked surprised. "I heard you on the porch." He opened his mouth to speak, but I put my hand up. "Raven told me Katie sent you here on a mission, but you'll have to convince her that I'm not up for a party."

Ethan stepped inside and closed the door. "Okay, don't worry," he said softly, "I'm not going to make you go if you don't want to, and I can handle Katie."

"I appreciate that," I answered through an unsteady voice. I felt a crying spell approaching.

Ethan took my hand and gently pulled me to him. "I can tell you haven't slept, and your eyes are swollen from crying." Tears flowed as he put his hand underneath my bangs to check for a fever. He stopped when he felt my scar. He removed his hand and pushed back my bangs to expose my forehead. He slowly rubbed my scar as he spoke in a whisper. "This is a pretty nasty scar. I can tell it's not very old. How long have you had it?"

"One year as of today," I answered and closed my eyes without fighting the tears.

He embraced me and whispered, "This is the first anniversary of something horrible, isn't it?" I didn't answer, but I knew I didn't need to. He kissed the top of my head. "No explanation needed. Try to get some rest. I'll come check on you later tonight. If you need anything, even just my shoulder, send me a text, okay?"

I nodded and wiped away my tears.

I spent the rest of the day moping, crying, and sleeping fitfully. A complete waste of a day. When I heard the first pop of fireworks, I wrapped up in a light blanket and took my pity party to the porch. The fireworks were beautiful. My brother, Rio, always called them "fire showers".

"Hey, partner. May I join you?"

"Hi, Ethan. I didn't hear you drive up."

"That's because I walked. You feeling any better?"

I shrugged. "A little. The tears have dried up. I think I'm dehydrated. My pity party was quite intense, and I'm exhausted now."

"I've thrown myself a few of those parties before, and they are exhausting, but necessary every now and then. Have you eaten anything?" I shook my head. "Well, I've brought you everything you need to end this party on the right note." He set a handled, reusable grocery bag on the floor. "First," he said reaching into the bag, "I brought you the best BBQ sandwich you'll ever have. Since you're really a Yankee, it might be the first BBQ sandwich you've ever had."

"You got that right. But I'm game," I answered as I unwrapped the sandwich.

"Then to wash it down, I have a fine beer brewed illegally a few miles down the road." I gave him a dubious look as he handed me a large mason jar of gold liquid. "It's safe. I promise. A great, light summer ale crafted by a master brewer, who just happens to be unlicensed." He pulled another mason jar from the bag, removed the lid and took a big sip. "This is my fourth one today. I'm still standing, so it's safe."

I took a sip. "Wow. This is awesome. So is the BBQ." While I ate, Ethan told me all about the party. I could tell he had a little buzz going. He was far more animated than normal. He was cute. "Raven and I won the parent/child egg race, and we came in second in the three-legged man race. Then she spent two hours on the slip 'n slide, ate two hotdogs and two pieces of apple pie. She passed out halfway through the fireworks show, so my folks took her home with them."

"You didn't happen to bring me any of that apple pie, did you?"

"Of course, I did," he responded as he pulled a plastic container from the bag. "I'll heat it up for you real quick. Don't move."

Ethan returned, and I devoured the pie. He watched me in amusement. "I can't believe how hungry I was."

He smiled. "Nice to see you're feeling better." He reached into the sack. "But, there's more to share. A little liquid relaxation. We're going to be naughty and have a few shots of Maker's Mark."

"I don't know, Ethan. That might not be such a good idea."

"Listen, I am older and clearly far more experienced at self-loathing and depression. Trust me, this is a proper ending to an exceptionally bad day." He filled two shot glasses and handed me one. "Have you ever done a shot before?" I must have looked highly unskilled. "Now take my advice. Don't sip it. Toss it back in one big gulp."

"Okay."

"On three. One, two, three."

We tossed back our glasses and I squealed. "I feel like my throat's on fire!"

Ethan laughed as he poured another round. "Just give it a minute, and it'll work its magic."

"I'm not having another one."

"Just one more," he argued. "With this one, you'll quickly feel all your muscles relax. All the knots and tightness in your body will evaporate. It's the poor man's version of a massage."

"You seem far too well-versed in this process, Dr. Moore," I teased.

"Sad, but true. Bottom's up, you novice."

We tossed back our glasses. I stood and waited for the poor man's massage to take hold. Suddenly, I felt relaxed and free. "I see what you mean, doc."

"Told you."

"You really are good for my soul, Ethan Moore. Thank you for helping me make it through one of the worst days of my life." I reached up and softly kissed his cheek. As I pulled away, I paused and looked into his dark eyes; they were pools of untapped emotion.

"You're welcome," he whispered as he played with a lock of my hair and leaned down to kiss me. It was unexpected but such a sweet kiss -- slow, tender, full of emotion. When I didn't say anything, Ethan apologized. "I'm sorry. I overstepped my bounds here." He hung his head in embarrassment. "I'll leave now."

"Wait. I don't want you to leave, Ethan. You just took me by surprise, that's all."

Ethan smiled self-consciously. "I haven't done that in a long time. It was probably subpar."

"Don't sell yourself short. It was a great kiss." I paused a moment before continuing. "What would happen if I had one more shot of Maker's?"

"Gutsy girl, eh? A third one is guaranteed to turn your limbs to putty and turn all demons to dust, at least until tomorrow. You'll sleep like a baby."

I grabbed the bottle and glasses and went inside, motioning for him to follow. I poured each of us a glass and raised mine for a toast. "To demon dust."

"To demon dust," Ethan repeated.

I sat on the sofa and patted the space beside me. "Keep me company until I fall asleep?"

"My pleasure," he said as he sat and rubbed my knee.

I stroked his face and pecked his lips -- a lingering peck so he would know I was interested. He seemed surprised. "When it comes to me, Ethan, I recommend proceeding with caution. You have no idea what a train wreck I am."

"I specialize in salvage work, kid." He kissed the top of my head and pulled me into his chest. I was asleep in three minutes. He was right; I slept like a baby.

****

The next morning I awoke on the sofa with a pounding headache. On the kitchen counter was a note and a bottle of Motrin.

> You'll probably need this today. I sure did. But it was worth it. You were sleeping peacefully when I left at 2 am. Manly snores and lots of drool. I'll call you later. Ethan.

Slowly, I showered and dressed. Coffee and toast subdued my queasiness. Once fortified, I headed to the barn for my morning routine. When I was done, I went to the house to check on Katie. I found her in the backyard cleaning up from last night's festivities. "Morning, Katie. Need any help?"

"Well, hey Dallas," Katie answered cheerily as she looked at her watch. "Goodness, the morning's almost gone. How did that happen? We missed you yesterday. But I knew Ethan checked in on you last night."

"He did and he brought me a BBQ sandwich and apple pie -- both were delicious. I practically inhaled them. I did see the fireworks. They were spectacular."

"I wish you could have found a way to make it yesterday. Raven was really disappointed that you weren't there to see her on the slip 'n slide, and she wanted you to do some of the games with her." There was a little bite in Katie's tone. I was in unchartered territory.

"Katie, you sound upset. The Fourth is a horribly painful holiday for me. I'm sorry, but I couldn't bring myself to be festive on a day that marks devastating memories."

"I'm not mad at you, Dallas. Hatch told me that he would be shocked if you came to the party. He told me not to push. I'm just concerned because Raven is completely attached to you. I know you're probably in the dark, but your presence has alleviated some of the damage Raven's mother caused her. I don't want her to be disappointed by another female. And I know Ethan has feelings for you, even if he won't admit them to me. But I'm not sure you feel the same way. They've been through a lot, and I don't want them to get hurt. I don't want you to get hurt either, Dallas. You're family to me now, and I worry about you, too."

"Katie, I would never willingly hurt Raven or Ethan, or you and Trevor for that matter. I adore Raven, and I recognize the fact that she's fragile. And Ethan, well yes, I do have feelings for him. First and foremost, I value and desperately need his friendship, but I'll admit that my feelings for him have been growing, and I've just repressed them. I don't have any confidence in my ability to handle feelings beyond friendship right now. But they're there. I have to go slowly. Does that make you feel better?"

Katie hugged me. "Yes, thank you for sharing."

"Why the sudden concern?"

"Hatch's visit. He seems very anxious to talk to you. But he seems stressed. I have a bad feeling that whatever news he shares will rock the boat, maybe even sink it."

My pulse raced. "Where is he?"

Katie looked toward the cabin. "I think he's that spot on your front porch. Better go find out."

****

"Detective Hatcher?" I called out as I approached the cabin. He waved and greeted me with a warm, fatherly embrace.

"Hello, Prov.., I mean Dallas." He shook his head. "I'm not sure I'll ever get used to calling you Dallas."

"I look forward to the day you tell me that I can be Providence Sanderson again and that I can go home." I kicked the porch post. "I guess it's not really home anymore, but what little I have left of my past is back in Philly. I did have a good job and great friends." Suddenly, my spirits brightened. "Is that why you're here, Hatcher? You haven't visited since you brought me here. It must be important for you to come all this way. What's going on?"

Hatcher sat down again. "I don't ever miss the Fourth of July bash at the ranch. I know yesterday had to be tough for you, so I didn't want to bother you. But there have been some developments, and I want to go through them with you carefully. I'm hungry. Any chance we could grab a pizza and beer?"

"Sure. There's a pub ten minutes from here, and the pizza is great. I'll go get the truck."

Fifteen minutes later we were seated in a corner of The Bluegrass Barn with a pitcher of Amstel Light and a large pizza with the works on the way. To say I was nervous is an understatement. Hatcher kept asking about my work with the horses.

I answered his last question and said, "Hatcher, you're stalling. Start talking about the developments you mentioned."

He sat back and sighed. "Let me start with the easy, more upbeat stuff. Remember I told you I had discussed your parents' estate with their attorney in Atlanta?"

"Yes, you said you thought she could free up some cash for me."

"Right," Hatcher nodded. "She's worked her magic, and now there is an account in your new name that has $85,000 in it." Hatcher pulled a sheet of paper from his wallet. "Here's all the information you need to access the account."

I took the sheet and glanced at it before putting it in my purse. "That is good news. Thanks for handling this. I'll have the $5,000 you loaned me last year wired to you." He nodded. "So, what's happened? You seem reluctant to update me."

Hatcher sighed. "How much do you know of your father's life before he married your mother?"

I couldn't imagine what this had to do with anything. "Not a lot, really. I know that Dad was an only child and that his parents died when he was in law school at Harvard. His parents were vacationing in the Bahamas, and their charter plane crashed on the return flight. There were no survivors. After law school, Dad took a job with some big firm in Denver where he met my mother, a paralegal. Two years later, they got married, traveled the world for a couple of years, then settled in Philadelphia, which is my mom's hometown."

"Most of that is true," Hatcher confirmed as he drummed his fingers on the table.

"Most?"

"You know we've been trying to find Parker, or rather James Cavanaugh, and had no luck. The hard reality is that the longer the case remains open, the less likely it will be solved, and the manpower devoted to the case diminishes. Three weeks ago, my partner and I were told that we were the only detectives authorized to work the case and that we needed to put it on the back burner and spend more time with new cases that were piling up, but we finally caught a break. Early on, we dug through Fielding's finances and nothing unusual popped out. But there was no way his job supported his lifestyle. You know how nice his house was. So we started digging into his parents. Only his mother, Candie Cavanaugh, was listed on his birth certificate. His father was listed as unknown. We started researching her background. It seems that she was a stripper in Boston, Massachusetts, before her son was born. After James arrived, she gradually became a raging alcoholic who floated from one clerical position to another, lasting no more than one or two months at each job. When she hit rock bottom, she moved to Philadelphia and tried to clean up her act. She committed suicide six years ago while her son was overseas. Despite her instability, she had a decent house and sent Parker to the best private school in Philly. So how did she pay for it all? We checked the school records, and it turns out that Parker's tuition was paid by your dad. Dallas, twelve years of private school were funded by your father."

I frantically twirled my long hair, a nervous habit from childhood. "Hatcher, are you trying to tell me that Parker Fielding is my dad's illegitimate son? Are you saying that I was engaged to my half brother?"

Hatcher grabbed my hand and gave me a reassuring squeeze. "No, far from it. I have learned that your dad was more of a saint than anyone knew. Except possibly your mother. Now you'll understand why I asked you about your father's past. Your dad was not an only child. He had a twin brother, an identical twin, and Parker Fielding (James Cavanaugh) is his son. The twin abandoned mother and son, and your dad tried to pick up the slack, at least financially."

My mind, as well as my heart, raced. "How do you know all this? I mean, about the twin brother?"

"When I contacted Ms. Dunn, the estate attorney, she shared with me a letter that your dad had included in the estate documents. It was marked to be opened only after his death. The letter explained to you and your siblings that you had an uncle with whom he had lost contact after law school. The letter included a picture of your dad with his twin, Hank, apparently taken at Harvard. He also mentioned that his brother had an illegitimate son that his brother failed to acknowledge."

"So, you're telling me that Parker is my first cousin and that he murdered the man who supported him? That makes absolutely no sense."

"No, it doesn't, but there's more to it. We had a theory, and after a conversation with Parker last week, I know we were right."

"Conversation! You got him? He's in jail now? It's safe to go home?"

Hatcher patted my hand. "Sorry. I didn't mean to mislead you. It's not in the least bit safe."

The server returned to check on us, and Hatcher assured him that we were fine. After he departed, Hatcher continued. "We know Parker did it; the problem is catching him. There was $50,000 left in his mother's bank account, so we froze it. We flagged the account to contact me if an attempt was made to access it, but Fielding hacked in and transferred the money to some Swiss account that we can't touch. Parker's ego, however, got the best of him. He contacted me."

"He called you?"

"Arrogant prick FaceTimed me on my personal phone. He said he wanted to call on July 4th to commemorate the one year anniversary of my failure, but he said he'd be busy with his girlfriend, a French model. He wanted to gloat. He obliterated the family, got the rest of the money and escaped, free and clear. He wanted to shove my failure in my face. I received the call while I was at work, so I went to an interrogation room so I could record the whole thing, but I'm not sure you want to see it."

"Show it to me," I demanded with conviction.

"Are you sure, because he is such a smug bastard. It may be easier for you if I summarize the relevant points."

"I want to see it." My tone was cold and unrelenting.

He found the video that he had apparently downloaded to his phone and handed me his cell. I hit play.

"Bonjour, Detective Hatcher." It was Parker Fielding, or rather James Cavanaugh, on the screen. Staggeringly handsome and confident. And then I saw it. Everyone who saw us together said we would make beautiful babies -- that our features were so similar -- that we just looked made for each other. I saw the family resemblance now -- blue eyes, high cheekbones. But his eyes were darker, and now I could see the sinister look -- the edginess.

"What do you want Fielding, or should I say Mr. Cavanaugh?"

"Ah, very good detective. You found my birth name. But even my birth name is a lie. Did you know that?"

"Yes, as a matter of fact, I do know that. Your last name should be Sanderson."

Parker clapped lightly. "Well, well. Kudos to you. I didn't give you enough credit, Detective."

"Let me ask you something, Parker, or do you prefer James?"

"Let's go with Parker. It's more unique."

"Fine. Let me ask you something. Why did you kill an entire family? Ten adults, one toddler, and a two-month-old baby. An innocent family who had done nothing to you."

"Detective, you disappoint me. You want to know why I killed that son of a bitch father who abandoned me, drove my mother to suicide, and went on to build a perfect family without me, as if I didn't exist?" Parker's tone started out flat, controlled, but became charged with bitterness as he spoke. "All of those people came after me. I was there first, and everything they had should have been mine. Seems pretty obvious to me why I took them all out."

Hatcher paused. "So you decided to seduce Providence Sanderson to work your way into their lives." Hatcher stated this as fact rather than speculation.

"Good plan, eh? Quite creative even if I do say so myself." Parker grinned, his sadistic pleasure obvious.

"Tell me, Parker. If you hadn't succeeded last year, would you have actually married Providence?"

"Anything for the mission," Parker answered, nonchalantly. "She's a looker even though she's my half sister. It's not like we grew up as brother and sister, so the hot sex didn't seem perverted, just hot." His lascivious smirk made my stomach lurch. I thought I might need to make a mad dash to the bathroom, so I paused the recording.

"I'm sorry, Dallas," Hatcher lamented. "I told you it was tough to hear. Do you want to turn that off and let me summarize the rest?"

"No, I need to hear everything, even if it's disgusting. Just give me a minute."

Hatcher reassured me. "No more disgusting comments left, but before you restart, let me give you a little background to understand what happens next." I nodded before he continued. "I took the ultimate risk. Obviously, he was overseas, and more than likely in France based on his comments. But we knew he wouldn't reveal his location so easily unless he was planning to change it. We couldn't get him even though he had just confessed to killing twelve people. He was well trained at deception and could create a new identity for himself without detection. The only way to nail the bastard was to plant a seed."

I was still queasy, but thought I could continue. I hit play.

"Parker," Detective Hatcher began, "Why do you think Cal Sanderson was the father that abandoned you?"

"Are you serious? You haven't figured that out? Guess I did have you pegged, Hatcher. I'll spell it out for you, moron. Daddy Dearest paid for my private school. Also, over the years I saw generous cancelled checks to my mother, and I saw the one picture she had of the two of them together."

Hatcher shuffled around his desk and then held a photograph up to the screen. It was a picture of two men, my father and his twin brother, obviously the photo from the letter Hatcher just told me about. They truly were identical except my father's eyes conveyed a brightness and hope, while his twin's eyes, though equally captivating, had a darker, more sinister hue. It was a subtle difference, but it spoke volumes. Parker had his father's eyes.

Parker looked confused. "Guess what dumb-ass," Hatcher began smugly. "Cal Sanderson was not the villain of your life. He was your knight in shining armor, the unsung hero, the identical twin brother of your bastard father. Cal Sanderson was the good guy who tried to make amends for his brother who abandoned your mother and you. Cal Sanderson tried to help your mother and make your life better. So you lose, asshole. Your father lives on oblivious to his bastard son. Daddy Dearest had no contact with his twin brother, so he doesn't even know that you wiped out the rest of his family. You, Parker, have yet to impact your dick of a dad in any way, shape or form.

Parker's face said it all. And with that, Detective Hatcher said, "Goodbye, you pathetic piece of shit."

There was so much information for me to process, I didn't know where to begin. I stared into my beer mug, as if the answers would emerge from the depths.

"You okay? I know this is a lot to take in."

"That's an understatement," I responded sarcastically. "I don't even know what to say."

"You've got to take some time to digest all this, but if my instincts are correct, Parker will be stateside as soon as he tracks down his biological father. I don't think you're in any danger. After all, he thinks you're dead. But his ego isn't going to let this go. He'll go after his father, and I'm sure his family as well."

I have an uncle. Obviously he's a horrible person if my dad felt it necessary to never mention him and take care of his illegitimate child. Maybe his family is nice. Maybe I have a kind aunt and nice cousins. "Has my uncle's family been warned?"

"We can't find them," Hatcher admitted. "Apparently Parker is a 'chip off the old block' because about the time Parker was born, your uncle, Hank Sanderson, seemed to fall off the face of the earth. My preliminary investigation is inconclusive. I can't find any evidence that he is deceased, but after he graduated from Harvard alongside your dad, there is no record of his existence -- no tax return, no bank account, no homeowner's deed, no active credit cards, nothing."

"Maybe he changed his name to hide from the stripper," I suggested.

"Possibly," Detective Hatcher conceded, "but if he did, we have no way to know."

We sat in silence. Hatcher stared out the window, but his gaze was not vacant. He looked uncomfortable; he was fidgeting, rhythmically opening and closing his left fist, rapidly bouncing his left leg, and grinding his teeth. My stomach flipped. "There's more, isn't there? What haven't you told me?"

He faced me and folded his hands. "I'm that transparent, am I?" He took a moment before responding, while I patiently waited for another scoop of bad news. "Charleston PD has officially closed the case. My superiors believe that since Parker confessed on tape that he murdered your family, he'll never come back to the States. I argued that his profile demanded that he return to correct his error -- to finish off the right man. But they said that other than giving his alias and photo to Interpol and airport authorities, there was really nothing more that could be done. I've been banned from spending any more department resources on this case."

The news was worse than I imagined. "So, that's it!" I exclaimed more loudly and angrily than I intended. A few heads turned to identify the source of the uproar. I lowered my voice. "I can't believe the police are okay with letting this lunatic get away with murder."

"They aren't okay with it, Dallas. As cold as it sounds, they have to play the odds, and they know that the odds of successfully apprehending a confessed mass murderer who has fled the continent are slim to none. If Parker really is in France, he will migrate to a country that will not extradite. Our homicide manpower and financial resources are stretched, so they have to direct their energy into the cases that can most likely be resolved."

"How nice," I commented with as much venom as I could muster -- a plentiful dose.

"I promise I'll keep working on this on my own time. The case is solved; we just need to track down Parker so we can prosecute him. Now that you have some of the money from the estate, you could hire your own investigators to find him."

"What about my life back in Philly? What about closure and justice?" I was frantic, and people were staring again. I hadn't realized how much louder I had become with every word.

Hatcher glanced around and spoke in hushed tones. "I've already spoken to the estate attorney, and she is confident that she can liquidate the estate and transfer the funds to the account we set up for Dallas O'Malley. She said it will require some creative legal proceedings and some signatures from you, but in time it can be done. The value of the estate is mostly tied up in real estate -- your parents' home and your grandparents' beach house -- neither of which has a mortgage."

I kept my voice under control, but not my temper. Through clenched teeth I declared, "I don't want either house sold. Those houses are all I have left of my family. I'm not about to give that up."

Hatcher tried to take my hand, but I jerked it away. He looked a little hurt, but continued. "If you keep the house in Philly and come back, it won't take long for the story to break that Providence Sanderson survived. You'll be hounded by the media, and even though

Parker now knows that he killed the wrong family, I don't think he has any remorse, and I'm confident he'll come back to kill you. To him, you were part of a mission that fell short of perfect. He can't accept that. He is an egomaniac and won't tolerate a subpar performance. And as much as you say you want to go home, sometimes you can't go back. Nothing will ever be the same for you there. Even your friends will treat you differently. You need to move forward, not look back."

"And I'm telling you that I can't move forward until Parker Fielding is either serving a life sentence for each member of my family or dead. And I'd prefer the latter." I glared at him. "Can't you trace the call?"

"We did, but he placed the call from Austria on a phone registered to some high school kid. Authorities interviewed the kid who said some guy gave him a thousand euros to borrow his phone. The man told the kid that he could find his cell again in one hour taped underneath a bench in a local park."

"Yet another dead end. Parker wins again." I stood abruptly and threw a twenty on the table, as well as the keys to the truck. "I need to take a walk. You can take the truck back to the ranch. Have a nice trip home." My tone was cold and ungrateful. Hatcher didn't deserve to be the target of my hatred, but I couldn't give him the kindness he had earned. Since I couldn't kill Parker, I killed the messenger.

****

I walked aimlessly for an hour, oblivious to landmarks and direction. I was consumed by an anger that rendered me incapable of sound judgment. I felt crazed, reckless, volatile. The situation was far too raw to generate any other state of mind.

As I ambled, I replayed all this new information: I slept with and almost married my first cousin; I have an uncle, my father's identical twin, who apparently vanished decades ago; the police have abandoned their search for my murderous cousin/fiancé; I can't return to my childhood home without making myself a target for my murderous cousin/fiancé; the Sanderson family was targeted in error. It all seemed too absurd to be fact. I screamed at the top of my lungs -- a long, piercing cry. Then I buried my head in my palms.

"Did that help?" Startled, I gasped and jumped at the sound of a man's voice. I turned toward the road. Ethan's truck was parallel to me, and he was staring through an open passenger window.

"You scared me. What are you doing here, Ethan?" I made no attempt to disguise my irritation.

"Katie called. She said Hatch had delivered some bad news and you probably needed a friend. She thought I was the best choice. I'm taking the afternoon off, so I'm all yours. Hop in."

I shook my head vehemently. "That's nice of you," I said in a clipped tone, "but I'm poison right now. Being with me would be a waste of your day."

"Friends are most important on the bad days. Now come on. We'll find a quiet spot, and you can unload."

I studied his face. It was kind, genuine. His eyes were warm, trustworthy. I knew I could tell him everything, but I wasn't sure the burden of my history would not be harmful to him.

He read my mind. "I'm a big boy. I can take it, Dallas."

"I think I'll need a few drinks to be able to tell you my story."

Ethan leaned over to the tiny backseat and retrieved a small plastic storage bin. "I got you covered." He opened the lid and showed me the contents. There was a large bottle of Maker's Mark and a large bottle of Patrón sandwiched between sweatshirts and rain slickers.

I climbed into the cab. "Not sure that'll be enough."

****

We drove in silence for thirty minutes before Ethan pulled onto a bumpy, dirt road and continued for another ten minutes. We entered pristine territory with rolling hills covered by lush grasses and a scattering of giant hardwoods. There was no hint of civilization in any direction -- no signs, no power lines, no houses or barns. The colors around me appeared more vivid -- the skies were bluer, the grasses a deeper shade of green. It was as if we had entered another dimension. I stuck my head out the window and took a deep breath. The air seemed pure and invigorating. For a moment, I felt as if I were the only human on an untainted planet. I had that sensation that comes with being out in the middle of the ocean -- lonely but profoundly aware of your surroundings and how beautiful life can be. Everything feels pure, unspoiled. Then Parker Fielding stepped into my mind, and I knew life would always feel tainted as long as we shared the same planet.

We drove off the dirt road into a group of hardwoods that nestled a tiny cabin. With massive trunks, the ancient trees towered like skyscrapers making the cabin resemble a dollhouse. It was old and run down, probably from the early 1900s. "Where are we?" I asked Ethan dreamily. "Does someone live here?"

He jumped out of the truck and came around to open my door. "Come on. I want to show you something." We went around the back of the house, and I gasped. A newly laid, wooden walkway meandered from a massive deck through the trees and sloped downward until it expanded into a dock on the edge of a stunning lake. We walked down to the lake.

"This place is spectacular. Aren't we trespassing?"

"It's okay," Ethan reassured me through a smile. "I know the owner." He set down the storage bin that he carried from the truck, opened the lid and retrieved two small, plastic cups and the bottle of Maker's. He poured each half full and handed me one. "You soak up the view and the booze, and I'll get the chairs from the truck." I nodded.

When he returned, Ethan worked silently setting up the chairs to face each other with the storage bin between them to serve as a footstool. "Dallas?" I turned and saw him motioning for me to take a seat. I sat and he topped off both of our cups. "Okay. Spill it. I can't help you if you don't share it all. Take as much time as you need."

"Time. What time is it?" I asked frantically. "I have a training session at four."

"Relax. When Katie sent me to find you, she said she would take care of all the afternoon activities. You're clear until morning and so am I, so we have all night if it takes that long."

I just stared at him, desperately wanting to tell him everything, but reluctant to share my pain and embarrassed by my stupidity in regards to Parker.

Ethan smiled. "Okay, it's obviously difficult for you to share your story, so let me tell you what I think I know based on some observations. First, you are supposedly Hatch's cousin from Sanibel Island, but you've admitted that you're truly a Yankee. Now, I've known Hatch for years. You probably don't know that Hatch was Trevor's fraternity big brother at UT, and Trevor's best man in his wedding. Hatch has not once mentioned a pretty, younger cousin from Sanibel Island. And, Hatch is a detective with the Charleston police department. So my skeptical mind is thinking that your connection is not as a relative but rather related to a crime that you witnessed or in which you became an unwilling participant. And, you mentioned that you wished your fiancé really had died in a mulching accident, so I'm thinking that somehow he used you in carrying out his crime and he got away with it. I'm also speculating that Hatch hid you at the ranch to keep you safe, so you can testify against your unmulched fiancé when they catch him. Finally, I'm thinking that today Hatch delivered some bad news regarding this scoundrel." Ethan took a long sip from his cup. "That's all I got. How'd I do?"

I took a gulp of my drink, though I knew I didn't need it. My head was already spinning from all the new details revealed today. "Pretty damn good, Ethan, pretty damn good." I took a few more sips and grimaced as the alcohol burned as it slid down my throat. "There's just so much more to the story. Some of it is unbearably painful and some of it makes me feel so stupid and guilty that I'm even alive."

"Dallas, I promise you can trust me." He looked around, surveying our surroundings. He pointed to the far side of the lake and whispered, "Look."

I followed his direction and saw three does and two fawns drinking from the lake. "They're beautiful."

Ethan kept his eyes on the deer. "Yes, they are. This place has magic, Dallas." He turned toward me. "At least for me anyway. Do you know why I brought you here?" I shook my head before he continued. "Because I know you've been betrayed and you feel isolated. I can see it since I've been down the same road. We are kindred spirits in that department. I brought you here because I wanted you to understand that you can trust me." Ethan stood and walked around the dock as he spoke. "I've known about this place since I was sixteen, and I've never brought anyone here. Not Trevor or Katie, not Raven, and not even my ex-wife, Amelia, with whom I was ridiculously in love. In twenty years, you are the first person to whom I've ever mentioned this place. That should tell you that you can trust me."

"I do trust you, Ethan. And I appreciate your faith in me. I promise I won't divulge this amazing place to anyone. How did you find it?"

He patted my head as he sat down. "You tell me your story; I'll tell you mine."

"Okay," I began slowing. "My name is not Dallas O'Malley. My name is Providence Sanderson, and my entire family was murdered by my ex-fiancé. The whole world thinks I'm dead, as well."

Ethan's jaw dropped. I told him every detail, even the humiliating reality that I had been engaged to, in love with, and had unwittingly made love to, on multiple occasions, my first cousin. I had to make a mad dash to the lake to throw up when I unveiled that embarrassing horror.

Ethan came to my side and wiped my mouth with his shirt. "I'm so sorry," he whispered. "What a cold-hearted bastard. The whole time he thought he was your half-brother, and he didn't care."

I cried in his arms for a long time. When I regained my composure and completed my story, I summarized. "So you see, I'm in no man's land. If I'm aggressive and move forward, I expose myself and probably make myself a target, as well as, endanger anyone else in my life. If I stay where I am, I have to abandon my past and let a horrible human being get away with murder." I looked at Ethan. "I'm screwed any way you slice it."

Ethan grabbed my hand. He pulled me into him and held me tightly for a long time. He rubbed my hair and rocked me, like he was comforting an ailing infant. I felt safe. Finally he said, "What do you want to do? What do you think your family would want you to do?"

I left the security of his embrace and sat. "My parents would want me to move on. They would want me to let fate run its course. They would encourage me to build a new life, even under the name Dallas O'Malley." I smiled as I thought of my parents. "They would say 'a rose is but a rose by any other name' and to live a full, productive life would honor them far more than an endless pursuit of their killer. My brother Rio, on the other hand, would tell me to go kick some ass. He would tell me to hunt Parker Fielding down and make him cry for his momma. My siblings would be divided --- some would think like my parents; others would take the Rio approach."

"And what approach do you favor, Providence Sanderson?"

I smiled at the sound of my real name. It was good to hear someone else say it after all this time. "Rio was always my favorite sibling. We thought alike."

Ethan nodded and smiled. "I thought that's what you'd say. So what's the next step?"

"I have to get justice for my family. I'll never be able to move on if that bastard gets away with what he did."

"If the case is closed, how can you do that?"

"I've got some money now. I'll hire a top rated, private investigative firm to track him down."

Ethan looked doubtful. "You know if he's eluded the police for this long, he'll be next to impossible to find."

"I disagree," I argued as I began pacing. "The police follow the law and private investigators are probably far more creative and take greater liberties when tracking someone. I bet they retrieve valuable information by hacking into databases that the police would never dare touch since it could get them in trouble. Parker will come back to the States eventually to take out his real father. He'll slip up. His ego will be his downfall."

"Maybe," Ethan conceded with skepticism, "but somehow you have to prepare yourself for the fact that he may never be found. You said your uncle disappeared without a trace. Maybe he's living abroad. Maybe he's dead. If you use all your time, energy and finances pursuing Parker, you'll never have a life of your own. You'll be stagnant -- living in a perpetual holding pattern. Trust me. I know what I'm talking about."

I knew Ethan was referring to his own demons who, for the most part, had failed to hold him captive. "I've unloaded my misery. Your turn now."

Ethan shook his head. "No. My troubles are a trip on a curb compared to what happened to you. I'll tell you, but not today. Let's just focus on you."

I reached up and brushed the hair back from his forehead. "You're a good man, Ethan Moore. Raven is a lucky little girl to have you as her daddy."

"Thank you," he said as he leaned forward and kissed me lightly on the lips. "I think you're an incredibly brave woman for dealing with this tragedy alone. You don't have to go through this by yourself, though. I can be your sounding board whenever you need me."

"I know, and I really appreciate it. I'm still in shock about everything. I think the alcohol is keeping it from sinking in."

"That's probably a good thing."

I was definitely past the buzzed stage and knew I'd regret it later, but I planned to keep drinking until I was completely numb. I knew that when I absorbed everything that I learned today, I'd fall apart.

I opened the bottle of Patrón and Ethan warned, "Um, are you sure you want to do that? You've already had lots of whiskey."

"What are you? My keeper?" I teased affectionately. "You sound like a responsible adult. Bor--ing! You're drinking it, too, doc."

I poured generously into two new plastic cups and handed him one. I raised my glass. "Here's to justice," I declared vehemently.

"To justice," Ethan echoed quietly. His eyes were focused in the distance. I got the impression that Ethan did not share my view of justice as the great emancipator.

****

We passed out in our chairs just after sunset. Ethan woke up around 12:30, walked me to the truck and then gathered our things. Luckily, it was a cloudless night, so the moonlight and Ethan's flashlight were adequate sources to guide us along the wooded path.

At my cabin, I vaguely remember Ethan carrying me upstairs, removing my shoes and putting me under the covers. I was a drunken mess, but I suppose Hatcher's revelations entitled me to a night of irresponsible behavior.

Little did I know that my inebriated slumber would be the last peaceful night I would experience for a very long time.

MARY CLAIRE

<u>Tuesday, July 29th.</u> Three days had passed since Andrew received the envelope that sent him into a tirade. Andrew had been exceedingly apologetic about his explosive behavior, but he refused to discuss the package. If I brought it up, he became sullen and barely civil. After two attempts, I stopped trying to get him to confide in me.

I decided that it would help me to attend clinic, even though I couldn't participate. I wanted to see the girls, and I was worried about Callie. I had texted and called a few times, but she had avoided me simply responding once that she was busy with a work deadline. I knew better. That was an excuse to avoid talking about whatever was bothering her, and I was confident that it concerned Jake.

As I drove into the club, Jake was walking across the parking lot. He met me at my car as I got out. "What the hell is this?" He pointed to my car.

"I've always loved a black Jaguar, and Andrew brought it home last night and said it was all mine." Jake rolled his eyes. "Jake, it's just his way of apologizing."

"You've got to be kidding. Mary Claire, that's all about him trying to ease his guilty conscience and nothing more."

"Now, Jake, everybody has his or her own way of saying 'I'm sorry'. This car is quite a big apology. I think it's a turning point."

Jake stopped in his tracks and turned to me. "So, you're going to once again forgive him?" I looked down at my feet and remained silent. Jake gazed into the distance and declared, "Just forget it. If you want to be stupid, then it's your choice. From now on though, leave me out of it."

He stormed off. I remained planted where I stood, like a scolded child, head hung in shame.

There I stayed until I heard a familiar voice behind me. "Mary Claire! What the hell happened to you?"

Alex stood in front of me eyeing my splint, bruises and swollen eyes.

I laughed uneasily. "I'm so clumsy. I tripped and fell down the stairs."

"Oh, you poor thing." Alex pointed to the splint on my left arm. "How bad is it?"

"Distal radius fracture. The doctor was able to move it back into the right place without surgery, but it was excruciatingly painful. Once the swelling goes down, they'll put on a cast."

"I'm so sorry."

"Thank you. I'm just going to watch today. I thought it would do me good to get out of the house."

We started walking toward the court, and Alex commented casually. "Damn, Mary Claire, you look like somebody beat the shit out of you. Are your stairs carpeted?"

"Unfortunately, no. That's why I look like a well-worn punching bag." I laughed. "Do you think I should leave? Maybe I look so bad that I'll be too much of a distraction," I worried aloud.

"Don't be silly. You're fine." We continued walking, and then Alex reflected, "I bet Callie shit a brick when you told her. I'm assuming you're out for these last two matches."

I answered slowly. "I'm definitely out for the rest of the season, but Callie doesn't know yet."

"What! You're going to catch her totally off guard today."

"I've tried to tell her," I defended myself. "She hasn't been available the past few days. Apparently, she has some big deadline. She might not even be at clinic today."

I was wrong. Alex and I rounded the corner and collided with Callie, who was walking briskly toward the court but had her head turned toward the clubhouse as she finished a conversation with someone. Her shoulder slammed into my chest. I gasped in pain.

Callie stopped abruptly and apologized as she turned to see whom she injured. "Oh my God, Mary Claire. What happened to you?"

As I recounted my mishap with a flight of stairs, we arrived at the court, and I had to go through the whole process again. The ladies were so kind and concerned. I was touched. "I didn't mean to disrupt clinic. I just wanted to get out of the house for a bit."

Alex looked around. "Well, since Jake isn't here yet, I have something I wanted to discuss with y'all. Girls, you know how much I despise that MKat, but really I think we need to cook a few meals and take to her. Her husband's been laid up for weeks with some mysterious illness, and now she's recovering from a snake bite. It's plain poor form not to help out."

I spoke up. "I agree, Alex. But I called her last week and told her I wanted to bring her a pan of lasagna, and she refused my offer. Quite frankly, she was belligerent. I felt as if I had somehow offended her."

Alex shook her head and slapped her racquet against the bench. "I'm telling you, something's off here. She's hiding something."

"Oh, Alex," I scolded gently, "you always think the worst of her. I think she has too much pride to accept help. I know it's silly."

"What's silly?" Jake asked as he walked up behind Mary Claire. Callie bristled noticeably and began rummaging through her tennis bag.

"We were just discussing the idea of doing something for Molly Katherine, but she adamantly objects to any help. Her husband is ill, and then there's the unfortunate incident with the snakes. Alex is right. We need to do something. I suggest we all make some dishes, take them to her house, and if she won't answer the door, we can leave them on her porch."

"You can count me out," Dallas said. "Don't be surprised if she greets you with a loaded shotgun. That woman is not stable." She trotted to the other court to retrieve a few stray practice balls.

"You oughta know," Alex muttered when Dallas was out of hearing range.

"Alex!" I reprimanded in a harsh whisper.

"Hey, don't get me wrong. I like Dallas. She's the best tennis partner I've ever had, but I wouldn't say she was intimately familiar with stability." Alex put her arm around me. "Not everyone can claim to a be a pillar of strength and serenity like you, Mary Claire." She lightly squeezed my arm, and I grimaced.

"I'm sorry. Did I hurt you? I didn't realize your upper arm was injured, as well."

"I'm fine, dear," I reassured Alex. "I'm sore all over."

"Well, I hope your husband is doting on you," Katlin commented. "You certainly deserve TLC right now."

Jake jumped into the conversation. "Oh, he's definitely treating her like a queen. He bought her a new convertible, black Jag to compensate for her misfortune." His tone dripped with sarcasm.

"You're just jealous, Jake," Amy teased. "I bet Olivia would buy you any toy you wanted. She's loaded and hot for you. She said she called you several times the other night. She must have had too many cocktails when she called, because she's never chased a man, that is until you."

Jake blushed and glanced at Callie, whose expression was a mixture of anger and pain. Unfortunately, Amy innocently added fuel to the fire. "Why, Jake, you're blushing like a school girl. I can't wait to tell Olivia. She does know how to make a man blush."

Jake ignored her and took control, though he spoke snippily. "You ladies can do your gossiping later. It's time for clinic. You have two matches left, and now you've lost a key player. I know you want to go to state. Hopefully your last two matches aren't against strong teams. Callie, this is your team, and you can do whatever you want, but I would recommend that Dallas play the 4.0 spot with you, Katlin play the 3.5 spot with Alex, and Amy and Kelly finish the season at 3.0. Even if Molly Katherine is available to play this week, she'll be rusty."

Katlin looked as if she wanted to protest, but Jake's dictatorial approach seemed to table her objections. Callie, with an equally no nonsense tone, affirmed Jake's recommendations. "I agree. Everybody's here, so let's get started on this new lineup."

I watched the clinic, studying the new pairings, and was impressed. I thought they would be fine, and I would definitely be their cheerleader on Friday.

As everyone packed up to go, Alex said, "Okay. Tell you what, Mary Claire. I know where MKat lives. I had to pick her up once for a match. Meet me here tomorrow at 11:30, and we can take everything to her. You do your lasagna and I'll do my chicken tetrazzini and Greek salad."

"I'll do some yeast rolls, too," I added.

"Can I just give y'all some money toward expenses?" Callie asked from the depths of her bag. "I can't make it tomorrow, but I'm happy to contribute."

"Don't worry about it, Callie. We've got it covered. Just putting up with this crazy group is contribution enough," Alex answered.

She grinned as she started to leave. "Y'all aren't that bad."

As she was walking away, Jake called after her. "Callie, can I talk to you for a minute?"

Without turning back she answered blandly, "No, I'm late for an appointment."

Jake and Mary Claire exchanged a concerned look. "Jake," Mary Claire began.

Jake held up his hand. "See you ladies later."

We both watched Jake walk away. "What just happened here?" Alex asked.

"Callie, wrecking the best thing that's ever happened to her," I answered sadly.

"Not sure I follow you."

"Trust me. You don't want to know. I'll see you tomorrow at 11:30."

"Okay," Alex muttered as I left the court. "Mary Claire, are you sure you want to do this? You're injured. We should be bringing you food."

"I'm good, Alex. Don't worry about me, dear. I'll see you tomorrow."

ALEX

The next day Mary Claire was already at the club when I drove up at 11:28 am. I had never known her to be late, frazzled, off-center, or the least bit out of sorts. Every hair was always in place. The woman was unnaturally perfect, even with her broken arm and spattering of bruises.

We transferred her food to my car and headed toward MKat's house. As I turned into the Harriman's drive, Mary Claire asked, "Are you sure you have the right house?"

"Absolutely. Why do you ask?"

"I think I attended a Christmas party at this house last year. It was hosted by one of my husband's law partners."

I put the car in park and grabbed my tray of food. "Maybe they sold it to MKat and poor Edward since then."

Mary Claire remained skeptical. "I think I would have known if they sold their house."

"Well, I am 100% sure this is MKat's house because I was so impressed by the landscaping. My daughter was with me, and we both commented on how much we liked her front entrance and that we had never seen a design quite like it."

"Hm," was the only response Mary Claire could muster.

Food in hand, we made our way up the stone walkway to the beautiful front entrance and rang the bell. An attractive, well dressed woman in her mid forties answered the door. "Mary Claire Jameson?" she greeted with surprise.

"Hello, Ariana, how are you?"

"I'm fine." Ariana looked at me quizzically. Mary Claire recovered. "Where are my manners? Ariana, this is my friend, Alex Anderson."

"Nice to meet you, Alex. Y'all please come in, get out of this dreadful heat."

"Oh no, Ariana. We aren't staying. I'm embarrassed, but we were taking food to a sick friend, and Alex was convinced that this was her house."

Ariana smiled condescendingly at me, the deranged lunatic. "No, we've lived here for over twelve years now."

I shook my head. "I know you think I'm crazy, but I swear I picked her up here not two months ago for a tennis match. Her name is

MKat, I mean Molly Katherine Harriman, and her husband is Edward Harriman. Do you know them?"

"No," Ariana answered with a shake of her head.

"I'm sorry we troubled you, dear," Mary Claire answered. "We'll be going now."

"Yes, so sorry. Nice to meet you."

Ariana waved goodbye and wished us luck as we took the walk of shame to my car. I started the car and turned to Mary Claire. "I swear to you that I am 100% sure that Avery and I picked MKat up here."

"Dear, I know you're confident, but how could she have possibly come out of a house occupied by another family."

I clapped my hands rapidly. "That's it!"

"What ever do you mean?"

"I picked her up AT this house, but MKat didn't come OUT OF the house. She was standing on the front porch when we drove up."

"Why would she be standing in front of a house that's not hers? She probably lives close by and her house is similar to this one. What will we do with all this food?"

"Mary Claire!" I was offended by her lack of faith in me. "I am not crazy! This is where I picked her up. We are taking this food to her and proving that I am not insane." I snapped a picture of the house and texted it to Avery with the caption "do you recognize this house".

"First things first. I have texted Avery to see if she can corroborate my story. Secondly, I remember MKat saying that poor Edward had a high profile position at a local bank...which one was it now?" I repeatedly slapped my forehead with the palm of my hand until the name jarred loose. "Bryant Bank, that's it."

I did a web search, found the number to the bank, and called on my cell. "Hi," I began when someone answered. "I'm trying to locate one of your managers, Edward Harriman."

"Mr. Harriman has been out of the office due to illness for several weeks now. Can I transfer you to his supervisor, Mr. Reynolds?"

"That would be great, thanks."

"One moment, please."

In less than one minute, a deep voice came through the speaker. "Jack Reynolds, here. How can I help you?"

"Hello, Mr. Reynolds. My name is Alex Anderson. Edward Harriman's wife plays on a tennis team with me. We understand that Mr. Harriman has been ill for several weeks, and recently Mrs. Harriman suffered an accident. We're trying to take food to them, but apparently we don't have the correct address. We were wondering if you could provide it so we could deliver this food."

"Mrs. Harriman is ill now as well?" Mr. Reynolds asked with concern. "No wonder she hasn't been returning my calls lately. We've been extremely worried about Edward. Yes, by all means, let me give you the address. Just give me a moment to pull up Edward's personnel file. Ah, here it is." I repeated the address aloud so Mary Claire could write it down. "Ms. Anderson, can you do me a favor?"

"If I can."

"Would you please call me after your visit and let me know how Edward's doing? I don't get much feedback from Molly Katherine, and it's not like Edward not to call. I haven't heard from him personally in about two months. He's been out for eleven weeks, and he will have exhausted all sick and vacation leave in one week. He's the most responsible employee I've ever managed. Everybody here likes him and is concerned."

"Of course. I'll be happy to call you. Shall I call the main number and ask for you?"

"You can, but let me give you my cell number as well."

I repeated the number to make sure I had it right. "I'll call you back shortly, Mr. Reynolds."

Just as I hung up, Avery's text tone pinged. I read it and handed it to Mary Claire. "See this?"

Mary Claire read aloud.

Hey Mom. Yes, that's the great house where we picked up your snotty tennis friend. Why do you ask?

Mary Claire handed me the phone. Her expression oozed confusion. I quickly texted my response:

Long story. Will explain later. Love you.

"This gets weirder by the minute." I entered MKat's correct address into my GPS and started the car. "And, I don't think we're even close to the truth yet." Mary Claire gave me an uncomfortable smile.

Ten minutes later, we pulled into the driveway of a nice, but small home. All the houses on the street were of similar size -- all well kept and modest.   We went to the door and rang the bell.   No one answered. I rang the doorbell three more times in rapid succession.

"Alex!" Mary Claire reprimanded. "Don't be so pushy. They may be napping, and we shouldn't disturb them. Let's leave the food here on the porch. We can call and leave her a message."

I stuck my face against the sidelight and saw MKat scurry like a frightened mouse down a hallway. I didn't imagine it; the bandage across her face stood out like Rudolph's nose.

"No way. MKat is here and awake. I just saw her running to hide. I'm going to go around back and take a peek in the windows."

"Have you lost your mind, Alex!" I turned and stared at Mary Claire.   She had actually raised her voice.   What happened to that absurdly calm and unruffled demeanor? Now her voice was frantic, and pitchy. "You'll be trespassing. Molly Katherine Harriman is bold enough to have you arrested if she doesn't want you here."

How amusing. Mary Claire unraveling. Wish I had this on video. "Relax. You can stay right here, and I will do the dirty work. MKat needs to explain herself. There's no reason for her to hide.   It's ridiculous. And rude."

"Fine. I'll go wait in the car. It wouldn't do for me to be involved in a breaking and entering scandal with my husband being a high profile attorney."

"Okay, prissy pants. I'll be back in a flash."

MARY CLAIRE

I returned to the car, frankly quite miffed with Alex. She had no business prying into the Harriman's affairs like a common peeping Tom. My agitation brewed for five minutes, but when I saw Alex running to the car, wild eyed, I half expected Molly Katherine to be chasing her with a shotgun, just as Dallas predicted at clinic yesterday.

Alex got in the car and locked the doors with great difficulty since her hands were shaking uncontrollably. "Alex, what's wrong?" She ignored me, started the car, drove down the street no more than five hundred yards and stopped.

"Where's my phone?" she asked as she dug through her purse.

"It's right here." I picked it up where it sat in the console tray and handed it to her. She yanked it from my hand and started dialing. "Alex, what happened?"

She ignored me. "Mr. Reynolds? Yes, this is Alex Anderson. We spoke about a half hour ago regarding the Harrimans. You need to come over to their house right now. It's an emergency. Thank you." She covered her face with her hands and released a frantic sigh as she slumped down in the driver's seat.

"Alex, talk to me," I demanded. "What happened back there?"

Alex looked at me as if registering my presence for the first time since she went to the back of the Harriman house. "I wish we had left. You were right. I should have minded my own business." She covered her face again. "I'll never be able to get that image out of my head."

"Alex, dear, just take it slowly and start from the beginning. What happened when you went into the backyard?"

"Dallas was right. MKat is totally unstable but far worse than we imagined." She took a deep breath. "When I went around back, I looked into the first set of windows. It was just the kitchen, and no one was there. Then there was a small deck with a grill, but if you walked onto the deck you could look through the back door and the windows and see the dining room and family room. Empty. The last set of windows ran across another deck, and there was a door with a screen. All the windows were open as well as the back door. Who opens their windows in this humidity? Anyway, I stepped onto the deck and immediately the foulest odor I've ever smelled hit me. I swear it could knock you off your feet. I knew something bad was about to happen, but I looked into the screen and saw poor Edward propped up in the bed. Mary Claire, he's dead."

"Dead! How can you be sure? He probably looks dead because he's sick."

Alex shook her head. "I tell you that was a dead body, and I assume it was Edward. I've watched enough CSI and NCIS shows to know what a dead body looks and smells like. The question is did he die of natural causes or did she kill him."

"Oh, Alex, you've obviously let your imagination get the best of you. What about Molly Katherine? Did you see her? Did she see you?"

"No, but she had to know someone was there. I don't think she ever knew who it was."

"Why did you call that Reynolds man?"

"Because he knows Edward and MKat, and he wanted to know their condition. I guess I really need to call the police."

I grabbed Alex's arm. "If the police are involved, I can't be seen here."

"But why? You haven't done anything wrong. You stayed in the car. You're an innocent bystander -- a do-gooder trying to bring a meal to a sick friend."

"Alex," I begged, "you don't understand the ramifications of my presence here if media or the authorities are involved. My sole purpose as Andrew Jameson's wife is to support him and his image as an attorney beyond reproach. My presence here would cast a shadow on that image, and he would be so disappointed in me. That cannot happen."

"That's ridiculous. I need you here as my friend, Mary Claire. I need your support. You are the rock of our group. You want to leave me to face this alone?"

"As you said, we have done nothing wrong, and you will have Mr. Reynolds."

"How can you be so cold?"

"I'm not being cold. I'm being a realist. You can't mention that I was here with you. You have to say you came alone. Please, I'm begging you. I wouldn't ask if it weren't necessary. It may not be unreasonable to say it is a matter of life and death."

Alex rolled her eyes. "I think you are being a bit overly dramatic here, Mary Claire, but fine. Go. Leave your food, and I'll tell everyone that I was the delivery person that came alone."

Alex started dialing again. "Who are you calling?"

"The police," she responded coldly. "Go ahead. Start walking."

I grabbed my purse and started walking toward downtown Homewood which I knew was only a few blocks away. I could grab a coffee at O'Henry's and take a cab home. With each step, I felt myself dissolve in my bubbling vat of compromise.

ALEX

I watched my rearview mirror hoping that either the police or Edward's boss would arrive soon. If MKat had murdered her husband, I didn't want her to get away, but I wasn't about to go back to that house alone.

Finally a car parked along the street in front of the house, and I backed up. I met the man in the car at the edge of the driveway and extended my hand. "I take it you're Jack Reynolds," I said as we shook hands.

"Yes, and you are Alex..Anderson, right?"

"Yes, and I'm sorry to bother you. After what I saw, I panicked, and you were the first person to come to mind."

He smiled. "It's not a problem. Tell me what you saw."

"Okay. I called the police, but let me catch you up to speed."

"The police? Is there some crime to report?"

"I'm not sure." I disclosed the details of my snooping.

He considered my words for a few minutes before commenting. "I hope you're wrong, but honestly Molly Katherine has been so evasive since Edward fell ill. But why would she lie and keep his dead body here unless she was a total lunatic?"

I chuckled. "Well, many of us think she isn't playing with a full deck."

He grinned. "I hear you. I wasn't around Molly Katherine often -- just Christmas parties -- but if there were ever a man that was henpecked, it was Edward Harriman. He was the most honorable man I ever worked with, but it was obvious that to his wife, nothing he ever did measured up. Edward was always kind, but there was such a sadness in his eyes."

"You keep saying 'was'. I take it you think Edward really is dead."

"I wouldn't be surprised. It would explain a lot."

About that time a police car arrived. The policeman introduced himself as Officer Bragg. He was young, but had an experienced, confident manner. Mr. Reynolds and I explained the facts as we knew them. Since I knew Mrs. Harriman and he knew Mr. Harriman, Officer Bragg asked us to accompany him to the house. At the front door, we rang the bell and called out to MKat, but no one answered. Officer Bragg identified himself as a policeman to compel her to answer, but there was no response.

We went around back and entered the house through the unlocked screened door. "Oh dear Lord!" Jack Reynolds exclaimed as he saw what was clearly the long deceased corpse of Edward Harriman. At that moment, MKat stormed out of a closet screaming "you bitch, you bitch" while waving a saber and charging straight toward me. Officer Bragg managed to tackle her before she decapitated me. Jack Reynolds helped by yanking my frozen frame out of the way.

Thirty minutes later, the coroner was hauling away poor Edward's decomposing body, and Officer Bragg was carting MKat away, hopefully to a padded cell.

Mr. Reynolds and I stood by our cars watching the remnants of the Harriman family vanish.

"Ms. Anderson," Jack said. "I think we deserve a little time to process this event. Can I buy you a cup of coffee? O'Henry's is just a few blocks away."

I hesitated only briefly. "Sounds like a good idea. I'll meet you there."

As I slid my car into a space on 18th Street, I saw Mary Claire slipping into a cab in front of O'Henry's. My blood curdled a bit at the sight. Then I saw Jack waving at me. I put Mary Claire out of my mind, for the moment anyway.

CALLIE

I shouldn't have left clinic yesterday without talking to Mary Claire. Here it was Wednesday night, and I hadn't bothered to see how she was doing. I've been in such a foul mood since Jake abandoned me on Saturday night, but that's no excuse for being a lame friend.

I picked up the phone and called her. "How are you feeling, Mary Claire?" I asked when she answered on the fourth ring. "I didn't wake you, did I?"

"It's only 7:15 in the evening, Callie. I'm not so old that I have to go to bed with the sun." Her tone was uncharacteristically defensive.

"Whoa, now, no need to get an attitude, girl," I explained. "I just thought you'd be on pain killers and might be sleeping more than usual."

She sighed. "I'm sorry. It's been an exceptionally bad day. Upon reflection, I've decided that I really don't like the way I handled a horrible situation today."

"It's okay. However, I can't imagine you being anything other than perfectly diplomatic. So what happened today?"

I poured myself a much needed glass of wine as she told me the story of her trip with Alex to deliver food to MKat. "That's insane. So you haven't talked to Alex to find out if poor Edward really is dead?"

"No, and I'm sure she won't reach out to me. She was obviously upset that I left her, and in retrospect, I don't blame her." Mary Claire's tone was regretful.

I proceeded warily. "I'm sure Alex will get over it, but I'm not sure I understand why you felt your husband would be mad over your innocent involvement in this situation."

A prolonged silence ensued. Finally, she began to speak, clearly choosing her words carefully. "I think I overreacted. Recently, Andrew has been on edge, easily agitated. He received some mail over the weekend that was obviously placed in the box rather than sent through the postal service, and it upset him deeply. In all our years together, I've never seen him so unglued. He refuses to discuss this envelope with me, and he has been...difficult...since he received it." She paused and added. "Callie, I'd appreciate it if that information stayed between us."

"Of course," I reassured her.

"Since I don't know the source of his discontent, I feared that my association with a potential scandal at the Harriman home might send him further over the edge."

I thought "feared" was an interesting choice of words, but I didn't pursue it. Mary Claire sounded as if she were nervous. I didn't want to add to her stress. "I'll text Alex to see how things went. If I know anything, I'll call you back."

"Okay, but Callie, before you go, I wanted to ask you about your date with Jake. How did it go?"

I stiffened, but decided to be honest. I needed a confidant. "Honestly, it was great. We had a great night out -- a fabulous dinner and equally fabulous conversation. When he took me home, we both admitted feelings, and things got...steamy. And I mean that in a good way. Things were escalating, but his phone kept ringing. He ignored it but finally decided he should check because several texts came through after he ignored the calls. Jake said it was an emergency and bolted. I told him I'd go with him, but he said that I couldn't. There was no doubt that he left very angry about the interruption, but I felt completely rejected. He hasn't texted or called since, and he seemed so angry yesterday at clinic. Until clinic, I had felt conflicted -- feeling like he didn't trust me on one hand and feeling like I needed to trust and respect him on the other. At clinic, though, it all became clear. I know who called him and why I couldn't go with him to his 'emergency'."

"You do?" Mary Claire sounded concerned. "Who called?"

"Didn't you hear Amy talking about how that Olivia Dunn woman had called him repeatedly over the weekend?" The line fell silent. "Hello? Are you still there?"

"Yes, I'm here," she answered slowly. "Callie, what time did Jake receive these calls?"

"I don't know, exactly, but it was definitely after midnight." I thought that was a strange question. "Why do you ask?"

"I think you're wrong. If Jake were upset, then that suggests that there truly was an emergency. Olivia lives in Atlanta, so how could Jake help when he's over two hours away?"

"Maybe the emergency was that she was camped out at his house, and he wanted to go be with her."

"Now that comment is ridiculously stupid. He wouldn't act mad if he were deserting you to go be with another woman. And he was still mad yesterday. Callie, Jake was very snippy with me. I think there's more to it. I think you're jumping to conclusions. Just because Amy mentioned that this woman had called him doesn't mean that his emergency had anything to do with her. You need to talk to him."

Through a sigh I admitted, "I really don't know how. Everything feels awkward now. It's like there's a bigger wall up than before. It's so weird."

"You need to address this head on," she advised. "Don't call him, Callie. Go see him and talk to him face to face. I'm telling you Jake's a good guy. If he left your date unexpectedly, then it had to be a true emergency that he could not avoid. Something has him upset right now. If you don't follow up with him, you'll regret it."

"I don't know, Mary Claire."

"Well, I do," she argued. "Jake deserves a second chance. He's certainly extended the same courtesy to you."

There was that snippy tone again, but she was right. Jake had been more than patient with me. I should have more faith in him. And us. "You're right, as always. I'll take your advice and let you know how it goes."

I immediately called Alex but didn't hear back before I fell asleep. On Thursday morning, I found a text from her sent at 11:45 pm last night.

> Hi Callie. Just picked up your voicemail. Didn't want to call since so late. The police hauled MKat to the psych ward after we discovered Edward's rotting corpse in her house. Don't know if she killed him or what. I think you can count her out for the duration. I'm still in shock. See you Friday.

Unbelievable. Could MKat have murdered her husband? As awful as the woman was, I didn't think she was a killer. Crazy. I called the club to see if Jake had any breaks in his schedule. He was open from 10-10:30, so I decided I would go to his teaching court around 9:55 to chat with him during his break. I was ridiculously nervous.

As I walked up to his court right at ten, he and his student were collecting balls. When he saw me, he was clearly surprised. "Hey, what are you doing here?"

I smiled. "They said you had a break at ten, so I was wondering if you could spare a few minutes to talk."

"Sure. Just a sec."

Jake thanked his student and then motioned for me to join him on the bench. Before I could say anything, Jake said, "I'm sorry about the other night. The last thing I wanted to do was leave you, especially at that moment."

"Wasn't exactly a gratifying departure for me either," I admitted. "You said you were going to call me Sunday afternoon and you never did. It's Thursday, and I still haven't heard from you. I'm confused, Jake."

"I'm sorry. I've been so angry about that emergency. The friend that it involves is being an idiot. It's a frustrating situation, and honestly, I've been struggling with the right course of action. But I think I know how to handle it all now." Jake tucked some stray hair behind my ear and smiled. "Sorry I shut you out."

I grabbed his hand. "It's okay, but if we're really going to have a relationship, we can't shut each other out. We've got to be able to lean on each other in the bad times."

"Callie Conrad," Jake spoke through a grin, "Listen to you sounding all grown-up and dare I say -- committed."

I punched him. "Don't make fun of me, Lenaghan. You know it's hard for me to go down this road."

He squeezed my hand. "I'm not making fun of you, I promise. It makes me happy to hear you talk about our relationship. Sorry the commencement ceremony was so rudely interrupted."

"Me, too. Can you tell me what the emergency was?" He squirmed. "I'm not trying to pry. It just seems like a bad start for us that you don't feel you can trust me with whatever happened. Jake, I can't imagine what trouble could possibly require you to flee at such a pivotal moment."

"You have to trust me. My friend swore me to secrecy long ago. She doesn't want her situation discussed with anyone. I totally disagree with her decision, but I have to honor that confidence."

"So this emergency is a recurring situation?"

He nodded. "It's happened before, but I have taken myself out of the equation. I've told my friend that I will keep her confidence but can no longer support her since I think she's being foolish."

Jake ran his fingers through his hair and leaned back on the bench. "It's not a matter of trust, Callie. I'd really like to tell you, but I know it would upset you, and you can't do anything about the situation. Just trust me to handle it on my own. Please."

start here

"I'm not sure I'm okay with that, but I'll try to respect your wishes since this is a situation that started before I came into the picture. But from now on, no secrets okay?"

"No secrets," he promised and pecked my lips.

"Answer one question, please."

"If I can," he responded.

"Is this friend a former girlfriend? Because, honestly, that would make me totally uncomfortable."

Jake laughed. "No, not a chance."

"Okay. Let's just move forward. On another note, I suppose it's a good thing that you wrote off MKat for tomorrow's lineup."

"Why do you say that?"

After I divulged the details of the Harriman scandal, Jake reflected, "I'm blown away. Do you think she killed him? He was such a nice man, but like I told you before, it was obvious that she wore the pants in the family. Maybe he crossed her somehow and she snapped."

I shook my head. "I don't know. I never liked the woman, but it's hard for me to see her as a murderer."

"Don't be naive, honey. Good people will go down dark paths to protect what's important to them."

"My, my, aren't you sinister?" I teased.

"Nope. Just honest," Jake said as he rubbed my arm. "Let me go grab those stray balls over there, and I'll walk you to your car."

As I stood by the railing where he left his keys and cell, I heard the ping of a text and instinctively looked down. I caught the name Olivia Dunn and couldn't stop myself from reading the text:

I need to talk to you. Possibly concerns a matter of life or death.

I turned and sprinted to my car. I could hear Jake calling after me as I peeled out of the parking lot.

****

The next day our match was in Gardendale, which is quite a drive from The Heights. Mary Claire texted that she was coming to be our cheerleader and offered to pick me up in her new black Jaguar. I had not called her back regarding my conversations with Alex and Jake, so I knew she was on a fishing expedition. But I felt defeated and needed a sounding board.

I was waiting on the front porch when she pulled up in my driveway. "This is the sexiest car," I gushed as I got into the Jag. "You must have been a very good girl to earn this ride. Your Lexus was quite nice and not very old if memory serves me."

The prim and proper Mary Claire cast aside any speculations of impropriety. "I can assure you that this car was not payment for any kinky sexual favors."

"Did I say that?" I defended innocently.

"Not explicitly, but you implied it. Did you ever talk to Alex?"

"Yes, just by text. Apparently MKat was taken to the psych ward. Edward is dead, but she didn't know cause of death. And she didn't mention you, so I don't know if that's a good thing or bad thing."

"We'll soon find out. I can't believe he's dead and that she stayed in that house with him for who knows how long."

"I know. It's beyond strange. The woman spent the entire season lamenting her ailing husband when more than likely he'd been dead the whole time." We drove in silence for a few minutes, each lost in thought.

"Callie, did you set things straight with Jake?"

"Well, yes, and no."

"What?"

I shared the details of my visit to the club up until I saw the text. "So we talked everything out. All the awkwardness evaporated, and we were back on track. Then I read a text from Olivia Dunn."

"You went through Jake's phone?" The usually calm, cool, and collected Mary Claire could not disguise her shock and disgust. "That's a dreadful invasion of privacy."

"Oh, relax, Pollyanna. I didn't go trolling through his phone. His cell was right beside me when her text came in, and I glanced down and saw what it said. It was an innocent breach of etiquette, I promise."

"So what was so upsetting about the text?"

"It said that she needed to talk to him about a matter of life and death."

"That's odd. What could she possibly be talking about?" Mary Claire pondered.

"Oh, come on. Don't be so naive. Think about it. Several weeks ago they have a blind date, and Amy goes on and on about how smitten Olivia is with him. Then the woman shows up unannounced in Birmingham, comes to the club and apparently makes it very clear that she is all his at any time. At some point they took a roll in the hay, and she's pregnant." I cracked my knuckles and looked out the window.

"That is ridiculous. I told you that the only reason Jake agreed to that blind date was to make you jealous. He knew Amy would babble on about it at clinic. He thought it might make you admit your feelings for him."

"Even if that's true, Mary Claire, Olivia Dunn is great looking, and no normal guy would pass that up if it's offered to him. Not even Jake."

We had arrived in the parking lot of the Gardendale Country Club. Mary Claire parked her Jag and turned to me. "I'm beginning to think that you don't deserve him."

"Excuse me, I.."

"Don't interrupt me, Callie Conrad." Mary Claire reminded me of my mother the time I snuck out of the house and found her waiting in the garage when I pulled in at 4 am. Indignant tone, wild eyes, and lots of gesticulation. "I have told you repeatedly what a kind, loyal gentleman he is. He always does the right thing. Katlin Hamilton tried to seduce him, and he passed, and that was before he knew you. That man has patiently waited for you to decide if you wanted to pursue a relationship with him, and now at the first little hiccup you think the absolute worst of him. The man is the closest thing to a living saint that I've ever known. You should be ashamed of yourself."

Mary Claire exited the car and slammed the door. I had never seen her so animated and openly hostile. This sudden character change hit me the wrong way. I got out of the car and grabbed my tennis bag. "What in the hell has crawled up your ass? You've been nothing but cranky and combative since you broke your arm. And what makes you such an expert on the chastity and perfection of Jake Lenaghan? You've always had him on a pedestal. What has he done for you that is so life-changing?"

"More than you will ever understand." Suddenly, she was steady and eerily serious. "Callie, you've been my friend for a long time now, but you know very little about me. All the signs are in front of you, and you constantly miss them. I don't know if you miss them because you're not as smart as I thought or because you're self-absorbed."

"Well, aren't you full of kindness today," I lashed out sarcastically. "I think I'll find a ride home with someone a little less caustic."

"That's mature," she snapped.

"Feisty is not attractive on you," I jabbed as I walked away.

****

We won the match 2-1. As expected, Kelly and Amy lost the 3.0 court badly. I was so distracted by my altercation with Mary Claire that I was definitely the weaker player on the court. But to be honest with myself, I think that Dallas would run circles around me even on my best day. She plays with an intensity that is so intimidating that it visibly disturbs her opponents. Communication is key in doubles, but Dallas gives and requires none. She asked me if I wanted the deuce or ad side before we started, and that was it until she said "great match" as she left the court. Her focus and ability to read the ball were phenomenal. It was humbling to be her partner.

We were done so quickly I was able to watch the last two sets of the 3.5 match. Alex and Katlin lost the first set 3-6, but it appeared that they had found their stride. In the second set, they switched sides. Alex took the ad side which is definitely the pressure spot in a deuce game. Alex played with a calmness that soothed Katlin, who was clearly feeling nervous about playing up. But Katlin surprised me. Her game elevated with a partner that encouraged rather than belittled her. Katlin seemed to follow Alex's lead with the instinct of a child who trusts and depends upon her mother.

They won the second set 6-4 and were off to the ten point tiebreak. Alex ignited Katlin's confidence after she ripped a shot down the line on an overaggressive poacher. Katlin took the same approach on the next shot, and they were up 2-0. The opponents adopted an overly aggressive strategy and charged the net after every return of serve. Katlin, intimately familiar with lobs at the 3.0 level, dropped three nice, deep lobs over the opponents' heads, and they led 5-0. Alex looked like a proud mama. The other team decided to take a defensive position. Both stood at the baseline for the next few points but were promptly deflated by Alex's drop shots that died two feet over the net. Sufficiently rattled, the opponents crumbled under the pressure of a 1-8 deficit and lost the tiebreak 1-10. Katlin and Alex embraced with joy.

"Congrats, girls," I applauded them as they left the court. "You saved the day. We got the win 2-1."

Katlin was beside herself. "I can't believe I won on a 3.5 court. It's all because of you, Alex."

"Don't sell yourself short, honey," Alex encouraged, "you played great. It's not uncommon for people to play better when they play above their ranking."

"I had so much fun playing with you. I'd forgotten what it's like to have a partner who's nice to you."

Alex hugged her again. "You're a great partner. I'm going to text Avery and tell her how fabulously you did."

"I can't wait to tell Sam about today," Katlin gooed.

"Still in love, I see," Alex commented. "You are going to bring him to Avery's wedding, right? We'd love to meet him."

"Yes, I plan to. I haven't mentioned it to him yet, but I'm sure he'll come with me. Gotta go now. See you later." Katlin ran to the sidelines where Mary Claire had watched. Mary Claire gave her a congratulatory hug, and they walked out together.

I turned to Alex. "Can you give me a ride home?"

"Sure. Did your car break down?"

"No. I rode over with Mary Claire. We had a nasty little spat, and I told her I'd find another way home."

"You're kidding!" Alex exclaimed. "What's up with her lately?"

"You've noticed a personality change too, I see." I felt vindicated.

"She abandoned me the other day when things got messy with MKat."

"If it makes you feel any better, she did tell me that she felt bad about that."

"I'm over it," Alex declared. "She was so worried about what her husband would think. I don't get it. Is she not allowed to be in the limelight? She seemed almost afraid of him. I've never met the man, but after the way she acted the other day, the thought crossed my mind that maybe those bruises aren't from a fall down a flight of stairs."

"Are you suggesting what I think you are?"

Alex shrugged. "The last woman I knew who had injuries like that claimed all her bruises came from a car accident. In reality, her husband was beating the shit out of her on a regular basis. Eventually, she shot him."

"How horrible! Was this someone close to you?"

"She was my mom's second cousin, not close to me, but it was quite the small town scandal. She hid it for years, and I don't understand why."

I remembered a book I edited about spousal abuse. "Because abusers won't let their victims go. They won't tolerate the rejection. Do you really think that's going on with Mary Claire?"

Alex waved the idea away. "It's just a thought that crossed my mind. I don't know her well enough to speculate. She's a bit unnatural though, don't you think?"

"What do you mean by unnatural?"

"She's never judgmental, always perfectly dressed, not a hair out of place, and she's ridiculously calm -- never gets angry or riled up about anything on or off the court. She's like a car in neutral. Nothing ever happens, nothing ever changes. One dimensional. Until the past week."

"Since she broke her arm," I added.

"Right. But like I said, I'm not close to her like you are. If she hasn't confided in you, it's probably just my wicked imagination."

THE SANDMAN CARRIES A PITCHFORK

Match 8 -- August 8, 2014

Named must your fear be before banish it you can.
....Master Yoda

MARY CLAIRE

Tuesday, August 5th. I woke up feeling relaxed and carefree, or at least that's what I thought I was feeling. In reality, I had no experience with those emotions. As a child, my days revolved around pleasing a tyrannical father. When I married Andrew, I thought I had escaped his bonds, but soon realized I had only graduated to a different level of imprisonment. Andrew provided the best of everything, but he was far more controlling and demanding than my father.

Andrew left two days ago for a ten-day business trip abroad, and I had spent those days reflecting upon my sadly subservient life and the realistic view of my remaining days. Now at the age of fifty-five, I decided that I wanted to take my life back. Actually, I never owned it, so it was more of a decision to eliminate my oppression. I was thrilled at the prospect and wanted to celebrate. I knew the perfect way to start.

Fifteen minutes before clinic was to begin, I walked toward Jake's court. The morning was spectacular. Cool, humidity-free mornings are unheard of in the deep South in August, but an unseasonable cold front that moved through the night before had left a pleasant gift. Jake sat slouched on a bench soaking in the sun with his arms and legs spread wide, head back, and eyes closed.

"You look like a beached whale," I called out playfully as I approached. He sat up. "Beautiful day," he commented without enthusiasm.

"Callie's avoiding you, isn't she?"

He nodded. "You know her well, don't you? Has she said anything to you?"

"Maybe." I sat beside him. "What happened?"

"Honestly, I don't know. Communication ceased after I abandoned her at a very inopportune time to deal with an emergency the other night. She showed up here unexpectedly on Thursday. We chatted and cleared the air. Reluctantly she accepted the fact that I couldn't discuss the details of the emergency or who it involved. After we hashed everything out, all was well. She was about to leave, so I told her I'd walk her to her car. I went to get some stray balls first, and the next thing I knew, she was getting in her car. I called and texted immediately, but she wouldn't respond. It makes no sense. She went from 'all is well' to 'mad as hell' in thirty seconds, and I wasn't even around. Maybe she's as crazy as Molly Katherine Harriman."

I laughed. "I don't think she's crazy, just insecure."

Jake shook his head. "The scenario I just described is loony."

"Jake, did you notice anything else after she left?"

He looked puzzled. "I don't follow you."

"You said when she left, you tried to text her. Before you sent her a text, did you notice anything unusual?"

"No, other than I received a weird text just before I sent my text to her." A look of recognition blossomed. "Did Callie see a text from Olivia Dunn?"

I nodded. "It was innocent. She glanced at your phone when the text pinged, and she couldn't avoid seeing it. She told me what it said. You have to admit that was a strange message."

"I can't imagine what it meant other than a desperate attempt to get me to call her. She's texted several times over the last few days. I don't think the woman is used to a man not being interested in her. I wish I had never gone on that blind date."

"Well, that text sent Callie's imagination flying. She's decided that Olivia was your emergency, that you had a one-night stand with her, and the life or death issue relates to the fact that she's pregnant."

"Damn, that woman IS crazy." Jake laughed hysterically. "I can assure you that if Olivia is pregnant, it is 100% impossible for it to be mine."

"Jake, you know I can fix this for you. Once she knows the truth, everything will be okay."

"I don't know. We may be at an impasse."

"Why do you say that?"

"Look how she reacted to that text? Why wouldn't she just ask me about it instead of running off like a sixteen-year-old and ignoring my calls and texts? We had just finished a conversation about trust and no secrets five minutes before the text arrived."

I grabbed Jake's hand and squeezed it. "Callie and I had a little spat Friday before the match. She rode out there with me but told me she'd find another way home. I guess Alex took her home."

"That sounds rather high-schoolish. What did you fight about?"

"A cute boy named Jake," I cooed through a grin and patted his cheek.

"Ha Ha. Seriously, what was the issue?"

"Seriously, it was you. I told her that she was an idiot for thinking you had created a love child with Olivia Dunn. I told her that you were a living saint."

"Oh, please," Jake protested and rolled his eyes.

"Callie asked why I was such an expert on your chastity and chivalry. She asked what you had done for me that put you on a pedestal. I told her more than she would ever understand."

Jake pulled me to him and kissed my forehead. "You're so sweet, but you need to take me off the sainthood list, because I meant what I said the other day."

I furrowed my brow. "Please refresh my memory."

"That I want to be taken out of the equation. You know that I regard you with deep affection, like a big sister, and that I want to protect you at all costs. But the next time you have to call me, I'm not coming alone."

"Ah, my valiant knight, this deeply indebted friend has decided to release you from your charge. I don't plan to ever again give cause for you to ride to my rescue."

Jake wanted to inquire further, but the ladies started arriving. He gave me a look of confusion and I whispered, "I'll elaborate later."

Once everyone was there, I said, "Ladies, I want to make an announcement before you get started. First, way to go on that win in Gardendale. I decided that we deserve to have an end of the season celebration. Saturday night, 7 pm, I'm hosting a party at my house. I'll email directions. Nobody needs to bring a thing. Y'all have a great clinic today, and I'll be around Friday to watch that final match. I have to run now to get a hard cast on this arm. See you Friday. And Jake, you're invited to the party as well."

Everyone seemed excited by the prospect of a celebration. Alex leaned over to Callie and said more loudly than she realized, "I swear I think some alien has taken over her mind. It's like somebody flipped a switch on her personality." Callie nodded.

I smiled and walked away. I had much to do before Andrew returned in eight days.

****

Friday arrived, and I sat courtside at The Heights for our last match of the season. From my vantage point, I could easily see all three matches.

"Are you going to explain yourself?" a voice called from behind me. It was Jake.

"Hello. What are you talking about?"

"At clinic Tuesday, you said you didn't plan to call me again. What does that mean?"

I smiled. "It means that I have decided to take charge of my life. I'm leaving Andrew." That felt so good to say aloud.

Jake could not contain his enthusiasm. "Mary Claire, I'm so proud of you."

"Thank you, Jake. I'm nervous about it, but very excited. Of course, you know I won't be able to play from The Heights after I leave, because I can't afford the membership."

"We'll figure something out," he consoled. "I don't want to burst your bubble here, but you know he'll fight you. He'll make it very difficult for you to leave."

"I know, and that's why I'm moving out Sunday. Andrew is out of town until Tuesday. I'm going to leave him a note. I know that sounds cold and cowardly, but I'm afraid he'll get out of control if I tell him in person."

"I think that's a good plan. Eventually you'll have to face him, but giving him time to absorb the idea is a smart move. Where are you going? You know you can count me in to help you move."

"Thank you. I'm not taking much, and I've already packed my things. I'm going to check into a hotel, so I was wondering if you would mind if I stored my boxes in your garage."

"There's no reason for you to go to a hotel. You and your boxes can camp out at my house until you have some concrete plans."

I started to protest, but Jake stopped me. "It's no trouble. I have a separate guest bedroom and bath, and it's all yours. Plus, I'm not home much. I insist."

"Jake, that's so sweet, but that's quite an imposition, and I need to learn to stand on my own."

"And you will. Look, I admire your bravery here, but I think this transition will be more difficult than you realize. Frankly, I don't think it's safe for you to be alone for a while. And, whatever money you've saved, you need to keep for attorney's fees. I guarantee you the minute he realizes he can't talk you into coming home, he'll cut off all your access to funds." Sweet Jake. He tried to be casual, but his voice conveyed concern.

"Are you sure?"

"Positive. I'll be at your house at ten on Saturday morning and load up your boxes. If you want to walk out the door at the end of the party, you can."

"You really are Saint Jake," I declared as I hugged him. "I appreciate it."

We stood watching the girls warm up for the match. "Look at Dallas. She's so driven."

"Yep. She's better than Callie now, and that's a major compliment. If she were younger, she'd be a dream player for the pro circuit. Her mental prowess is rock solid, and that's the biggest battle from a coach's perspective."

"She's only thirty. That's not too old is it?"

"Thirty!" Jake exclaimed. "I thought she was at least forty."

"Anger and sadness age you quickly. I think I'm the only one who understands her. She's really a sweet girl, but she's very troubled. She's opened up to me a little, but in general, she's very closed off. I'm not giving up on her, though."

"She's a hell of a tennis player. Callie's lucky that she asked to be on this team."

"Speaking of Callie," I began, "have you heard from her?"

"Not a word," he replied, disappointedly. "What about you?"

"No, but I plan to tell her on Sunday. Once the air is cleared, I think all will be fine between us and you as well."

"Look, I want you to tell Callie everything, but only if you're doing it for you. You need to tell her because you're friends, and you need her support. Quite frankly, I'm surprised that she hasn't figured it out by now. I've had a lot of time to think about things. You know how I feel about Callie, but if she can't trust me, it's a huge hurdle. This whole situation makes me wonder if she'll be constantly paranoid and always second guessing me. I don't want a relationship that requires me to report everything I do. Everybody needs some space. Does that make any sense?"

"Yes, it makes more sense than you know. Hang in there. I'm sure it will all work out. Somehow."

"We'll see," he answered. "I have a lesson now, so gotta run. Hope they win. See you tomorrow at ten."

"Okay." As I watched him depart, I ached for him. I really did understand Jake's mindset. Since childhood, everyone in my life demanded that I explain my every move. It was exhausting and eroded my sense of self. I didn't want that for Jake, and Callie was insecure enough to be that demanding. Jake deserved better.

CALLIE

We won our last match -- all three courts. Everybody was visibly excited, except, of course, Dallas. Her celebratory escapades culminated in a high five to me and a "well done" to Alex and Katlin. I did notice that she stopped to chat with Mary Claire before leaving. That relationship still baffled me. Katlin glowed with child-like elation. She and Alex took pictures arm-in-arm and texted them to Avery with the news of their victory. Amy grabbed Jake and had Alex take a picture with Jake standing between Kelly and her. No mystery to whom she'll send that photo, I thought.

As I drove home, I contemplated the satisfaction of having reached my goal. I set out at the beginning of the season to have a team that could go to state, and we did it. Despite the fact that I was thrilled, it seemed anti-climatic since I was at odds with the two people with whom I really wanted to share my excitement.

Once home, I grabbed a water bottle, sat on the sofa and checked my phone for messages. There was a text from Jake:

> Hey Conrad. Well done today. You should be proud of yourself and your team. Congrats.

I responded:

> Thanks, Jake. I'm sorry I've been silent. I miss you. I couldn't get truly excited today because it all seemed a bit empty without sharing it with you and Mary Claire (she's a bit annoyed with me right now, but you probably know that). Please come to the party tomorrow and let's talk.

Ten minutes later, he answered:

> See you tomorrow night :)

I needed to get in the shower, but stretched out on the sofa to rest for a few minutes. I wallowed in all the negativity that Mary Claire unleashed last week. Her declaration that Jake deserved better haunted me. What did she mean that I didn't really know her, that I was blind to all the signs? What signs? I remembered a conversation with Jake where he suggested that I have a talk with her because something was going on with her. Was Alex right? Could the famous Andrew Jameson be abusing his wife? It all seemed preposterous, but I vowed to be more vigilant. My eyes felt heavy, and soon I fell fast asleep.

I awoke in complete darkness -- not a sliver of light to provide even the slightest degree of visibility. It was the unyielding darkness that the blind endure -- void of distinction, infinite. "Why did you put me here?" I screamed in anguish. No one answered. I yelled again, this time a ranting, with the most wretched string of expletives I could fathom -- a classic toddler's tantrum times one thousand. No response.

Exhausted from my tirade, I sat, legs crossed, with my back to the wall, willing my heart to settle into a less frantic pace. I felt the wall behind me. It was slimy and rough. As I rubbed the surface, my hand kept slipping into pockets. It must be formed of stacked stone, I thought. I needed to know more about my surroundings, so I removed my shoe and placed it against the wall to mark my starting point. I stood and paced off my environment while hugging the wall. I counted roughly twenty feet when I hit my shoe marker. My brief journey took me in a circular motion. I was in a freaking well. I don't remember how I got here, but I sure as hell knew who put me here. Jake.

I sat down again with a sigh of defeat, knowing that he would not come for me. No one would. It was up to me to claw my way out. If I went slowly and used the pockets in the rocks as holders for my hands and feet, I could climb out and reenter the world. I realized, though, that I couldn't survive a fall, and it would be so easy to slip on those slimy stones. And only Heaven knew what ghastly creatures resided in those pockets poised to retaliate upon a home invasion. I took off my jacket and rolled it up into a makeshift pillow. It was safer to just lie down. I didn't have the energy for the fight. I knew I would lose. What would be the point in trying? Complacency was less risky.

I woke up in a cold sweat, breathing heavily. I headed to the shower, for I had no desire to resume my slumber.

MARY CLAIRE

<u>Saturday, August 9th</u>. As I pulled wine glasses from the cabinets and set up the food, I hummed a Four Seasons favorite, *Big Girls Don't Cry*. What a great day it had been. Jake had moved all my boxes to his house. It took him three trips, that sweet man. I spent the rest of the day preparing for the party. I smiled as I thought of how appalled my husband would be that I entertained without his prior approval.

Promptly at seven, the doorbell rang, and I was surprised to see that my first guest was the least social of all. Dallas stood awkwardly at my front door holding a bottle of red wine and a box of Publix chicken fingers.

"Hi, Dallas. Come in," I said as I held the door fully open. "You didn't need to bring anything, but that was thoughtful of you." Tentatively, she walked into the foyer and looked around in slow motion. Her expression was indiscernible. "Is something wrong?" I implored as I led her to the kitchen to deposit her wine and chicken.

"No, no," Dallas replied, my voice seemingly pulling her from a trance. "Your house doesn't seem to go with you."

I smiled and said, "Well, this is more my husband's style." I grabbed a serving platter and starting arranging the chicken fingers in symmetrical rows. "He's very particular about things. Through the years I've tended to cater to his decorating desires."

Dallas was studying me. "Clearly you and your husband have very different personalities."

"You could say that. I think I mentioned to you before that he's ten years older than me. I was a few months shy of nineteen when we married. In the beginning of our relationship, I felt his judgment was superior to mine; therefore, I often conceded." I smiled. "When you get married, Dallas, be careful not to concede too much. It tends to become a pattern."

Dallas seemed uncomfortable, so I offered her a glass of wine to change the subject. I asked if she wanted red or white. She picked up the proper glass for white wine and handed it to me with the comment "I prefer white". For a social misfit, Dallas was clearly well versed in proper etiquette. I had observed this on the occasions when we dined together. From the placement of the silverware to signal completion of a meal to placement of the napkin when leaving the table to go to the restroom, Dallas was well trained.

The doorbell rang again, and I excused myself. When I opened the door, a huge poster board colorfully adorned with the words "I'm Sorry" hid my guest's face.

Callie lowered the poster. "Please forgive me for my childish behavior, Mary Claire. I'm an idiot."

I reached out and grabbed her with my good arm. "Water under the bridge, Callie. Everything is fine. Come in and let's celebrate."

"Thanks so much for opening up your home. This team needed some levity." Callie handed me a lovely bottle of Sancerre and proclaimed, "A peace offering."

Once Callie said hello to Dallas and had a glass of wine, she began surveying her surroundings. She strolled from the kitchen to the living room and studied the furnishings and the view of the backyard. She turned to me and shook her head. "I have to say, partner, never in a million years would I have placed you in this house." I felt offended by the comment, and I guess it showed. Callie quickly explained, "Oh, don't misunderstand me. I think your home is lovely. Actually worthy of a magazine but this stoic, contemporary look does not fit you. I would've thought you'd have warm colors, soft lamps, lots of inviting pillows. It just doesn't seem like you."

I turned to Dallas, who gave me an "I told you so" look. "Dallas expressed the same sentiment a moment ago. Andrew always handled the decorating through an interior design client. I was too young and inexperienced when we married to know what my style was. And once precedents are set, it's hard to change them."

The doorbell rang. Saved by the bell. My husband was the last topic I wanted to discuss. Tonight was dedicated to celebrating a team victory and personal liberation. Amy and Kelly arrived together. Katlin told me it would be between 8 and 8:30 before she could make it. Jake said not to expect him before 8:30, so everyone had arrived except Alex, who had promised to bring a surprise.

When she did arrive, Alex did not disappoint. Her surprise was a laundry basket of squirming puppies. I was delighted because I find all types of babies mesmerizing, but I have to say those were the goofiest looking puppies I'd ever seen.

As I studied the litter, Dallas walked up. She smiled, a grin that suggested a sarcastic thought, but she repressed her comments and picked up a puppy. She pressed its face against hers, and in a voice that conveyed kindness and innocence, qualities I had never seen from Dallas, she cooed, "And what kind of creation are you, baby?"

Alex appeared shocked as well. In the short time I'd known Dallas, I had witnessed anger, confusion, distrust -- nothing loving and carefree. Baby talk from Dallas seemed incomprehensible. Alex recovered as she watched her interaction with the puppy. "Izzy, that's our Boykin Spaniel, is a little tramp. I've seen all kinds of dogs wander into her domain, so we aren't sure who the 'baby daddy' is. Based on the looks of these pups, though, I think it's our neighbor's Dalmatian. Duke struts around the neighborhood like a fifteen-year-old who's just discovered his manhood. Typical male. Hope the pups have Izzy's brain, but not her taste in one-night stands."

"How old are they?" she asked.

Six weeks as of yesterday. There were seven in the litter, five boys and two girls, but my husband gave one to a girl in his office. They are free to anyone interested, provided they offer a good home, of course."

Dallas, the damaged girl who rarely smiled, glowed with a joyful expression. "Really? You're giving them away?"

Hesitantly, Alex responded. "Yes. Do you want one? You can take one tonight if you do. They're old enough to be away from their mother." Alex looked at me. I could tell she was shocked by what we were witnessing, a crack in the armor of our most hard-core gladiator.

Dallas was positively exuberant. "Wow. I think I'm in love with this little guy. I would love to have him if you trust me with him."

"Absolutely," Alex appeared elated to have inadvertently inspired a flash of emotion from Dallas.

"Thank you." Dallas gently cradled the puppy who had settled into a slumber in her arms. "I know the perfect name. Justice."

"Justice. That's a serious name for a dog that looks like a hobo," Alex proclaimed lightheartedly. "How about INjustice because it's a crime for a dog to be so ugly."

"Listen to Alex," Dallas cooed to the dog. "Such a comedian. Ignore her. Justice is a perfect name for you."

"Justice is a great name for a dog. It's solid, stately, dependable," I commented approvingly. "Don't you agree, Alex?"

"Indeed. I'm thrilled that my tennis partner will go home with a pup tonight." Alex looked toward the kitchen where everyone else had congregated. "I'll see if anyone else is interested in a spontaneous adoption." She picked up the basket where the remaining five puppies huddled together in a massive ball of snoozing fur.

"Who likes puppies?" she appealed to the crowd in the kitchen. She set the basket on the floor and oohs and aahs followed as one by one the pups were cuddled by our teammates.   I watched as the group seemed to collectively melt under the spell of the canine infants.

CALLIE

By the time Jake arrived, the party was quite lively -- a seduction of puppies and wine. Everybody was having a great time, even Dallas. Jake found Alex and me huddled together whispering about the inexplicable transformation of Mary Claire.

"What are you two ladies conspiring about over here?" Jake inquired as he sat beside me.

"We've been watching Mary Claire," I responded. "Look at her flitting about, laughing and drinking. She's on her third glass of wine. Neither of us has ever seen her so whimsical and tipsy. She's always the picture of southern gentility. Tonight she's...I don't know... like someone just released from a long prison sentence."

Alex commented, "More like somebody flipped a switch and she's become a new person."

"Like a butterfly breaking free of its cocoon," Jake declared as he studied Mary Claire.

"Perfect description," I said.

"That, ladies, is exactly what Mary Claire is doing, breaking free. It takes guts to take chances that you know will be hindered by a multitude of obstacles. She's a brave woman," Jake proclaimed with admiration as he walked over to her and embraced her. He whispered something in her ear. She blushed, and he returned to my side.

Now I was a little tipsy and had no idea what he knew about Mary Claire and I didn't, but I was so happy to see Jake that I spontaneously planted a big kiss right on his mouth. It was not a passionate kiss but rather a territorial mark, and I was clearly the aggressor. By the time our lips parted, the room had grown silent.

"About damn time," Alex declared loudly.

"Amen," Mary Claire seconded.

That kiss clearly disturbed Amy Morard who obviously still harbored visions of Jake wedded to her beloved Olivia. "Well, Jake, I don't think Olivia is going to be too happy about this incident. What should I tell her?"

Jake grinned and pulled me to my feet. He encircled me with one arm and cupped the side of my face with his free hand. As he pulled me into his body, he delivered the hottest, longest, most passionate kiss imaginable. When we parted, he looked at Amy and said, "Does that answer your question?"

Jake grabbed my hand and led me toward the backyard. The girls, rendered speechless, watched us exit. Just before we closed the door I heard Alex moan, "Damn, that made me horny. Sly's getting lucky tonight!"

Jake plopped down in a lounge chair and settled me next to him. "Comfortable?"

"Perfect actually. That was some kiss."

"Thank you. You make it easy."

"Not that I'm complaining, but what was that all about?"

Jake gently stroked my arm as he spoke. "I was making a statement. If that kiss doesn't get rid of Olivia Dunn, then she's a stalker."

"I think Amy got the point." I turned so I could look at his face as I spoke. "Jake, I'm sorry I went off the deep end about the text I saw. I'm sure Mary Claire told you I read it. And I wasn't snooping."

"I know you weren't, but why didn't you just ask me about it instead of storming off? We had just finished a conversation about trusting each other and having no secrets."

"I know. I was wrong. I'm so stupid." I sat up. "And I'm wrong to transfer the bad facets of past relationships to you. You know how they say history repeats itself?" Jake nodded. "I've never had a relationship that didn't end badly. It's hard for me to believe that I can have a good one. I'm terribly insecure, and I know that's not fair to you. Mary Claire told me that she wasn't sure I deserved you."

"She didn't mean it the way it sounded. She's protective of me, like a big sister."

"You're right about that, but as much as those words hurt me, I know she was right." Jake started to speak but I stopped him. "Let me finish. What she meant was that you don't deserve someone who constantly doubts your sincerity. You don't deserve someone that is so insecure that you have to constantly explain yourself. That's the way I've behaved, and you deserve better than that. I had this nightmare yesterday. I woke up, frantic, my heart racing, and I realized that the bottom line is that I don't think I deserve anything good, and I'm tired of getting hurt. But this nightmare, in which you shoved me in a well, by the way, made me realize that it was my choice. I can either fight for what I want and live in the light, or curl up in the darkness, guaranteed not to get hurt, but also guaranteed to miss everything good. I want to live in the light, with you, if you still want me."

"Callie, first of all, if you were ever at the bottom of a well, I'd be the one to climb down and pull you out, not the one to put you in it. And, I get how your history makes you skeptical about the success of any relationship, but answer this question. Have you ever felt about anyone the way you feel about me?"

"Not even close," I answered without hesitation.

"What's the difference?"

"Because you're the only person I've ever fallen for that I considered my best friend. You're the first person I think of when I have something to share -- good or bad. In past relationships, I never considered the fact that I wasn't getting what I needed out of the relationship. I was always making sure my boyfriend got everything he needed from me. I guess when they would leave, or cheat, or lie, I always wondered what more could I have done. I gave everything I possibly could to the point that I almost lost my own identity. With you, I feel like I can be a better version of myself. You enhance me."

"Those are huge differences. There's no way our history will mirror the past." Jake sat up and took my hands. He pulled me up to face him. "I'm in love with you, Callie Conrad. And I have been for a long time. I'm nothing like your past boyfriends, and I don't want to be compared to them. I want to make a go of this, with a long term goal in mind, but I don't want to go down this road if you can't feel confident that you can trust me and talk to me about anything." We just stared at each other. "Are you in or out?"

"I'm in, Lenaghan," I promised as I pushed him to a prone position. "All the way." I kissed him, hungrily. It was obvious that we both wanted more. I was about to suggest that we sneak away when I heard Alex scream, "Oh shit!"

We bolted upright and dashed back inside. "What's wrong?" I asked with concern.

Alex pointed to a puppy that had escaped the basket and was peeing on the floor. "Mary Claire will have a fit. I bet this rug cost a fortune."

"It did cost a fortune," Mary Claire confirmed nonchalantly as she entered the room with a full glass of wine. "And I despise this rug. I've hated it from the first day Andrew insisted that we purchase it. He just wanted it because it has some snotty history that he could babble about while entertaining." Mary Claire took a big gulp of wine. "Alex, I like that dog. He has good taste. May I have him?"

"Sure, Mary Claire, he's all yours."

Mary Claire picked him up and gave him a big kiss on the head. She turned to Jake. "You don't mind, do you, Jake?"

Everybody looked at Jake who awkwardly answered, "Not a problem for me." Jake took the puppy from Mary Claire and placed him in the basket. He picked up the basket and turned to Alex. "I bet they all need a potty break. I'll take them out."

"Wait, I don't want to mix my little guy up with the rest," Mary Claire fretted. "How can I tell him apart?"

"That's easy," Alex responded. "He's the only one in the litter with a pink nose. We've been calling him Rudolph."

"Love it," Mary Claire approved.

"Dallas, do you want me to take yours out too?" Jake asked. Dallas had guarded Justice since she claimed him.

"I'll bring him out and help with the others," she replied.

As they headed to the backyard, the doorbell rang, and Katlin entered simultaneously. "Hey. Sorry I'm late."

"Not a problem, dear. Come in," Mary Claire encouraged cheerily. "Come with me to the kitchen, and we'll pour you a glass of wine and get you some food."

They disappeared for a few minutes. By the time they returned, Jake and Dallas had come back inside and placed the basket of puppies in the guest bathroom, away from the commotion. Dallas reluctantly left Justice to snuggle with his brothers and sister. Unlike his siblings, Justice had a white patch shaped like an uneven star between his eyes. Distinguishing him from the crowd would not be an issue.

With everyone back in the living room, I decided to make a toast. I canvassed the room and saw that everyone had a full glass except Jake. I went to the kitchen, poured him a glass of red, and handed it to him when I returned. "I'd like to propose a toast," I announced. Once I had their attention, I continued. "This has been the most bizarre season I've ever experienced. Early in the year, I asked Jake to pull together a team that he believed could go undefeated, or at least perform well enough to win a bid to state playoffs. We finished the season 8-0 and no team came close to us in sets won. Vestavia finished second with a 7-1 record, but we still won 8 more sets than they did." Everybody cheered. "Now we accomplished all this despite an impending wedding, a broken arm, a snake bite and a corpse. So let's raise our glasses to Jake for assembling this crazy team and to each other for finding a way to bridge our differences and win week after week." Everybody clinked glasses and said cheers.

Katlin took the floor. I noticed that Amy made a face at Kelly. "I have a question that I think the whole team would love answered. As you know, I was with MKat when she decided to go snooping on the side of the road and ended up with a snake attached to her nose. Admittedly, I was a wimp and passed out. Luckily, Alex saved the day. But no one seems to know why Alex had the skills to remove the snake attached to MKat's nose. Alex's daughter saw the whole thing on YouTube, and she had no clue how her mother knew what to do. Alex was fearless. So Alex, would you please explain to us where you got your snake handling skills?"

Alex examined her captive audience and rolled her eyes. "Oh, just give me a moment, and I'll tell you. Jake, you and Callie come help me with something. You, too, Mary Claire."

We went to the kitchen where Alex asked Mary Claire for eight shot glasses. She pulled a bottle of North Carolina moonshine from her giant bag. "Y'all each grab some shot glasses and pass them out."

"If you girls want to know the story, then first you have to 'man up' and take a shot of some redneck refreshment. As you all know, because you should all have invitations, my one and only baby is getting married two weeks from today. My precious cousin, Noah Hargrove, sent me some North Carolina moonshine to sooth my pre-wedding jitters."

"Did you say Noah Hargrove is your cousin?" Dallas interrupted. "The Noah Hargrove that writes for travel magazines?"

"The one and only," Alex answered with pride. "Do you know him, Dallas?"

She shook her head but turned deathly white. "No, I'm familiar with his work. He's very talented."

"I'll be sure to pass on your kind words. Noah's the best. If he weren't my first cousin, I probably would've married him. Come to think of it, marrying your first cousin used to be a common practice in the Old South." Alex poured the moonshine in each glass. "Anyway, you've got to be in touch with your redneck side before I can share this story. Down the hatch."

I thought my throat would disintegrate. Everyone, even Jake, looked as if they had swallowed fire.

"Okay, this story doesn't leave this room. You got it? My husband is mortified by this part of my history, and Avery doesn't know. When I was seventeen growing up in Hartford, Alabama, there wasn't much to do. Noah and I were tight as ticks, and we'd sneak out all the time and do all sorts of stupid things which I shall keep to myself. Anyway, our moms, the Baker twins, decided we needed to spend the summer before our senior year at Baker Boot Camp. Baker Boot Camp consisted of a summer with their parents, MawMaw and PawPaw Baker, the two meanest humans on the planet. They lived on Compass Lake in the northwestern part of Florida, which back then was a snake and gator infested hellhole. Noah and I were slave laborers, but we still snuck out at night with the local teenagers. We met these locals, a brother and sister named Dale and Daphne Danforth, and Noah and I each fell head over heels. They were gorgeous teenagers, but dumb as dirt. We didn't care; we would follow them anywhere.

"One day they asked us to go to church with them, and it turned out to be one of those crazy snake handling churches. Noah decided his affection for Daphne wasn't strong enough to endure reptile wrangling. Not me. As much as I hated snakes, the thought of giving up Dale was unbearable. I learned how to handle copperheads and rattlesnakes. I hated every moment of it, but I was bored at Compass Lake, and Dale was the best kisser ever, or so I thought.

"After about six weeks, I was pretty good with the snakes, and Dale asked me to help him transfer some to another church. Turns out he just wanted to unleash them at the local Methodist Church during the eleven o'clock service as a joke. An eight-year-old boy picked up a rattlesnake and tossed it in the air because, as he said during his television interview, 'I thought it'd be fun to see a snake fly'. Charming boy. Unfortunately the flying snake landed on the choir director and bit his arm, and the preacher's wife suffered a heart attack in all the chaos. Then during the stampede to get out of the church, a man with a cast on his leg couldn't keep up and was trampled. Everyone survived, but lots of legal horrors followed until my innocence was proven. Needless to say, it was a blot on our good family name."

"Wow, Alex," Katlin commented, "that's nuts."

"Yes, indeed. Not my finest hour."

"What happened to Dale Danforth?" Jake asked.

"Dale, who was eighteen at the time of this unfortunate incident, was sentenced to three years in prison but was out in one for good behavior. I ran into him a few years ago when I was in Orange Beach visiting friends. He left Compass Lake after his legal troubles and went to work for a port-a-potty company on the Gulf Coast. He was fat, bald and missing most of his teeth."

"Aren't you glad you dodged that bullet," Kelly commented.

"Yes, I hit the jackpot with Sly. He's the best," Alex complimented her husband.

"Alex," Mary Claire began, "do you have any more information on MKat's situation?"

"Not much. Poor Edward's boss at the bank did share a little with me. The results from the autopsy are still pending, but MKat isn't speaking at all."

"What's going to happen to her?"

"I really don't know. Apparently, she has no living relatives that are close by, only distant cousins that haven't kept in touch since childhood. Edward had a brother and sister who are still living, but they both despise MKat and say they hope she rots in a padded cell. They say they tried for years to get him to leave MKat because she was so awful, but he wouldn't hear of it. Edward's siblings are convinced that she killed him."

"She was an evil tennis partner," Katlin commented.

Suddenly, the puppies started crying, and Dallas went to retrieve them.

"Is that a dog I heard?" inquired Katlin.

"A whole litter, actually," Alex explained. Dallas returned, set the basket on the floor, and removed Justice from the wad of puppies. "I'm giving away puppies to good homes. I've got four left. Dallas is taking one, and Mary Claire has claimed Rudolph here." Alex pointed to the dog with the pink nose.

"Why didn't you leave them home with your husband?" Katlin asked as she stared at the puppies.

"I told Sly to go have a boys' night out since I'd be gone. I brought the puppies because I was hoping you girls would drink enough to think they were cute and you'd adopt them all. But I don't think we have enough alcohol."

Katlin kept her eyes locked on the puppies, examining them with consternation. "Alex, your husband's name is Sly?" Alex nodded. "That's short for Sylvester, right?"

Alex laughed and answered playfully, "No, honey. Sly is what he is. His fraternity brothers nicknamed him Sly because he could charm the ladies. And the name stuck, much to his mother's horror. Everyone except his mother called him Sly. Since college, she's the only one who still calls him Sam."

Alex picked up a puppy and moved it close to Katlin's face. "Please take me home, Katlin," Alex cooed in a silly voice.

Katlin took the puppy and placed it on her lap. "Are there any more to choose from? I mean is this the whole litter?"

"We had seven," Alex answered as she picked up a whining puppy. "I brought six tonight. Sly gave one to a girl in his office yesterday. I fussed at him because he took the cutest one (not that any are cute), but he said he wanted to surprise this girl because he knew her boyfriend was a selfish jerk. We called her Bugs because she had bulging eyes."

Katlin, who had turned stark white, put the puppy back in the basket, and ran to the bathroom. When she returned, she apologized. "I'm sorry, ladies. I ate some oysters earlier today, and now they're doing flips in my stomach. I think I'd better go."

"Are you okay to drive?" Alex asked.

"I'm okay, thanks. I'm not far from here."

"Are you sure you don't want to take a puppy with you? They're so ugly they're cute."

"No thanks," she said and hurried out.

"Well, I hate that she had to leave," Mary Claire lamented cheerily.

"Me, too," Alex reiterated, "but she did look a little green around the gills. Those puppies seemed to bother her. Maybe she's allergic."

"I love that song," Mary Claire announced as she turned up the volume of her Bose stereo. Adele was belting out *Set Fire to the Rain* and everyone, even Dallas, was engaged in conversation.

Abruptly, the music ended and a man's voice bellowed over the cackle of females. "What's this?" he said, the tone friendly but with an unmistakable edginess.

It was Mary Claire's husband, Andrew. I recognized him from the one brief meeting we had when he watched us play a match. I knew he was sixty-five, but he was still strikingly handsome. Tall, fit, immaculately dressed with perfectly manicured hands and salt and pepper hair. Cold, dark blue eyes dominated his handsome, chiseled face. You could tell he was a man who held himself in high regard. His countenance exuded confidence. There was no doubt in my mind that he was formidable in the courtroom.

As Andrew Jameson commanded the room with his presence, Mary Claire seemed to wither like a rose thrust into a subzero freezer. Talk about a sobriety check. Everyone seemed to instantly stand at attention before Andrew Jameson. Everyone that is, except for Jake, who stood beside me, shoulders back, alert, a bull ready to charge. Mary Claire recovered slightly and approached her husband with a manufactured smile. "Hi, honey. I thought you weren't returning home until Tuesday morning."

"Obviously," he retorted in a chilly tone as he cut his blistering eyes toward Mary Claire. His displeasure escaped no one, especially Alex.

Alex extended her hand toward Jameson forcing him to reciprocate or appear rude. She gripped his hand firmly and did not abandon the shake or eye contact as she spoke. "Hi. I'm Alex Anderson. It is such a pleasure to meet the man who is lucky enough to have snagged Mary Claire. She is an angel." Mary Claire, still with a "deer in the headlights" expression, gave Alex a weak smile that said "thank you".

Alex dropped her hand and continued. "This group of women you see before you forms the currently undefeated tennis team of which Mary Claire is a crucial part. We've had a tough week, and we needed to unwind a bit, so we decided to have a get-together. Mary Claire was gracious enough to offer your exquisite home as a gathering place. And might I add that you have an impeccable decorating eye. Mary Claire gives you all the credit for this fabulous home."

I decided Alex didn't need to go it alone, though she was doing an outstanding job. I walked up and said, "Hello, Mr. Jameson. I'm Callie Conrad, and Mary Claire has been my doubles partner for the past five years. She's the best partner I've ever had."

Jameson seemed to relax a bit, and his charming facade emerged. "Welcome to my home." The "my" did not escape me. Now, he became the consummate politician and worked his way around the room introducing himself to everyone except Jake. Clearly Mary Claire's husband saw Jake but somehow managed to avoid him without being blatantly obvious.

When he saw Dallas, however, Andrew Jameson looked unsettled. With a dead, but disturbingly penetrating glare, Dallas introduced herself but refused to accept his extended hand. Her eye contact was searing -- like a drill boring through his skull. Clearly, he was shaken by her gaze. "Have we met before?" he inquired in a cautious tone.

Dallas, in an unemotional tone, responded, "We've never met, but often people are connected in ways they've never imagined." Her menacing stare didn't waver. You could have heard a pin drop. Everyone was watching this eerie encounter, riveted to the pair like magnets to a fridge.

Seemingly at a loss for words (which I'm sure was a rare occurrence), Andrew backed away from Dallas and returned to Mary Claire's side. He put his arm around her and squeezed her left arm.

Mary Claire tried to suppress a grimace, but she was obviously in pain. "Well," her husband addressed the room, "it was a pleasure to meet you all. I'll let you return to your festivities. I wish you continued success with the rest of your season."

I positioned myself behind them, out of sight, but able to overhear what he said when he whispered in her ear, "I'm going to shower. These people better be out of my house when I'm done." Now all smiles, he exited with a final wave and "good night".

At that moment, Mary Claire was frozen. I went into my control freak mode. "Okay, everybody. I didn't realize it was so late. Please grab your stuff and let's give Mary Claire some peace and quiet. If anyone still wants to stay out, I'm buying a round of drinks at Grey Bar." But everyone said they were calling it a night.

Only Amy, Kelly, and Dallas left. Jake, Alex, and I surrounded Mary Claire. Clarity slapped me in the face -- the inexplicable long sleeves in the dead of summer, the obsession with perfection, her reference to the signs, the black Jaguar given after the fall down the stairs, Jake urging me to talk to Mary Claire about what was going on with her. It all made sense. Andrew Jameson abused his wife. I took a moment to wallow in self-loathing, "Oh, Mary Claire, I'm the worst friend in the world." I embraced her gingerly and cried, "I'm sorry I didn't see it until now. Please forgive me."

Jake interrupted. "Look, we all know what's going on here or we would have left. We can hash this out later, but for now, we've got about two minutes before he realizes that all of Mary Claire's things are gone. Alex, grab your puppies and go home. Callie, you and Mary Claire follow me to my house."

Mary Claire looked alarmed. "Jake, the kitchen is a wreck. He'll go crazy if everything isn't in place."

Alex responded, "Who the fuck cares! I don't think you live here anymore."

ALEX

That motherfucker really has been abusing Mary Claire, I thought as I drove home with my basket of sleeping babies. I knew those bruises didn't come from an accidental fall down the stairs. What a total piece of shit Andrew Jameson was, and what a bitch I am for calling her a Stepford wife. It made perfect sense now why Mary Claire seemed so unnatural to me and why she freaked out about being at MKat's when all hell broke loose. The woman lived in fear of her husband. She had to fly below the radar to avoid setting him off. Shit, you really don't know why a person behaves a certain way until you've walked in their shoes. I was ashamed of myself, but more than anything, my heart ached for Mary Claire.

I glanced at the sleeping puppies. They calmed my heart -- so sweet and innocent. They make you remember the good in the world. Sly will be happy that we are down to four babies. But as I surveyed the litter, I counted five. Rudolph, the one Mary Claire chose, was still in the basket.

I pulled my phone from my purse and called Callie. "Hey. It's Alex. Have you gotten back to Jake's place yet?" She answered that they had just walked in the house. "Listen, I have something that I think will help Mary Claire. If it's okay with you, I'd like to swing by and drop it off. Could you give me the address?"

Jake came out of his house just after I pulled in the drive and turned off the car. He met me in the walkway. "Hey, Alex. What's up?"

"Is she still awake?" I whispered.

"Yes, Callie's getting her settled. She's calm because I think she consumed four times the amount of alcohol that she normally does, but I think she's a bit displaced. She was all set to leave him but wasn't going to be forced to face him for a while. His impromptu arrival shook her newfound strength, but she'll be okay."

"You're right. She will. We'll all be around to help her. You're a good man to give her a place to stay."

Jake shrugged and smiled. "What are friends for."

"Just a sec." I went to my trunk and retrieved a bag, then opened the passenger door and picked up Rudolph. I handed Jake the puppy and a small bag of puppy food. "Here's your other roommate and his food. I always have some in the car in case of a traffic jam or other emergency. Look, Mary Claire was probably drunk when she claimed Rudolph, but I know in my heart that this little critter will help her get through this awful mess. I know it's a burden on you, Jake, but.."

He put his hand up and said, "Say no more. You're right. This little guy is the perfect medicine for her. Since the moon seems to be full," Jake pointed skyward to confirm his statement, "and lunacy is afoot, I think I'll give Rudolph a companion. Can I take a peek at the others?"

"Really?" I was shocked, but he nodded. I opened the car door, and he surveyed the four pups remaining.

He seemed at odds. "Do you mind if I conduct a little experiment?"

"Knock yourself out."

Jake removed the basket of puppies from my car. One by one he lifted them from the basket and set them in his front yard. Then Jake set Rudolph down. Without hesitation, Rudolph waddled toward the smallest puppy, a brown boy that had splotches of white on his right side. We watched the puppies interact for five minutes, but Rudolph never left the smaller pup's side.

Jake smiled and said, "Perfect." He picked up Rudolph and the runt. "This little guy will be Callie's....and mine. We can share custody. And, since his best bud is Rudolph, Mary Claire can help out."

"Jake, are you drunk, or do you really want to do this? I mean if you change your mind in the morning, I won't hold it against you."

Jake shook his head. "Alex, I had one glass of wine and your moonshine shot. I'm totally sober. Thanks for the pups and the food."

"Okay, if you need some vet recommendations, just let me know."

"Thanks. It was really sweet of you to drive out of your way. Please send me a text when you get home so I'll know you've arrived safely."

"Will do, Jake." I opened my car door as he strolled up the walkway with the two puppies. "Oh, Jake," he turned when I called out. "You and Callie gonna make beautiful babies." I winked and got in my car.

****

Once buckled up next to the three remaining pups, I picked up my cell and saw that I had one missed call and two texts from Avery. The first text said:

What happened to Katlin?

The second read:

Call me. Doesn't matter what time it is.

It was 11:15 and the text came in at 11:08. I texted Sly:

Should be home by 11:45.

Then I called Avery. "What's up, baby girl?"

"Mom, I'm so worried about Katlin," Avery fretted.

"Why? I saw her two hours ago. We had a tennis party, but she wasn't there long. She was having some stomach problems and left pretty quickly."

"There's something else going on with her. She texted me a little while ago and said she's breaking up with her boyfriend tomorrow when she's not completely hysterical. She said she'd found out tonight that he wasn't a good guy after all. She said he'd been lying to her all along. I called her, but she didn't answer. I texted her to please pick up the phone, but she texted back that she was too upset to talk. Her texts didn't make much sense. She said she couldn't come to my wedding and that she was so sorry. She said, and I quote, 'I'm so sorry. I promise I didn't know. I didn't know'."

"That is strange," I admitted.

"Mom, Katlin told me yesterday that her boyfriend had a previous commitment the date of my wedding, but she would be coming alone. She said she wouldn't miss it for anything. Now, less than twenty-four hours later, she's hysterical. It's okay if she doesn't come to the wedding, but something really bad has happened. I'm worried about her. Can you check on her? She's really a sweet girl, not stuck up like I thought she was. She's been so happy even though her boyfriend is old enough to be her father. I can't imagine what's going on with her."

"Honey, do you think she's suicidal. I mean do I need to barge into her apartment right now?"

"No, she told me that she went to her parents' house to spend the night because she was so upset. When she texted me, she said that her mom was curled up next to her, and this is the weird part, giving her the strength to tell me that 'she didn't know'."

"That is strange. Things can be misinterpreted in texts, though."

"Katlin had not introduced her boyfriend to her parents for two reasons. First of all, he's close to her dad's age, so she thought they would freak out about that."

"Gotta say, as a parent, that's understandable," I admitted. "I mean if the first time you brought home Travis, he turned out to be 48 instead of 28, I'd be concerned, no doubt."

"I get it. The second reason she hadn't introduced him to her family is because she was dating him under a false name. Everybody knows the Hamilton family is loaded. She's worth several million, and she wanted to make sure he cared about her, not her money. She told him her name was Kate Carter and that she taught second grade at some school in Prattville. He must be stupid. Who would live in Birmingham and commute over an hour one way to teach in Prattville?"

"You'd be surprised, honey. If you're desperate for a job, commuting doesn't seem so bad. But that's beside the point. Katlin was so worried about being loved for her, and not her money, that she gave a false name. Is that the story?"

"Yep, she told me last week that she was ashamed to admit that her past relationships were embarrassing. She said she'd had an affair with a married man, chased an older hot guy who totally blew her off even though he was unattached, and had dated three guys her age, but they were fixated on her name not her."

"Avery, why was she telling you this? You've been friends now for what, two months? Seems like she's divulging a lot of information to someone she doesn't know well."

"True, but I think all her friends were born with silver spoons in their mouths. They're all college-educated, but I'm her only friend that works and lives in the real world. We had this long conversation a few days ago about relationships. She wanted to know how I knew that Travis was the one. I told her that I knew we had the proper foundation for a lasting relationship -- friendship, attraction, humor, devotion, and real love. You and Dad are my example of the formula for a happy marriage."

I was touched. "Sweetie, that warms my heart."

"But I don't understand why Katlin said that her mom was giving her the strength to tell me that she didn't know. She promised that she didn't know. What do you think that means?"

Snippets of the evening yanked my mind, and I felt mentally weighted. "Avery, is Travis there?"

"No, he's at his brother's house this weekend. He's having a bachelor party with his friends from high school. Why?"

"I was curious if he had an opinion on the situation -- you know, a man's view -- but you probably haven't discussed it with him."

"No, I won't talk to him until tomorrow. What do you think I should do? I want to be a good friend."

I smiled, so proud of my kind-hearted daughter. "Honey, I think Katlin's okay. She's obviously confided in her mother, and nobody takes care of a daughter as well as her momma. But I promise you that I will check on her and get back with you. Just send her a text tomorrow -- an 'I'm thinking of you' text. Don't push, okay."

I pulled into the garage. "Avery, Katlin's boyfriend...or rather ex-boyfriend. He's around my age, right?"

"Yes," Avery confirmed. "Why do you ask?"

"Well, if he's a peer, maybe I know him or can find out something about him. Do you know his name?"

"Yes, I do remember because his name is catchy. It's Sam Flaherty." My hand flew to my mouth, and I subdued a cry. "Do you know him, Mom?"

I swallowed hard and pulled myself together. "No, baby. Listen. I've just gotten home. Don't you worry about Katlin. She'll be fine, and I'll check on her and get back to you, okay?"

"Thanks, Mom. Can you believe this time two weeks from now I'll be leaving on my honeymoon!"

"Hard to believe, baby girl." I squeezed my eyes tightly, but tears still found an outlet. "Listen, I think Noah will be here early. He'll probably be in town before you are."

"Really?" Avery could not contain her excitement. She adored her Uncle Noah.

"Yep. Hey, I gotta run now, but I'll talk to you tomorrow. Don't worry about Katlin. Avery, you're a good friend."

"Thanks. I love you."

I got out of the car and let the three remaining puppies waddle in the grass to do their business. God, they were ugly. I decided I'd keep one. I collected the puppies and went into the house with a heavy heart. "Sly. I'm home. Three down and three to go." I found him in the living room stretched out on the sofa, channel surfing. "Hey," I greeted.

Sly looked up and gave me a sleepy smile. "Hi, honey. Who took three puppies?"

Sly made room for me on the couch. I sat down and freed the remaining puppies on the floor. Izzy appeared. She knew her babies were home. She also knew that some were missing.

"Look at Izzy. She knows something's not right."

"She's okay." Sly rubbed my thigh with his foot. "Who took the puppies?"

"Shockingly, my cold as ice regular partner, Dallas, melted at the sight of these ugly ducklings and took one. She named him Justice."

"She must be an attorney."

"No, don't know why she named him that. Then Mary Claire adopted Rudolph because he peed on an expensive rug that her husband picked out. She hated the rug, and her husband too, so it seems." Sly laughed nonchalantly. "Jake Lenaghan took the runt."

"It's late. Must have been a good party," Sly observed.

"Oh, I think enlightening is a better word."

Sly gave me a quizzical look. "Enlightening? What earth shattering things did you learn at a tennis party?"

I crossed my legs Indian style, and got comfortable on the couch. "Lots of secrets wormed their way out of the crevices tonight."

Sly chuckled. "Oh yeah? Like what?"

I stretched and said, "Gosh, there are so many. Where do I start? Okay, I'll go in order. First, Jake, our pro, professed his desire for our captain, Callie Conrad, by sticking his tongue down her throat in the most provocative kiss I've ever witnessed. Apparently they've been dancing around their feelings for each other for years. I predict they'll be married within a year."

"Is that a good thing?"

"It's a fabulous thing," I confirmed. "They belong together. And that kiss. Geez, it made me so horny I almost left to come jump your bones."

Sly gave me a lustful look, shoved his foot between my legs, and dug his toes into my crotch. "I'm all yours, baby."

"Hold on, tiger," I teased as I removed his foot from my personal space. "There's more to this story, and you don't want to miss it."

"Really? Do tell." Sly turned off the television and gave me his undivided attention.

"Let's see. Oh, yes. Mary Claire Jameson hosted the party at her house. Do you remember her husband, Andrew Jameson?"

"That prick of a lawyer who acts like he's better than everyone else?" Sly had picked up a puppy and placed him on his belly. He rubbed his back and the baby was asleep in thirty seconds. He smiled. "Works on canines, too."

I smiled. "Yes, I remember how you did that to Avery when she was a baby. You could lay her on your stomach, rub her back and she'd be out in no time."

Sly wiggled his fingers. "Magic," he declared in a whispery voice.

I smiled. "You're a good daddy, Sly."

"Thanks, babe."

"Anyway, back to all those secrets. Who were we talking about? Oh, yes. Mary Claire Jameson is the wife of the snotty lawyer, Andrew, who you've run into from time to time at The Heights." Sly nodded. "Turns out that Andrew is not only a royal prick, but he's been emotionally and physically abusing his wife for years."

"What!"

"Yes, it's shocking but true. She's left him, but I'm sure the worst is yet to come."

"Wow, that is a big secret."

"Indeed," I agreed. "Shocking, actually. You just never know who people really are."

Sly moved the puppy to the floor and abruptly pulled me on top of him. He began rubbing my back. "Now it's time for me to work my magic on you." He kissed my neck. "But I have no intention of putting you to sleep."

He moved his hand under my shirt, but I stood up. "Oh, honey, I'm not done with my story. You don't want to miss the best part now." I headed to the kitchen and called out, "Noah sent me some North Carolina moonshine to soothe my nerves about the wedding. Want a shot?"

"Why not," he answered, defeated.

I returned with two shot glasses and handed him one. "To a beautiful wedding for Avery," I toasted. We clinked glasses, and I sat down in a chair across from Sly.

"Okay, so here's the best, or rather the most disturbing, secret revealed. It's disturbing because the parties concerned were innocent bystanders in this secret. They were victims."

"Sounds juicy," Sly feigned interest. "Do tell so I can take your clothes off."

"My, aren't you a horny toad," I teased. I returned to my story. "We found out that one of the young girls on the team, a girl who has actually become good friends with Avery, has been dating a man that claimed to be recently divorced, only he's not. You've heard of the Hamilton family, right?"

"You mean the multi-millionaires that live in a palace on top of Red Mountain?" I nodded. "Of course, I've heard of them. Who hasn't?"

"Right. Well, they have several children, and the youngest, Katlin, is Avery's age. She's on our tennis team. Turns out Katlin and Avery have a mutual friend, and over the past couple of months, they've become good friends. Katlin is coming to the wedding."

"Fabulous. A local celebrity at the wedding. Bet she'll give a great gift."

"Anyway, turns out that she's been dating someone that she's crazy about. She said he was 'the one', but apparently he's married, and she didn't know it."

"That's awful," Sly commiserated.

"Yes, indeed it is. Avery says she's devastated. I hate it for her." I retrieved the moonshine and poured each of us another shot. "By the way, Sly, how's the puppy doing that you gave to the girl in your office?"

"Fine, I guess. She hasn't mentioned it."

"Have I met this girl before? Maybe at the company Christmas party? What was her name again?"

"Kate. No, you haven't met her. She's only been with the company a few months. Why do you ask?"

"Oh, I just like to know where the babies end up."

"The baby is in a good home, I promise." Sly stood up, walked to the back of my chair and began massaging my shoulders. He whispered in my ear as his massage moved toward my chest, "You still horny? I had oysters for lunch today, so we're on the same page."

It took every ounce of restraint in my body not to grab his hands and bend all his fingers backwards. At the moment, all I wanted to do was hurt him. But I kept my cool. He was still clueless, and I had the upper hand. I wiggled out of his grasp and sighed. "First I want to show you something. Katlin Hamilton has been my doubles partner for the past two weeks, and we took the cutest picture after we won yesterday. I meant to send it to you." I pulled up the picture on my iPhone and handed it to him. I thought his eyes would pop out of their sockets. "Kate Carter is actually Katlin Hamilton." Sly hung his head in shame. He had nowhere to run.

"Alex, I don't know what to say. I'm so sorry. She doesn't work at my company. I met her in a bar when I was out with the guys from the office. I don't even know how it happened. It started as a joke, a dare that I couldn't get her number, and things got out of control."

"You destroyed a young girl, a girl your daughter's age, and wrecked your marriage on a dare?" I was no longer calm.

"Honey, calm down so we can talk about this," Sly pleaded cautiously. Wrong choice of words, but then again all words were bad choices at that moment.

"Don't tell me to calm down, Sly. I don't want to see your sorry ass much less talk to you right now. So here's what's going to happen. First of all, Avery's not going to know anything about this. You will do everything I tell you to do for the next two weeks, and she will have the perfect wedding that she deserves. After the wedding, when I feel like it, we can talk. Right now you have ten minutes to pack a bag and get the hell out of here. Don't call, don't text, don't drop by. I'll let you know when Avery's coming home, and we'll go from there."

"Alex, I love you. Please don't do this."

"Your begging is no more attractive than your lying. Get out of my sight." I dismissed him with a wave and went back into the living room. I pulled out my laptop. There was only one person who could help me through this nightmare.

CODE RED. I REPEAT CODE RED. *If your skinny ass isn't in front of my face in 24 hours there will be hell to pay. Get here NOW. Whether by train or plane or boat or goat or bus or....what mode of transportation rhymes with bus? You get the point, Dr. Seuss. Let me know where and when you'll arrive, and I'll be there. But be warned, this will be our darkest hour in our journey of life. Prepare yourself for drama.*

I heard the back door close, the garage door open, and Sly drive away. I lay down on the sofa with Izzy and her puppies and sobbed uncontrollably until I was completely spent.

Blanketed by Izzy and her litter, I drifted into a fitful sleep which took me to Avery's wedding reception. Avery looked stunning and happy. The weather was perfect, well as perfect as it can be on a southern August night. The food looked fabulous. The band was great. Everyone appeared to be having such a good time.

The night was exactly as I dreamed it would be -- a fairly tale for Avery. I saw Sly chatting with a small group and walked up to join them. I reached for his hand, but mine literally passed through his, like moving through fog. "Sly," I called out in a panic, but he didn't hear me. No one did. I screamed, but still no one heard. I was there, but apparently in spirit only. I could hear everything that was said, but no one could see or hear me.

I watched Sly laughing and smiling with the group. He put his arm around the woman next to him, and I gasped when I saw it was Katlin. I cried out in agony, but to no avail. They kissed and stared in each other's eyes, like newlyweds. I looked at her left hand and it was adorned with a stunning rock twice the size of mine. She wore a wedding band of diamonds and rubies, the band that I always wanted.

I floated around the room listening to snippets of conversations. I stopped beside a group of Sly's business associates and their wives. Lance Griffin was saying, "I feel somewhat responsible for the whole thing. I'm the one who dared Sly to approach that girl, and now he's left Alex and married Katlin. It was just a dare. I never meant for it to blossom into an affair." Lance's wife, Monica, consoled her husband. "Oh, honey, don't blame yourself. It was inevitable. Alex used to be so pretty, and now she's fat. She really let herself go. Look how dreadfully tight her dress is." I followed their gaze to a table by the band. There I sat huddled with Noah, the beautiful dress clearly showing the stress of being pulled beyond its natural elasticity. It hugged my excess flesh in a most unflattering way. Jim Preston commented, "Yeah, Alex used to be a real hottie. Poor girl." Monica reproached, "That's what happens when you stop taking care of yourself. Look at Sly. He's as fit as a thirty-year-old. No wonder he upgraded to a sleeker model." I threw my drink in Monica's face, but of course, she didn't feel it. I always hated that pill-popping, anorexic socialite.

I felt a warmth spread across my belly and awoke to find, Chunk, Izzy's most portly pup, peeing on me as he slept splayed on my stomach. Nice job, Chunk.

I took Izzy and the puppies outside and then tucked them away in their bed in the laundry room. Then I took a shower unable to escape the reality of that nightmare. I had gained a lot of weight. It's not like I started eating or drinking out of control. My doctor said it was a menopausal thing -- that I had to eat less and exercise more. I repulse myself every time I get in the shower, so it's logical that Sly would be repulsed as well. Let's face it; what handsome, fit, successful man wants to be accompanied by a woman built like his mother. Still, there's no excuse for what he did. It was cowardly, selfish, and the timing couldn't have been worse. He started all this up on the eve of Avery's wedding. What a jerk.

I got out of the shower, wrapped myself in a towel, and sat on the edge of the bed. I never thought I'd be one of those women whose husbands leave them after the kids are grown. And I knew plenty. The feelings of rejection and abandonment sent some of them over the edge. But they didn't have good relationships with their husbands, not like Sly and me.

I sighed and went into the closet. My dress for Avery's wedding stared accusingly at me. I knew it wouldn't fit. I knew Amber of Amber's Alterations was the only seamstress in town that might be able to help. I'd go see her first thing Monday morning. I refused to add fuel to the fire by trying it on now. I'd been peed and pooped on enough for one day.

I dressed for bed and checked email to see if Noah had responded.

> *Holy shit, Alex. I about had a heart attack when I saw CODE RED. Luckily I'm between assignments so chilling at home in NYC. I'm on an 11 am Delta flight to Atlanta. I should be available for pickup by one central time, but I'll text you when we land. I'm assuming that Avery's betrothed has flown the coop and the wedding is off.*

I responded:

> *OMG Noah, DO NOT contact Avery. She and Travis are blissfully happy and the wedding is a go. I do NOT want her to be aware of any SHIT that is going on. That's why I need you by my side to make sure her wedding proceeds flawlessly. I'll fill you in tomorrow.*

I couldn't bring myself to sleep in the bed that I shared with Sly. I went to Avery's room and curled up on her bed. Sleep eluded me until the sun was rising.

DALLAS

I stopped at Wal-Mart on the way home from the party to buy puppy food for Justice. I think Alex said they ate Iams. While I was there, I picked up some small dog bowls for food and water, as well as a cozy dog bed. Once home, I got Justice settled. Then I relaxed on my bed thinking about the party. What a night. I can't believe that Alex's cousin is Noah Hargrove, the writer who saved my life. What a small world. I smiled remembering how passionately Jake had kissed Callie. I was happy for them and hoped that they'd share a happily ever after. I'd like to believe that happy endings exist. I thought about Ethan. I missed him and wondered what might have been if I hadn't left the ranch. He warned me that letting my anger drive all my decisions would lead to more pain. Maybe he was right, but I knew I couldn't let it go.

Justice whimpered, so I picked him up and cooed, "If we were still at the ranch, Ethan would be your vet. And Raven would be so excited to play with a puppy." I placed Justice beside me. He burrowed into my side and quickly returned to a peaceful slumber.

I looked at the boxes in the room. My entire life as Dallas O'Malley could be consolidated into three moving boxes, two carry-on pieces of luggage, and one fire safe. When I moved to Birmingham, I knew it would be temporary, so I rented a fully furnished apartment. In three days, I'd be in my car headed where -- I had no clue.

I thought about my last days at the ranch. Five days after Hatcher's disturbing and explosive visit, I had purchased a laptop, secured a WiFi connection, and hired a highly regarded investigative firm in New York City. Within thirty days, I was $20,000 poorer and had no valuable information from my investment.

The investigators found the woman Parker was living with in Paris, Simone Piccard, a beautiful, intelligent heiress born with three silver spoons in her mouth. Simone loaned Parker (though she knew him as James Cavanaugh) 400,000 euros to invest in an exclusive B&B on Lake Como, a famous vacation spot in Italy. The money was earmarked for the renovation and expansion of the B&B's quaint yet inadequate restaurant-bar.

Parker was a masterful con artist. He showed Piccard multiple documents on this business venture, and she even had it checked out independently. Her contacts confirmed that he had been in negotiation to become an investor in the project. According to Piccard, Parker had been working on the deal for months, and the plan was for him to finalize the investment on June 30th. After he signed the documents, Parker planned to spend the next few days searching for a villa on Lake Como. He would develop a "short list", and Simone would join him on July 4th so they could decide together which villa they would purchase. They planned to be married in Lake Como and make their home in the newly purchased villa.

Parker's conversation with Detective Hatcher occurred on June 29th. Apparently he left Paris as planned on June 30th, but Simone never heard from him, and the investors at Lake Como said he never showed. The 400,000 euros had disappeared with him. I wondered if Parker had really intended to go through with his Lake Como life but had changed his plans when he found out that he had murdered the wrong Sanderson family. Miss Piccard should be grateful that she had escaped marriage to a devil.

There was no trail after Parker left France, and with 400,000 euros in cash, there would be no chance of a trail for a long time. I was convinced that he would come to the States to track down his father, but the investigators could find no evidence of his departure. He probably altered his appearance and adopted another alias in order to evade detection by the authorities both domestically and abroad.

The news was devastating. How would I secure the justice I craved? My nightmares escalated, and the pain of knowing that he was free was unbearable. Anger was the only emotion that thrived. Everything else withered swiftly. After Hatcher left, he continued to call every two weeks, but I was cold. I recognized the fact that my attitude was irrational and immature, but I held him singularly responsible for the failure to capture Parker Fielding. Once the NYC private investigators failed to produce anything, I stopped taking his calls. What was the point?

Finally Hatcher mailed me the contact information for Olivia Dunn. I emailed her and told her to hold everything as is -- that I wasn't ready to liquidate. In his letter, Hatcher swore that he had not given up. He admitted that he had limited financial resources, but on his own he was digging into things when he could. I scoffed at his meager offering.

My mood was readily apparent to everyone around me. Granted, I did my work and interacted appropriately with the kids I was training, but I no longer tried to be friendly. I shied away from all opportunities to strengthen relationships, even the ones that I cherished. It was obvious that Trevor, Katie, Raven and Ethan all felt my withdrawal. I wasn't trying to hurt them; I was trying to protect myself. What was the point of getting close to them? Everyone I ever invested in emotionally was ripped from my life. I didn't want to go through that ever again, so I shut down.

I recognized what was happening and embraced the resulting isolation like an old friend. That's the saddest part. I was surrounded by people who cared about me. In my corner, I had a really good man who was a fabulous friend and a precious little girl who, for some reason, adored me and blossomed because of our relationship. I had these wonderful treasures at my fingertips. They represented a second chance at life, but I couldn't move forward. I could focus only on a tragic past and the man who caused it. The only emotion I cultivated was the hatred I felt for the man who took everything away from me.

I abandoned the Thursday night ritual and even Sunday tennis with Ethan. Ethan tried to help, but he didn't push. He knew his ability to reach me was limited. I was cognizant that I was destroying every positive facet of my life, yet I kept doing it. My anger boiled, and the fact that I had no outlet, no hope to subdue it, ate at me like a cancer. I grew numb to everyone and everything except that anger; it consumed me. I was morphing into an empty shell, unfit to shelter anything viable. All that I ever liked about myself was dormant or dying.

By the end of October, it was all I could do to get out of bed every morning. I knew I couldn't continue this way. I remembered Ethan's warning about "living in a perpetual holding pattern". A perfect description of my existence, and I was miserable.

One afternoon I asked Katie if I could borrow the truck. She replied, "Sure. Where are you going?" She tried to be peppy, but I knew she was asking out of worry. Normally she would have never asked.

"Just need to escape for a bit.... going to a secret getaway. Thanks."

I made a few wrong turns, but eventually I found Ethan's sanctuary. I parked by the cabin and began my walk to the lake. My mood lightened slightly as I succumbed to the solitude of nature.

When I reached the end of the dock, I sat and dangled my feet in the cold, clear water. I breathed deeply and felt a sense of calmness I had not experienced since Ethan shared his hidden world with me three months earlier. I closed my eyes and soaked in my surroundings.

It was six in the evening, and nature's orchestra was warming up for its nocturnal symphony. The bullfrogs were doing their scales; the crickets and cicadas were tuning their strings; the geese and mallards, the percussion section, practiced their symbols; the owls perfected their hypnotic vocals.

The symphony alleviated my anger. It was incredible to feel something other than darkness. It had consumed me for so long and suddenly, in this magically medicinal environment, everything became perfectly clear. My pursuit for justice failed because I followed the wrong approach. I knew exactly what I had to do now. The sense of clarity was staggering.

I looked up and gasped. Directly across the lake stood an unsuspecting group of horses. The youngest couldn't have been more than six months, a stunning chestnut filly frolicking in the water. I felt privileged to witness their evening stroll.

"They're breathtaking, aren't they?" a voice from behind beckoned.

I turned and saw Ethan standing a few feet away, hands in his pockets. He was smiling as he watched the horses.

"Hi, Ethan," I said awkwardly, and began to stand. He motioned for me to sit down. He removed his shoes, rolled up his jeans, sat beside me and stuck his feet in the water. "Yes, they're mesmerizing. Are they wild?"

"For the most part. There's a good story behind their presence here, but another time." Ethan focused on the ripples that he was creating with his feet. "So, have you made a decision?" Ethan asked.

"A decision? About what?"

"About your life. Your future. You wouldn't have come here unless you were at a crossroads and seeking answers." He smiled unassumingly.

"You're right. I haven't felt good since the day you brought me here." He was such an insightful person. I longed to swim in the dark pools of his eyes. I missed his occasional kisses and soothing embraces that disappeared as I pushed him away. Deep down in the sliver of me that fought to survive, I knew that if circumstances were different, I would want to pursue a relationship with this kind and patient man. Unfortunately, it was clear to me that unless I was avenged, I couldn't explore anything. This was my pathetic reality.

I looked at him and admitted, "I really miss what we were building, but every day, I slip a little deeper into darkness."

Ethan grabbed my hand. "I can empathize, trust me. I've seen you slipping away a little each day for weeks now, and it kills me, but I know there's nothing I can do to help. Only you can change. Watching you sink into despair made me realize the hell my parents and friends went through when I was where you are now. It's horrifying to watch someone you love fall into a black hole and be helpless to save them."

"What happened to you, Ethan? You've never told me your story."

"I tried to tame a wild thing, and it bit me." He chuckled and rubbed my arms. "Look, at this point my story is irrelevant. Dallas, you have an insatiable craving for justice. Maybe what you seek is really revenge, and this unbridled desire is smothering the good person that you are. One day you'll wake up and not recognize yourself in the mirror."

Ethan used his thumbs to gently wipe away my tears before he spoke again. "Even if you get justice, you'll still be broken. You'll still have all the scars. Your family will still be gone. And you will still be forced to rebuild your life. Let it go and redefine yourself here with the people who care about you."

"I can't give up until I know everything possible has been done."

"Dallas, be realistic. The police haven't found him, and the private investigators had no luck. Maybe it's time to let go and move on."

I shook my head. "Everything you say is true, but I can't give up yet. I think I've found a better way to tackle this manhunt. Parker is too good, and nobody is going to find him. But there is no doubt in my mind that Parker will find his father. So instead of spending my time and energy looking for a chameleon, I need to find my uncle. As long as I locate him before Parker does, I'll get him."

Exasperated, Ethan argued, "Your uncle is either dead or has changed his identity. How are you going to find him?"

"A plan is unfolding in my mind."

"That's definitive," he commented sarcastically. "What will you do if you find him? I don't think he'll welcome you with open arms. He probably doesn't know you were ever born."

"I don't know yet. I don't have the details worked out in my head. Right before you arrived, I came to the conclusion that I've been chasing the wrong ghost all along. It will be much easier to find my unsuspecting uncle than his evil offspring."

Ethan placed his hands on my shoulders. "Dallas, this quest is an obsession, and it's going to kill you."

"You don't know what it's like to have everything ripped away from you," I screamed at him. "Don't you dare judge me."

Ethan buried his face in his hands and screamed into his palms. "Okay. You do what you have to do to be happy." He kissed the top of my head. "And I'll do the same." He kissed my cheek and walked away.

Over the next three evenings, I meticulously outlined a plan to leave the ranch without a trail and begin a search for my estranged uncle. On the third evening, I packed my few belongings in two carry-on suitcases and arranged for a cab to pick me up at 7 am. I copied my contact list from my phone onto a piece of paper -- that didn't take long since there were only four names -- and stored the list in my wallet. I wrote letters to Ethan, Katie and Trevor, and Raven explaining as best I could why I had to leave without saying goodbye. To my fire safe, I added a picture I had from my time at the ranch and the first note from Ethan.

When the cab arrived at 7 am, I took my two suitcases and the small fire safe and loaded them in the trunk. Then I taped the letters to the front door and left the phone on the doorstep. It was time to disappear.

****

I instructed the driver to drop me at Side Bar Grill in downtown Lexington. Although I planned to pay for everything in cash, I decided that I needed an alias until I was clear of Lexington. I combined the names of my two favorite horses at the ranch to become Olive Weasley. Once seated, I had a quick snack and asked the server to call a cab for me. I had the second cab drop me at the bus station. I had already researched the schedules, so I quickly purchased my ticket to Cincinnati in cash. Upon arrival I took a cab to the Hilton Cincinnati Netherland Plaza, checked in as Olive Weasley, and paid in cash.

Once settled, I poured myself a shot of bourbon from the minibar to steady my nerves so I could face my next step. This was going to be very difficult for me. I knew that I had to hide from Parker Fielding, and I thought chances were strong that our paths might cross as we searched for the same man. He wouldn't recognize the name Dallas O'Malley, but he would recognize me. I pulled the styling scissors and box of L'Oréal hair color from my suitcase. I cried as I cut my blonde locks to the base of my neck. Then, I shortened it further by layering it like a boy's haircut. I felt like Anne Hathaway in Les Misérables though my end result looked far better than hers.

The sun kissed caramel shade of brunette wasn't so bad, but once the color was set and I dried my hair, I didn't recognize myself in the mirror. I suppose that was the point.

The next morning, I loaded my things in a taxi that took me to a used car lot close to the hotel. I had already selected online a five-year-old Nissan Rogue with 52,000 miles, paid cash and set my newly acquired Garmin to the address for the Harvard Square Hotel. Harvard Law School was the last place the Sanderson twins were known to exist as brothers; thus, my search would begin there.

Once acclimated to the area, I went to the law school library. With the help of a student, I was able to secure a copy of the first page of the "S" section of the 1974 yearbook that profiled the graduating class. On the top row, immortalized for history, were Cal and Hank Sanderson, side by side, looking exactly the same except for subtle differences in their blue eyes. Despite their identical nature, there was some quality in the infamous Uncle Hank that drew your eyes to him rather than my dad. He exuded a drive or confidence that was captivating.

I took this copy to the registrar's office and crossed my fingers that someone could help. I explained to the secretary that I was developing a family history for my mom as a Christmas present, and I was having difficulty tracking down information on her twin cousins who graduated from Harvard Law School in 1974. I showed her the picture and pointed to the Sanderson twins.

The secretary, who was no more than twenty-five, explained, "Unfortunately, I'm not at liberty to disclose any information from our student files." I think she picked up on my desperation. She glanced around the office and spotted an older woman at the copier. "You see that lady back there?" she spoke in hushed tones as she pointed. "Her name is Miss Duvall, and she's worked in this office for forty-five years. She has a mind like a steel trap. It's amazing really. She's retiring this year, and she loves to tell stories about former students. At ten o'clock every day, she walks over to the cafe down the street and has coffee and a blueberry muffin while she reads her *New Yorker* magazine. If you just casually ran into her at the cafe and engaged her in conversation, I wouldn't be surprised if she could share a little information, particularly if there are any interesting stories related to these twins. As hot as those guys were, I bet there are some stories."

"Thank you."

The next morning, I was at the cafe at 9:45 am waiting patiently for Miss Duvall to arrive. Promptly at ten, she walked through the door. After she ordered, I nervously approached, hoping that my tactics would work. "Excuse me. You're not Miss Duvall, are you? The Miss Duvall that works at the law school?"

She pulled her reading glasses to the tip of her nose and looked up at me. "The one and only, dear. I don't know you, do I? I rarely forget a face."

"Oh, no, we've never met, but one of the students told me that you were probably the only person on campus who could help me solve a mystery."

"Which student?" she inquired.

"Unfortunately, I'm not good with names, so I don't remember. Could I trouble you for a moment of your time?"

"Yes, please, do sit down. I like a good mystery," she commented as she set aside her magazine and reading glasses to give me her undivided attention.

"Thank you. My name is Dallas O'Malley, and I'm from Sanibel Island, Florida. For several months now, I've been tracing my mother's family history. I want to give it to her as a Christmas present."

"What a charming gift," Miss Duvall commended.

"Thank you. I'm excited about it. She's said for years that she wished she had the patience to conduct some genealogy research. What I think she really wants is to reconnect with some of her favorite relatives with whom she's lost touch over the years."

"And, I bet she has a long-lost relative that attended Harvard Law School."

"Actually, two. She had twin cousins, boys, who she talked about as her favorite childhood playmates. I think they were second cousins. Anyway, they moved away when she was around ten, and they lost touch. All she knows is that the boys attended Harvard Law School." I extracted the yearbook photocopy from my purse and spread the paper in front of Miss Duvall. "See these guys here," I pointed to their pictures, "Cal and Hank Sanderson. They graduated in 1974."

"The Sanderson twins!" Miss Duvall clutched her chest. "My, I could never forget these stunning men. I wasn't much older than them, so I witnessed much of their extracurricular activities because I frequented the same spots that the students did. The stories I could tell. I could write a scandalous novel. Maybe I'll do that when I retire, which is very soon."

"You don't look old enough to retire!" I exclaimed, trying to win her trust, but in reality, she really did look far too young for retirement.

"You're sweet...Dallas, right?" I nodded. "Told you I don't forget much."

"I'm impressed," I stroked her ego and smiled.

"Now back to the Sanderson twins. Those two boys were like night and day. I mean they looked exactly alike. If you didn't know them, the only way you could tell them apart was by their eyes -- both blue but very different." She paused and studied my eyes before continuing. "I see Cal's eyes run in your side of the family. That's a compliment."

"What do you mean?"

"Cal's eyes were kind, full of joy and goodness, while Hank's were cold and unyielding. Like I said, despite being identical twins, they were nothing alike. They were both brilliant, but it's like when that cell split in their mother's womb, all the good character traits shifted to one side of the cell -- the side that became Cal." Miss Duvall paused, contemplating this genetic anomaly. "Despite their differences, though, they were close. Cal looked after Hank as if he were a much older brother. If Hank got in trouble, Cal always found a way to bail him out."

"Miss Duvall, you don't happen to know how I can locate these cousins, do you?"

"Cal Sanderson was a devoted contributor to the school and even came back on occasion as a guest lecturer. And he rarely missed a reunion. But I'm sad to say that Cal and his entire family were tragically killed in an explosion on a boat in Charleston. It was about fifteen months ago on the Fourth of July. There was speculation of foul play, but last I heard the case was never solved."

Miss Duvall appeared alarmed when she saw tears streaming down my cheeks. "Oh dear, I'm sorry. I didn't mean to upset you."

"Sorry," I said as I wiped my tears. "I know my mother would be so upset to hear that news. What about Hank Sanderson? Do you know where he went after law school?"

"Well," Miss Duvall whispered as she looked around the restaurant for potential eavesdroppers, "that's another mystery, and it all came about the summer after they graduated."

"What happened?" I asked.

"I never knew how Hank made such outstanding grades because he was always busy chasing the girls. Actually, they were always chasing him. Cal was the real catch, but girls at that age seem to gravitate to the bad boys. Anyway, spring of their third year, Hank became a regular at a trashy strip joint off campus. He started sleeping with this stripper. I hate to be crass, but he didn't date her, he just screwed her after his drunken nights at the club -- and there were many drunken nights. The story is that the girl thought Hank really cared for her, but Hank left Cambridge after he graduated and that was the end of that. Cal and Hank were hired by separate firms in the Boston area and began working right after graduation. Hank's stripper girl turns up pregnant, tracks down Hank at his law firm, and makes a huge scene in the lobby of the firm. Hank tells her that he doesn't love her, he doesn't want the baby, and to basically get lost. He screamed at her that she was just a common whore with no brain in her head. She threatened to sue him for child support and lost wages because pregnant strippers don't get paid. Anyway, the stripper lawyered up, and Hank flew off to Paris never to be heard from again."

"Don't you think he eventually returned to the States?" I asked, hopeful that she might have some information.

Miss Duvall shook her head. "The last time I saw Cal, which was the 2009 reunion, I asked if he had ever reconnected with his brother. He said no. Poor Cal stiffened at the mention of his brother. So heart wrenching."

I must have looked like I was about to cry again. "I'm sorry, Dallas. I hate to disappoint you."

"Thank you. My mom would be heartbroken, so I'm not sure I'll share either story," I continued my ruse. "Miss Duvall, I want to make every effort to see if perhaps Hank Sanderson returned to the US. Is there anyone at the school that students reach out to after they've left? Like a professor who was really popular with the students?"

Miss Duvall pondered. "Most of the professors would be deceased by now, but there is one professor who is still around that has always maintained a rapport with many of his students after they graduated. His name is Byron Larkin. He's down to teaching two classes now, so he's here only on Tuesdays and Thursdays."

"Do you think he would talk to me?" I asked excitedly. "I know it's a long shot, but I'd like to try."

"Don't get your hopes up, but I'll chat with him and arrange a time for you to meet. It's Friday afternoon, so it will be next week. If you give me your cell number, I'll call you."

"Oh, I'm without a phone right now, but here's my hotel number."

"Okay," she said as she folded the paper and put it in her purse. "Expect to hear from me Monday afternoon between 3 and 4." I rose, extended my hand and thanked her for her time and help.

At 3:45 on Monday afternoon, Miss Duvall honored her promise and called to tell me that Professor Larkin had agreed to meet me in his office at 10:30 on Tuesday morning.

Anxiety overwhelmed me as I knocked on his door the next day. If he didn't know anything, what would I possibly do next? It would be like looking for a needle in a haystack. The door opened and an adorable old man greeted me. Professor Larkin was tiny, frail and no more than five foot five. He had a thick head of silver hair, piercing emerald green eyes and a smile that revealed charming dimples.

"Professor Larkin?" He nodded. "I'm Dallas O'Malley. Thank you for agreeing to see me."

"Come in, please," he invited as he stepped aside for me to enter. His office was lined on three walls with shelves fully loaded with law books, textbooks and other works. Every surface was occupied except a small rectangle of space in the center of his desk. He offered me a cup of coffee and pointed to a chair that was covered with file folders. "Goodness, I can't expect you to sit on top of those files," he said as he moved them to the floor. "Now how can I help you? Miss Duvall said you were a distant cousin of the Sanderson twins and that you were trying to get information on them for your mother's genealogy chart."

"Yes," I confirmed, "I'm sure you are aware that Cal Sanderson and his family were murdered a little over a year ago."

"Murdered? I wasn't aware there was foul play. I thought it was a boating accident. An explosion of some sort."

"That's true, but there's evidence that the explosion was from a bomb."

"A bomb! Unbelievable. Why would anyone want to harm Cal Sanderson? He was among the finest students to grace our hallowed halls. I wouldn't find it hard to believe that someone might murder his brother Hank, but not Cal."

"That's an interesting comment," I reflected aloud.

"How insensitive of me. I apologize. After all, he is a distant cousin of yours, right?"

"Yes sir, but no need to apologize. Why do you say that a plot to murder Hank wouldn't surprise you?" He looked at me hesitantly. "Please be perfectly candid with me," I reassured. "Just because I know the sordid truth doesn't mean I'll share it all with my mother. I will certainly take her feelings into account. I wouldn't want to ruin any fond childhood memories she has of her twin cousins."

"Very well. In a nutshell, Cal was a saint, and Hank was a sinner. Hank was brilliant, more naturally gifted intellectually than Cal, but he was a womanizer and a selfish bastard who thought of no one but himself. He was ruthless in mock trials. He would easily befriend a witness on the stand, making him feel completely comfortable, and then viciously turn on that witness all in the matter of a few moments. If he continued practicing law, I'm confident he became quite successful as a trial lawyer. Soon after he graduated, though, he went to Europe in an effort to avoid a scandal that I'm sure Miss Duvall divulged. I don't think he's been heard from since."

I felt deflated but not ready to give up. "Professor, based on how you and Miss Duvall have described Hank Sanderson, he sounds like the type of man whose ego would compel him to return home, eventually. If he waited a year or two, he could return under an assumed name and completely avoid detection by his jilted stripper. I know that former students occasionally contact you for advice. Do you ever remember being contacted by someone that you didn't know, but who seemed familiar? Maybe the voice or demeanor rang a bell? I realize it's been forty years and that my theory is a long shot, but is there any call or email you can remember that struck you as odd?"

I sipped my coffee and patiently waited as he scrolled through the files in his brain. Suddenly his eyes sparkled. "I do recall a strange phone call I received several years ago from a charming gentleman who claimed to be a former student. I didn't recognize the name, but then he said that he was in the class with Hank and Cal Sanderson. Anyway, he questioned me about some obscure legal technicalities, and he thanked me for my time."

"I don't follow. What's so odd about that call?"

"After I hung up, I was curious to place the name with the face, so I looked him up. He didn't exist."

Instantly, I knew that was my uncle. "Do you remember his name, Professor Larkin?"

"Oh, dear. My memory isn't what it once was. Not like that Miss Duvall who sent you here. That woman is a walking encyclopedia of Harvard Law School students."

"She's impressive," I commented trying not to sound impatient. "But do you remember the caller's name or law firm?"

"It's been so many years, and it was just that one phone call," he defended himself. "Now I'm confident that he didn't tell me his firm's name, but his name was...Andrew...or Andrews...Either his first name was Andrew or his last name was Andrews. But I'm positive that Andrew was part of his name."

Great. I have to search for every attorney in the United States with the first name Andrew or the last name Andrews. At least it was a start, I reminded myself. "Professor, do you remember anything else about the phone call that might be helpful. Like something that might indicate what part of the country he was calling from?"

Professor Larkin strummed his chin. "Let me see. I did tell him to look me up at the next class reunion. He said he hadn't been back to Cambridge since graduation, but that he sure did miss the weather and the culture. He said he'd love to walk down the street in the summer without being drenched in ten minutes and that he wished he were surrounded by more enlightened people. I thought that last part was quite arrogant. I suppose that's why I remembered."

He's in the South and obviously not a big city like Atlanta or Miami or an artist's haven like Charleston. "Professor, thank you for your time." I rose and walked toward the door.

"Miss O'Malley, if you do find that Hank Sanderson returned to the States, would you let me know? I'm curious to hear what kind of life he led."

"I will, sir. Have a lovely day."

For the next ten weeks, I conducted an exhaustive search for any attorney in the South with the first name, Andrew, or last name Andrews. I googled and researched in every way possible to eliminate attorneys. If I couldn't eliminate in this manner, I called the law firm I was researching and described his age, looks or even faxed the yearbook photo from 1974. A few secretaries would not engage in such a conversation, but most were kind and indulged me. For those I could not eliminate, I made a list. If necessary, I would drive to each law firm and make an appointment with each Andrew/Andrews. I would find him.

My biggest mistake was starting with Florida. I don't know why I didn't start with the smaller southern states. If I had, I would have hit the jackpot much sooner. But I wasted four weeks on Florida before moving on to Louisiana, Mississippi, and Arkansas. It was a tedious process that, in retrospect, led me down a self-destructive path. First of all, it was an obsessive, miserable undertaking that isolated me further from humanity. The tedium drove me to take frequent breaks in the form of trips to the mini bar. I had copious amounts of take-out delivered to my hotel room. I ate and drank almost anything. Since I slept so fitfully, my munching breaks occurred around the clock. My trips out of my hotel room were infrequent; I left only for money and new clothes to cover my ever expanding girth. When I needed money, I had it wired to a branch in New York City or Connecticut, and I would drive to that bank. In case anyone was trying to track Dallas O'Malley, it would lead him to the wrong state. Thus, I secured large sums of cash to avoid frequent drives out of state. During the three months I was in Cambridge, I had money wired only four times.

I isolated myself to the point that I was oblivious to the real world. Thanksgiving and Christmas passed without much thought. I rarely thought about my life at the Roberts Ranch in Kentucky. Ethan, Raven, Katie and Trevor seemed like a dream to me, part of another world. All that mattered was finding my uncle, because I knew he would lead me, at some point, to Parker.

By the time I located him, I hated my uncle as much as Parker and had convinced myself that he was equally responsible for my family's deaths. I wanted father and son to pay.

On February 1, 2014, I loaded my SUV, paid my final bill at Harvard Square Hotel and headed to Birmingham, Alabama. I didn't realize it at the time, but I had truly redefined myself as Dallas O'Malley -- severely introverted, thirty pounds overweight, and driven by the desire to destroy the two people responsible for crushing my world. There was nothing left of Providence Sanderson.

****

Now here I am, a little more than six months later, ready to avenge my family and hopefully reclaim my life as Providence Sanderson. Justice whimpered beside me, so I picked him up and kissed his slimy nose. With my puppy curled up on my stomach, I drifted into a light sleep. I was in Mary Claire's house holding a gun to Andrew Jameson's temple. Mary Claire was seated directly across from him pleading with me not to kill him. I told my wicked uncle to tell his wife the truth. I wanted her to know that he was a bigger monster than she realized.

When I glanced away from my captive, I found Detective Hatcher, Katie, Trevor, Raven and Ethan encircling Mary Claire. Wearing desperate expressions, they simultaneously begged me to abandon the gun and let the police take control. I told them I wasn't going to shoot him; I only wanted Mary Claire to know the truth about her husband. After all, I reminded them, the police can't prosecute a man for fathering a mass murderer or being a coward.

I turned to Andrew Jameson. "Tell them who you really are, Hank?" Suddenly my uncle lunged and knocked me to the ground. The gun fired upon impact, and a bullet lodged itself between Raven's eyes. I cried out in horror, but Ethan's scream dwarfed mine as he caught his daughter's lifeless body in his arms. Enraged, he dove for Andrew who had recovered the gun from the floor. As Ethan tackled him, Jameson fired two bullets directly into Ethan's chest. I screamed and yanked the gun from my uncle's hand. I knew there were three bullets left, and I emptied the chamber into his chest.

When my uncle fell, a sinister laugh erupted behind me. Parker Fielding smiled at the sight of his biological father's lifeless form. "Lady, I don't know who you are, but thanks for doing my work for me. Although I'm a little pissed that you robbed me of the pleasure." He walked over to his father's corpse and looked down. "Maybe this will make up for it." He put the barrel of his own gun directly between his father's eyes and pulled the trigger. "That's better," he said and walked out.

I sat up with a gasp and looked at my clock. I had been asleep for only ten minutes. Slumber now held no appeal. I turned on the TV and began channel surfing.

CALLIE

After I got Mary Claire settled in Jake's guest room, I returned to the living room to find Jake sprawled on the floor with a puppy. "I could swear I just left Rudolph in the bed with Mary Claire."

He turned the puppy to face me and pointed to his nose. "This isn't Rudolph. He's yours. Well, mine too. He's ours. What do you think?"

"I think I can barely take care of myself, much less a dog." I picked him up. "He is adorable in an 'off the beaten path' sort of way." He laughed. "You really want to do this, Jake?"

"Absolutely. Dogs are soothing companions. I've wanted one for a while. If we tag team, it'll be easier. And this little guy is Rudolph's best friend, so it would be a crime to separate them."

"And, you thought you could dump him on Mary Claire if need be," I teased.

"I wouldn't take advantage of her. Besides, it works both ways. If she needs a break from Rudolph, he can hang out with this guy. They can entertain each other."

"Does he have a name?" I asked.

"Alex didn't mention one. What do you want to call him?"

"Let's do something tennis related," I suggested. "Seems appropriate under the circumstances."

You want to call him Fed, don't you?" he teased, knowing that Roger Federer was my all time favorite tennis player.

"Not bad. But I wouldn't be opposed to calling him Mac, after one of your favorites."

"Thank you." Jake smiled and pecked my lips. "Those are options, but we can come up with something more original. Come on Callie; you're the wordsmith."

I laughed and punched his bicep lightly. "Nothing like a little pressure to stall the brain cells. Let's deliberate overnight."

"Okay."

I propped myself against a chair across from Jake. "Mary Claire didn't fall down the stairs, did she, Jake?"

"Yes, ma'am, she did fall down the stairs..after her loving husband pushed her."

"I started thinking about the timing of certain events. Mary Claire's alleged fall occurred the same weekend as our date. She was your emergency, wasn't she?"

"Correct." Jake exhaled a deep sigh. "I'm relieved you finally know. She was in a lot of pain when I arrived, and, of course Jameson was gone when I got there. 'Hit and run'. That's his MO. I took her to Druid City Hospital in Tuscaloosa (where the Jamesons are known to few), claimed she was my spinster sister, Claire Lenaghan, who fell down the stairs. No, she didn't have insurance since she lost her job two years ago. I would pay the medical expenses. Same drill, different hospital, all to protect the reputation of a wife-beater. They kept her overnight to monitor her concussion. We didn't get back to Birmingham until late afternoon the next day. That's why I didn't call you."

"You've done this before?"

Jake nodded. "That was the fifth time over the past ten years. Each time we go to a different hospital."

"Jake, I can't believe you haven't reported him." My tone was incensed. "He could've killed her."

"Callie, I tried to get her to turn him in, but she swore she wouldn't testify against him. She's the classic abused wife. She made excuses for him and blamed herself. But I told her the other day that she was an idiot to stay with him, and if she called me again, I wasn't coming to her rescue without backup."

"So the long-sleeved shirts in the dead of summer?" I began.

"To cover up bruises. Jameson has always abused Mary Claire, but it used to be more emotional abuse than physical. Over the past two years, I think the physical abuse has increased. I don't think she really understands why. Nor do I. The catalyst could be stress at work or maybe an affair. Who knows."

I covered my face. "I can't believe she's been going through this all these years, and I never saw it. You tried to point me in the right direction by suggesting that there's more going on with her than she discloses. You told me I should talk to her, and I did that but she dismissed my concerns, and I let it go. I'm a horrible friend."

"Don't beat yourself up. I'm not sure I would have seen it if she hadn't confided in me. She does an Oscar worthy performance as the well-bred, poised, and gracious wife of a highly successful trial lawyer. She's Birmingham's own Jackie Kennedy. And Jameson was the one who trained her. He played God with a young, impressionable woman and molded her into his image of the ideal wife."

I was appalled. "Before tonight, I'd been around him only once, and I didn't care for him. Way too arrogant and opinionated for my taste. But attraction is an inexplicable force, and Mary Claire seemed so happy and together. I actually envied her marriage."

"You know the old saying, 'you never know what someone else's life is really like until you walk in their shoes'," Jake reflected.

"Yes, I'm familiar with that tune of misperceptions and its many verses -- 'the grass is always greener on the other side'."

"Indeed," Jake commented as he rose to his feet. "I'm going to take No Name out one last time and then let him sleep next to Rudolph. Mary Claire will probably wake up with a pounding headache and think she's seeing double."

"Jake," I called as he turned toward the back door. "Why do you think she decided to leave? It seems like the older you are, the harder it would be to leave. Alex and I both noticed that she became very grumpy, almost hostile, since she broke her arm."

He shrugged. "She's the only one who can answer that question, but honestly, I think she looked in the mirror and didn't like what she saw anymore."

"If it's okay with you, I think I'll stay here tonight in case she needs anything."

"I think that's a good idea."

"Do you mind if I use your shower?"

"Knock yourself out."

****

When I got out of the shower, I found Jake sitting in the guest room, watching over Mary Claire. Undetected, I stood in the doorway and studied him with admiration. A guardian angel, he looked at Mary Claire like a parent holding vigil over his ailing child. The unmasked tenderness and warmth enhanced his manliness. I was so in love with this man and was thankful that he had patiently waited for me to figure that out. I wasn't sure I deserved someone this wonderful, but I knew that from this day forward, I would refrain from taking him for granted.

"How is she?" I whispered.

He looked in my direction and smiled. "That t-shirt never looked that good on me."

"Thanks," I said as I moved toward his chair. "I thought it looked comfortable." There was plenty of room in the wide lounge chair, so I straddled him and kissed him. I poured every emotion I had into that fervent kiss. I knew it conveyed the depths of my feelings far better than words.

"Wow," he moaned as he opened his eyes. He started rubbing my thighs. "I like it when you speak without words."

I smiled. Jake's caresses moved up my thighs and under my shirt but stopped when he unexpectedly hit bare skin. He stared at me longingly. "Are you sure about this?"

"Positive," I whispered and slowly kissed his neck.

Jake stood up, keeping me wrapped around his waist by supporting my bottom with both hands. "Not in front of the kids," he said playfully, and nibbled my ear.

He carried me into the bedroom and laid me on his bed. I have no idea how long we were there, but we spoke volumes without uttering a syllable. Our eyes, our lips, and our bodies did all the talking. Jake lay down beside me on his stomach and gently stroked my face and neck. I closed my eyes and immersed myself in the hypnotic pleasure of his touch. He moved to my arms and legs, never rushing, giving equal attention to each limb. When he slipped his hand underneath my shirt and touched my breast, I moaned as I ached for him to be closer.

I sat up and removed his shirt. I caressed his lean but ripped biceps and admired the subtle definition of his abdomen as I moved my hands slowly down to his shorts. He watched me intently as I slowly removed his shorts and boxers, ceremoniously touching every inch of him in the process. He obviously enjoyed the process. Unabashedly, I soaked in every inch of him. Jake was a beautiful man. He removed my shirt and performed a similar ceremony, lingering in areas known to arouse pleasure. Oddly, I didn't feel shy or self-conscious. I trusted him and was fine with him touching me as he pleased. He pulled me on top of him and the sensation of our bare skin touching was intoxicating. He held my face and kissed me hungrily. I kissed him back, conveying an unmistakably insatiable craving for more.

The kiss unleashed a powerfully emotional and erotic dance. There was no awkwardness, no jockeying for dominance. We held nothing back, just two bodies flowing together in perfect unison. It felt as if our bodies and souls melded into one undulating form, losing ourselves in the various rhythms of our dance, sometimes feverish in intensity, sometimes breathtaking in simplicity.

I had never experienced anything even remotely close to this level of pure physical and emotional unity. It was like entering another world -- a dimension free of boundaries and inhibitions. Provocative, unadulterated.

We lay in each other's arms, legs intertwined. I broke the silence. "You have no idea how many times I've fantasized about making love to you."

"Really," he commented, obviously flattered by the admission. "That's a little intimidating since fantasy typically far exceeds reality."

I smiled. "I'll admit that my fantasies about you were HOT, very awesome, but you're the exception to the rule, because in this case, the reality is far better than the fantasy."

"Thank you," Jake said and kissed me tenderly. "I'll admit I've had a fantasy or two about you."

"Only two?" I asked disappointedly.

"Maybe a few more than that. The ones that hit me during clinics were wicked. It's very difficult to conduct a team clinic when I'm having inappropriate thoughts about the captain."

I laughed. "Was that callous of us to get so wrapped up in each other with Mary Claire in the other room?" I asked guiltily.

"No," he answered with a laugh. "If she heard a moan or groan, she would have cheered us on."

I belted him playfully in the abs. "You're bad."

"Dreadful, I know."

"I thought of the perfect name for the pup," I offered. "Let's call him Poach."

"Is that what you were thinking about while I was giving you my best moves?"

"Of course not. I thought of that while I was in the shower."

"Well, in that case, Poach it is."

ALEX

As I drove to the Atlanta airport on Sunday morning, I made a call that in a million years I never would have dreamed would be necessary. I reached out to my husband's mistress.

The phone rang four times before a voice answered, "Hello, this is Katlin Hamilton's phone. May I help you?"

The voice on the line was formal but clearly protective. I assumed it was Katlin's mother. I knew that Katlin had me in her contact list, so when my name popped up, Mama Bear took control to protect her cub. "Mrs. Hamilton? Could I please speak to Katlin?"

Again the voice was pleasant, but guarded. "I'm sorry, but she's not feeling well. She's resting now."

"Mrs. Hamilton, this is Alex Anderson. We met when I brought Katlin to the hospital after the snake debacle." She didn't respond, so I continued. "Please understand that I'm not calling to upset Katlin. Last night all the stars aligned to reveal that my husband, with whom I have cherished every moment for thirty years, is having an affair with your daughter. I know that you're aware because of a conversation I had with my daughter last night. My daughter is completely in the dark in this situation, but as Katlin's friend, she is deeply concerned about her. I know beyond a shadow of a doubt that Katlin was not aware that she was falling in love with a married man, and worse, her tennis teammate's husband, and her friend's father. My daughter's wedding is in two weeks, and Katlin was so excited about coming and bringing her boyfriend, Sam. I know she's devastated and innocent, but I need to talk to her."

"I must say, Mrs. Anderson, you seem surprisingly calm about this situation."

"Calm?" I repeated. "Far from it, Mrs. Hamilton. I'm in shock, and I'm numb. I haven't had a chance to process this nightmare, and I can assure you that this has hit me as unexpectedly as it has your daughter. But my focus for the next two weeks is 100% on my daughter, Avery, and making sure that NOTHING interferes with her wedding. Her father and I will find a way to appear completely together so that she gets the perfect day that she deserves. So I need to make sure that Katlin steers clear of Avery. I don't think she can talk to Avery without breaking down."

It was quiet on the other end. "Mrs. Hamilton, are you there?"

"Yes, I'm still here," she answered, her tone a little more friendly. "Katlin really is asleep. She cried all night and finally drifted off about an hour ago."

"Don't disturb her, but I'd really appreciate it if you had her call me when she wakes up."

"I will." There was a long pause. "Mrs. Anderson, I appreciate your kindness toward my daughter. Katlin's made many mistakes in matters of the heart, but I do believe she was sincerely duped in this situation."

"We both were. Thanks for your time."

****

When I saw Noah emerge from baggage claim, I felt the weight on my shoulders lift a little. Noah always found a way to lighten the severity of bad times. I got out of my car, walked to him, and smothered him with a tight embrace.

"Oh God," he commented worriedly. "It must be really bad. You didn't call me fart-face."

Since we were ten years old, I had greeted him with "hello, fart-face". That is, until today.

"It's bad, Noah." We loaded the car, and I headed toward I-20 West to return to Birmingham. "How was your flight?"

"Bumpy, but I made it. Just give it to me straight. Spit it out now."

"It's not that easy, Noah. I'm still in shock. It's hard for me to believe."

"Alex, it's me. Just say it."

I sighed heavily. "Sly's been having an affair with a twenty-seven-year-old."

"No fucking way!" Noah screamed. "I don't believe it. It's no secret that Sly and I aren't buddies, but I've always thought he adored you. Never would I peg him as a cheater."

"The details will blow your mind. What a tangled web we weave." The phone rang. It was Katlin. "I have to take this." He nodded.

"Hi, Katlin. Thanks for calling me back." She cried uncontrollably. "Sweetie, this is not your fault, okay. I'm angry and hurt, and mostly in shock right now, but I'm not upset with you." I continued talking as she sniffled. Noah stared at me, confused. "I know that you're innocent. I don't understand how he could do this to me and to you, but I don't want to focus on that right now. I'm not going to deal with this subject until after the wedding. Katlin, Avery cannot know what her dad has done. It will destroy her, and she deserves a fairy-tale day. Please send her a text and tell her that you're better. She'll ask what you meant when you said, 'I'm sorry, I promise I didn't know'. Just tell her you meant that you didn't know a breakup could be so devastating that you couldn't find a way to come to her wedding." Katlin struggled to say a few sentences. "That's probably a great idea. I hope it helps." I hung up.

"Were you just comforting the enemy?" Noah asked, shocked.

"She's not the enemy, Noah," I corrected through a tired smile. "She's a victim." I looked at the clock. "We've got another hour and a half before we're home. Do you want me to spill it now or when we get to the house?"

"Depends. Will Sly be there?"

"Hell no. I kicked him out last night and told him to stay away until he hears from me."

"Then let's wait until we get to your house and get comfortable. Why don't we talk about Avery. That's a happy subject."

"Ah, I need to call Avery." I picked up my phone and dialed. When she answered, I greeted, "Hey, baby girl."

"Hey, Mom."

"I'm just checking on you. You sounded really upset last night."

"Sorry. I was so worried about Katlin. It was such a shock to hear her say that things had gone bad with the boyfriend. She seemed so happy -- almost euphoric. She even thought he was going to propose the other day."

That comment caught me off guard. "Propose! They haven't been dating very long, have they?"

"Around two months, I think. He kept telling her he had a big surprise for her. She never told me what it was, but obviously it wasn't a ring."

"Suppose not. Listen, honey, I called Katlin today, and she's okay. She's very hurt, but she'll recover."

"Did she tell you what went wrong?"

"No, she didn't go into it," I lied. "Her mother is taking her on a trip to the Caymans, and she won't be back until the day after your wedding. She feels horrible about missing your big day, but I told her a wedding is no place for a girl with a freshly broken heart. I told her you'd understand."

"Of course. I'm glad she's getting away from everything. And I hope that Sam Flaherty gets his due."

"Something tells me he will." I was sure I'd scoop out a big dish of evil for him before it was all said and done.

"What a jerk," Avery declared vehemently.

"A complete scoundrel," I confirmed. "Oh, by the way, I'm in the car driving back from Atlanta. I picked up a colorful surprise for you." I handed the phone to Noah, and the two chattered away for the next fifteen minutes.

During the rest of the trip, we covered Avery's wedding details and Noah's recent travels. When we crossed the Georgia-Alabama state line, Noah said, "Now that we're in God's country, I'm craving some southern caviar. Please stop at the first roadside stand."

"I hate to disappoint you, babe, but you've got to be a lot farther south before you'll find a boiled peanuts stand on the side of the road. Most people who live above Montgomery have never tasted one."

"What!" Noah was appalled. "That stinks. Guess I'll make them myself. Can you buy unshelled peanuts in the store?"

"I'm not sure. It's not on my radar when I'm grocery shopping."

Noah crossed his arms in a huff and vowed, "I can't visit this part of the world without having my favorite southern delicacy, damn it. I have a mission now."

"I'M your mission, fart-face," I reminded him.

Noah laughed. "Fart-face. There's my girl. Don't worry. You are my number one priority. But I'll still find a way to have some damn boiled peanuts, even if it requires a road trip."

"I'm sure you will, you obsessive freak," I responded affectionately.

When we got home, Noah settled into the guest room while I took out Izzy and the three remaining pups.

"Lawd!" Noah gasped when he saw the babies. "Those are the strangest looking critters I've ever seen." Izzy barked. "Well, I'm sorry girl. Truth hurts."

Noah selected a bottle from the wine rack. He handed me a glass with a generous pour and then equipped himself with the same. We each found a comfortable spot in the family room, and I spilled all the details. Noah interrupted on occasion to ask questions, but for the most part, it was a soliloquy. I didn't shed a tear. What does that mean?

When I was done, Noah spoke. "I gotta say, Alex, I'm blown away. I would've bet my savings that he would never cheat on you."

"Me too. So we'd lose and be in the poorhouse together," I said through a snicker. "I feel stupid because I had absolutely no clue. Sly's behavior has been normal, except that he's been entertaining for work more than usual. But he hasn't acted unhappy, moody or distant. We've been the same old Sly and Alex. Maybe I've been so wrapped up in Avery's wedding plans that I've been blind to it."

"No, I don't think so. It all sounds more like an out-of-control midlife crisis. What fifty-year-old man isn't going to be bolstered by a hot twenty-seven-year-old paying attention to him. After all, he used his Sam Flaherty bar alias when he met her, and you know what that means. Sounds like Sly got a dose of attention that drove him to succumb to temptation."

I stretched out on the sofa. "I remember the night I met Sly at Gillette's. The place was packed. Bama had crushed UT that afternoon, so everybody was out celebrating. Sly came up to me, introduced himself as Sam Flaherty and asked if he could buy me a beer. We chatted for an hour before my friends were ready to leave. As I started to go, he grabbed my arm and told me that he was really Sam Anderson, but everybody called him Sly. When I asked him why he was telling me that, he confessed that he used Flaherty in bars so no whacky sorority girls could track him down. He said he was giving me his real name because he wanted me to find him."

"I remember that night vaguely. You called me at 2 am to tell me all about the charming frat boy you met at Gillette's. If you recall, I thought the whole Sam Flaherty alias was cheesy, but you thought it was charming."

"Yes, I remember," I conceded. I sat quietly for a few moments before continuing. "This affair may have started as an innocent flirtation, Noah, but I think Sly developed real feelings for her. And their relationship changed her. When I met Katlin at the beginning of the season, I wasn't impressed. She seemed to live up to her reputation as a spoiled, entitled brat. But as the season progressed, I saw positive changes in her personality -- tolerance, humility, kindness, patience. She really matured. I know she fell in love with Sly. Hell, she was talking about marrying him because he was 'the one'. The most hurtful thing to me is that deep down inside, I know that Sly genuinely cares for her, because I don't think he's capable of faking it that well." Tears rolled down my cheeks as I spoke.

"Or maybe," Noah speculated, "Katlin is slightly delusional and sees what she wants to see rather than reality. You've heard only her description of their relationship, not Sly's."

"My gut tells me otherwise," I argued. My tears grew heavier, and my lip started quivering. "I think maybe he really loves her. Why not? I've gotten fat, and he still looks like a Greek god." Noah gave me a look. "Think about it, Noah. Avery's about to get married, and they're moving to Italy. Although she'll always be Daddy's little girl, things are never the same once you get married. Your focus is on building your own family...as it should be."

Noah sat next to me. "Okay, you listen to me. I get it. I don't even like Sly, and his indiscretion has rocked me to the core. So I know it is a million times worse for you. You've started doubting your self-worth, and that's ridiculous. Alex, I am here through the wedding. I'm not going anywhere. And then right after the wedding, we're going back to my place in New York and play for a few days before we go to Arizona for that four day assignment. I'm your sounding board for at least the next three weeks."

I liked the idea of Noah taking care of me for an extended period. He continued his pep talk. "For the next twenty-four hours, you're allowed to have a pity party. You can cry, drown in self-deprecation, and carry on in whatever fashion suits you. After that you have to talk to Sly, one on one, if for no other reason than to figure out how you'll deal with each other so you don't spoil Avery's day. Once Avery has left for her honeymoon, you can sit down with Sly again before we leave for New York. I'm making arrangements for a late afternoon flight on Sunday, August 24th. That will give you Sunday morning to get your stuff together and talk to him."

"I love it when you take charge of my life, Noah," I said sarcastically, but in all honesty, I really was glad to relinquish control. I didn't feel as if my head were clear enough to make good decisions.

"Hang on a sec, Shirley," Noah said as he headed for the kitchen. It was comforting to hear him call me Shirley -- like a walk through our childhood. When we were kids, he said I was an annoyingly perky girl like Shirley Temple. It infuriated me, as was his plan, but it stuck.

Noah returned and handed me another glass of wine. "Now you sit right here and mope or come into the kitchen with me. You can watch me pretend to know how to cook. I'm famished. I'm going to make something disgustingly fattening."

"I don't need fattening. I'm already fat enough," I fretted.

"You are not fat, but it's your pity party so say what you want." Noah opened the refrigerator and started rummaging through the shelves and bins. "It's normal for a fifty-year-old woman to gain weight with all those hormonal changes. Cut yourself some slack."

"My dress for the wedding doesn't fit. I've got to take it tomorrow to see if my seamstress can work a miracle. If not, I'll have to find a new one."

"It'll all work out, Shirley." He grabbed a can from the shelf. "Ah ha!"

"What's so exciting?" I asked unenthusiastically.

"Rotel. I'm making my world-famous nachos."

"Goodie. Just what I need, another 10,000 calories for my belly."

"Shut up. One day of decadent eating won't derail the train. You don't need to be worrying about losing weight in a crisis. After the wedding, you can focus on a diet if you want."

"Okay, okay," I said as I raised my hands in a defensive motion. "You're the boss."

I went to the bar and pulled out the moonshine that we drank at the party last night. I poured two glasses. "If we're going to be decadent," I stated as I handed him a glass, "we might as well make it a doozie."

"Here, here," he agreed as we clinked glasses. "Ah," Noah said. "Good old redneck juice. Is this the bottle I sent you a few months ago?"

"Indeed it is."

"Good stuff, Shirley. I done good," he praised himself.

"You always do, baby."

Noah cooked ground beef, then added it to melted Velveeta and Rotel. He poured the mixture over blue corn chips and topped the dish with chopped tomatoes, lettuce, purple onions, black olives, jalapeños, and sour cream. Like I said, 10,000 calories, but it was divine.

As we devoured the nachos, I quizzed Noah. "I'm curious as to why you don't like Sly. I mean I get why you don't like him today, but in general you've never warmed up to him. And it's mutual. He's always remained distant with you. Every time your name comes up, I can see the tension on his face. Did you two have words a long time ago, and I'm in the dark?"

"Maybe. Sort of," he conceded reluctantly.

Noah remained silent. "Do tell," I urged.

"After your rehearsal dinner, a bunch of the guys, including the groom, went out and had too many drinks. After a couple of hours, it was just Sly and me doing shots. He said he didn't know what possessed him to get engaged at twenty-two, that he couldn't believe he was getting married in less than twenty-four hours."

"What! Sly was having second thoughts the day before our wedding."

"Oh, come on, Alex. I've never been married, but it's got to be scary to think about how drastically you're changing your life. I think his comment was about his fear not about his choice of a bride."

I acknowledged his point with a shrug. "So what did you say?"

"I was too drunk and stupid to understand the comment like I do now. Back then it pissed me off, and I ripped into him. I told him that he didn't deserve you, that he wasn't good enough for you. I told him that the honorable thing for him to do would be to call it off that night to spare you the agony of having him as a husband."

"You're making this up!" I accused.

"No. As I live and breathe, I said it."

"I can't believe Sly never told me, after all these years. But I'm more surprised that you never told me how you felt. Why? We've always told each other everything."

"Because I knew I was being completely selfish. He was taking you away from me, and I was jealous. You and I had been joined at the hip since birth. We had the perfect friendship. We made each other laugh, helped each other through bad times. We had no secrets. Ours was the perfect partnership, just without sex. I was losing that, but I loved you enough to let you go because I knew he made you happy. I was angry that you were leaving me behind, but it was easier for me to be mad at him than you." Noah looked remorseful, like a little boy caught in a lie.

"Noah, honey." I stood and held him close. "You've always been my rock. Nobody can touch the bond we have. I'm so sorry you felt like I was leaving you. I thought I was just adding to my life, not replacing you. That's impossible. You are irreplaceable."

"Ain't that the truth," he commented, cockily. "You don't need to feel bad. I soon came to realize that I hadn't lost you. You had only moved on to a different phase of life."

"Why haven't you ever gotten married? You've dated, but I've never known you to be serious about anyone. There are those who speculate that you're batting for the other team, which is completely okay with me, but I would think you would've told me by now."

"Is Sly one of the speculators as to my sexual preference?"

"Actually no. I'm referring to some of our classmates. I've been to a few reunions over the years, and everybody asks about you. A few of the Neanderthals have thrown out that idea from time to time, and I've always told them they were barking up the wrong tree."

"Do you really think that marriage is for everyone?"

"No, but you are an awesome companion, and you love kids. You've traveled extensively, and I'm surprised you've never met anyone you wanted to build a life with. It's not a criticism, just an observation. I would hate to think that you missed out on something that you wanted."

"Don't think that, Alex. I've had a great life, seen spectacular sights, met fascinating people, forged great friendships. I never wanted to compromise, and it's not fair to travel the world and leave a family behind only to swoop in on occasion. Plus, I never wanted to settle. I never met a woman with whom I had the kind of relationship I wanted."

"What do you mean?"

"I've cared about and lusted over a few women, but I want the kind of relationship where you're an open book. You feel like you can be completely yourself. A relationship like ours, plus sex of course."

"Until yesterday, my relationship with Sly was great, but it's not the same closeness that I have with you. Nothing will equal that. It doesn't mean my relationship with Sly isn't, or wasn't, fulfilling, it's just different."

Noah sighed, exasperated as he threw back his head. "I've had enough depth for one night. Let's go watch mindless movies. Nothing sad, nothing sexy. I haven't seen a movie in two years, so it should be easy to find something."

We watched *Identity Thief* and *The Heat*. Levity thrived with a double dose of Melissa McCarthy.

DALLAS

<u>Tuesday, August 12th</u>. The day of reckoning had arrived. I hoped that the events of this day would prove as cathartic as I envisioned. I was ready to shed the unappealing shell in which I lived an obsessive, self-loathing life.

By 11 am, I had loaded my SUV and turned in the keys to my apartment. I drove to Tuscaloosa, secured a room at Hotel Capstone, and took Justice to a local vet to get any necessary shots. Justice would spend the night there, and I would pick him up when they opened the next morning. I drove back to Birmingham and made a quick stop at The Heights before heading to the firing range to practice one last time with the revolver I'd purchased earlier in the year. I planned to use it today, but without firing it. I purchased it for protection and power but thought it wise to be proficient in handling it. If Parker Fielding crossed my path, I'd be ready. I had the advantage since he wouldn't recognize me.

By 3 pm, I was at Starbuck's in Mountain Brook, pretending to read a book while I drank four double espressos. By 5 pm, I parked across the street from Mary Claire's house, waiting for Andrew Jameson to come home. At 7 pm, his BMW 760 Li pulled into the drive.

I called Mary Claire's cell. "Mary Claire? Hi. It's Dallas. Are you home?"

"No," she answered. "Dallas, you sound nervous. Are you okay?"

"Not really. Listen, I'm at your house, and I need to talk to you and your husband about something very important. Your husband just arrived home, and I'm parked across the street. Can you please come now, and we can go in together?"

She was silent. Finally she spoke, "Dallas, I'm afraid of my husband. I left him after the party the other night and haven't spoken to him since. I left behind a letter telling him that I wanted a divorce. He's emotionally and physically abusive, and I can't take it anymore."

"I know."

"What do you mean, you know?"

"It was obvious to me when he interrupted the party the other night. I know I'm asking a lot for you to face him now, but I promise he won't be able to hurt you, and I think that what I have to say will make it easier for you to leave him. Please. It's very important."

After a long pause, she answered. "If it's that important. I'll be there in fifteen minutes."

After we hung up, I called Detective Hatcher, but the call went to voicemail. "Hatcher, it's me, Providence. It's 7 pm central time in Birmingham, Alabama. I tracked my uncle here. I've been living here for the past six months trying to devise a way to approach him and waiting for Parker to arrive. I've met my uncle once, and he's a horrible man. The apple doesn't fall far from the tree. Speaking of the apple, Parker is here. At least, I'm fairly confident he is. On a couple of occasions, I've caught a glimpse of a man that resembles Parker, though he's much thinner, and his hair is shoulder length and dark. He didn't recognize me because, well, I don't look like me anymore. I'm about to confront my uncle, and in two hours I'll be headed away from here. I suppose I can't come back to Philly since Parker is still out there, but I'm tired of running. I'll get a little closure tonight. Thanks for everything." I also sent him a text telling him to check his voicemail.

As I finished the text, Mary Claire pulled up behind me. I grabbed my bag and met her at her car. "Dallas, what's this all about?"

"You'll see soon enough. Thank you for coming."

We walked to the front door, and she inserted the key. I noticed that her hand shook badly. She walked in ahead of me and Jameson, who must have heard the door opening, yanked his wife toward him. I walked behind him, stuck my revolver into his temple and warned, "No, no, no. Those days are over. Let her go."

Jameson didn't dare turn his head to identify his assailant, but he released Mary Claire. I slowly guided him to a chair and ordered him to sit. I told him to place his hands behind the chair. I took a rope from my bag and tied his body to the chair. I bound his hands behind his back with duct tape. Once he was secure, I lowered my weapon and walked around the chair to face him. He looked at me with that same eerie sense of familiarity that he had at the party two nights before.

"Dallas, what are you doing? I don't understand." Mary Claire's voice was frantic.

"It's time for tough confessions. You're about to find out how deep your husband's evil streak runs."

I turned my attention to my prisoner. "Let's start with something easy. Please state your full name?"

"Andrew Jackson Jameson III."

"I'm sorry. I didn't ask the question correctly. What is your real name, not your alias?"

He didn't answer.

"Oh, come on now, you can't remember what name is on your birth certificate?"

He didn't answer.

"I'll help you with this one, but you'll have to answer the other questions if you want to keep all your limbs." I turned to Mary Claire. "Mary Claire, meet your husband, Henry David Sanderson. Everybody called him Hank."

"What are you talking about?"

"Do you remember the picture you showed me? The one you said you found in your husband's car? The one that you liked because his eyes were so kind?"

"Yes, of course."

"The reason you've never seen his eyes look that way is because that picture is not of him. It's his identical twin brother, Cal Sanderson."

"What? Andrew is an only child," she corrected.

Jameson stared at me menacingly. "I know who you are. I knew it the minute I saw you the other night."

"Really," I said, curious as to what he thought he knew.

"You're the one who sent me the envelope with the newspaper article."

"Well, that is true. I stuck that in your mailbox to torture you."

"I don't care what happened to my brother. We haven't spoken in almost forty years. I didn't even know he had gotten married, much less had kids."

"Dallas, you're the one who put that envelope in the mailbox?" Mary Claire implored. "What was in the envelope? Please tell me. That's what led to my fall down the stairs."

"Are you saying he pushed you down the stairs after he looked in the envelope?" I felt horrible.

"Yes, please tell me what was in it."

"It was a picture from a Philadelphia newspaper of Cal Sanderson and his family. They were killed in a boating explosion in Charleston. Twelve people, an entire family, including a four year old and an infant. I wrote the words 'YOU DID THIS' on a piece of paper and attached it to the article."

"That's horrifying," she said sadly.

"Yes, it is," Jameson said condescendingly, "but as I said, I've had no contact with my brother in close to forty years. If you think you hurt me by sending me that article, you failed."

"If I failed, why did you push your wife down the stairs after you opened the envelope?"

"She fell."

Mary Claire jumped up and pointed a finger at her husband. "You know damn well you pushed me. Why did you change your name? Why did you abandon your own brother?"

He shifted in his chair. It was odd to me that he displayed no fear. Like he was exempt from retribution. The height of arrogance. "We had a disagreement about how to handle a problem. Ultimately, we parted ways." Jameson delivered his answer calmly, vaguely, as if he were completely innocent. A seasoned trial lawyer applying his tried and true testimonial tactics.

"Must have been quite an argument if you felt it necessary to change your name. What happened?" Mary Claire demanded.

"It doesn't matter. It was a long time ago." His answers basically dismissed his wife. He turned to me with a cold stare. "If you think you're getting a dime from me, you're crazy."

"You think I want money?" I asked rhetorically and laughed. "I don't want money, I want justice. You are a horrid person, and I hold you personally responsible for the murders of Cal Sanderson and his family."

"That's absurd. You can't hold me responsible for an accident."

"The explosion was caused by a massive, high grade bomb designed, set and activated by your offspring."

"Your offspring?" Mary Claire shouted. "You have a child?"

Again, Jameson ignored his wife. "You think you gained power over me by killing my brother?"

"What?" I uttered in confusion.

"I know you're the stripper's child," Jameson declared unemotionally.

"Wrong," a voice disputed from across the room. Leaning against the doorway, Parker Fielding sneered at us. "I'm the stripper's child. Hello, Dad." Venom spewed from his lips as he spoke.

Parker looked at me. "Are you Dallas O'Malley? What is your relation to dear old Dad here? Are you one of his abandoned children, too?"

"Hello, Parker," I said coolly. I was stunned that I could remain calm at the sight of him.

"You know me?" a shocked Parker took a few steps forward to study my face. "God, is that you, Providence?" He couldn't conceal his shock. "You're supposed to be dead."

"Thanks to a Good Samaritan, I survived your annihilation."

He surveyed me from head to toe. "Damn, girl, you got fat. And what's with the butch haircut and the dark hair? Not flattering, sweetie."

"It kept me hidden from you. How did you know my name was Dallas O'Malley?"

"Clever, Providence," he praised admiringly. Parker made himself comfortable in a leather chair and rested his legs on the matching ottoman. "You changed your looks and assumed a new name in case our paths crossed. Excellent job," he commented nonchalantly. "When I found out I'd killed the wrong Sanderson, I started searching for Hank. Once I found a way back to the US, which quite frankly proved to be an arduous task, I started at Harvard looking for records on the whereabouts of Hank Sanderson. The ladies in the registrar's office thought it was odd that only a few months before a sweet young woman named Dallas O'Malley came looking for him as well. I assumed that Dallas O'Malley was a Charleston detective or a PI working with Hatcher. When I determined that Dallas O'Malley was not a detective, I decided she must be a PI. The most effective way to find a PI is through gun registration. Bingo, Dallas O'Malley registered a gun three months ago in Birmingham, Alabama. When I got here, I couldn't find a PI named Dallas O'Malley. Then it was clear to me that this mystery woman must have some personal vendetta against dear old Dad. That meant he was here. I took his yearbook photo to the top firms in town, and on my third firm visit, someone told me he looked just like the successful attorney named Andrew Jameson. Since then, I've been studying him and his wife -- acquainting myself with their patterns so I'd know when to strike. Waiting for just the right moment. Providence, I guess I have you to thank for making it easy to find my father."

"And why is today the right day for you to attack, Parker?"

"Because today would have been my mother's sixtieth birthday. No better way to spend the anniversary of your mother's suicide than sharing it with the man responsible for her death, right Providence?"

Mary Claire was so confused. Her husband sat strapped to his chair, a smug, superior expression on his face.

"You're Andrew's son?" Mary Claire asked Parker innocently. "He abandoned you and your mother?"

"Yes, before I was born. You mean Daddy didn't take his own wife into his confidence? For shame, Dad, keeping secrets from the beginning."

Mary Claire ignored his sarcasm. "But why did you kill his brother and his family?"

"Oh, my dearest stepmom, a case of mistaken identity, I'm afraid. Turns out my Uncle Cal was a bit of a saint. He tried to make up for his brother's transgressions by giving my mom money and paying for me to attend private school. After my mom killed herself, I started digging into her finances. All this money came from Cal Sanderson, a mystery man. When I found a bio of him online, he looked just like the man in the photograph my mom had of her and my father. I made some honest assumptions which unfortunately sent me down the wrong path."

Mary Claire, stunned by the onslaught of information, turned to me. "So how do you fit into all this, Dallas? Are you a friend or enemy?"

My heart sank as I realized she doubted the sincerity of our friendship. "Mary Claire, I loathe your husband, but I care deeply for you. Your husband is my uncle. I am Cal Sanderson's oldest child, and I never knew my father had a twin brother until this past October." I pulled a copy of the newspaper article that I sent Jameson from my bag. "Do you see the girl on the bottom row, second from the left, with the long blonde hair?"

Mary Claire studied the picture. "Yes, based on the picture, she's part of the family that died."

"The police let everybody believe that she died, but that girl, Providence Sanderson, is me." She looked doubtful. "I know it's hard to believe. The stress of losing my family and trying to find my estranged uncle resulted in a feeding frenzy. I used to be very petite. When the police dropped the case, I tried to change my looks as much as possible as I searched for my own brand of justice. I would have died as well, but a couple of seconds before the bomb exploded, I stepped out of the boat to pick up a bag that I'd left on the dock. My injuries were life threatening, but the first one on the scene knew what was required. I'm told if he hadn't been there, I would have died. Sometimes, I wish I had."

"Oh, Dallas, I'm so sorry. I can't imagine the pain." Mary Claire spoke with tears running down her cheeks.

"It gets worse," I warned. "Parker, care to explain how I know you?"

Parker adjusted his posture in the leather chair and crossed his legs on the ottoman. His mannerisms mirrored a guest at a dinner party who was about to regale the crowd with an entertaining story. "I must say I'm quite proud of the creativity behind this piece of the saga," he said as he crossed his hands behind his head. "I decided that to avenge my mother and my miserable life, I would take out my father and his entire family. Again, unfortunately, I thought Cal Sanderson was my father. I wasn't sure how to take them all out at once, so I decided I needed to find a way to get close to the family. At the time, four of the five Sanderson kids were either married or heavy into a relationship. But Providence, or Dallas as you know her, was not. So I studied her. I learned her habits, interests, hangouts, and when the opportunity arose, I interjected myself into her life via a chance meeting. We were madly in love in no time. I knew what she wanted to hear, and let's face it, from the exterior, I'm a pleasing package. I got my looks from my mom, fortunately. Anyway, I gave Providence, who by the way was smoking hot two years ago, the emotional and mental connection she craved. In no time, we were engaged. Our relationship is how I knew that the Fourth of July, when the entire family gathered, was the perfect day to take them out." Parker looked at me. "By the way, cuz, I really enjoyed our numerous romps in the sack. You know what they say, incest is best."

Mary Claire cried out through tears, "you beast" at the same time I pointed my revolver toward his head. I wanted nothing more than to see his brains splattered across the walls. "What's your grand plan now, Parker? What had you decided to do here today?"

Parker stretched and yawned. "This little family gathering has definitely put a kink in my plans." Parker pulled a knife and a tiny pistol from his back pocket. "I planned to make Dad suffer by watching me torture his wife. First I would scalp her with this hunting knife, then shoot her extremities with this very ineffectual, but pain-inducing pistol. I would eventually end her misery with a bullet to the temple."

At this point, Mary Claire was cowering in the corner, hands over her face. I'm not sure why she didn't run. I turned to Parker and said, "That plan would be a waste, because your father doesn't give a damn about her. He's been abusing her for years, and she was completely clueless about you, your mother and his alias."

"Yes, I see that now," Parker conceded, apparently perplexed. "My stepmom is clearly as much a victim as my mother, so I would take no pleasure in torturing her. Providence, you're more like me than I realized. You've studied the situation, targeted the victims, just like I targeted you. Kudos to you. If you didn't look like a dike, I'd be so hot for you right now."

"I'm flattered," I answered flatly. "If you value my opinion, let me make a suggestion."

"Oh, by all means. I'd love to hear it," Parker agreed enthusiastically.

"You've already ruined my life, so killing me just puts me out of my misery. As for Mary Claire, her life with your father has been one of manipulation and control. She's never been allowed the freedom to be her own person. She deserves a second chance at a life without your dad. Let her go. I don't give a shit what you do to him. In my opinion, he's the reason you're demented, and he's worse than you are. So torture him all you want. Matters not to me. Just let her go." I walked over to Mary Claire and helped her stand. As I did, I whispered in her ear, "When I tell you, run to a neighbor and call the police." Slowly I walked toward the front door.

"You know," Parker began, "I actually think you're right on all points except there's one thing that bothers me about your plan."

"What's that?" I asked as I inched myself, with Mary Claire behind me, directly in front of the door.

"My stepmom is obviously a sweet person, but a law abiding citizen. If I let her go, she'll go straight to the authorities, and it will be hell to get out of the country. It was a bitch to leave Europe. I went through 100,000 euros in bribes and traveled on four freight barges to get back to the US. I've been through another 100,000 euros since I've been here."

"You have my sympathy," I commented sarcastically.

Parker laughed. "I like this feisty version of Providence far better than the one I seduced in Charleston."

A wave of nausea overwhelmed me. "You can take all the credit for the change in my disposition, Parker. Now what's it going to be?"

Parker turned toward his father, obviously deliberating his demise. As he looked away I opened the front door and told Mary Claire to run. Parker whipped around as he heard movement. He fired a shot at Mary Claire as she moved into the doorway. I repositioned myself to block her body and felt a pain rip through my left shoulder. I knew Mary Claire had stopped in mid-flight, but I managed to push the door shut and lock it before I fell to the floor. Hopefully, she had the good sense to run to a neighbor's house.

"Providence, shame on you. That was not a wise move on your part." As he walked toward me, Parker fired a shot at my hand that was holding the far more powerful revolver. When the bullet entered, the gun flew out of my hand. I screamed in agony.

Suddenly, I heard sirens close by, but there was no way they were for us. Mary Claire had not been gone more than thirty seconds. As I lay on the floor, I saw a thin object under the sofa. There was a light emanating from it. Suddenly, I understand that the sirens really were headed to this house.

With a renewed awareness, I felt a surge of energy and bolted out the door as Parker went to pick up my revolver. I was in the middle of the street when I heard four shots fired -- ten seconds between each round. I could hear sirens but had no idea how far away they were. Then I saw Parker coming out the front door pointing my gun at me. I jumped in my car and peeled away from the curb. In my rearview mirror, I saw Parker get in Mary Claire's Jag. I'm not sure if he found a key or he hotwired the car, but when I turned the corner away from Mary Claire's street, I saw the Jag pulling away from the curb.

I depressed the accelerator and went as fast as possible down Cherokee Road. I turned right onto Highway 280 heading toward UAB Hospital. I knew my wounds were not life threatening, but if I reached the emergency exit at UAB, policemen would most likely be around, and Parker would not dare stop. As I flew up the ramp to Highway 31, the black Jag was only a few yards behind me and a police car was just behind the Jag, sirens blaring. Silently I prayed that the police would follow the Jag, not me, after I exited onto 8th Avenue South.

There was little traffic to worry about at this time of day, so I merged onto Hwy 31 with no trouble. As I drove 85 mph, the black Jag floored it and hit my right, rear bumper. My SUV spun out of control and hit the guardrail. With an impact at that velocity, I was instantly airborne over the rail. I flipped three times before an oncoming car barreled into the driver's side. Everything went dark.

POST SEASON

CAN YOU SEE THE LIGHT?

Labor Day Weekend

Wicked storms are often followed by exquisite days.

CALLIE

August 14th, 2014 -- 2:30 am. By the time Officer Bragg returned to the waiting room, an hour had passed. It was 2:30 am. "Hey, Miss Conrad. Sorry to be gone so long. Miss O'Malley was still in surgery when I got up to the OR. Then I received an update on the black Jag that was chasing your friend."

"What's going on?" I asked anxiously.

"It's a little convoluted at the moment. Other officers intercepted the black Jag on Interstate 65 North, an hour outside of Birmingham. The driver was a male, in his late thirties or early forties, but he had no ID on him. The car registration is to Mary Claire Jameson, wife of an attorney here in town. We thought perhaps the car was stolen from the residence. Officers went to their Mountain Brook home and found the front door ajar. They found Mr. Jameson strapped to a chair, dead. He had been shot four times."

"Oh God, how horrifying."

"Yes, it was a brutal murder. One bullet went to his privates, one to the right kneecap, one to the abdomen, and one between the eyes. It was clearly a murder designed to inflict pain until the final shot to the brain."

"Do you know who did it?" In the back of my mind I feared that after years of abuse, Mary Claire snapped.

"It's too early to know," answered Officer Bragg, "but it was either Dallas O'Malley or the unknown occupant of the black Jag. The revolver that shot Jameson was registered to Miss O'Malley. The guy's not talking, so we are clueless at the moment." Officer Bragg looked at the envelope in my lap. "Is there anything in that envelope that could shed light on this story?"

"There's a letter and a key. It says that the key belongs to a locker at Birmingham Heights Country Club. I have a friend who works there. He can let me in so I can access the locker. The letter from Dallas says that the contents of the locker will explain everything."

"If you can go there now, it would be helpful since the driver of the black Jag isn't talking."

I nodded. "How can I reach you if I find anything?" He gave me a cell number. "Is Dallas still in surgery?"

"She came out of surgery just moments ago," he answered. "The doctor says she suffered a lot of abdominal damage from the wreck.

Her prognosis is a little better than originally anticipated. The next twenty-four hours are crucial."

"Do they need blood for her? I'm O positive."

"I'll let the nurse know," Officer Bragg offered.

"In fact," I added, "I'm positive there are several others who would be willing to give blood, so please let the nurses know."

"Will do," he assured me.

****

When I exited the parking lot, I called Jake. No one answered before voicemail picked up. "Come on, Jake, pick up. I know you're home."

I dialed again and on the fourth ring, a groggy voice answered. "Hello?"

"Jake. It's Callie."

There was a long pause. "It's 2:45 in the morning. Somehow I doubt you're calling for phone sex."

"Honey, why would I opt for phone sex with you when I can have the real thing?" I took a moment to enjoy his response and then became serious. "Listen, Jake, I need to get into the women's locker room at the club. Do you have a key?"

"Yes, but can't this wait until a decent hour?"

"Sorry, no. It's an emergency. And Jake, you need to bring Mary Claire with you. Andrew Jameson has been brutally murdered, and Dallas has been in a horrible car accident. Somehow, I don't know how, the two events are connected. I think there's something in a locker at The Heights that will explain everything."

"I found a note from Mary Claire when I got home at 9:30. It said that she had fed Rudolph and Poach, but had left at 7:15 to meet Dallas at her house. She said that Dallas seemed nervous but had something important to discuss with her. She wasn't back by the time I crashed at 10:30."

I heard Jake scrambling from his bed. "Shit, Callie. She's still not here. You don't think she killed him, do you?"

"Let's not panic. I know she wasn't with Dallas in the car accident or with the guy that stole her car."

"Somebody stole her car?"

"Yes. Details are sketchy. She wasn't at home when they found Jameson's body. It doesn't make sense. Look, you get dressed and meet me at the club. I'll call the police and see if she's turned up."

After we hung up, I pulled into the Wendy's parking lot, picked up my cell, and began dialing. "Officer Bragg," I said when a voice answered. "This is Callie Conrad. Listen, I'm on my way now to open the locker, but Mary Claire Jameson is missing. I'm not going to mince words here. Mary Claire has been my friend for five years. Just last week I found out that her husband has been abusing her for years. She finally got the courage to leave him, and she's been staying with a friend. I just spoke with him, and he said that she left him a note at 7:15 saying that she was meeting Dallas at Mary Claire's house. Nobody knows where she is. Can you do something to find her?"

"Will do," Officer Bragg stated. "Obviously this is all related. Hopefully the contents of that locker will help."

I exited the parking lot. Once at The Heights, I parked and waited in my car until Jake arrived.

When I met him at his car, he grabbed my hand and started walking toward the clubhouse. "I haven't heard from Mary Claire, have you?" I shook my head. "This is insane," Jake said. "Andrew is dead. Dallas is in the hospital, and Mary Claire is missing."

"Jake, Dallas was shot twice before the accident -- once in the shoulder and once in the hand with a low caliber pistol. Her severe injuries came from a car accident. Some unidentified man was chasing her in Mary Claire's Jag. The police caught him on I65 North, but he had no ID and won't speak. And it gets worse. The gun that killed Andrew Jameson is registered to Dallas."

"None of this makes any sense," he commented as he unlocked the clubhouse door.

"According to Dallas's letter found in her car, the contents of locker 44 will explain everything."

We entered the women's locker room, and I located locker 44. I inserted the key and pulled out the contents -- a thick envelope with yesterday's date. When I opened the package, I found a lengthy, hand written letter that began "My name is not Dallas O'Malley. I am Providence Sanderson". Over the next ten pages, Dallas laid out all the circumstances that brought her to Birmingham. It started with falling in love with Parker Fielding in a restaurant in Charleston, South Carolina. I cried as I read her gut-wrenching story. I passed each page to Jake as I finished and heard him mutter, "horrible" and "unbelievable" more than once.

"Jake, look at this picture of Dallas's whole family." It was a color copy of a photo from a Philadelphia newspaper. "Can you believe this is Dallas? She looks twenty years younger and beautiful. So happy and at ease. This whole situation is incredible."

Jake's phone rang. "Hello," he greeted anxiously. He obviously didn't look at the caller ID.

"Olivia, why the hell are you calling me at 3:30 in the morning?" Jake saw the look on my face and put the call on speaker.

"Hi there, handsome. What are you doing up at this hour? Dreaming of me, I hope," she responded seductively. Her voice was a poor imitation of Marilyn Monroe.

Jake rolled his eyes, and I put my hand over my mouth to muffle a giggle. "Actually, I'm in the middle of a crisis. What do you need, Olivia? Obviously, you haven't spoken to Amy recently."

"Actually, I have, Jake. She said you used your tongue to probe some girl all the way to her toes. I have to admit I was a bit jealous I wasn't on the receiving end of that kiss. But Amy can be a tad bit dramatic. I wanted you to tell me directly if you're off the market or if that was just a silly, drunken encounter."

Jake locked eyes with me as he answered. "Olivia, it was not a silly drunken kiss. It was a passionate declaration of my feelings for an incredible woman with whom I hope to build a relationship that ultimately ends at the altar. Is that clear enough for you?"

"Crystal, Jake. Sorry if I've been overbearing. I'm accustomed to being chased. Not to sound cocky, but your lack of interest was baffling. Unchartered waters, if you will. I suppose I haven't been sure how to proceed. I guess the competitive side of me took over."

"I wish you the best, but did you really call me at 3:30 in the morning to have this conversation? Seems a bit drastic."

"Sorry, no. Listen, Jake, I sent you a text last week that said matter of life or death and now that truly may be the case based on the phone call I received just before I called you."

"What are you talking about?" Jake sounded exasperated, but it was clear to me that Olivia Dunn has switched gears; the seductress had yielded to the attorney.

"When I watched Amy play her match a few weeks ago, there was a woman playing next to her that looked somewhat familiar to me. Do you remember who played next to Amy and Kelly?"

"I definitely don't know the opponents, but our team players that day were Alex Anderson and Dallas O'Malley."

"Oh my God, Dallas O'Malley. Jake you need to find her and put her somewhere safe. She's in danger."

"Why? Because she's really Providence Sanderson?"

"How do you know that?"

"This conversation is coming a few hours late, Olivia. Dallas was shot twice tonight, and whoever shot her caused her to have a car accident. She just got out of surgery and is holding her own. The guy who ran her off the road is in custody but has no ID and isn't talking."

"Listen to me, Jake. Find the officers in charge. Do not let that man go. He is most likely a mass murderer. Tell the police to ask him if his name is James Cavanaugh or Parker Fielding. See how he reacts. A Detective Hatcher from the Charleston police department will be in Birmingham as early as possible tomorrow. I'm giving him your cell number. What police department is holding this guy?"

"Birmingham PD," Jake replied.

"Tell them under no circumstances are they to let him go. If they need a reason to hold him, give them my number. "

"This was obviously very important. Amy could have told you who played next to her that day. Why didn't you call her last week when I didn't respond to your text?"

I heard her sigh. "Because it was an excuse to get you to call me. Now I wish I had left my emotions out of it and called Amy. Maybe if I had, all of this wouldn't have happened." There was a long pause. "Goodbye, Jake." Olivia's tone was serious and final.

I picked up my phone, hit the last number dialed and handed it to Jake so he could share Olivia's comments with Officer Bragg. Just as Jake hung up, his phone rang. "Yes, this is Jake Lenaghan."

He listened intently for a few minutes and responded, "I'll be there in fifteen minutes."

Jake grabbed my hand. "Come on. We've got to lock up here and go pick up Mary Claire. She's okay but in shock. She's at the Mountain Brook police department."

We secured the clubhouse and Jake said, "Let's take my car. I don't think either one of us is getting any more sleep tonight."

"Okay, but let's not forget the last line of Dallas's letter."

Jake looked at me, confused.

"It said, 'if you are reading this, please pick up Justice. He's at the Bama Animal Clinic in Tuscaloosa. I know you'll give him a good home'."

"We'll get him tomorrow. Callie, it's almost 4 am. Can you take the day off?"

"Sure."

"There's a lot to deal with here, and I was thinking about leaving a message for Janice to cancel my lessons. Let me go inside now and leave a note."

When he returned, we headed to pick up Mary Claire. "Does she know about Dallas's accident?"

"I don't know."

When we entered the station, Officer Bragg greeted us. "Hello," I said, surprised to see him. "Jake, this is Officer Bragg." They shook hands. "What are you doing here? I thought you were with the Homewood police."

"I am, but Mrs. Jameson mentioned Dallas O'Malley and eventually I was contacted."

I pulled the letter from my purse and handed it to him. "I need a copy of this, but it sheds light on this situation. When you read it, you might think that Dallas had motive to kill Andrew Jameson, but I don't believe she would do that."

Officer Bragg put up his hands. "You don't have to worry about that. We've already determined that there was no gunshot residue on your friend's hands, and there is on the guy that stole her car. Plus, the phone recording puts everything in perspective."

"What phone recording?" Jake inquired.

"Apparently Mrs. Jameson had the good sense to silence her phone but call 911 when Dallas pulled a gun on her husband. She also put her camera on video/record while Dallas was busy tying him up. Then she pushed it under the sofa so no one would see it. She thought Dallas was the bad guy until the conversation revealed the sordid details. So the entire confrontation was recorded via 911 on Mrs. Jameson's phone. That's why the police arrived when they did. The whole story is too crazy to believe but too insane to have been fabricated. You're free to take Mrs. Jameson home."

Mary Claire looked haggard. As she approached, I whispered to Officer Bragg, "Does she know about her husband?" He nodded. "How did she take it?"

"Stoically," he replied. "She became quite emotional when I explained Dallas' condition."

Mary Claire melted in Jake's comforting embrace. Officer Bragg returned a copy of Dallas's letter to me. Once in the car, no one spoke. Jake headed back to his house, but Mary Claire insisted, "Take me to see Dallas, please."

"She's not awake. There's nothing you can do for her," Jake explained.

"When she wakes up, she needs to see a friend. That child has no one but me, and it's all because of my husband. I will be there when she wakes up."

Her tone was decisive, so Jake didn't argue. Dallas was in ICU; consequently, we couldn't sit in her room. We stayed in the ICU waiting room, and at 7 am, a doctor greeted us. He said that Dallas was lucky to be alive and that most people with her injuries wouldn't have survived the night, but she was strong and was showing signs of improvement. He said that she was still critical, but if she made it through another twenty-four hours, he felt that she would fully recover.

Every time she was allowed in the room, Mary Claire sat beside Dallas, held her hand and talked softly to her. As it turned out, she had the same blood type as Dallas, AB negative, so she donated her blood. Mary Claire left the hospital only to shower. She slept in the waiting room, and Jake and I stayed with her as much as possible. When Dallas finally woke up two days later, she saw Mary Claire and said with relief, "You're okay." Mary Claire told her that Parker Fielding killed his father and that Parker was now in the custody of a Detective Hatcher of the Charleston police department. It was okay to be Providence Sanderson again. According to Mary Claire, Dallas smiled and fell back to sleep.

ALEX

By the time Avery's wedding arrived, everyone knew the full story of Dallas O'Malley, even Katlin who was still vacationing in the Caymans. When I shared the story with Noah, his mouth flew open. The day the Sanderson family died, Noah called me and shared what he had witnessed. The fact that he had tried and failed to save the one possible survivor had haunted him for two years. To know she had survived gave him great peace of mind.

Mary Claire graciously buried her husband and played the role of the grieving widow. She allowed Andrew Jameson to be buried with his dignity intact. The sordid story of his illegitimate son was buried with him. She was unbelievably strong throughout the whole ordeal, but she couldn't bring herself to return to the Jameson house.

By the time Sly and I talked, my pity party had passed, and I focused on a plan for the future. I had no idea how Sly fit into that future and needed to give myself time to ponder the subject. We spoke on Friday, and Avery arrived home the next day, Saturday, August 16th, to spend the entire week before the wedding. We agreed to make Avery the priority. Sly moved back in thirty minutes before Avery arrived, and we faked our way through the week for our daughter's sake. If Avery sensed any discord, we told her it was just sadness at the thought of our baby being married and moving so far away. Noah's presence was instrumental in mitigating tension.

I indifferently told Sly that I had no idea how I felt about him and that I needed time to think. I informed him that after the wedding, I would be working with Noah full time and would be staying with him in New York when we weren't on assignment. He agreed to stay in the house and take care of Izzy and any remaining pups. I had decided to keep Chunk for myself, but until I really had my head on straight, Jake and Callie said he could stay with them.

August 23rd arrived, and the weather was perfect. The wedding and reception surpassed my expectations. Everyone from our team except Katlin and crazy MKat attended. Dallas had been released from the hospital two days before, so Mary Claire, her self-appointed caregiver, brought her to the wedding and to the reception. They didn't last long, but Dallas got to meet Noah. She cried and confessed, "I used to hate you, Mr. Hargrove, because I would have died with the rest of my family if you hadn't been there. Instead, I lived and I suffered. But now I want to thank you for saving my life."

After the wedding, Dallas and Mary Claire relocated to Dallas's family vacation home in Rosemary Beach for an indefinite stay while Dallas recuperated. Now that she could be Providence again, she could take possession of the beach house and her childhood home in Philadelphia. She invited everyone to come stay at the beach over the Labor Day weekend. No one refused.

Around seven on Saturday of that weekend, we all gathered on the beach with blankets and a few pitchers of margaritas to watch the sunset. Justice, Rudolph, Chunk and Poach frolicked in the waves crashing along the shoreline. Eventually they waned, and Jake was able to round them up for a siesta amongst the group.

Callie sat between Jake's legs and leaned against his chest; Jake had his arms wrapped around her. Clearly, they were meant to be together. I smiled as I remembered being similarly intertwined with Sly on our many trips to the Gulf. Mary Claire sat next to Jake and doted on Dallas who sat on her other side. Kelly and Amy lounged next to Dallas.

Katlin sat next to me, our secret, twisted bond still known only to Noah. I admired this privileged young woman, who the night before snuck into my bedroom and told me exactly how she felt. "Alex," she said, "I fell madly in love with your husband and really thought I would be marrying him. I want you to know that even if you leave him because of this betrayal, I want nothing to do with a man who mistreated you and Avery. I value my friendship with Avery and you and would never choose Sam above y'all." I thought Katlin was becoming a substantial young woman.

"Ladies," Jake addressed the group, "it's been a hell of a season. You kicked ass on the courts, but off the courts...WOW...talk about having to deal with some spin. Life has stressed you all to a breaking point -- more fragile and frayed than well-worn racquet strings -- but you've all tackled those challenges admirably. Now, you have a decision to make collectively. At the end of September, you're scheduled for the state playoffs in Gulf Shores. If we don't have at least six players, and the right mix of levels, we need to give up that spot. So, let's take a vote."

Callie started. "I'm in. What about you, Alex? Aren't you leaving with Noah for Australia soon?"

"We don't leave 'til mid October, so I'm ready and willing. What about you, Katlin? You can play 3.0 or you can play 3.5 with me, if Dallas isn't up for it."

Katlin smiled and said, "Count me in." She looked at me and mouthed the words "thank you". I winked at her.

"We're up to three now," Jake said. "Dallas, I'm sorry, Providence, I know you'll play, but will the doctors let you? Or are you going home before the state playoffs?"

I'm staying here for a while. I'll be okay to play by the end of the month, but I'm not sure I'll be very effective. I'm game though."

"Mary Claire, what are your plans?"

"My cast comes off next week, so I can play. Like Providence, though, I'm not sure how effective I'll be. But count me in."

"Okay, you need one more 3.0 player, but better to have two. Amy, Kelly, are you in?"

They both nodded.

"Awesome, we're going to state," Callie cheered. "Y'all want to try and break MKat out of her padded cell? She'd add some color to the occasion."

"Heavens to Betsy! Don't we think this group has enough color, Callie?" I teased. "But let's toast to state and kick some butt in honor of poor Edward."

We all raised our glasses. "For poor Edward," I declared.

"For poor Edward," the gang repeated.

People broke into individual conversations, and I laid down pretending to be sleeping. Mary Claire and Dallas (rather Providence - I'll never get used to that) were close by. I heard Mary Claire say, "I guess you'll be heading back to Philadelphia after the playoffs. I know you're anxious to see your friends again."

Providence shook her head. "You know, for the past two years, all I've wanted was to go back to Philly. A long time ago, in another lifetime, a good friend told me that sometimes you just can't go back. You have to let go and move forward. He was right. He also told me that even if I got the justice I sought, I'd still feel broken inside. He was right about that as well. Smart guy. I have to rebuild, and I need a healthy environment for that. Philly would not be healthy for me."

"I know what you mean," Mary Claire agreed. "I haven't been back to my house since that horrible day. I just can't face it. Luckily I had already moved out all the things that mattered to me when I left him.

But I feel like I need a new environment -- somewhere totally different from home -- somewhere away from the bad memories."

Providence smiled. "Do you like horses?"

ABOUT THE AUTHOR

Donna Roberts grew up in Dothan, Alabama, and graduated from the University of Alabama, Tuscaloosa, in 1985 with a BS in accounting. After many years in public and corporate accounting, she is now pursuing her passion for writing. Currently, she lives in Birmingham, Alabama, with her son, Austin, and is working on a second novel involving the characters from FRAYED.

Made in the USA
Charleston, SC
07 April 2015